THE REIGN OF THE BEAST

a DI Wiggins Adventure

THE REIGN OF THE BEAST

a DI Wiggins Adventure

~ Book One ~

IAN C. GRANT

For Grace

The first one's for you.

I hope you would have liked it ~ Dad

For Valerie

You continue to inspire me

Contents

Chapter 1 - The Beast (London, 1913)

"The highest type of man may revert to the animal if he leaves the straight road of destiny."

Sherlock Holmes - The Adventure of the Creeping Man

It sat crouched on the stone ledge, snarling at the crescent moon that struggled to break through the dense cloud of a bone-chilling London night. It tore with its jagged, yellow-stained incisors at the raw meat held in its taloned claws, swallowing the flesh with an unquenchable relish. The feasting made a repulsively sickening sound, the mastication of meat interspersed with the crunching of bone. Its long arachnoid legs were pulled close towards its body in a tight crouch that mirrored that of the gargoyles that adorned the building. Carved stone sentinels that sat silently gazing down upon the murk of the Thames, surveying the great river and guarding the building against unseen assailants. A pigeon fluttered down from the night sky and landed on a precarious ledge near the gorging Beast. The bird looked inquisitively at the creature, ruffled its wings and edged its way towards the looming black shape. The Beast looked up from its repast, blood and saliva dripping slowly from an engorged mouth and turned its head towards the encroaching bird. Ink black, red-rimmed eyes stared at the pigeon causing it to cease its head-bobbing movement, unsure as how to proceed. Its primitive instinct at once urging it to approach the feasting figure in the anticipation of scraps but also urging it to flee from a stare that signalled absolute danger. The Beast wrinkled its muzzle and growled a low leonine rumble that rose from the pit of its core. The pigeon flew off, its tiny brain impelling it to flight.

The Beast tore rabidly at another swathe of flesh, gorging greedily upon its feast. A beam of moonlight escaped through the snow heavy January clouds and glinted brightly off the razor-sharp steel of its claw-like hands. The Beast caught sight of its own reflection in the glint of metal. An inhuman countenance sneered fiercely back. The face of some demonic monster, its eyes stygian dead pools. It smiled at the sight grotesquely, growling loudly in appreciation of its accursed ungodliness. Lifting its talons to its mouth it ran a serpentine tongue along the length of the blades, licking at decaying stains of dried, coagulated blood.

Far below the monstrous feast, the early morning stragglers of the Metropolis' nightlife mingled with shift workers, some anticipating a welcoming home fire, others heading towards market, mill or dock. The Beast stood upright and stretched to its full height, its steel claws reaching as if to scratch the sky. Its muscles stretched and its joints cracked a splintering, sinewy snap as its spine straightened. It arched its neck backwards and screeched at the night sky. The shriek was a prolonged unholy scream that increased in volume until it became a high-pitched howl of absolute evil. Birds bolted from their roosts, dogs began to scratch and howl, and children pulled their bedclothes over themselves in fear. Mothers comforted their crying babies and men looked long and hard at themselves in their morning shaving mirrors, inwardly testing their masculinity.

Fully sated with its grisly meal and satisfied with its salutation to the night, the Beast darted down the stone edifice of the building and dropped into the still quiet of a side alley. It scuttled on all fours like a giant black leather-backed cockroach for a few yards then gradually stood aloft and walked on bipedally in the manner of a sophisticated man. The Beast hissed and spat as it stepped over the prone figure of an inebriated drunk lying unconscious on the cobbles. As it approached the entrance to Victoria Embankment it halted, conscious of the small number of people strolling its length. It looked fleetingly from side to side, madness dancing in its opaline eyes, a smiling snarl playing across its blood swollen lips. It strolled out amongst the human traffic, awkward in its enforced gait, seeking the riverside pavement. As it did so it collided with a young smartly dressed couple making their way home from some happy event.

"I do beg your pardon Sir," uttered the gentleman gallantly in an effort to impress his young lady. "My fault entirely dear chap."

The Beast whirled instantly, its black cloak rushing through the air like the wing of some giant bat. Its monstrous face turned ferociously towards the young man who shrank back with revulsion at the gruesome countenance that now sneered back at him. The young man stumbled back and put a protective arm around his Innamorato. The Beast fell to all fours like a great black beetle and scuttled over the Embankment wall and disappeared into the gloom.

Chapter 2 - The Crime Lord

Harry Filch slithered through the damp night, coughing into his ill-fitting sleeve as was his habit. The fog was a thick mustard yellow and Harry could feel it seeping heavily into his already chronically damaged lungs.

"Bleedin' fog," he cursed under his breath. Just then sleet began to fall. He knew his chronic bronchial wheezing and coughing was beginning to compromise his competency, not to mention his safety in his chosen profession. Harry was a thief for hire. He hated the fog, he hated the cold, he hated the sleet and he hated the damp. Most of all he hated being summoned to a visit by Mr King. He dreaded the now customary call and what usually followed, a visit to Pakapuh.

Pakapuh was ostensibly a Thameside restaurant dealing in noodles, soup, pancakes, dumplings and other such Chinese dishes, all of which Harry, quite frankly, regarded as completely inedible foreign muck. Harry was a pie and mash man whenever he had the coin to afford it. In reality, Pakapuh was the centre of an abhorrent spider web of corruption, opium dealing, prostitution, thievery, kidnapping, extortion and murder, at the very epicentre of which sat Mr King, the ruthless Chinese crime lord who oversaw London's foulest business empire.

Pakapuh sat plumb on the waterfront at Shadwell Basin along Pelican Wharf and boasted a small private pier which extended into the murk of the Thames. The pier was set on pilings driven deep through the stone shingle and into the heart of the muddy riverbed. If one had closely examined the stretch of shingle beach from the Pelican Steps to the underside of the pier, one would have seen a mixture of bones, crushed and rounded by the continual ebb and flow of the river, dispersed among the pebbles and bricks. Heavy chains hung from the side of the pier rattling in the wind, the shackles attached to their ends hinting at their macabre purpose. The pier was deserted save for a small boat tethered to one of its main posts.

'*Right old dump,*' thought Harry as he plucked up the necessary courage and knocked the prescribed number of knocks at the desired tempo on the ramshackle door of the ultimate den of iniquity. The pier bell clanged back and forth in the gloom, a muted death knell which accompanied Harry's rasping breathing as he waited, shuffling from one frozen foot to another. A small viewing hatch in the door snapped open suddenly and a pair of enquiring oriental eyes met Harry's.

"Harry Filch to see the King. I'm expected," wheezed Harry hugging the collar of his coat ever more tightly against the pervading damp. The viewing slot shut as sharply as it had opened, and Harry could hear multiple locks being unbolted from within.

"You come this way," instructed the toothless Asiatic who had granted his entry, scuttling away in short sharp staccato steps. Harry recognised him as one of King's murderous henchmen. They were all either Burmese Dacoit stranglers, Indian Thuggees or Chinese assassins, all highly skilled in the art of murder. Harry only hoped that the most feared of them all, the Chinese Giant, was elsewhere this evening. He could certainly do without making his acquaintance again.

"I know me way me old china," chortled Harry, inwardly happy with his little joke in the face of his growing disquiet. Unsurprisingly no customers were eating in the front restaurant. In all his visits Harry had never seen anyone eating in the front restaurant. The only occupants of the ornately decorated room were two tough-looking Asiatics with sharply sculpted angular features who sat at the bar drinking hot saké. One was picking his teeth with what to Harry looked like the sharpest knife he had ever seen, the other was singing nonchalantly to himself. Harry recognised these two as the Shang brothers, a pair of cutthroat twins and long-standing employees of Mr King. *'No doubt some song 'bout killing someone under a cherry blossom tree,'* thought Harry to himself, always the joker. The two men both stared at Harry with an underlying menace that chilled him to his core.

"Through here ain't it lads," nodded Harry with fake jocularity towards a back door in the restaurant, now eager to leave the presence of the sinister twins. Harry passed through the door as quickly as he could without appearing terrified and walked through a small kitchen populated by one tiny, wizened oriental woman whom Harry reckoned must have been a hundred years old if she was a day. The little woman's skin wrinkled like parchment as she smiled benignly at Harry, unveiling a mouthful of battered brown teeth, and bowed to him as he entered the back room. *'Teeth like lampposts,'* thought Harry, *'One every hundred yards.'*

The smell of opium struck his nostrils and stung his eyes immediately as he opened the door. Plumes of smoke made their eager escape from the squalor of the smoking-room as if searching for freedom and fresh air. The room resembled a small wooden-clad stable with wall mounted bunks on all sides from floor level to ceiling, some three bunks high. Each compartment held a lost soul, a hollow carcass, each devoid of any outward feeling, engulfed in an opium-induced torpor from which, Harry speculated, some may never wake.

Harry shuddered. Lifelong criminal though he was, he had never been tempted by the Chinese Poison that was openly pedalled here. Beggars lay side by side with respectable middle-class folk and no doubt some of even higher breeding. All were united in the despair of their helpless dependency on the ruinous opiate and its supply by the satanic King. In the corner of the room, as ever, sat Wang, the impossibly rotund master of the Opium Den, pipes and paraphernalia lying prepared and ready for distribution in front of him.

"You want some hit, Harry? I make special pipe for wheezy old weasel like you," sneered the spherical Wang.

"No thanks Wang, old mate, you'll never get me on that old brain rot. I'll have a gin later on maybes," offered Harry with a wink. Wang slowly smiled a knowing smile that split his face like a knife would a ripe tomato and sent a shiver down Harry Filch's spine. "Upstairs Harry," pointed Wang. "Mr King waiting for you and you know he not like waiting. Last man kept Mr King waiting, he no waiting anymore," giggled Wang with glee, his fatty shoulders jigging up and down in delight. "He end up hanging on the river chains."

Harry shrugged, mounted the unsteady rickety timber staircase, and reached the first floor. He walked down the corridor past the rooms on either side, each of which held nothing but a bed and a working girl. Some doors were open showing the girls inside in the most explicitly unglorified positions, the others were blessedly closed. Harry had no desire to witness whatever degenerate practices were going on within those rooms.

At the end of the corridor, Harry knocked four times on a heavy oak door and coughed nervously to clear his throat, fidgeting with anxiety, every fibre of his being screaming at him to run and get out of this hell hole and to never return. But where could he run to? King was everywhere, London was his. Well, at least the London that Harry moved in. The Crime Lord's poisonous tentacles extended to every corner of the sprawling metropolis. Even the Great Detective had not managed to catch him. He was as clever and as shrewd as the Devil himself. '*Perhaps he could run to the Leper Dutchman out West*,' thought Harry, '*but what use would he have for a common thief such as little old Harry Filch?*'

As these thoughts were racing through his head the door slowly creaked open. He was ushered into the room by a human hand the size of a builder's shovel. Harry swallowed hard and entered the opulently decorated room, his worst fears rising at the sight of the gargantuan hand. Oriental rugs and tapestries covered walls and floor and a large Chinese chandelier hung from the centre of the ceiling. Cloisonné decorated bowls of incense hung suspended from timber beams located sporadically throughout the room. The focal point of the space was a large oblong table inlaid with carved images of jade-eyed dragons and serpents, cranes and tigers. Harry recalled having heard somewhere that the ancient Chinese had believed Jade to be the dried saliva of dragons. At the head of the table dressed in green satin robes sat the diminutive but demonic figure of Mr King, his serpent-like eyes boring into Harry. King slowly brought an ivory cigarette holder up to his pencil-thin lips and inhaled from a pungent smelling cheroot. Harry removed his hat and stood before his employer shivering, awaiting instruction.

At Mr King's left-hand side sat Madam Huai, head of his London-wide prostitution ring. She was a faded beauty whose now hard-edged face and deep grey eyes emanated an underlying menace that Harry found more than uncomfortable. To King's right sat the Poisoner, a lithe pockmarked, lizard-like man whose name no one knew. He oversaw the Dacoits and Thuggees and his fearsome reputation was based upon his ability to devise ever more ingenious and undetectable methods of assassination.

One look at this triumvirate convinced Harry that today was not going to number amongst his best. The door closed behind him and Harry was nudged powerfully forward by the enormous hand in the small of his back towards the only vacant chair at the table directly opposite Mr King.

"Welcome, Harry. Take a seat," oozed Mr King blinking his reptilian eyes and languidly exhaling the putrid smoke from his cheroot.

"Thank you, sir, I'd sooner stand if you don't mind," quaked Harry, already regretting his answer. Instantly he was pushed down into the chair with enormous force. Harry gulped. He knew just exactly who was behind him. Out of the corner of his eye, Harry could see the shape of the enormous figure move past him and take its position standing directly behind Mr King. Hercules Chin! The Chinese Giant. Harry shuddered once more. If Chin was here, Harry was in real trouble. The size of Chin was simply petrifying. An eight-foot-tall giant of enormous strength who served King with unquestioning loyalty. Harry knew for a fact that Chin had personally killed dozens of men, mostly with his bare hands. Those enormous hands, the huge square shoulders, the low browed forehead shadowing the dead looking eyes blanched by habitual drug use. Harry had heard that King had bought Chin from a travelling circus in China and moulded the abused youth from a sideshow freak into the terrifying monster of a man standing before him.

Harry coughed. Twice.

"And therein lies my dilemma Harry," whispered Mr King, his voice so quiet as to be barely audible.

"What do you mean sir," stammered Harry.

"A bronchitic thief, Harry. What use is a spluttering asthmatic thief to me Harry? Too easily discovered. Too easily heard. Some may say a liability, Harry."

"But I ain't never let you down Mr King," pleaded Harry, now seriously frightened.

"Better not to eat a rotten lychee than to see what it tastes like Harry," smiled King, exposing his horrific teeth, filed to points like the canines of a wolf. "A test Harry. You have five minutes."

"What do you mean sir? Five minutes for what? What test?" asked a completely confused and now entirely petrified Harry.

"Why, five minutes during which not to cough Harry. Put my mind at rest you may say."

"Oh," gasped Harry stunned. Terrified. Harry was no fool. Twenty-five years of thieving for a living had made sure of that. He knew that there was no way past Chin and that the murderous Shang twins blocked his return journey. He was utterly trapped.

"Shall we start, Harry?" enquired Mr King rhetorically, turning to Madame Haui who produced a large oriental timepiece from somewhere amongst her ample cleavage, flipped the lid and pressed the timing button, all the while staring directly at Harry.

"Now."

Harry swallowed hard. 'Keep swallowing,' he thought to himself, 'keep bloody swallowing.' Maybe the saliva would lubricate his throat like a clarinet's reed, and he could get through this ordeal. A minute passed. Beads of sweat appeared on Harry's forehead. He had heard about these Chinese maniacs' unique forms of torture, but little had he ever imagined that he would be the victim of the most unique of all. 'Keep swallowing Harry old boy, keep swallowing.' His mouth was rapidly drying up. The beads of sweat now trickled down his face as he felt the first traces of a tickling cough surface.

"Two minutes Harry," laughed King "Very good, I am impressed."

King took another long inhalation from the foul-smelling cheroot and exhaled the acrid smoke forcefully in the direction of Harry's face. Harry's throat now felt rougher than sandpaper. The more he thought about it the more arid his throat became. 'Swallow Harry, swallow.' The seconds ticked away like minutes and each minute passed like an hour. The tickle was silent, but it was all he could do to counter its rasping rise at the back of his throat. Unbearable.

'Only another few minutes, Filchy old boy,' agonised Harry. And then it happened. The tickle. That tickle! He could not stop it. He felt it rising, rising. 'Try to ignore it Harry. Try to ignore it Harry. Swallow. It will go away.'

"Three minutes Harry. Is it painful?" enquired the merciless King gleefully, blowing yet another plume of poison in Harry's face. The tickle became an itch. He could feel it catching at the back of his throat. 'Don't do it, Harry. Don't do it!'

He did it. He coughed. The instant the cough left his lips, Mr King's satanic eyes lit up under his raised eyebrows and his hand slipped under the table to a hidden lever activating a razor-sharp sword two feet in length that shot up into Harry's rectum from the chair on which he had sat his last. Harry screamed in agony as the blade entered his bowel and intestine. His head hit the table and was then lifted by Hercules Chin who crushed poor Harry's neck vertebrae with a single chop of his massive fist.

"Pity, another minute and I may have tired of this game," dismissed King, repeatedly clapping his hands together with child-like glee. "Take him to the pier and deposit him into the river Chin," ordered the Crime Lord. Harry Filch would cough no more.

Harry Filch would filch no more.

Harry Filch's body was slipped into the inky cold blackness of the Thames, the river that had spliced his life together for the last forty-four years finally welcomed him and swallowed him up. Moments before the giant lumbering figure of Hercules Chin had carried Harry under his arm down a timber staircase affixed to the exterior of the opium den where Harry had met his brutal end. His corpse was deposited into Old Father Thames' arms through a frequently used trapdoor at the rear of the pier.

Hercules Chin emitted a low, rumbling grunt of self-congratulation at another task accomplished. Not the most challenging task he had ever done for Father King; as easy as snapping a matchstick to the huge man. He took a moment to look around at the now unusually fog-free London night sky, turning his head towards the Cheshire cat moon that shone and smiled down upon him and all the other denizens of the original Gotham. Chin felt as if the moon was smiling at him, telling him that it was happy with the job he had just accomplished. A feline smile of admonishment. Chin shrugged his gigantic shoulders and slowly sat down on the pier edge, the timbers creaking under his great weight. He crossed his massive arms, stroked the pronounced tramlines at the side of his mouth absent-mindedly and began to subconsciously kick his legs back and forth, one after the other, like a child on a swing whilst still looking at the night sky. '*How could it be so dark with so many lights up in the sky,*' he thought to himself. It made no sense to him. He gently started to hum a lilt in the deepest of rumbling tones emanating from the back of his throat.

'*Where had Jaio gone?*' he puzzled. He missed her with a longing that hurt his heart every day. An ill-understood emotion that he was not at all at ease with. '*Why could liking someone hurt so much?*' Father King had told him that she had left him. Fled from his ugliness and brutality. What pretty lady, after all, would want to be around an unnatural freak like him, King had laughed. Chin shook his giant head slowly and stared at the moon. He knew enough to know that the same lunar smile was shining down on Jaio somewhere and that solace made him feel warm despite the bitter chill of the night which enveloped his huge mass.

His head began to hurt again. He knew the medicine that Father King gave him was bad for him, but it helped the pain go away. He always felt much better after he had taken it, and always wanted more when the pain came back. King told him that the medicine stopped him growing and that without it he would be the size of the houses and the trees, and what woman would want a man the size of the giant clock tower. That made sense to Chin.

There was a glug from the Thames as Harry's body momentarily bobbed to the surface. It was as though the river had belched in disagreement at the unusual meal it had just been served. Chin had carried out disposals often enough to know that it would sink again within a few seconds, the last remnants of air leaving the corpse, then it would be gone forever. He knew this river was nowhere as mighty as the rivers he remembered from his childhood back in the other land, but it was still deep. Chin knew the river was tidal and fast flowing and it would soon carry the man's body an exceptionally long way away, maybe even delivering it into the great sea. He remembered his old land, the muddy rivers and purple mountains, his parents, his brothers and his sisters. The time before the circus. A time before King.

Chapter 3 - The Killing

"PLEASE GOD, NO! HELP ME! SOMEONE HELP ME!"

Tears of terror spilled from her panic-stricken eyes. Eyes that had been pretty only moments before. Eyes that were now fixed upon the most abominably horrific face only her worst nightmares could imagine. A foul, blood curdling, ghastly vision of absolute evil. Perspiration matted her hair to her forehead. Hair that had been pretty only moments before. Her heart pounded violently within her heaving chest as she gasped desperately for air.

Her piercing screams echoed around the foreboding, dark East London streets. She shrieked frantically for help. Screams so terrifyingly tangible as to wake the dead. Penetrating aniridial eyes returned her terrified stare. Black, shark-like eyes, soulless and devoid of emotion. The expression was demonic, a ferocious mask of ugliness that foretold the savagery to come. A single embodiment of evil.

"HELP ME! FOR GOD'S SAKE HELP ME!"

The monstrous vision loomed sickeningly closer, the Beast's lips snarling back to unveil pink fleshy gums and sharp yellowing teeth. Its hot putrid breath clung disgustingly to her face like a death shroud. She could smell its meat fetid breath and began to pray soundlessly for mercy. Its head now blocked out everything else, the faint amber of the gas streetlights that tried to penetrate the curtain of the London fog, lost behind a stomach-churning visage. Bubbling saliva dripped from the demonic mouth. This face was to be the last thing Mary Harrison would ever see.

"PLEASE GOD MAKE IT QUICK!"

The sharp high-pitched shrill of several whistles penetrated the heavy smog-laden air.

Running. Two men running frantically, pistols in hand, towards the screams that pierced the night. "Run Pyke, we must get there. Faster, faster!"

Ba dum ba dum. Mary Harrison's heart beat uncontrollably as the tongue of the Beast, long and slender, slowly licked at her jugular notch, up the front of her neck and across her jaw then up to her earlobe. She shuddered, staunching the nausea, and screamed once more.

"PLEASE GOD MAKE IT PAINLESS!"

Legs pumping. Arms thrusting. The two men accelerated even further, their lungs gulping air to fuel their muscles. "Faster, Pyke," again shouted the taller and more athletic of the two men, knowing that his shorter, stronger companion was quicker.

Ba dum ba dum. Mary Harrison's heartbeat echoed those of her would-be rescuers. She kicked out violently and scratched frantically trying to claw at the eyes of the Beast. Her wrists were grasped with such ferocity and force that she felt each of them snap in opposite directions with a bone splintering crack. She shrieked in agony. The Beast raised its eyebrows, threw back its head and laughed.

Sparks flashing from hobnail boots on cobbled streets. '*Must get there,*' demanded Detective Sergeant Jem Pyke to himself. He gritted his teeth as he heard the tortured cries of the woman reverberate around the brick walls of Narrow Street. Where was she? North side or riverside? It was almost impossible to tell. The thumping of his heart and the bellows in his chest confusingly masked the exact source of the screaming.

Ba dum ba dum ba dum. Mary Harrison's heart now close to bursting. "Please don't kill me," she pleaded, her voice a trembling whisper, her mouth close to the Beast's malodorous ear.

Calves screaming. Head bursting. Shoe leather skidding over cobbles. Detective Inspector Albert Wiggins could feel his diaphragm cramping causing a stabbing painful stitch to develop in his side. His lungs were burning, and his heart hammered out a rhythm like a Coldstream snare. '*Need to get there,*' he ordered inwardly. "Go, Pyke, Go!" Wiggins encouraged breathlessly several yards behind his colleague.

Ba dum ba dum ba dum. "Please don't kill me," whimpering, Mary again beseeched her attacker, her body now paralysed with terror.

The shorter of the two men accelerated further, his coat tails flapping in his wake. He almost slid to the ground as he bulleted around a corner, steadying himself from falling by stretching his hand out onto the cobbles.

In a sudden outburst of fury, the Beast's talons slashed and ripped at her flesh. Its teeth biting and wrenching at exposed skin, flaying it from her neck like one side of a peeled banana.

Ba dum ba dum ba dum ba dum. Her legs thrashed and her arms flailed in a last despairing effort to free herself from the gnawing feasting Beast. "OH GOD, NO!" she screamed. "Sweet mother of Jesus," she then whispered.

Ba-dum. Blood gushed from her carotid artery as a bestial claw penetrated her abdomen and ripped upwards.

Ba-dum. Mary Harrison's body convulsed, twitching violently as frothy blood-streaked sputum exploded from her mouth.

Ba-dum. The Beast lapped at the bubbling blood foaming from her lips.

Ba. Her heart worked its last, deprived of oxygen-enriched blood as her life ebbed finally from her now mutilated body.

Silence. The Beast smashed her ribcage like brittle dry sticks and pulled the now redundant heart from her chest cavity, holding it aloft like some victorious trophy. It howled at the dark night sky.

The two running men came to a breathless skidding halt, crashing into each other at the entrance to Thames Path, just off Narrow Street. The dimly lit alleyway framed a gothic scene of unbelievable horror and violence. The two gasping figures stood in rigid disbelief at the incomprehensible sight they were witnessing. A huge shadowed figure hunched over a lifeless bundle of rags. It rose slowly, deliberately, like a lengthening shadow. Its head turned, the motion almost imperceptible like the minute hand of a clock to reveal the most frightening face imaginable, turning to stare directly back at their gaze. The face was that of a demon, its ink-black eyes beneath dark hooded lids was bordered by an immaculate silk top hat and the high collar of a black gabardine cloak; beauty framing its bestial countenance. Stygian pools of death locked upon shocked eyes. A grotesque half-smile played on the fiend's salivating blood-soaked lips. Deep grooves curtained the malevolent mouth as it bared its teeth and snarled. The Beast howled and laughed with an animalistic glee as it bit a chunk of the still warm heart of Mary Harrison before hurling it towards the two exhausted policemen. It came skidding to a halt at the toe of Wiggins' left boot. Both men looked disbelievingly at the object, instantly recognising it for what it was.

Both men looked up, each brandishing their pistols, but the apparition had gone, absorbed into the oily fog. The fiend had sprung away so rapidly and so silently that the men would later wonder if it had been there at all. This was all too much to process. They edged toward the bundle of rags only to discover the remains of the body of Mary Harrison encircled by an ever-increasing halo of blood. If it were not for the victim's clothing it would have been impossible to discern any gender. The face had been torn away and the throat lacerated into ribbons whilst the torso had been ripped apart and eviscerated.

Detective Inspector Albert Wiggins made the sign of the cross and fell to his knees.

Chapter 4 - The Force

After what he had just witnessed, Detective Sergeant Jem Pyke decided a drink was the satisfactory prescription to settle his nerves and allow him some sleep, so he headed to his preferred watering-hole, The Grapes. The Grapes was one of the many rough house pubs, come whorehouses in Whitechapel that never closed its doors if there was a penny to be made or a trick to be had. Pyke entered the smoke-laden atmosphere and drew a stool rasping across the dusty stone flagged floor and settled into his accustomed position hunched at the bar. He ordered a whisky from the formidable landlady Hungry Mary.

"Mind if I join you Sarge?" came a voice from Pyke's right as he fumbled in his pocket for some coins.

"By all means Pottsie," grunted Pyke indicating the adjacent stool to the young off-duty constable. "A little bit of company would be appreciated lad."

"Another two Mary if you don't mind," motioned Pyke with a nod of his head, "Make them large ones."

"Nasty business tonight by all accounts Sarge," offered Potts tentatively swallowing the firewater Hungry Mary offered up as whisky with a grimace.

"You bet your Grannie's last farthing it was lad. I ain't never seen nothing like it. Shook me from me bollocks to me boots I can tell ya. What I can't for the life of me understand is how that Beast vanished into thin air so damn quickly. It was a blasted dead-end! Nothing at the end of London Path but a drop into the river," added Pyke, running his grubby hands through his sweat-matted hair.

"Two more Mary when you're ready Luv," asked Pyke wiping his chin with his sleeve. "Why, you're in the mood tonight and make no mistake Jem?" observed Mary inquisitively.

"Just thirsty Mary," shot back Pyke, whilst at the same time rebuking the proposal of one of the Grapes' many regular working girls. "Not tonight Sally, got other things preying on me mind, even worse things than spending the night with you," he winked. Just as Mary turned to reach for the whisky bottle the narrow double doors of the pub burst open almost knocking over a slightly built, ratty-faced man who was staggering to a table with a tray laden with glasses of cheap gin.

An inebriated rabble of half a dozen ruffians spilled into the bar. The ugly mob, fronted by a hard-faced thug, flowed towards the bar in a torrent of chaos. Swearing, shouting, people being kicked from chairs and women leeringly snatched from laps.

"Drinks for me and me mates," hailed the apparent leader as he strutted his way towards the bar, the fingers of his huge calloused hands playing with his fob watch as he approached. He rested his elbows on the bar, wiped his nose with the back of his hand, and looked to his left where Pyke sat, already on his fourth Scotch and seemingly unaware of the change in atmosphere at the mob's entrance.

"LESLIE Pyke, as I live and breathe! I ain't seen your ugly mush since that business down in Kimberley. I thought that was you when I clocked the war wound," leered the heavy-set drunkard pointing to the sickle-shaped scar exposed on Pyke's forearm. Pyke acknowledged the man with the slightest nod of his head.

"I hope you ain't going to be causing no trouble Pricey," mumbled Pyke looking unconcerned by the larger man's reflection in the long gilt mirror hanging behind the bar. Mary was hurriedly clearing glasses whilst anxiously looking at Pyke's mirrored reflection, an uneasy unspoken assessment of the potentially ugly situation set out before them. Pyke winked at Mary reassuringly. The wink said, 'no need to worry, I have this under control.' He returned to his whisky and conversation with Constable Potts.

"So that's where you got the scar then Sarge?" enquired the young Bobbie inquisitively. "The Siege of Kimberley during the second Boer war?" he added, somewhat enthusiastically.

"Well, what do you expect from a damn Russki Son!" proffered Pyke.

"So, Leslie, how many ragamuffins 'ave you locked away today then? Hey! Leslie and Kimberley kinda match huh lads, both girls' names," sneered the thug turning to his mates and joining their laughter.

"The name's Jem," replied Pyke in a deep-throated growl, slowly emphasising each word whilst contemplating his whisky.

"Say, LESLIE, how's your old man, Sarah, and your old lady, George, these days?" laughed the ape-like leader of the mob as he wiped away the remains of the first slake of gin from his lips. He pushed his cap back from the front of his head and rubbed the back of his heavily rolled neck with his broad-fingered hand.

THWUUMP! Alf Price did not see it coming. Pyke's mammoth fist rammed home like a slab of granite. His meaty paws were chiselled like a Michelangelo creation; huge, muscled, kinetic. The uppercut trajectory of the bolt-hard knuckles at first parted the man's upper lip before continuing their upward path and snapping his nose. He was unconscious before the back of his skull crashed sickeningly against the stone-flagged floor. His right foot twitched convulsively in submission.

Immediately Pyke turned towards the other men in the mob who now stood before him. Pyke knew these were all street-hardened brawlers who knew their way around a bar fight. '*No Marquis of Queensbury rules here,*' he thought to himself, relishing the prospect.

The first man to reach Pyke felt a bone-crushing left hook shattering his ribs followed instantly by a right cross to the temple which rendered him senseless as he hit the glass laden table before slipping to the floor. A third assailant managed to land a hard right jab to the mouth of Pyke jolting his head sideward. Pyke used this momentum and spun around like a bovine shouldered ballerina, snatching a bottle from a nearby table and in a single spinning movement smashed it backhanded into the face of his foe who crumpled in a bloody mess.

"Let's be havin' you lads," he snarled, beckoning to the remaining three ruffians as a mixture of blood and saliva dribbled past his clenched teeth and down his chin towards his now loosened collar. "One at a time or all at once. Makes no odds to me!" Pyke smiled as two more men flew towards him. Pyke straight-legged the first man's kneecap hyperextending it at an acutely painful angle then dispatched the second with a head-butt to the face; a manoeuvre that his Chief Superintendent would have described as an exquisite 'Glaswegian Kiss'. The final attacker was the easiest to dispatch as he ran out of the pub wailing like a baby taken from the breast.

"Heavens above Sarge!" stammered a wide-eyed Potts. "Have you ever heard the term to chew iron and to spit rust? All I can say is that I'm sure glad you're on our side." Pyke grinned and turned back to the bar, gulping back his whisky. "Call the station lad and have the Paddy Wagon come and scrape up this scum. A night in the tank should clear their sorry bonces."

"Nobody but me sainted mam can get away with calling me Leslie," muttered Jem to no one in particular. He straightened his coat, took his brown derby from the hat stand, placed it upon his head, tipped the brim and shot Mary a good-humoured wink with the slightest of bows as he made his exit. For once in her life, Hungry Mary had completely forgotten to charge a customer.

'*A few more on the way home wouldn't hurt,*' he thought to himself as he headed into the damp, foggy London night.

The rays of a crisp January morning woke Pyke early the next day. He was still fully clothed minus his boots, coat, hat, and part of a tooth. A church bell was going off in his head accompanying that of nearby Saint Botolph's Church in Aldgate, and his mouth tasted like he had consumed the contents at the bottom of a particularly rancid birdcage.

'*Should have given those last few a miss,*' he mused as he rubbed the back of his neck and headed to the bathroom to empty his uncomfortably swollen bladder.

As he shaved, he looked at the man staring back at him. Rugged and moustachioed with the squarest of chins. The neck and shoulders of a bull inherited from his Blacksmith father and further developed through his early apprenticeship in the family forge in Shadwell Docks. He remembered the intense heat and physical exhaustion of the workplace. Long days and painful nights. The reverberating ringing of metal on metal, relentless exertion on arms and hands, hammering, shaping, gripping, the sweat constantly being wiped from stinging eyes, sizzling as it dropped onto the hot metal.

Scar tissue littered his face as if a caustic chicken had walked uncertainly across it, each scar a reminder of his many battles within the boxing ring and in the arena of war with the Royal Artillery. Sergeant Pyke, always Sergeant Pyke. Never Leslie! He recalled the words he had uttered over a decade before when he had pledged his oath to the Police Force of Metropolitan London.

'*I, Leslie Jeremiah Pyke, being appointed a constable of the Police Force of the Metropolitan District of London, do solemnly, sincerely and truly declare that I will serve our Sovereign, King Edward, and in all respects to the best of my skill and knowledge, discharge the said office faithfully according to Law.*'

'*According to Law,*' he chuckled inwardly. '*Well, that's been stretched enough on occasion.*'

His eyes were those of a clever and commanding man, confident in his abilities, experienced and settled within his own skin. A man who knew that he could outfight and outwit most of the human debris he encountered on a daily basis.

He combed his once thick sandy-blonde hair which was beginning to show signs of thinning, a recent development for which he held little appetite. Changing into some fresh clothes, he quickly shined his boots on the back of his trouser legs, grabbed his coat, warrant card and billfold, and his ubiquitous derby. He spat in the grate of the fire and headed for the door. He relished the early start which meant he could fill his lungs with the freshest part of the London day and would avoid the weekly visit of his landlord, an insistent Jew by the name of Levinski.

Better to face the debrief of last night's events with his boss the Scottish bulldog Chief Superintendent Magnus McDonald, than the veiled threats and sly pleadings of Levinski. Pyke laughed to himself at the conflicting images now in his head. Images of his landlord and that of Battling Levinski. One a hunchbacked money grasping crow, the other the strapping young American pugilist, destined, in Pyke's opinion to be World Light Heavyweight champion at some point. '*Not one single thing in common between these two men,*' thought Pyke with a snigger. He drew a deep breath, tugged at the front tails of his waistcoat, and headed off to the Station.

Detective Inspector Albert Wiggins and Detective Sergeant Leslie Pyke of the Metropolitan Police CID sat on a long wooden settle outside the office of their boss, Chief Superintendent Magnus MacDonald. One man sat shoulders hunched and head bowed, the other fiddled with his felt derby. Both men looked tired and drawn after the exploits of the previous night. A dreadful, sickening night. A night the two officers now inexorably shared. They sat in silence continually reviewing and recalling the details of the previous night's chase and its horrific conclusion. Both men had slept fitfully due to the shared memory of the two faces they had witnessed only hours before. Faces that were now forever burned into their consciousness. One face evil and ungodly, the other gruesomely stripped of any features whatsoever.

"Been to The Grapes again Sergeant?" asked Wiggins breaking the silence.

"I guess my bust lip and bruised countenance forbids any denial Inspector?" acknowledged Pyke with a sideward grin.

"That, and the awful rank of Mary's cheap whisky," added Wiggins. "Try to abstain for the duration of this investigation Pyke. I need you here and on form with your wits fully about you, not brawling and whoring every night. We need to solve this dreadful case as a matter of urgency."

Pyke nodded. "How do you think His Nibs will be, sir?" questioned Pyke.

"Not best pleased, I'm sure. Just state the facts the best you remember," Wiggins told Pyke.

"Them facts still seem impossible Sir to be fair," replied Pyke.

"State them just the same Jem."

Just then the office door adjacent to them suddenly swung open revealing a squat, somewhat stocky man in his second half-century. "Come on in the pair o' yeh," barked MacDonald in a brusque Scottish brogue.

Magnus McDonald was a twenty-eight-year veteran of the Metropolitan Police Force of London. A son of the rugged but beautiful Highlands of Scotland, he had risen sharply through the ranks of the Met from junior beat bobby to Chief Superintendent, due to a keen razor-sharp intelligence aligned with an unforgiving strength of character and determination verging on the brutal. He commanded the respect of his officers and the fear of the criminal population of London.

Wiggins and Pyke entered the sparsely furnished office and waited for their superior to indicate that they could be seated. MacDonald reached into his pocket and pulled out a small horn snuff pouch and proceeded to administer two successive inhalations after which he dabbed his nose with a grubby Paisley handkerchief.

"Sit doon then gentlemen. Inform me of last night's events please DI Wiggins."

"A stranger and ghastlier thing I have never seen Sir," he intoned. "Undoubtedly, we are dealing with the same creature that murdered the prostitute Louise Smith three days ago, just off Victoria Embankment. The two witnesses who called into the Yard that morning were a young lady and gentleman who described encountering a large, black cloaked beetle-like creature in the very vicinity of the first murder."

"Beetle?" queried MacDonald looking querulously at Wiggins. "Perhaps the young gentleman had overindulged."

"There were also reports of howls and shrieking, as those of a wild animal, that same morning."

"Foxes, perhaps?" questioned MacDonald with a raised eyebrow. "The Irish believed their mating shrieks to be those of the banshee you know."

Wiggins swallowed. "The description given by the young couple somewhat matches what myself and DS Pyke witnessed last night. I am convinced that both these murders were committed by the same culprit, Sir. Until last night we had not caught sight of the perpetrator of these fiendish murders and I must admit that I would rather not set eyes upon his face again any time soon."

"Damn devilish looking he was Sir," added Pyke, leaning forward to emphasise his point. "The injuries inflicted in killing this girl were truly horrific. Would put old Jack himself to shame." Wiggins kicked Pyke imperceptibly under the desk before continuing, "We were alerted to the approximate whereabouts by the whistles of two Constables that were in and around the Limehouse area of Docklands so we headed as fast as our legs would allow towards the shrill. This was at approximately eleven-thirty last night. If the night had not been so smoggy and slippery underfoot, I would like to wager we could have saved the poor girl and I cannot rid my thoughts of this possibility." Wiggins paused, drew a deep breath, and continued. "The scene we came upon was ... was ...well, indescribable Sir, for the want of a better word. The Beast pulled her heart from her chest and after taking a bite from it, hurled it towards us, Sir." The three men exchanged glances, not knowing how to continue.

"Why in Heavens did you no' draw yer pistols and shoot the damned abomination?" interjected MacDonald tersely.

"I'm ashamed to say, Sir, that my senses were not altogether working as they normally would have. I was having the utmost difficulty processing the scene that we were witnessing and by the time I'd regained some sensibilities and remembered to draw my pistol, he was gone. As quick as electricity he was," explained Wiggins.

"Electricity Sir sure enough. Mercury himself could not have caught that fiend. Faster than lightning and quieter than the grave so he was. Makes old Spring-Heeled Jack look like a one-legged pony!" quipped Pyke fingering his moustache anxiously. "Left me shaking like a shitting dog so he did!"

"Now, now Pyke, this is not the time to make light of such devilish matters," admonished Wiggins, his flaring nostrils belying his smile.

"Sorry Inspector. Rest assured that poor gal won't be 'aving an open casket to be sure," said Pyke shaking his head ruefully whilst fiddling with his hat.

"So, it's still out there?" spat a ruddy-faced MacDonald. "After all this, he's still at large? Still free to commit his atrocities on good, god-fearing people?" he added through gritted teeth.

"First Louise Smith and now this latest poor unfortunate! Neither were sexually molested nor raped but both ripped to shreds on my streets, gentlemen! Slaughtered with their throats and faces torn asunder by this Beast. What about suspects?" Wiggins and Pyke exchanged an uneasy glance, neither willing to offer anything at this stage of the investigation.

"Well? Suspects! Give me suspects gentleman," roared MacDonald, a wormlike zig-zagging vein pulsing above his left temple.

"There is the Russian. He is definitely a person of interest Sir," suggested Wiggins hesitantly. Pyke bit his lip.

"We must tread carefully in that respect, gentlemen," warned MacDonald sitting back in his chair. He slid open a desk drawer and produced an ancient looking briar. "Radasiliev is an envoy of the Russian Empire and a preeminent member of his country's consulate here in London. As such his diplomatic protection is a very real barrier to us acting on any suspicions we may have regarding his involvement in this or any other case."

"I fancy him for it, Chief," coughed Pyke. "He's a nasty piece of work and no mistake. I know that he has violently raped at least two and possibly three women in the East End. My informants tell me that they were all lucky to survive given the ferocity of the attacks. Yet none were willing to raise a complaint against him. Word is that he prowls the area looking for compliant victims, confident in the protection his status affords him. It is said he has something of a Mesmer about him." MacDonald nodded sagely as he lit his pipe, "Go on."

"His description could also match that of the Beast we saw last night, tall, slender, a forbidding presence. Perhaps he was even wearing some mask or disguised his features in some way," added Wiggins. "It is conceivable that he has escalated his behaviour to murder."

MacDonald sucked on the stem of his pipe for what seemed to Pyke and Wiggins to be an inordinately long time. "Bring him in for questioning. Tread cannily mind, he could bring the weight of Westminster doon upon oor heads. In the meantime, I would also recommend that it is time the pair o' yeh paid a visit to a certain Mr Van Hoon."

Chapter 5 - The Enigma

The house stood almost unseen, surrounded as it was by other large, but less resplendent villas in the Belgravia area of West London. A high, ivy infested, red-bricked wall topped with ornate cast iron spiked railings surrounded the sprawling grounds. The wall offered up one single entry gate, which Wiggins presumed also represented the only visible exit once inside.

As he and Pyke approached the gate Wiggins felt as if the weather had suddenly changed for the worse. Somehow the temperature seemed to have dropped and the very air around him became more electrically charged as if a thunderstorm was threatening from the now oppressive sky. Brushing aside some interfering ivy which crept over the face of the gates resembling a grotesque nest of intertwined rat tails, Pyke discovered a verdigrised brass bell button on the right-hand column of the double gate. The gate was of solid oak construction and was bolstered by huge iron hinges. The Blacksmith in Pyke admired the intricacy of the craftwork.

"Be my guest" offered Pyke to Wiggins who pressed the bell button twice. After a few moments, the securing chains were unlocked, and the gate was opened by a short, stooped figure shrouded in a hooded garment that seemed to envelop his entire body. A white macramé belt was tied at the waist. The figure extended a scrawny, pock-marked arm indicating that they enter and proceeded to guide the two men down the relatively short but wide gravel pathway that led to the mansion dwelling ahead.

The two detectives walked down the pathway, gravel crunching underfoot. The surrounding gardens were immaculate in their planting and design and were obviously tended to an exceptionally high and expert standard. The borders of the garden were shrouded in exotic trees of a type neither of the two detectives recognised. Brilliant red Japanese acers were interwoven with huge date palms, majestic cypresses, willowy eucalyptus trees and woolly trunked prehistoric-looking trachycarpus. Ferns, lilies and giant gunnera resembling spiky felt-covered umbrellas gave the overall impression of an exotic grove within a tropical jungle supplanted slap-bang in the middle of the most exclusive part of London. '*All quite remarkable,*' thought Wiggins.

The house that confronted them was just as outstanding as the gardens it stood within. A gothic revival extravaganza of turrets, rotundas, buttresses and balconies encapsulated by the most ornate Parisian style railings rose before the two approaching men. Turkish inspired copper turrets rested precariously on a roof that was pitched at an Eiger-like angle. The roof itself was covered in dull grey slates which made Wiggins think of the scales of a pangolin. At least two dozen large shuttered sash windows framed a central stucco portico of enormous stature. On each side of the portico stood a marble statue of a leonine and aquiline creature standing in a rampant pose. The two companions glanced briefly at each other with shared raised eyebrows as they mounted the Mediterranean hued terrazzo steps towards a gargantuan bronze door. A door inlaid with elaborate Arabesque figures and motifs.

Wiggins' investigative brain immediately recognised that the architecture and design of the building turned it into an elaborate fortress, difficult to access, and he suspected, even more difficult to exit once inside. The servant who had ushered them towards the house had disappeared.

"Your turn," said Pyke indicating with a nod of his head to the brass button set in the centre of a bronze coiled serpent fixed to the stonework of the arched door architrave. Wiggins nodded and pressed the button.

"Be prepared for a bit of a shock Pyke," warned Wiggins as they awaited a response. "Dante Van Hoon is an extremely eccentric and indeed dangerous character. He is the richest and most enigmatic individual in London if not all the land." Wiggins lowered his tone to a conspiratorial whisper, "Some say he is Dante Alighieri himself, kept alive these last six centuries by being in league with the Devil. Others say that he is Count de Saint-Germain, Louis XV's supposedly immortal Court Alchemist. Others say that he is Saint John the Apostle cast out from heaven by Saint Peter to walk the Earth in torment forever. All poppycock to be sure but what we do know for certain is that he heads one of the largest extortion rings in the world, operating from behind a cloak of respectability. How he exerts such power over the great and good remains a mystery but his connections range across the highest strata of modern society, from the English nobility to the Royal Families of Europe, Americas richest tycoons and beyond. He is the serpent in today's Garden of Eden, seemingly untouchable like his army of pox-ridden informants and spies. He exists in a hinterland between the law and the underworld. In the past, Van Hoon has assisted us in certain delicate cases which we at the Yard had been unable to, how would you say … conclude satisfactorily," continued Wiggins. "Always for the same recompense, that is, his continued immunity from persecution and prosecution with regards his business operations, along with a very singular end fee which involves no financial transaction but rather the provision of some unique collateral."

Pyke was just about to enquire about this collateral when the huge door heaved open with surprisingly little noise. Inside they were greeted by yet another stooped and severely pock-marked figure, this time dressed in the finest livery of a footman or butler.

All houses have their own distinct and individual aroma and this gothic mausoleum was no different. Incense could be seen burning from wall-mounted sconces dotted at an elevated level around the bare but dressed stonework walls. Huge elaborately detailed medieval tapestries depicting scenes of battle were suspended from ornate brass rails. Each sconce was fashioned in the shape of a different animal; here a snake, there a lion, an eagle, a peacock and an ape. The atmosphere was dense with the scent of eastern aromatic oils. The aromas of patchouli and sandalwood being the most prominent. Wiggins' impression was that the sheer volume of incense was unwarranted even for the odours of Georgian London. Perhaps such a cloak of perfumery was there to mask an underlying, and as yet unidentified smell.

"DI Wiggins and Sergeant Pyke of Scotland Yard to see Mr Van Hoon," offered Wiggins presenting his warrant card.

"The master is expecting you gentlemen," lisped the scarred manservant whilst ushering them into the hallway. "Please walk this way." A fleeting and unspoken joke played upon the detectives' eyes, but neither man seized the opportunity to imitate the gait of the stooped man shuffling ahead of them.

"Crikey, boss," whispered Pyke out of the side of his mouth. "I ain't never seen anything like this outside of that Natural History Museum."

Wiggins nodded, looking furtively around whilst trying not to look as awestruck as he felt himself. They found themselves surrounded by hardwood framed glass cases containing a wide variety of stuffed creatures. Sloe-eyed lemurs stood alongside lugubrious looking sloths, South American peccaries and a huge tapir whose oily fur gave the impression that the animal was still alive and perspiring. At the centre of the grand entrance hallway stood an encumbered grizzly bear the height of which must have exceeded nine feet and stood nearly half the height of the decoratively carved wood-panelled ceiling above them. Wiggins inwardly noted that the standard of the taxidermy on display was of an exquisite, museum level quality and must have been produced by the hands of an absolute master of the craft.

The two policemen were guided past the foot of a huge sweeping bronze staircase, whose twin newel posts were each in the form of a dragon holding a limp lion in its gaping jaws, and on into a large imposing drawing room which was in the manner of a glasshouse adjoining the main building. The room was full of yet more exotic plants no doubt propagated from some far distant rain forest. Among the verdure, Wiggins spied several brilliantly coloured hummingbirds flitting from one iridescent bloom to another. Butterflies occasionally appeared randomly kissing orchids and lilies, and the room echoed to the background trilling of insects unseen or perhaps unrecognised within the foliage. Tiny green lizards darted across the windowpanes skidding through the droplets of condensation racing each other to nowhere.

Wiggins was unable to shift his gaze from the walking stick resting in the nearby umbrella stand. He was unsure of what species of wood it was carved from, but the entire shaft was a yellowish-brown highlighted with dramatic dark stripes. He was transfixed by its strikingly heavily grained body and the several knots that appeared like squinting eyes returning his gaze. There were clearly defined sections getting incrementally smaller the closer they got to the tip. Like everything else in the house, it was of astonishing quality and looked to have some genuine age. The carving was extremely intricate and ornate showing a heavily detailed castle, and he could make out a rendering of Aeolus, the God of wind blowing plumes of air forth from his puffed cheeks. There were vile mythological creatures and writhing human bodies, effigies of cardinals and demons. There was a boat of some description, and a circle of flames leapt from the final section before ending with what looked to Wiggins like a platinum ferrule. But the most impressive aspect of the room was the figure who greeted them upon their entrance.

"Good afternoon gentlemen, I am Van Hoon," he announced in a toneless and rather hoarse timbre. He had a slight but indeterminate foreign accent, although his English was impeccable and his diction precise. The resplendently clad figure sat in a high throne-like chair, more ecclesiastical than royal, behind a huge walnut desk in the centre of the room. He rose slightly as Wiggins and Pike entered and indicated they sit on a patent leather chaise of enormous proportions on the opposite side of the desk.

The figure that confronted them was a truly remarkable one. Van Hoon was a man of indeterminate age but the clothes he sported exuded the finery of an eighteenth-century dandy. He wore a deep blue high-collared velveteen suit over a gold vest adorned with natural seawater pearl buttons. Around his neck was draped a gold-coloured neckerchief of the finest Mulberry silk which was loosely clasped with a black sapphire serpentine tie pin. His shirt appeared to be of white lace with ruffed cuffs and a stiff collar. His blue-black hair cascaded in waves from his high forehead onto his shoulders framing a face that exuded extreme intelligence and strength of character. High cheekbones curtained a strong jaw and square chin.

There were two other striking elements of this remarkable face. Van Hoon removed a pair of modernistic 'penny piece' round pink coloured spectacles to reveal the most remarkable pair of eyes that either of the two policemen had ever encountered. One eye was a brilliant shade of verdant green and the other was as milky white and clouded as that of a dead fish. By far the most remarkable aspect of Van Hoon's countenance, however, was the leprous scarring etched into the left side of his face and neck. Like the grotesque yet beautiful fractal scars created when struck by lightning.

"Bocote wood DI Wiggins," announced Van Hoon walking towards the detective. "I could not help but notice your attentions to my walking cane. More of a stick to be accurate but the term 'cane' is so much more refined for such a remarkable example don't you think?" Van Hoon picked up the cane and slowly rotated it in his grasp. "The wood itself originates from the flowering Cordia plant, native to parts of southern Mexico. I believe it was carved sometime in the fourteenth century and I am especially fond of the Mexican fire opal knob. Its orange translucency I find rather splendid. The cane, as I am sure you have noted, depicts the nine circles of Hell as described in The Divine Comedy."

"Written by a namesake of yours," observed Wiggins.

"Yes indeed, Dante Alighieri. You show profound knowledge," retorted a somewhat taken aback Van Hoon.

As they all took their seats Van Hoon detected Pyke's ill-disguised revulsion at the sight of the extortionist's scarring.

"You spied my affliction. Leprosy, though now contained by a medication of my devising. Most all sufferers view the condition as a curse, however, I gentlemen, regard it as a blessing. It gives me unprecedented access to the denizens of London's leper houses. They are my Pestilent. My Untouchables. They can come and go whenever and wherever I need them to be without fear of interference. What man dare stops to question a leper? So long as I hold the medicinal solution to their affliction within my power, they serve me with unquestioning loyalty and deference." "At the same time allowing you to blackmail and extort huge sums from the misadventures of unfortunate and misguided nobility," interjected Wiggins with a thinly veiled degree of venom.

"Perhaps Inspector. I am a man of many passions," laughed Van Hoon. "Science, botany, philosophy, travel and of course … money. It is my only vice. I am also, as you can see an amasser of curios," indicating around the room with an elegant flourish of his hand. "I am at heart a collector, gentlemen, not only of substantial amounts of money but also of the souls of the departed made new again in the preservation of their former selves."

"Yes, I buy and sell information and protect those who need my protection, but disambiguation remains my greatest passion." Van Hoon paused, circumflexed an eyebrow, "Taxidermy to you. A fascinating term don't you agree. It comes from the ancient Greek, 'taxis' and 'derma.' The literal translation being 'to move skin'. Rather splendid don't you think gentlemen?"

Van Hoon pointed his ornately carved cane and directed their gaze towards a free-standing glass case to one side of his desk which contained a stuffed armadillo.

"The culprit gentleman," announced Van Hoon indicating the Armadillo. "The very animal from which I contracted my condition whilst hunting for specimens in the Argentine. You see, armadillos are the only creature known by modern science to be a carrier and spreader of leprosy to humans." Van Hoon trilled looking admiringly into the glass case. "This creature bestowed me an everlasting affliction, and in return, I gave it everlasting life. Quite fitting don't you think?"

Wiggins and Pyke glanced at each other momentarily, bemusement passing unsaid between them. '*This bloke's off his bleedin' rocker,*' thought Pyke. Just then Van Hoon's panegyric regarding the South American armour shelled mammal was interrupted by the appearance of a diminutive oriental servant girl carrying a tray of drinks which she placed on the highly polished walnut desk. Wiggins noticed she was wearing a macramé belt just as the hooded fellow that opened the gate had sported, only green in colour. After a brief bow and a smiling glance at Pyke, the girl departed the room tiptoeing demurely and almost silently.

"Jiao defected to our Family of the Pestilent from her previous employer," nodded Van Hoon, noticing the slight flirtation that had flashed between his servant girl and the pugnacious police sergeant. "That yellow-skinned, opium fuelled scourge, Mr King."

Pyke straightened his tie and clicked his jaw. "I take it you and King don't see eye to eye then? Suppose two master crime lords in one city is one too many for both of you?"

Van Hoon smiled sardonically as he reached for the crystal decanter. "King is no threat whatsoever to me, gentlemen. We move in disparate circles. He is, however, as you both well know, a very tangible threat to the safety of every citizen in this Metropolis. His network of Dacoit thieves and assassins are a plague on our society. His poisonous opium houses pray on the carnal desires of weak-willed and vulnerable souls. In short, gentlemen, he is the rat that needs to be cleansed from our sewer."

"And leave the way clearer for your activities," bit back Pyke. Wiggins placed a gently restraining hand upon his colleague's tensed forearm.

"As, if I suspect, you came here seeking my assistance Detective Inspector, I suggest you reign in your Hound," grinned Van Hoon, pouring them each a substantial brandy into a crystal cut glass. "Have a Cognac please, it is my only vice."

"Thank you," smiled Wiggins accepting the glass and nodding to Pyke to do likewise.

"We have indeed come seeking your assistance with an ongoing investigation."

Van Hoon savoured the subtle tones of the Le Burguet '65 whilst Pyke downed his brandy in one swift swig and replaced it on the silver tray rather more forcibly than was necessary. *'I'd like to knock Dutchy's clogs off! One round in the ring and I'd knock that arrogant head off his fancy-Dan shoulders,'* he thought inwardly.

"The celebrated Beast I have been hearing so much of I presume?" shrugged Van Hoon raising his cadaverous eyes from the rim of his glass to meet those of Wiggins. Wiggins nodded. "We are experiencing some difficulty in identifying and apprehending the individual in question I have to admit."

Van Hoon sat back in his chair and clasped the fingertips of his hands together under his chin. "A monster indeed. Jack reincarnate they say. A worthy prize. Consider my interest piqued gentlemen. I assume that should my contribution in this endeavour prove successful, the customary collateral would be forthcoming as my fee?"

"The customary collateral," nodded Wiggins. The pupil of Van Hoon's undead eye dilated ever so slightly at the prospect.

The Belgravia night was unseasonably balmy for winter, with an abnormally warm breeze tickling through the fronds of the ancient Trachycarpus upon which Dante Van Hoon rested his head. He gazed at the night sky, mentally identifying a remarkably considerable number of stars. *'Many of these stars are billions of years older than the Sun that feeds our planet,'* he mused. *'Incalculable age, incalculable numbers.'* The enigma appealed to the ageless leper. How many of these sparks had spat out their last candela of light during the course of his lifetime he wondered? How many worlds snuffed out? The light he was studying was already millions of years old. Time travel in effect. The fact that he was observing light from stars that no longer existed fascinated the leper tremendously. His mortality or otherwise a mere speck amongst the panorama displayed above him. An old Arabic saying strayed into his mind, *'The thoughts of one who sleeps indoors rise as high as the ceiling. The thoughts of those who sleep outside rise to the stars.'*

Van Hoon was impervious of the night temperature as he scratched behind the rough-haired ear of the Thylacine which rested its head upon his bare chest. The creature made a catlike purring rumble, its diaphragm resonating with pleasure as it stretched its long neck closer to Van Hoon's hand. The male, Ingomar, having noticed the gesture of affection, lifted itself from where it lay curled at Van Hoon's unshod feet and began to nuzzle his master's neck, keen to receive similar attention to its mate, Parenthia. *'Imagine the astonishment of those fools at the Regents Park Zoo if they realised that a pair of the world's rarest carnivorous marsupials were lying on a lawn not three miles from its very gates,'* smiled Van Hoon.

Van Hoon's attempts to breed the pair had thus far been frustratingly fruitless and he dreaded the prospect of these majestic animals fading away before they could reproduce. He had toyed with the idea of experimenting with some serum, reasoning that if it worked on humans, why not, given some modifications, on animals also. A project for another day he had decided, hoping nature's course would be the preferable and ethical option.

Van Hoon scratched each tiger simultaneously, a wide smile spreading across his singular face. He was never more content than when he was with his animals, stroking and massaging the short fur of their striped hindquarters. Relaxing, enjoying their unconditional devotion. Both tigers had offered their bellies for attention, nature's most vulnerable area, revelling in Van Hoon's scratching. He felt a warm gently rasping tongue roll across a scar that traversed his abdomen from west to east. He glanced down and saw Mayerhofer, his wolf husky, jealous at the attention bestowed upon the Tasmanian tigers, licking at the cicatricial tissue. Van Hoon laughed aloud. The wolf always seemed to be drawn to the scar, lapping at it as if to aid its healing, now long since passed. How ironic, he thought, given the nature of how the horrific wound had been bestowed all those years ago one night in Budapest.

How idyllic and contented he was. His three favourite companions paying homage to him on a beautiful star-speckled night. He knew his face was spilt with a smile from ear to ear.

Van Hoon's mind returned once more to the idea of treating the Thylacines with life-prolonging serum. He would much rather lengthen the lives of these majestic animals than those of the worthless Illuminati who paid him a King's Ransom every year for the provision of his miraculous elixir. The richest people in the world fed him money, gold, bonds, jewels, land and property in order to live one more year of their useless, degraded lives. Kings and Emperors, tycoons and nobility. The public never seemed to question why it was that these people tended to live to extraordinarily old age in comparison to their less affluent counterparts. The consensus being that a life of privilege and being waited upon enabled them to outlast their less fortunate brethren. Only Van Hoon knew the truth. Only his was the power to grant longevity or to curtail existence. Only he held their very lives in his hands.

Chapter 6 - The Morgue

"We very much appreciate you dropping by the Station Doctor Bleak. Your expertise in such matters is always greatly appreciated. I think from what you've told us that we can safely confirm the poor fellow's demise was as a direct result of the unfortunate head injuries he received from the falling cargo of wine crates at Victoria Dock."

DI Wiggins shook the doctor's hand vigorously and proceeded to lead him out of the station morgue. At that moment, the detective hesitated and momentarily turned again to the doctor and enquired, "That reminds me, could you possibly spare a further few moments of your valuable time Doctor Bleak?"

"Yes, I'm sure I can," replied the doctor, checking his fob watch with an agreeable smile. "Always a pleasure to help, Inspector. How may I be of assistance?" Wiggins sensed that agreeable, though he appeared, the good doctor would be more comfortable elsewhere. He led the doctor back into the morgue and through into a slightly smaller tiled antechamber. In the centre of the room stood what appeared to be two tables draped with jute. The detective uncovered the first table revealing the mutilated body of a middle-aged lady positioned supinely within a shallow zinc trough.

"Laying before you my good doctor are the remains of Mary Harrison aged 34 years," detailed Wiggins. "She was an actress of some repute and was found two nights ago in a narrow street in the Limehouse area, not only with a severely fractured skull but with her throat and most of her face torn asunder. Although she is in a frightful condition, we can clearly see what appear to be teeth marks where her throat once was. What we now need to decipher whether these injuries were inflicted by a human or an animal. If so what type of animal did this so we can then perhaps discover if any beasts matching your thinking have presently escaped the Zoo at Regent's Park."

Doctor Bleak looked intently at the body in front of him whilst removing his overcoat and rolling up his shirt sleeves. He fumbled in his waistcoat pocket and produced a small pair of wire-rimmed spectacles which he perched on the end of his hooked nose. "I am without my tools so evidently this is not the ideal situation for

THE REIGN OF THE BEAST: A DI WIGGINS ADVENTURE

me to conduct a comprehensive examination but on preliminary inspection, there would seem to be massive haemorrhaging due to a combination of biting and of slashing." Wiggins raised his eyebrows and cocked his head for a closer look as Bleak motioned to the neck and chest areas where ragged ripped flesh was underscored by long slits and incisions. "Judging by the destruction here I would initially suspect that the unfortunate victim was sliced several times with some form of sharp blade, an open razor perhaps, and subsequently this slashed flesh was then ripped apart by the teeth, not of a wild animal, but of some dog, possibly a bulldog or a pinscher, judging by the bite dimensions." The doctor then carefully turned the corpse over from her waist up. "There is no doubt in my mind that the head trauma you mentioned was a subsidiary result of her falling backwards immediately during the attack onto the flagstones that pave Narrow Street."

Wiggins uncovered the second table, diverting his eyes as he did so. "And this is Louise Smith, an erstwhile prostitute who was murdered only a matter of days before Miss Harrison. Would you have an opinion as to the nature of this unfortunate woman's attacker, Sir?"

Wiggins could see that even Bleak, a doctor of many years' experience was shaken by what he saw. "The poor woman," lamented Bleak. "She has similar, but more widespread injuries than those of Miss Harrison," he stuttered. "In this case, the creature has evidently eaten or removed the visceral organs. Perhaps a wolf rather than a dog Inspector? Quite a ferocious animal I would think."

"My initial postulations also. Yet, if the same creature killed both Louise Smith and Mary Harrison, then that creature was undoubtedly a man," postulated Wiggins.

"I find this hard to countenance given the injuries I see before me Inspector," countered Doctor Bleak.

"Yet I saw the culprit of this killing with my own two eyes, Doctor Bleak. A man. An unholy Beast, yet a man none the less." Doctor Bleak shook his head in disbelief and hastily began to put on his overcoat and gloves. He looked pale and visibly shaken. "This is most upsetting. A man you say? What type of devil could have committed this level of atrocity? Please understand that I am a general practitioner and surgeon and therefore forensic medicine is not my particular area of expertise. I suggest if you need any further advice to contact a Doctor William Willcox. He is the best man currently in London to enlighten you regarding chemical pathology, toxicology and forensic medicine. You will most probably find him at Saint Mary's Hospital during daylights hours," offered Bleak adjusting his top hat, before bidding farewell and exiting the Station.

"Thank you again, Doctor Bleak," shouted DI Wiggins at the already departed doctor. Wiggins stood contemplating the bodies before him, rubbing his chin through his neatly clipped beard.

Chapter 7 - The Heap

Pyke was soaked through. He felt as though his skin was a sodden greatcoat draped over a frame of frozen, brittle bone. The hour was late, and the night was chillingly cold. He clutched at the collar of his coat as his breath formed wraith-like condensed steam clouds that drifted behind him as he strode down the alleyway. Every surface around him was covered with a sheen of glistening moisture; the street cobbles, the brickwork of the buildings' walls, all highlighted by the fuzzy light emanating from the fog-shrouded streetlamps. Even at this time of night, the stench emanating from Smithfield Market pervaded the air, a mixture of blood, viscera, death, and fear. The particular slaughterhouse that Pyke and Potts were headed for was not known for upholding best practice as regards current legislation. Pyke knew for a fact that it dealt in untraceable carcasses and was numbered amongst the most unhygienic abattoirs in London. As such it tended to deal in clandestine underground cash-only transactions and had a turgid reputation of selling on cheap, rotting and infected meat. Pyke had also had reason to suspect over the years that not all the meat that passed through it was purely of the animal variety.

"You're in for a treat tonight, Pottsie," grinned Pyke as he hunched his shoulders even further forward into his collar. "Jesus! It's as cold as a stepmother's kiss tonight. You'll be glad you volunteered for this one. Grimley's Slaughterhouse is arguably the most revolting shit hole in Smithfield bar none, I reckon."

"I've heard that tannery was the foulest of all jobs Sarge, ain't that right?" offered Potts, teeth chattering back the chilly night.

"No two ways 'bout it mate. Still is. All skin, fat and guts. The stench of lime and dog shit is deplorable. Absolutely putrid job. Even worse than a tosher or a leech collector in my book. Give me ten hours a day at my Old Man's Smithies forge any day of the week." Potts laughed. He well knew Pyke's background and was sure that his upbringing had been equally as hard and grim as that of a tanner's lad.

As they approached the large timber double gates of the knacker's yard, Potts glanced upwards at the wrought iron lettering arching overhead. *Grimley's International Abattoir*, he read, inwardly grinning at the inappropriateness of the grisly sounding title. Pyke pounded the door with a gloved fist. "Let's be havin' you lads! CID!"

After what seemed like the longest minute of Pott's young life standing in the downpour the door rattled open. An enormous, near toothless, mole polluted head peered around the gates. "Whatchoo want copper?" it snarled.

"Health inspection," demanded Pyke showing his warrant card and shoving the ugly giant of a watchman in the chest as he pushed passed him through the gates. "Hoy, you can't just waltz in 'ere pigskin!" argued the watchman, trying to hold back Constable Potts. Without any further preamble and without breaking stride, Pyke slammed a haymaker of a right-hand square on the ogre's upper lip. The giant toppled and landed flat on his back, gurgling in the muddy street.

"That should have taken care of those last two tombstones you call teeth, Stonesy," muttered Pyke as he beckoned Potts to follow him across the yard towards the main slaughterhouse building.

Archibald Stone, sat on the cobbles rubbing his bloodied mouth, the arse of his trousers now soaked through. "Ain't no need for that Sergeant Pyke, I was letting you in, wasn't I?" he mumbled to no one but himself.

Two angry Rottweilers strained at their neck chains which were secured to a ground spike, barking uncontrollably as the two police officers strode across their yard. "Shouldn't we have some more back up Sarge?" stuttered Potts glancing around nervously. He had had a mortal fear of dogs since being nipped as a small child by Whisky, his Great Aunt Lilly's aptly named west highland terrier.

"Not to worry Pottsie. This shouldn't take very long. Just a bit of a fishing expedition, albeit in the foulest knacker's yard this side of Gomorrah! All you need to do is look like a policeman, don't inhale through your nose and leave the rest to me." Pyke raised a booted foot and kicked open the main door. The stench hit them like a club hammer. The air was rotten with blood and guts, decay and death. The atmosphere was putrid and noxious causing Potts to dry retch. Pyke produced a small jar of peppermint oil from his pocket and offered it to his young colleague. "Here you go Pottsie me lad, dab a drop of this on your upper lip. It'll mask the pong a bits."

The nightshift was in earnest progress. Most of the tanners and butchers had looked up from their work as the door had flown open. The tanners stopped stirring their pits of foul-smelling liquid and scraping at the hanging animal hides with tanner hooks. "No cause for concern lads," shouted Pyke, again flashing his warrant card, "routine health inspection."

Potts realised that they were in a potentially perilous situation. Most of these men were armed with meat cleavers, knives and butcher's hooks. He grasped the head of his truncheon reassuringly and hoped that Pyke was carrying his service pistol. Pig and cow carcasses hung swaying from rows of meat hooks suspended from the ceiling. Blood pooled on the blistered concrete floor. The tension in the air was as thick and sickly as the sweet metallic pungency of the blood in their nostrils. Half a dozen of the larger framed butchers pushed their way past the suspended carcasses as if parting grotesque curtains and approached threateningly brandishing various weaponry. The carcasses swung from side to side dripping blood in spirals on the killing floor.

"Sarge?" questioned Potts, looking increasingly nervously at Pyke, who seemingly unworried drew his pistol, took careful aim and gently squeezed the trigger. The bullet hammered home into a pig carcass situated between the two most fearsome looking antagonists. The group came to an uncertain jerking halt. "Next bullet is for one of you ladies. Up to you which one. First to take another step wins the cigar and gets hung up next to old Daisy there."

"Let them past," came a rumbling voice from the far end of the room. "We have enough killing here." The butchers' arms dropped to their sides and the group stood aside allowing the two policemen to approach where the rumbling voice had emanated. As they moved forward Potts realised that any potential retreat was now cut off from behind by the assembled mob. Glancing behind him he could also see the ogre, Stones, re-entering the building, blooded lip included. The Rottweilers were straining at a chain in each of his hands and were being driven wild by the scent of fresh blood. Potts had never been so afraid in his entire life. He glanced once more at Pyke who seemed as cool as ice. Potts could see a faint mass take shape from the emergent darkness of a corner of the vast concrete bunker of the room. It was an indistinct shape at first but as they got closer the silhouette became gradually more defined. A darker smaller shape shifted within the darkness of the corner. Potts saw what appeared to be a huge flabby arm-like appendage reach upwards towards the ceiling and pull on a single downward hanging cord. With an audible click, the shape before them was bathed in electric light. Pott's eyes widened and his jaw visibly dropped, his stomach almost turning at the sight before him. The largest, most obese human form he had ever seen sat in front of them, bare-chested on a huge timber chair. Its pendulous breasts hung glistening with sweat, saliva and blood. The chair it sat upon was constructed of scaffold boards, joists and other timbers large enough to support the tremendous weight of its occupant. The eyes in the huge bald head that sat atop a mass of quivering blubberous, blood-stained fat, were almost entirely lost in the glutinous folds that engulfed them. The beady eyes met Pyke's unmoving gaze. The eyeballs tremored incessantly as though they were darting rapidly around at tremendous speed, desperately in search of something they could never find. The man before them, if man it truly was, reminded Potts of a tuskless walrus. He mentally wagered that a walrus would smell sweeter and weigh far less than this abomination.

"Constable Potts, make the acquaintance of the Heap," declared Pyke with a flourish towards the corpulent mass of human obesity. "I would make the introduction more formal, but nobody actually knows his real name, ain't that right Heap old boy?" teased Pyke.

The Heap shrugged his massive fatty shoulders and grunted nonchalantly. The movement created a sticky, sickly sound as if two sides of a rotten fruit had been prised apart. He eagerly picked up a leg of mutton from his lap and chewed on it as if ravenous. Within a few seconds, all but the bone had been swallowed before it was given a last disgusting lick before sucking the marrow from within. It was then tossed aside towards a pile of bones at his enormous bloated bare feet. His legs were patterned with festering ulcerated sores that seeped clear fluid. 'Human juice,' thought Potts in disgust. The Heap wiped the grease from his hands on his huge stomach and belched loudly. The hands appeared almost as paddles so fat and swollen were his fingers with deep dents where knuckles should be.

"The Heap sat down here more than eight years ago and ain't moved a muscle since, except to eat of course!" explained Pyke with a chuckle in his voice. Potts stood motionless, his mouth still agape, unsure of what to say or do.

"What do you want Pyke, can't you see I'm busy," spluttered the Heap, pieces of mutton and spittle flying from his rubbery swollen lips. "Who's your girlfriend? She would make a rather pretty gift. Maybe a bow or a ribbon here or there." Potts' cheeks puffed somewhat uneasily, and his head clouded at the unimaginable thought.

Pyke removed a half-smoked cigar deliberately from his inside pocket, struck a match and puffed until the cigar end produced a satisfying glow. He shook the match and discarded it casually on the floor where the still hot tip fizzled in a puddle of blood. He blew a dense blue-grey smoke ring which ghosted its way towards the Heap. "Disgusting habit. Put it out," slobbered the Heap.

"You got to be pulling my chain, Heapie. This stogie is the least disgusting thing in this entire sluice house," replied Pyke.

"It'll be the end of you Pyke, you know it's bad for your health," belched the Heap, picking up a boiled chicken and ripping it in two, pimpled slimy skin flying in all directions.

"I can safely say that your meat will get you before my tobacco will get me," grinned Pyke deliciously exhaling another huge plume of smoke.

"No one ever died of eating meat, so far as I know," stated the Heap, sucking dry the second half of the chicken and tossing the carcass onto his pile.

"No one ever scoffed meat the way you do, Heapie. Half a stone a day of any foodstuff is going to clog you up old mate, never mind half a stone of that stuff you flog as meat." Pyke turned to Potts. "You remember we stated there couldn't be a more disgusting job in the world than being a Tanner? Well, I suddenly remembered that there is!" Pyke nodded at a forlorn young lad who stood in the shadows to the side of the Heap holding a heavily soiled towel and a yard brush. Potts could feel his lunchtime sausage sandwich surge upwards to make an imminent reappearance.

"What do I want? Good question, Heap old fellow. I want to know what you have heard about the madman who trawls our streets murdering our good citizens," demanded Pyke.

"Women, Pyke. Murdering our good women," corrected the Heap, wiping saliva from the multiple rolls of fat that served him as a chin and as a makeshift bib. He cast a lascivious eye in the direction of Potts.

"I am aware of your, how can I put it, intimate preferences," said Pyke, glancing at the forlorn figure of the young lad in the shadows. "But these women are citizens of this good city just as I, or even you are, Heap. Don't forget that my job is to protect everyone out there. Even low lives such as you!"

The Heap grunted and tried his best to slightly shift his enormous bulk, wind loudly escaping from his rear as he did so. "A wolf is what I've heard. Or a man with a wolf. Or a Man-Wolf, like you 'ear them old nightmare stories about. Not that I've seen anything mind, I don't get out as much as I should these days you understand." The Heap roared with laughter and sprayed small pieces of masticated chicken on to his gigantic sagging breasts. He was still roaring with laughter and slapping a thigh the size of a man as Pyke and Potts made their exit out into the welcome freshness of the night air. The laughter of the huge mass of adipose tissue still ringing in their ears.

"Cor blimey Sarge," blurted Potts gulping in the London smog as if it were a life-giving elixir. "I think I might try that vegetarianism them Suffragettes all go for. I ain't never going to be able to look at another sausage or pork chop as long as I live and breathe."

"Another box ticked in your training lad. You have now been officially acquainted with the Heap," Pyke laughed and put his arm around the younger man's shoulder as they strode off into the gloom. "Let me take you for a drink. How's about a swift half or two in the Red Pig?"

"Easy on the pork scratchings, Sarge!" joked Potts.

Chapter 8 - The Viscount

Egyptian and Sudanese antiquities and artefacts of all size and description peppered the spacious Georgian drawing room. A green siltstone bust of an unnamed pharaoh created the impression it was attempting to decipher the hieroglyphs on papyrus scrolls that were displayed in nearby walnut cabinets. An intricately carved bronze scarab beetle looked as if it was scuttling gingerly around the limestone sculpted paws of the cat goddess Bastet, the Egyptian goddess of domesticity. There was also a solid gold effigy of an empty funeral boat alongside a bluestone amulet depicting the eye of Rah. In one corner stood an unopened rather plain sarcophagus bearing no inscription.

The drawing room was lavish but not ostentatiously so. Hunting scenes and traditional landscapes decorated each wall and Persian and Turkish rugs adorned the hardwood floor. One painting which stood out from the others, however, was done in a modern cubist bravura style. It was of a strangely confusing portrait, at once inviting head turning and the process of thought to understand the peculiar angular features. The ancient antiquities and antiques were displayed with modern works of art in a tastefully dichotomous yet harmonious way.

A long-limbed, broad-shouldered man with grey hair sat on a tan leather button-back library chair. He wore a smoking-jacket of Paisley print over an informal slate grey sack suit. He looked comfortable in himself and his surroundings. Black Italian leather brogues bore a mirror shine with even the soles displaying a highly burnished polish. Lord Randolph Jasper Harkness had just been served afternoon coffee and the smell of Arabica beans now percolated the corner where he sat reading his morning newspaper.

"Dreadful business this beastly fellow," remarked Lord Harkness as he angrily crumpled the newspaper closed. He turned his pained arthritic neck towards his butler. "What possesses a man, for it will be a man I can assure you, Jeffers, to commit such heinous atrocities?" he boomed in his deep baritone voice. Jeffers remained silent in the knowledge that this question was purely rhetorical, and his opinion was not required at this juncture. There was always an unmistakable tone in his master's voice that signalled when a reply or opinion should be forthcoming.

"I suppose if we truly understood *why*, father, we would be no better than the monster himself," replied his eldest daughter, Agatha Harkness, who had entered the drawing room just as her father had launched his tirade.

"Oh, you're back Aggie. How did this week's mission go?" asked the Lord lowering his voice and smiling attentively. His ice-blue eyes glinted with inner pride as he regarded his daughter.

"Very well father. With everyone's assistance, we distributed three crate loads of clothes this morning. The poor unfortunate people of London's darkest East End are so dreadfully poor. Spitalfields today was even more poverty-ridden and tragic than last week's venture into Limehouse. Your heart almost freezes solid when you see the children's haunted expressions brighten at receiving a second-hand coat or a pair of used shoes. And the simple toys only go to make the smiles last a little longer. Bless them, some have never possessed a pair of shoes let alone a toy in their young lives. These are not the faces of children but the defeated time-weary faces of old age. The simple act of Constance and I distributing clothes at least keeps them from dying from something as avoidable as the cold. If only we could supply them medication to lessen their illness and pain. It is perhaps something we should investigate the possibility of a little deeper."

"Indeed, but talking of death, I would rather you and your sister did not frequent the poorer areas of the City for the time being Agatha. These dreadful occurrences in Whitechapel and Limehouse give me the fear," specified her father pointing once more at the newspaper. "I know your deeds are meritorious and well-intentioned but to possibly endanger yourself and Connie for the sake of clothing some drunks and ne'er day wells does not rest well with me in the slightest I must confess."

Agatha Harkness thought for the briefest of moments. "When you witness the deprivation, it is of no wonder that some individuals resort to alcohol stupors father, or theft or even indeed prostitution for that matter."

"Aggie!" retorted Lord Harkness in a mixture of embarrassment and admonishment.

"I am sorry father, but if you desperately required income to feed your hungry child you would employ whatever means at all possible."

"That is as well may be," Lord Harkness grumbled quickly changing the subject. He reopened his paper with a flourish. "And another thing, Jeffers, why do the reporters insist on giving these murderers glorifying designations I ask you? The Ripper, the Whitehall Murderer, the bloody Beast for heaven's sake!" Jeffers again remained silent.

"You know Aggie," the Lord mused. "We must endeavour to do all we can to help the authorities rid us of this maniac and any other such monsters that may be lurking to strike."

"What can we do to help in such matters that the police are not only capable of but are already attending to?" Agatha asked her father.

"Funds!" he proclaimed. "Why, we as a family have the financial position and strength that our beleaguered Force can only dream of. It is my philosophy that if you throw enough money at a problem, that problem will invariably be resolved, sooner rather than later."

"This cannot always be the case, Father," responded Agatha in a rather prickly fashion. "You need only look at the endemic poverty of which we spoke. This is a problem that society needs to address through governmental policy, education and health provision. How can we possibly think of such forward-thinking reforms whilst we continue to struggle merely to obtain political franchise for women?"

The Viscount nodded sagely, his hooded eyelids closed as the tips of his fingers came together as if in deep thought. "No doubt you are correct, my dear," he admitted, "but this Beast, as the scandal sheets call him, concerns me deeply. He must be apprehended and dealt with, and we must do what we can to assist our valiant police force. I will make enquiries with the Commissioner, as to who is leading the investigation." The Viscount pondered further. "Perhaps, Aggie, you may want to act as my envoy in this matter?"

"I will do whatever I can to assist, of course, Father," acquiesced Agatha.

"Then I suggest you pay a visit to Scotland Yard and offer them our unconditional support."

Chapter 9 - The Interrogation

Pyke could feel the anger well up inside him, a volcanic rumbling deep within his very core that was set to erupt at any second. What was it about this man that made him so angry? For starters he was a damned Russian, Pyke reasoned, glancing at the sickle-shaped scar on his forearm which now seemed to throb and blaze an alarming shade of scarlet in response to his rising resentment. He had interrogated hundreds of men, many of whom had raised his temper, but not one of them had offered such an instant and furious effect upon him. The Russian had done nothing wrong as far as the evidence suggested and he had said very little, yet an instant dislike had turned very swiftly into an irrational hatred, not of what they suspected Radasiliev of having done, but of the very man himself. Something primal, something base. Sheer hatred and loathing were intensifying within Pyke. He tried to swallow back the poisonous emotions, but every fibre of his being was urging him to clobber the man's smiling supercilious head clean off his noble shoulders.

"What brings you to our shores Mr Radasiliev?" questioned Wiggins.

"Many ventures and reasons demand my presence here, none of them murderous I may add," calmly retorted the handsome Russian. "As you are aware, I am an envoy of the Russian Consulate here in London. As such I enjoy a certain level of protection from the laws of your country." Luca Radasiliev was an individual of striking countenance and regal bearing. His ebony dark hair was shot through with a distinguished silver at the temples and his intelligent grey eyes sat within a face of noble features. His presence exuded confidence and extreme self-belief.

"We have reason to believe that an individual, very much resembling yourself has been responsible for at least three violent attacks upon women in the Whitechapel and Limehouse areas. Do you have any response to this suggestion?"

Radasiliev raised a single eyebrow. "You think me to be your Beast, Inspector? How laughably absurd." Wiggins thought the Russian looked genuinely surprised.

"We ask the questions 'ere Ivan," interrupted Pyke, straining to withhold his anger. Wiggins threw Pyke a look. "I do not speak of any Beast but of a number of sexual assaults in the area, Mr Radasiliev. Nonetheless, you raise an interesting point of consideration regarding the murders." Wiggins felt a general disquiet begin to creep over him, an uneasy feeling of uncertainty. The Russian threw back his head and laughed. "I have found London women, particularly those of your lower classes to be, how can I put it, very accommodating to new experiences, shall we say." Pyke moved forward as if to grab the Russian. "Stay your hand, Sergeant Pyke!" barked Wiggins. "Mr Radasiliev is here at our invitation and benefits from diplomatic protection."

"I know what this piece of scum did. He's a sadistic rapist and I will see those women avenged," spat Pyke his face almost nose to nose with the still calm Russian. Radasiliev turned his gaze towards Wiggins. "And do you have any statements from these women you talk of, Inspector? Anything that corroborates your colleague's outlandish accusations?"

"We have anecdotal evidence that would suggest you as a person of interest," responded Wiggins feeling the confidence slowly ebbing from him. "So, your answer is therefore in the negative, Inspector," oozed Radasiliev.

Wiggins' sense of unease was growing with the passing of each minute. His analytic psyche and logical train of thought were fighting a battle against a general feeling of inadequacy that was creeping insidiously over his self-confidence like a shroud. Certainly, the evidence against Radasiliev in terms of the recent murders was extremely circumstantial, to say the least. However, reports from Pyke's informants identifying him as a serial rapist seemed to Wiggins to hold more substance. Rumours had also begun to abound throughout London's criminal underworld regarding the mysterious Bolshevik. Rumours that he was the Beast, rumours that he was evil beyond evil, a man who walks with demons or was, in fact, a demon himself. A night shade, a Vampyr, a corrupter of souls as well as bodies.

"As for being your Beast, my dear Inspector, unless I am able to have been in two places at the same time, I cannot be your killer," submitted Radasiliev in his heavy Russian accent. He flipped open a thin dossier with an indifferent flick of a finger, turned it upside down and slid it across the roughly hewn desk that served as a barrier between himself and Wiggins. The dossier contained sworn affidavits from the Russian embassy attesting that Radasiliev had been in the North of England at the time of the first murder and was in a night-long consultation meeting with the Ambassador and several colleagues on the occasion of the second atrocity. Wiggins began to read over the dossier again, but his eyes struggled to properly focus on the text. He read the same paragraph once, twice, three times over, his normally forensic eye seemed to fail him and the information on the page was not embedding itself in his brain. He looked up at the Russian who sat calmly returning his gaze with his dark grey eyes staring unflinchingly into those of the Detective. Wiggins tried valiantly to return the Russian's stare but his will failed him and his eyes fell lazily back towards scanning the words in the file in front of him. The letters seemed to swim and dance around the page making each word unreadable, each image blurred as though he were reading it under water.

"Take your time, Inspector. I am in no immediate hurry this evening. You must be comfortable with the facts laid out before you," added Radasiliev crossing his arms. As Wiggins struggled to properly decipher the words in front of him, behind him prowled Pyke, stalking agitatedly from one side of the room to the other like a caged panther. Pyke glanced at the clock hanging on the wall behind the Russian. Each tick of the second hand seemed to create a clamour in his brain as if it were the thunderous peel of Big Ben. Each ticking second seemed to correspond with his increasing heart rate. Radasiliev stroked back his sleeked, greying temple hair and rubbed the back of his neck. A huge, confident smile split his handsome face from ear to ear. "On the occasion of your first killing, Inspector I was, as you can see from the file in front of you, attending an ambassadorial conference in Liverpool."

"Yes, I can see that!" snapped Wiggins angrily and uncharacteristically. Pyke was now imagining the noise of the second hand to be that of an executioner's axe wedging itself into the executioner's block, time after time, each chop getting louder and louder. He felt not only the urge to batter the life out of the Russian, but he was now beginning to feel an irrational hatred towards Wiggins. '*Why was he stalling, stammering, beating about the bleedin' bush? Why not just slam shut that damn file and give this smart-arsed diplomat the beating of his life. Pull him bleeding from the interrogation room and throw him in a cell with some homicidal pansy brute and keep him there until he wailed for mercy.*'

"… and on the second occasion I was attending an all-night meeting of the most confidential import," added the dislikeable diplomat pointing his index finger dismissively towards the file. Wiggins nodded, lifting his head wearily from the document in front of him. Once again, their eyes met, and Wiggins could feel the last ounce of confidence draining from his being. '*It is him, he thought, he is doing this to me. Somehow, he is affecting my senses, my very judgement. Hypnotising and sapping my confidence as a sadist would a vulnerable child. As a cat toys with an ensnared mouse. He is somehow bringing out the worst weaknesses of my character and empowering them over my strengths.*' Wiggins drew several deep breaths and once he had recognised what was happening his logical brain rapidly began to counter battle against the mesmeric influence of the Russian.

An explosion of noise awakened him fully from his mental turmoil. Pyke had slammed both of his granite-hard fists onto the surface of the desk. "Pull yourself together Bert or I will personally wallop some sense into you!" roared Pyke. He turned to Radasiliev who had calmly stood up and coolly retrieved his hat from the back of his chair. Pyke lunged violently towards him, each hand grabbing a neatly pressed lapel of the Russian's immaculate Jermyn Street suit.

"I don't fully understand why, but I have the greatest notion to break your Red neck here and now." Sweat was pouring down Pyke's forehead, blinding his adrenalin-fuelled eyes. Rage was coursing through his veins like the energising steam through the pistons of a locomotive. Pyke could feel the Russian's icy cold hands grip his wrists and with what appeared to be very little effort whatsoever, he removed them free from his clothing. At the touch of Radasiliev, Pyke's fury accelerated to the point where he felt that he would explode with rage. Once his hands released, a comforting sense of calm seemed to envelop him. Pyke was stunned, '*Ain't no man in London could do that,*' swore Pyke, inwardly recalling how effortlessly the Russian had broken his grip.

"Jem, stand aside," came Wiggins' assured tones. He had placed a restraining hand on his colleague's shoulder. "I feel we should detain Mr Radasiliev no longer. He did after all come here under our invitation without any resistance, and of his own free will."

"My thanks, Inspector," responded Radasiliev bowing slightly as he straightened the now somewhat crooked lapels of his jacket." I must admit I have found our little tête-à-tête most illuminating. I feel that we now understand each other a little better. Got inside each other's heads as you quaintly say in this country. It has been, how can I say, an experience I sincerely hope we do not have to repeat in the future. May our next encounter be under entirely more amenable circumstances. I bid you, good evening gentlemen." With that, the Russian swivelled on his resplendently shining heels and exited the interrogation room, delicately closing the door silently behind him.

Pyke slumped into the chair recently vacated by the Russian. As he did so a faint surge of the anger, he had previously felt again rose within him, but gradually subsided within seconds. "What just 'appended here Boss?" he asked, looking at Wiggins with imploring eyes.

"Incredibly Jem, I think somehow, we have been in the presence of an individual who can literally bring out the worst in someone," replied Wiggins, stroking his beard with a sense of incredulity. "I could feel that he was draining my confidence and energy whilst it was physically obvious that your naturally suppressed rage was being rapidly unleashed. Fascinating really. Mesmerising in fact. How can it be that a man can elicit such a reaction from others without outwardly doing anything? It is as if he can recognise and accentuate the worst traits within an individual and bring them boiling uncontrollably to the surface. Such a man must prove to be an extremely dangerous and crafty adversary indeed. Just think, Jem, what mayhem such a man may create amongst the masses of our Society."

"Surely this is fantasy, Sir. I lost me temper and you may have lost your nerve a bit. Happens to us all," countered Pyke reassuringly.

"Maybe you are correct, Jem, although I have never encountered any individual unshackle themselves from your clutches as he just did," reasoned Wiggins. "How do you feel now?"

"Back to normal Sir. I have a clear head and a thirsty throat. Gagging for a pint to be truthful. Do you fancy joining me for a quick one … or a few?"

"Why not, indeed," replied Wiggins smiling. "I feel perhaps, a couple of drinks uptown may be in order. It has been another long and challenging day. The Ship and Shovell may offer the perfect antidote to a rather traumatic last half an hour." Wiggins headed towards the door of the interrogation room with Pyke following closely behind.

"I'll get me hat, Guv," declared Pyke.

As Pyke closed the door, he glanced at the chair in which he had briefly sat after Radasiliev had vacated it and recalled the sudden surge of rage he had experienced as he did so. It was as if Radasiliev had left an imprint of energy behind upon the chair. He hesitated for a second or two before closing the door behind him.

The following morning Wiggins was greeted by an exasperated Pyke as he entered the incident room at New Scotland Yard.

"God-forsaken machine!" spluttered Pyke as his index finger missed its intended target for the umpteenth time, this time jamming between the G and B keys. "Why does everything need to be documented on a typewriter these days, boss? Takes an age to type what would have taken just minutes using a bleedin' pencil. Nobody's ever gonna read this anyway!"

"Firstly, for your information, my ham-fisted friend, it is the latest model of Imperial typewriter. The manufacturers, based in Hull if I am not mistaken, state that not only is it accurately efficient but it is also the speediest brand of its type. No pun intended. It is after all, not the machine's fault that you possess fingers that resemble bloody Bratwursts," Wiggins teased his companion. Pyke extricated his finger and continued to type erratically, his tongue involuntarily protruding between his lips in concentration as he pecked one-fingered at the keys.

Wiggins continued, "Secondly, if all the facts and data are properly documented and filed, it is all the easier to cross-reference and revisit the information for future investigations. So, you see your endeavours now will save time in the long run. You just need to use more than one finger Pyke!" sniggered Wiggins. "Digitus tardi, as an old acquaintance of mine would say."

"Yeah, yeah. How the Dickens do you spell Radasiliev again?" grumbled Pyke in frustration. "Why can't some clever dick like that Marconi fella invent a gizmo you could speak the letters into, and the words would type themselves?"

"A somewhat fanciful idea Pyke but one that I am positive will come with time. Perhaps, I suspect, not during our lifetime unfortunately for you and your bruised digits. Remember it is only a few years ago that we thought fingerprint signatures were a rather far-fetched concept and now we employ their use routinely."

"And effectively Sir," added Pyke without looking away from the typewriter. "In the name of all that's holy, how the hell do I stop the words all being capitals?" he fumed.

"Perhaps it is prudent if you leave the report to me, Pyke, whilst you go and investigate that report of a bull in the china shop," winked Wiggins at his frustrated comrade. They both laughed as friends do.

Later that day a sturdy knock rapped at the door of Wiggins' office interrupting him from his studies.

"Lady to see you sir," smiled Pyke, poking his head around the door, the half-smoked cigar he was chewing bobbed up and down as he spoke. "Miss Agatha Harkness no less," he added in a lower, more conspiratorial, would-you-believe-it tone.

"Well show her in Pyke. What are you waiting for?" urged Wiggins, smartening his hair and straightening his tie.

"As you wish Guvnor," clipped Pyke, somewhat mischievously, knowing that Wiggins somewhat disliked the sobriquet. Agatha Harkness entered the room with a rustle of dresses as if she were entering the ballroom of a stately home, completely at ease in herself and her surroundings. She offered a confident gloved hand towards Wiggins who took it and not quite knowing the protocol of greeting a Viscount's daughter, he decided that a gentle shake and the slightest nod of his head were the best and safest form of acknowledgement.

"Please be seated, Miss Harkness. How goes the pursuit of suffrage?" asked Wiggins offering his guest a chair and wondering if he had overstepped the mark with the familiar nature of his enquiry. '*How would the Superintendent have greeted a person of such standing?*' He questioned himself, feeling slightly uncomfortable.

"Oh, it is a constant struggle my dear inspector," she replied smiling. "In this modern age we should not be forced into radicalism and have to resort to violence and hunger strikes merely for the privilege of gaining the vote and improved jobs don't you feel?" quizzed Miss Harkness. "Only yesterday I heard the authorities had thrown several of our valiant ladies into your jails and worse still, others are being force-fed through funnels!"

"I agree that your cause is a worthy one, I am sure," nodded Wiggins waiting until his visitor had made herself comfortable before he sat. "So, what can we help you with today?" he enquired, pulling his chair closer to the desk to find its customary position. He swiftly examined his desk to ensure that every item was in its correct position. He slightly adjusted his blotter so as its lower edge was in alignment with that of the desk.

"I should like to know how you and your resourceful department are progressing with the hunt for this Beast that terrorises the just women of our great City," enquired Miss Harkness in a rather forthright manner. Wiggins coughed. He had not been expecting so direct an enquiry, particularly on such an evocative subject. "We are pursuing several lines of enquiry Ma'am and hope to make a significant breakthrough in the coming days," Wiggins detailed rolling out the hackneyed stock answer and wondering if he should have termed her My Lady. Miss Harkness straightened slightly at the glib response, recognising it for what it was. "I speak of course for my father, all my colleagues in the movement and for those of lesser determination when I say that we are all living in fear and that the sooner this fiend is caught and removed from our society, the sooner we can all get on with our daily business and rest easy in our beds. Those of us who have one of course. I trust that all your efforts are being focused to this end Inspector."

Wiggins recognised this as a statement rather than a question. "Of course, Miss Harkness, we have all our best detectives and constables working around the clock on the case. I am sure my superiors will be keeping your father informed of any developments of import as they happen."

"I am encouraged. Now I must not encumber your research Inspector," said his guest indicating the map on his office wall. "Please know that we are all behind you and wish you well with your endeavours in our prayers."

"Many thanks my lady," offered Wiggins bowing slightly, and, feeling rather absurd in having done so, he escorted the young woman out of his office and back into the less refined protection of Sergeant Pyke. "My colleague Sergeant Pyke shall see you to your car, Miss Harkness. I bid you good day."

Five minutes later Pyke crashed into Wiggins' office with a knowing grin on his face. "Bit of a looker Guv, but far too Mayfair for the likes of you."

"Calm yourself, Pyke. This is a Police Station, not one of your bordellos and as you well know I am a happily married man, and I suspect Miss Harkness may not be of my persuasion if truth be told."

Chapter 10 - The Russians

"I will Sir." Constable Potts carefully replaced the telephone receiver in its cradle and looked up at DI Wiggins who was standing at Pyke's desk. The two men were closely reviewing their transcript of the interview they had conducted with the mysterious Russian, Luca Radasiliev, the previous day. "That was Mr MacDonald, Sir. The Boss wants to see you in Commissioner Gregson's office in ten minutes," announced Potts. Wiggins and Pyke exchanged knowing glances. "The Russian," nodded Pyke throwing his pen to the desk. "I knew he'd make trouble. Might as well light MacDonald's pipe with this now," added Pyke flourishing the document in front of him. "Stay your hand Jem," afforded Wiggins. "Let us not jump to any conclusions just yet." Pyke threw the interview transcript across his desk and sat back disgustedly in his chair.

Wiggins climbed the three flights of stairs to the top floor of the building and approached the door of Commissioner Gregson's office. The armed uniformed constable who stood sentinel outside nodded to Wiggins, "Sir," and rapped upon the door on behalf of the detective then returned smartly to his original standing position.

"Enter!" came the forceful response from within. Wiggins obeyed the command and strode into the office. Commissioner Gregson stood from his chair as Wiggins entered and offered him a seat opposite his desk between the other two occupants of the office. Gregson sat, brushing a stray grey hair from his brow. "You know Superintendent MacDonald of course, DI Wiggins. Let me introduce you to Sir Edward Grey, Foreign Secretary for His Majesty's government."

Wiggins turned to the stately strigiform looking figure seated to his left. "An honour, your Lordship," acknowledged Wiggins with a slight bow of his head. He had, of course, recognised one of the pre-eminent members of His Majesty's government the moment he had walked into the room. He mentally noted that Sir Edward's stern, yet youthful countenance somewhat belied his years.

"I hear great reports of your prowess, Mr Wiggins," said the great Statesman. "You are held in high regard at the uppermost levels of the Department."

"I am indebted to your Lordship, but I am but one part of a team of very talented and committed officers working for Superintendent MacDonald." Wiggins felt satisfied by his off the cuff answer.

"Modest as well as talented, I see," smiled Sir Edward. "I am, to some extent, aware of your history and your early association with the greatest of all the practitioners of your trade." Gregson coughed and rubbed an index finger subconsciously around the inside of his collar as if it had suddenly become a band of iron. Wiggins looked at Sir Edward. "I was doubtless fortunate in my tutelage. May I ask, to what do I owe this honour, an interview with a statesman of your import?" enquired Wiggins, safe in the knowledge that he already knew the answer.

"Forthright and to the point, as I would have expected," accorded the Foreign Secretary. "My visit here, as you may already have anticipated, regards your recent interview with a certain Mr Luca Radasiliev of the Russian diplomatic delegation."

"You have presumably received some communication regarding our conversation I take it?" enquired Wiggins. Sir Edward nodded wisely, his demeanour suddenly switching from one of inclusive camaraderie to one of manufactured concern. "You are very perceptive, Mr Wiggins. I have indeed received a call from His Excellency, the Russian Ambassador to the Court of Saint James, Count Benckendorff, during which he muted some very real concerns regarding your communications and interview with said Mr Radasiliev."

Wiggins straightened. This was exactly what he was expecting. "In my defence, Your Lordship, the individual concerned is a valid suspect who fits within our current line of enquiry with regards the recent spate of vile attacks on women that currently corrupts our City."

"No doubt," interjected Commissioner Gregson, "but we must realise that the gentleman in question is an envoy of the Russian Empire and as such is entitled to the respect that his diplomatic status affords." Wiggins nodded, feeling that the direction of this conversation was beginning to slip away from him.

"You must realise, DI Wiggins, that the signing of the Anglo-Russian Entente, which subsequently led to the Triple Entente a few years ago, has made Russia one of, if not, the most important international ally of His Majesty's government," explained the Foreign Secretary proudly. Wiggins bit his lip. "It is not his nationality that is in question, rather information we have received from some extremely reliable sources. I can only reinforce that it was a pertinent line of enquiry, Sir. Mr Radasiliev remains a person of pronounced interest in our investigation." A brief silence descended upon the room.

"I agree, Mr Wiggins." Lord Grey broke the silence enigmatically. Wiggins was visibly taken aback by the politician's unexpected response. The Foreign Secretary cleared his throat and continued in an almost conspiratorial tone. "I have, gentlemen, regular discussions with Mr Churchill over at the Admiralty on a variety of subjects, and, being a military man, he has a very apt saying to describe our immediate situation. The First Sea Lord describes official, on the record discussions as 'Hats On' talks. This gentlemen, as my illustrious colleague would say, is very much a 'Hats Off' conversation. May I insist that *this* conversation is strictly confidential. Indeed, if any mention of it emerges beyond these walls and into the public realm, it will be stalwartly denied by His Majesty's government, and I will personally see to it that everyone in this room is relieved of their duties forthwith. I can also see to it that your pensions be withdrawn. That is a promise by which you can regard the extreme seriousness of this situation."

The three policemen looked at each other but no words were exchanged. "I am certain I can safely speak for my colleagues, Sir, when I say that we will adhere to your Lordship's wishes," stated Commissioner Gregson breaking the silence whilst canvassing his fellow officers with an inquisitive glance. Both Wiggins and MacDonald nodded their consent. "Pray continue your Lordship," prompted Gregson.

"Very well gentlemen, let these walls be our only confidante." The politician unbuttoned his gloves, removed them, and placed them deliberately on Gregson's desk as if drawing a line in the sand that was under no circumstances to be crossed.

"We have, at the highest level of government, for some days now, held some very genuine reservations as to the intent of our colleagues at the Russian Embassy. Our normal lines of diplomatic communication have been, how can I say, strained to say the least. Considering the previously mentioned Entente, this downturn in collaborative discourse has caused great alarm at the very zenith of the Realm." Wiggins leaned forward with his hand raised thoughtfully to his chin. Lord Grey now had his undivided attention. Wiggins sensed a connection here, a link of some description.

"We have made discreet enquiries and have heard peculiar rumours pertaining to your Mr Radasiliev. His provenance seems speculative at best, but his influence appears to be omnipotent. I have requested personal meetings with Count Alexander Benckendorff on several occasions over the last few days and have received either rebuttals or silence from the office of a man whom I would normally have regarded as not only a colleague but a friend. There is something very definitely amiss at the Embassy gentlemen and I would welcome your department using your investigation into Mr Radasiliev as a lever into discovering exactly what is going on within the delegation of the Russian Empire."

"I consider it an honour to serve, Your Lordship," confirmed Wiggins, relieved that this hitherto unexpected turn of events very definitely gave him license to pursue his line of enquiry regarding the mysterious Russian. "You have my word that we will proceed with all due reverence to the diplomatic sensitivities you have outlined and report back to your office through the appropriate channels." He laughed inwardly as he imagined Jem Pyke paying *due reverence to diplomatic sensitivities.*

"I am delighted to hear it Mr Wiggins," announced Lord Grey as he stood and pulled on his tan gloves." I leave this room a more confident man than the one who entered. Good day gentlemen."

Wiggins, Pyke and Constable Murray stood on the polished marble steps of the Russian Embassy in Chesham Place in the heart of Belgravia. Their knocking upon the black gloss painted panelled door had gone unanswered as had their attempts at ringing the large brass pull bell.

"Curious that nobody answers don't you think?" questioned Wiggins of his colleagues. Pyke made a low rumbling noise that seemed to emanate from the depths of his throat. Wiggins could see that Pyke involuntarily rubbed his left forearm which he knew sported a large sickle-shaped scar, reputedly the result of some hand to hand combat with a Russian during a skirmish in the Second Boer War. "I swear, DS Pyke, that you would be distrustful of any man who did not sport a union jack tattooed on one arm and carried a bulldog under the other." Murray stifled his chuckle whilst Wiggins again pulled on the bell more forcefully and sustained this time.

Pyke grinned at his boss' description of him and removed the remains of a well-smoked cigar from his mouth and spat a symbolic brown globule on the steps of the Embassy. Wiggins rolled his eyes skyward as Pyke grinned again like a cheeky little child. Just as Wiggins was about to admonish his fellow officer, the door slowly and silently opened. A stern middle-aged woman of formidable build stood before them, her head strangely cocked to one side, wordlessly awaiting the policemen to announce themselves. Wiggins broke the awkward silence but not the stare of the woman. "Good morning madam. I am Detective Inspector Wiggins, and this is Detective Sergeant Pyke and Constable Murray of Scotland Yard. We are here to call on Mr Radasiliev. We have a few questions that we would like to ask of him."

The three men moved forward brandishing their warrant cards. As the woman stepped aside to allow them to enter, Wiggins noted the deadness of her eyes. Blank, emotionless eyes, devoid of life or any animation or emotion. Without uttering a word or even acknowledging their presence, the woman turned her back on the officers and proceeded to walk somnambulistically out of the front door and made her way down Chesham Place in the direction of Belgrave Square. The three colleagues exchanged perplexed looks. "Best you follow her ladyship there and make sure she is safe. Seems as though she is in a trance-like stupor," suggested Pyke to

Murray. Murray nodded and headed off after the sleep-walking pedestrian, somewhat relieved to have been given such a seemingly simple task.

A large, chiselled concierge in military uniform sat at a desk in the entrance hall of the building. He sported a long bushy beard and his eyes also appeared sightless and his manner as one in a waking sleep. Pyke thumped the desk with a powerful fist. "Wakey, wakey, Sergei! What you doing sleeping on the job there? You got the morbs mate? The Tsar would 'ave your guts for garters, Russkie me lad," he shouted, recreating his best Sergeant Major voice. The guard remained unflinching and silent as if hypnotised, completely unaware of anything or anyone around him. "Does nobody speak the King's English round here?" asked Pyke to his boss.

"Most peculiar," pondered Wiggins. "What do you suppose has happened here?" "Radasiliev," countered Pyke. "That's what's happened here. Let's have a gander around."

The first room they found themselves in was what appeared to be the ground floor general office. Pyke threw back the timber window shutters, and the mid-morning sunlight flooded into the room illuminating as bizarre a tableau of humanity as either man had ever witnessed. "I thought Van Hoon's gaff was weird but this …" expressed Pyke his words tailing off. Dust particles swirled in the newly released sunlight and danced around the space like a million microscopic lace flies swarming over a pond.

"Bleedin' hell" murmured Pyke. The room was occupied by four people but was as quiet and as still as a mausoleum. Nothing moved but the stirred dancing dust, its accompanying music being the muted ticking of a clock lost somewhere amongst the madness of the room. One man, presumably a Clerk sat at his desk, his neck craned outwards and downwards, his teeth biting forcefully into the mahogany of the bureau. His teeth were clenched fast to the timber, biting into it for all his worth. Sweat poured down his forehead and the tendons on his strained neck stood out like stressed cables. Another older man, stood at his colleague's side, his eyes clenched tightly shut. He held one arm aloft in the most awkward of fashions, the muscles twitching, close to atrophying as he reached on tiptoes for some unseen object above him. A woman stood face pressed as closely against a wall as she could possibly be, with her legs and arms spread-eagled in a senseless saltire-like embrace. The last occupant was no more than a boy, the office junior reasoned Wiggins. He was crouched in a corner of the room, his head buried between his knees, rocking backwards and forwards as if in a metronomic fit. The policemen looked around them, trying to mentally process the silent bedlam of the scene.

"Their heads, Jem. Look at their foreheads," breathed Wiggins, calling his colleague by his first name now that Constable Murray was no longer present. Each individual sported a blood-encrusted pentangle within a circle, scored into their brows. "What sort of devilry is this?" whispered Wiggins as he lifted the lad's head to see the same five-sided star etched into his brow.

"Radasiliev. That's what it is," spat Pyke. "How long did you say the Foreign Secretary said it had been since he had heard from the Russians?"

"He stated a few days, and by my book that is at least three days, possibly four," responded Wiggins.

"I know Russian food is rotten but surely that geezer ain't been gnawing on a table for four bleedin' days Guv?" winced Pyke.

"See if you can find a telephone and call for medical assistance Pyke," ordered Wiggins still surveying the insanity in front of him.

"There's one on the desk right in front of the gentleman eating the table Guv." Pyke carefully approached the telephone sitting on the desk directly in front of the clerk whose teeth were clamped firmly to the table edge. Both men's eyes met. The Russian's eyes looked pleadingly from his sweat-stained, reddened face. Pyke offered a reassuring smile at the deskbound man. "Don't worry Sir, help is on its way," he encouraged the stricken individual.

"The Ambassador!" Wiggins suddenly exclaimed. "We must find the ambassador." Pyke quickly made the most bizarre telephone call of his life and then raced after Wiggins who had already sprinted upstairs. They both stepped over the bodies of two men on the half landing where one lay trembling convulsively, legs kicking at fresh air as if riding some invisible bicycle, whilst the other knelt facing the corner with his hands placed squarely on his hips. Pyke shook his head in disbelief. "What sort of man has done this?"

"Unlike any man we have yet encountered, I fear," responded Wiggins.

The door to the Ambassador's top floor office was locked from the inside. Pyke stood back and rammed the lock side with his shoulder, mustering all his weight and force behind it. The door flew open and Pyke steadied himself by grabbing the splintered door frame, which stopped him from falling through, narrowly missing colliding with a moustachioed middle-aged man who was slowly circumnavigating the room in a slow ceaseless shuffle.

"Mr Benckendorff, Sir?" implored Wiggins, placing a restraining hand on the elder man's shoulder. Benckendorff, it seemed, was oblivious to any external stimuli and shrugged off Wiggins assistance without breaking stride and continued his endless shuffling around the room's perimeter. Wiggins could see that this interminable orbiting had created a distinct circular pathway trampled into the deep pile carpet of the room. "Mr Benckendorff!" shouted Wiggins more forcibly.

The diplomat turned his head slowly towards the sound of Wiggins' voice whilst continuing walking. "Help me," he whimpered pleadingly. His forehead was encrusted with the same satanic branding as his colleagues displayed downstairs.

Trails of dried blood ran from the devilish tattoo, over his bulbous nose and traced their way down its deep philtrum, continuing down his neck and running beneath his loose-fitting collar. "Help me," he again pleaded. The two policemen looked at each other, the glance communicating their bafflement as to how to proceed. Pyke shrugged his shoulders, strode towards the mesmerised Russian and caught him squarely on the chin with a powerful jab. The Russian's eyes rolled upwards, and he collapsed in an unconscious heap on the now well-trodden carpet. Wiggins looked at Pyke in horror. "Jem! What on God's good Earth do you think you are doing? You have just knocked out the most senior representative of the Russian Empire on British soil."

"Stopped the poor bugger walking didn't it?" countered Pyke, outstretching his arms in an imploring innocence. "Anyways, I think you'll find this is officially Russian soil, what with it being their Embassy an' all." Wiggins shook his head in disbelief whilst trying hard to suppress the smile that was brimming within him. '*So much for diplomatic sensitivities,*' he thought.

"No sign of Radasiliev either at the Embassy nor at his official residence in Highgate next to the Russian High Commission's administrative centre," concluded Wiggins. He stood alongside Pyke in Commissioner Gregson's office, looking back and forth between Superintendent MacDonald, the Scotsman's superior officer, Gregson, and the Foreign Secretary. "He appears to have somehow escaped. Vanished without trace."

"And you suspect that this Radasiliev is somehow responsible for the remarkable condition in which you found these poor desperate people?" enquired Gregson wearing the sternest of concerned looks.

"Indeed, I do, Sir," confirmed Wiggins, "Not only the unfortunates we found in Chesham Place but also those in Highgate, and also the poor lady Constable Murray eventually detained trying to scale a lamppost in Cundy Street."

"There was one poor blighter in Highgate who'd drowned himself in a bucket of water," interjected Pyke with an emphatic nod of his head. Wiggins threw Pyke a warning look, silently imploring him to remain quiet. Pyke pursed his lips and shuffled his feet awkwardly. Lord Grey stifled a muffled cough. "I see. I also understand that you used somewhat strong-arm tactics to subdue His Excellency, the Ambassador of the Russian Empire, Sergeant Pyke? So much for my instruction that this operation be conducted in the most sensitive of manners." The Foreign Secretary turned his imperious gaze towards Wiggins.

"Begging your pardon, Your Lordship, but his Excellency would still be circling the room like a comatose chicken if I hadn't have given him a slap," countered Pyke. Lord Grey nodded and looked to the ceiling, trying desperately to subdue a smile. "I am sure you did exactly what was called for at that required moment Sergeant Pyke. Now the question is gentlemen, what do we do regarding this man Radasiliev? We have the Tsar of Russia asking serious questions in the highest levels of the Realm and we have a complement of his most eminent diplomats and staff undergoing medical and psychiatric treatments for a baffling number of physical and mental ailments. If Radasiliev has committed such inexplicable acts against his own people, then Lord only knows what else he is capable of doing."

An uneasy silence fell upon the room. "He is in the wind, gentlemen," stated MacDonald breaking the silence. "But rest assured we have the wherewithal, one way or another to track down and banish this malignant scourge from our City. We fight a war on three fronts today. This Russian, the Beast whose murderous rampage terrorises our good people and the organised crime syndicate of the Chinaman which is indiscriminate and preys upon good and bad alike. I can vow here and now that we will remove each of these cancers from oor Toon or perish in the trying."

Chapter 11 - The Confession

He dreamt of sparks of molten metal. Rivers of liquid steel chasing at his heels like chariots of fire. He tried desperately to run but his legs would not move, could not move, his feet were encased in large ferrous ingots. The heat was intense, so hot he could feel his hair singe and clothes ignite, his belt and boots began to melt, becoming a liquefied part of himself. Huge riveted fists, shaped like anvils, battered him on his body and face repeatedly. The thumping numbing pain was as severe as anything he had ever experienced, hammering him in and out of consciousness. The thunderous clanking noise of the fists sounded like the Noonday booms of Big Ben. A wild, feral pain streaked from one side of his head to the other.

"Mr Pyke. Mr Pyke, Sir." He could hear a distant tiny voice as the relentless thumping continued unabated. He opened his eyes carefully and shook his head groggily. His eyes hurt and stung due to the dehydration engulfing his body. He recognised the ceiling above him by the blistered paint which looked like the contours of countries on a map. He heaved a huge sigh of relief. He was in his own bed. He shook his head again to brush the alcoholic cobwebs aside. '*Not too bad,*' he thought. There was the hint of a hangover still developing but nothing that he could not handle. Bang, Bang! That thumping again. "Mr Pyke, Sir." A boyish voice accompanied the knocking on the door. "I have a message from Mr Heap, Sir."

"Just a minute lad," shouted Pyke easing himself up and fumbling for the switch of the bedside lamp. As he did so he heard a slight groan and felt a movement beside him in his bed, reminding him that he had not spent the night alone.

"Mmmm don't go yet Jem, it's still dark outside," mumbled the shape beside him. She turned over and reached out for him, but Jem had already sat up and swung his legs around to dress. He ruffled his hair as he looked around for his underwear. '*Nora? Norma?*' He could not quite remember her name but decided he would take a gamble on the latter. '*Please let her not be an ugly old crow!*' He patted the plum-shaped backside of the redhead. "Settle back down Luv. Whatever this is it shouldn't take me too long." He thought he would chance his arm, "I'll be back to warm yer feet before you knows it Norma."

"Norma! You really are a one Jem Pyke," responded the flame-haired woman feigning slight annoyance. "You know fine well my name is Noreen."

'*Shit!*' he thought. '*I should have remembered. At least she's not an ugly old crow,*' he smiled.

"I'm only jesting with you, Noreen." More rapping on the door. "Mr Pyke, Sir, I has a message for you from Mr Heap."

"Stand fast lad, I'll be with you in a minute." He reached for a vest, sniffed at it a couple of times, decided it would pass muster and pulled it over his head all the while yawning. He unlocked the door and ushered in the messenger boy. Pyke instantly recognised him as the young lad he and Potts had seen attending the Heap during their visit to the slaughterhouse a few days earlier. The odour was unmistakable but thankfully toned down to a certain degree.

"What's the message then Son?" asked Pyke, looking the boy up and down. It had been impossible to make out much of the lad at their previous meeting given that he had been mostly scurrying around in the shadows. He would place his age at about thirteen and he was as fat as a string. A mop of curly matted black hair topped a grubby freckled face that skewed slightly to one side as he spoke as if always uttering a secret.

"Mr Heap says to tell you that a geezer is going around telling anyone who will listen that he is the Beast Man you hunt."

"Is there now?" questioned Pyke stroking his stubbly chin. "And what makes Mr Heap think that this geezer is any different to any of the other lunatics that have admitted to being the Beast?"

"I don't quite rightly know Sir. He only tells me to get the message to you," replied the boy craning his neck around Pyke in an attempt to gain a glimpse of the stirring shape within the bed behind him. Pyke moved sideward to block his view.

"Keep your eyes on the floor and off the lady Son. What's your name?"

"Billy."

"You only got the one name like Houdini then? Billy what?"

"I don't rightly know Sir," answered Billy looking at his shoes and trying desperately to resist lifting his eyes. "Mr Heap, he never told me what my other name was. The lads at the slaughterhouse calls me Billy Skew on account of me face, see." Pyke gritted his teeth and screwed up his face and turned to send Noreen a look that demanded '*stay under those bedsheets, darlin.*' Pyke turned again to look at the boy noticing that he had taken the opportunity to sneak another swift glimpse at the lovely Noreen. "Don't you be slinging no butchers hook at that fine lady now Billy." He grinned to himself at the unintentional reference, given the nature of Billy's employment. "How long have you been ... attending to the Heap anyways then Billy?"

"Ever since I were a nipper, Sir. He's the only family I can remember, Sir," eyes still firmly rooted to his tattered and worn shoes.

"Are you related then? enquired Pyke. "I'm not rightly sure Sir, I think we must be. Why else would he look after me?" quizzed Billy.

"Are you sure it is not you that looks after him, Billy? Would you stay with him boy or would you want to further yourself outside the confines of the slaughterhouse? Maybe have a chance in life. An opportunity so to speak?" asked Pyke. Billy's feet shuffled restlessly from one to the other as if the floor below him was tickling at his toes. He lifted his eyes to meet those of Pyke's. "Why I should like to be like you, Sir, I should," he whispered, returning his eyes instinctively once more to the floor. Pyke ruffled the boy's hair playfully and exhaled deeply through his nose. "Look at me Billy." Billy looked up at the stony-faced Pyke. "Why does The Heap give me this information?"

"He ain't an 'orrible man, really Sir. He looks 'orrible and smells 'orrible and though he sometimes makes me do 'orrible things, it's just the way he is you see. He don't want to see no more ladies cut up and killed, like," said Billy again trying to peer around Pyke.

"I understand Billy," replied Pyke. "And what is the name of this man who boasts of being the Beast?"

"Cripes, Sir. The geezer goes by the name of Cripes," confirmed Billy, his chest swelling with pride now that he had successfully delivered the message.

"Thank you, Billy, you're very brave to have come here and delivered the message. I'm not even sure I could have done what you have at such a young age," admitted Pyke endeavouring to extol Billy some pride in himself and his actions. He reached over to his mantelpiece and picked two sixpences from the pile of shrapnel that he had thrown there the previous night. "Here, take this Billy and whatever you do, tell the Heap that you only got one sixpence for your troubles. He will no doubt take it from you."

"Thank you, Sir. Thank you ever so much," smiled the young urchin.

Pyke returned the smile and gave Billy's hair another ruffle. "You come and see me any time you want lad. You understand? We might even make a Bobbie out of you in time. And call me Jem in the future, Sir is far too formal for mates."

Billy replaced his hat and turned for the door. "Thank you again, Mr Pyke … erm, Jem and thank you Miss!" he shouted cheekily as he bowed, at the now awakening Noreen. Pyke laughed and playfully booted the lad's behind shoving him off the premises. "Any time, now remember Billy," shouted Pyke.

"The Beast you seek now stands before you, Sergeant. I have come this judgement day to confess of my heinous crimes and to face the court of law and that of Our Lord, Jesus Christ himself," proclaimed the lisping voice. A tall slender man of approximately fifty years of age stood in front of the Desk Sergeant. His short white-blonde hair and eyelashes were almost albinoesque in their paleness as though bleached by the sun. His skin bore a waxy sheen giving his face the reflectiveness of a China doll. His hands were gnarly and heavily scarred displaying years of heavy manual labour. He was immaculately attired although in inexpensive clothes and his shoes were scruffy and in urgent need of a skilled Cobbler. The overall impression, thought the Desk Sergeant Ash, was one of an individual with misplaced airs and graces. An individual strangely out of time and place in this new age Georgian London.

"I beg your pardon, Sir?" asked Sergeant Ash with an intrigued expression whilst simultaneously surreptitiously signalling Constable Bunce to guard the station entrance.

"I said, I am the killer you seek, and I freely give myself up in the name of the Holy Spirit," repeated the albino expressing every syllable in his lisping tongue. "... and there will be no need for any such tactics Sergeant, I am not going to attempt escape. Why should I? Am I not here of my own volition?"

"Detain this man Constable," ordered Nosher Ash. The man freely offered his wrists which Constable Bunce secured with a set of Hiat D-style handcuffs whilst further restraining him by holding his upper arm by forearm and bicep.

"Name?" ordered Sergeant Ash.

"Nathaniel Cripes, aged fifty-two, Church of England," came the slow deliberate response.

"Occupation?" asked Ash.

"I am currently not in employment although my trade is that of Butchery," added Cripes.

"Place of residence?"

"I would rather not say at this time."

"You bloody-well will say!" demanded the Sergeant angrily.

"Well, if I must," the hissing of the harshest consonant being longer than was necessary. "I currently find myself residing with my late mother."

"Your *late* mother you say?" blustered a' suspicious Ash glancing up from his notetaking.

"Yes, it is a most unfortunate trait, she is always *late* for everything," came the unemotional and practical reply.

"So, you're some type of music hall comedian now then are ya? A real Dan Leno you are. Address ... NOW!"

56

"Number 61a Narrow Street, the one with the yellow curtains, and there is no need for your rudeness Sergeant. *Therefore, all things whatsoever ye would that men should do to you, do ye even so to them, for this is the law and the prophets.* The twelfth verse of the seventh chapter of the Gospel of Matthew, unless you had forgotten."

"Poppycock! Take him to the cells at once Bunce. And for your information Mr Cripes, that'll be the one with the iron curtains."

"Inspector, Ash here, Paddington Nick. We've got some nutter here by the name of Cripes saying he's the Beast. Turned 'imself in. Spouting holy scriptures and such. Bonkers conkers if you ask my opinion, but there was something about him, Sir. I thought it best to detain him. He's in a holding cell as we speak, Sir. Thought you may be interested."

"Really!" exclaimed Wiggins in an excited tone. He cupped the speaker of the telephone in his hand and turned to Pyke. "Nosher Ash from Paddington, he has Cripes in custody. He turned himself in."

"That's the bleedin' character I was just tellin' you 'bout Boss. The young lad, Billy, delivered the Heap's message to me first thing this morn," enthused Pyke.

"We will be there within the half-hour Sergeant Ash. Nutter or not, we still need to investigate what he is claiming. Does it not take a madman to commit such atrocities in the first place, Sergeant Ash?" Wiggins advised the desk sergeant.

"I suppose it does, Sir." Nosher nodded his head thoughtfully to himself. "Probably best we don't understand the ways such minds work Sir, or then we would be thinking just like they do themselves!" he added shrewdly.

"Come, Pyke, let us go see what our Mr Cripes has to say for himself," ejaculated Wiggins. Pyke rose from his chair. "I'll get me hat."

Nathaniel Cripes sat bolt upright on the solitary stool in holding cell G of Paddington Station. His feet were planted squarely on the cold stone floor, ankles together with his hands placed symmetrically upon each of his knees. His stare never vacillated as he sat, motionless, staring straight ahead at an indeterminate fixed point. He was so quiet and still that it was as though he was not even breathing. The clanging noise of the cell door being unlocked and opened failed to divert his unflinching stare.

"My name is Detective Inspector Wiggins, and this is my colleague Detective Sergeant Pyke. I believe you are a Mr Nathaniel Cripes, aged fifty-two years, a butcher by trade, and of no fixed abode," stated Wiggins matter-of-factly.

"I must interject there Sir, I am in fact a *master* butcher and I reside with my sainted mother. She is an Angel you know. A real angel," interrupted Cripes in his relaxed and collected manner.

"Very well," appeased Wiggins. "Can you tell us how many victims you have murdered and why you have chosen to come here today?"

"Three in total, representing the Holy Trinity, all female," Cripes paused momentarily.

"Three, you say Mr Cripes. Of this you are sure?" interjected Wiggins.

"Yes, Sir, three. But you must realise Detective Inspector that it is I who is the victim in all of this. I did not choose to slaughter these women, and neither was it I who decided today to admit to the killings. Rather it was Jesus Christ my Lord and Saviour that decreed as such. He has promised to forgive my sins and grant me eternal life at his side in Heaven."

"I'll grant you eternal death you abomination!" snarled Pyke.

"Easy soldier," steadied Wiggins, familiar with the good and bad routine they had successfully built up over their years interrogating suspects together.

"Ah, you are a soldier Constable?" intoned Cripes. "May I then enquire just how many people you have killed?"

"I am a Sergeant and no, you may not enquire and no matter the number, it may well increase by one in the next few minutes if you don't start answering our questions properly," retorted Pyke, his voice gaining volume with each word.

"I was merely hastening their passage into the Kingdom of Heaven and eternal life you understand. A promise of never-ending love. They *will* thank me when I next see them."

"Do you know of an individual called Mr Heap?" asked Wiggins attempting to prise any connection between the pair.

"Ah yes, good old Mr Heap. I was in his employ for several months before I realised that he had absolutely no morals and no comprehension of the meaning of scruples. A non-believer whom I do believe has intentionally and indecently broken or ignored each of the Decalogue as laid before us by the prophet Moses at Mount Horeb. He is disgusting and dishonest and does not care what he fills his bags o' mystery with. I understand he still exists somewhere in the bowels of Spitalfields, his vile butchery most probably still killing the good citizens of this city like a silent, unseen plague. I am delighted to inform you that our paths have never again crossed."

"So, let me get this sorted," demanded Pyke pointing at Cripes. "You state that the absence of morals and being slightly unhygienic are worse than murdering three innocent women in atrocious and vile circumstances and that it is, in fact, an act of kindness in the eyes of your God?"

"Correct Constable. You are a quick learner and really should be a sergeant," tested Cripes.

"I am a bleedin' Sergeant you cretin!" spat Pyke leaning his face closely towards that of Cripes. "And you will remember my name when you are walking your last walk. You can put that in the bank."

"Three you say?" interrupted Wiggins. "Yes, Sir. Three. The Father, the Son and the Holy Spirit," oozed Cripes creepily whilst crossing himself. "No more than three you say?" continued Wiggins, labouring the point. Cripes continued to stare straight ahead, his neck seemingly immobile. "Yes, Sir. Just the three."

"And why have you turned yourself into Paddington station when Leaman Street would have been more convenient to your place of residence?"

"Tis an unholy place Leaman Street. The Devil stalks the streets of Whitechapel and has done for many years. The Lord pervades in Paddington, the churches, the chapels. I was called to testify here by the lamb of God."

"Surely then Saint Paul's?" questioned Wiggins, trying to make sense of the deluded man's thought process.

"God has set a day in which he purposes to judge the inhabited earth. Acts seventeen, thirty-one, and this is the day and place he chose for my judgement. I have nothing to atone for as I did only His bidding."

Pyke violently and without warning lifted a tin cup from the cell bench and hurled it forcefully at Cripes, missing his head by mere inches. It rang against the brick wall and rattled to a circling halt on the stone floor. Cripes' head remained still, unflinching, his immobile eyes still focused on something unseen in the middle distance.

"Your mother, what is her name can I enquire?" Wiggins continued his barrage of questions.

"Of course, you can enquire. It is your job to do so. My mother is an Angel. A blessed Sainted Angel," restated the albino pompously.

"Let me hazard a guess. Your mother's name is Mary, am I correct?" prodded Wiggins. For the only time since the three men had met, Cripes' gaze for once shifted to the face of Wiggins, a slight tremor flickered across his left eyelid.

Wiggins and Pyke walked away from the locked cell door behind them.

"What do you think Jem?" asked Wiggins.

"I'm not so sure, Sir," ruminated Pyke. "He's clearly mad enough and he possesses the skills needed to butcher but I'm not completely convinced. I would not have thought our man would walk into Paddington Nick and start talking about his sainted mother. However, he does bear more investigation than all the other Johnny nut jobs we've had claiming responsibility."

"Yet he maintains he has murdered three women. We know of only two, Mary Harrison and Louise Smith. However, it is wholly plausible that there may be a third, as yet, undiscovered victim out there. Did you notice how Cripes did not blink Pyke? Not once," enquired Wiggins.

"Can't say as I did Sir to be truthful," responded Pyke, slightly embarrassed that he had failed such an observation test.

"A remarkably unflustered mien," continued Wiggins. "We blink far more rapidly the more stress we become exposed to, but he did not blink once during the entirety of our conversation. His nervous system is obviously operating on a lower level than normal. It has a trancing effect once you notice it and it shows that Cripes has an amazing ability to focus and not react to external distractions. Staring, or more specifically non-blinking, is a very predatory trait. One need only observe birds of prey to appreciate that. This unnerves me to a certain degree. Remarkable really when you think more deeply about it."

"I say we leave him to stew for a couple of days, maybe throw a twenty stone Jessie boy in with him. See if he still wants to test our good judicial system after forty-eight hours of that sort of attention," suggested Pyke with a conspiratorial wink. "I'm sure I could arrange for Syphilis Phyllis to be picked up. He'll be down Victoria Dock right now swinging his boa about."

Wiggins could not suppress a laugh. "A capital idea, Jem. Get a couple of uniforms to pick him up within the hour. Meanwhile, I wouldn't mind taking a look at number 61a Narrow Street. We could even partake of a beer on the way back?"

"Don't need asking twice Boss. I'll get me hat," smiled Pyke.

It was nearly eight o'clock by the time the two policemen reached the shabby front door of 61a Narrow Street, complete with bright yellow curtains. Pyke had insisted on personally supervising the arrest of Syphilis Phyllis, taking great relish in the prospect of introducing him to the religious zealot trapped in holding cell G of Paddington Station.

"But I ain't done naffink, Sergeant! I were only out for me evening constitutional," pleaded Phyllis. "Doctors orders. It's me chest you see, it ain't quite right." Phyllis' deep rumbling baritone was in sharp contrast to the pink petticoats and red stockings that he sported.

"There's a lot more that ain't quite right about you other than your chest Phil," retorted Pyke with a distinct laugh in his voice.

"But it ain't fair, Jem, I ain't done naffink wrong," Phyllis reiterated as he struggled with the two constables who were trying to squeeze the twenty stone, lavender-scented streetwalker into the back of the Paddy Wagon.

"Resisting arrest and wearing a pink frock in public, Phil. That gets you two nights in chokey luvvie," laughed Pyke. "Don't worry, we got some nice company lined up in there for you. Very accommodating, so I've heard." The doors of the wagon slammed closed on a still protesting Phyllis as Pyke and Wiggins doubled up in laughter. "Cripes doesn't know what's gonna hit him, literally," chuckled Pyke.

"You are a wicked man Sergeant Jeremiah Pyke," added Wiggins.

"You don't know the 'alf of it Boss," winked Pyke.

Over the years the door to number 61A had been painted red, blue and black in turn, that much could be seen from its revealing layers of peeling paint. Wiggins reached for the splendidly ornate Crucifix door knocker and gave several sharp raps. One, two, pause, one, two, three. Pyke grinned at his boss' habitual knock. They waited a few moments without reply. Pyke cupped his hand to a grimy ground floor window and strained to peer inside whilst Wiggins repeated his customary knock. No answer was forthcoming.

"Mrs Cripes!" shouted Pyke as he thumped heavily on the door, instinctively ignoring the iconic knocker. "Police, Ma'am. Open up please!" The house remained as silent as the cast of a shadow. "Time to enter, I feel, Jem," nodded Wiggins towards the door, stepping back in expectation of what he knew was about to unfold. Pyke took one step back and aimed a powerful kick at the lock area of the door. The frame splintered slightly. "One more should do it," puffed Pyke and threw another full-blown kick at the door. This time it cracked again and flew open only to be stopped abruptly. Through the gap between door and frame, Wiggins observed a chain secured on the inside. "Someone is inside Jem," he reasoned. Pyke took several steps back and this time launched himself shoulder-first at the door. It crashed open and Pyke stumbled through, stopping his run at the farthest end of the hallway stairs. "That was a stubborn one," smiled Pyke rubbing his shoulder. "That'll be bruised come tomorrow."

Both men looked about them. Wiggins searched for a light switch without success. Pyke reached up and lit a gas mantle with his flint lighter. "Whiffs a bit don't it Guv?" sniffed Pyke screwing up his face at the strong, pungent, sickly-sweet odour. "I sometimes think that your sense of smell is the only sensitive thing about you Sergeant Pyke," joked Wiggins.

The hallway was gloomy and sparsely furnished. Another crucifix adorned the wall, this one much larger than the door knocker. The Christ looked pleadingly downwards, and Pyke got the eerie sensation that the eyes followed his every move. The pair walked into the parlour, lighting mantles as they proceeded. The room was filled with religious iconography, wall hangings of various biblical scenes, statuary of the apostles and taking pride of place a large home-made grotto, a shrine to Our Lady Mary, mother of God. Candles and small mirrors cluttered the fireplace, table and mantelpiece. Wiggins found an old hand-held paraffin lamp. Once lit, he held it aloft and peered closely at the grotto. "I can't quite make out what this is made from, some sort of plaster de Paris perhaps, Papier-mâché even," he mused.

Pyke was diligently scanning the room. "There are some photographs on the dresser here Sir. Looks like there were three of 'em, all remarkably similar looking. Triplets I would guess," he said taking a frame in hand and showing it to Wiggins who took the photo, brushing some dust from the glass. "By Jove, I think you are right Jem. Two boys and a girl, all identical, all albino. How exceedingly rare. I presume that this is the mother standing beside them. No sign of a father I see." Three wraithlike, ghostly pale faces stared at him through a sepia mist. Each more serious than the last as if trying to outdo each other to see which could look least happy sitting still for the photographer. "There is something haunted and empty about these children, Jem. There is no joy here, no soul, no love."

"The Holy Trinity he spoke of perhaps?" ventured Pyke. Wiggins nodded in agreement. Both men looked at each other, then again at the photograph. Wiggins wiped the remaining film of filthy dust from the glass with his coat sleeve and replaced the frame on the dresser. "What became of the other two I wonder?"

"I could venture a guess, Sir," replied Pyke, "… and I'll wager the answer ain't a pleasant one neither." At that moment they heard a distinct creak from the floorboards upstairs as if some weight had been shifted on the upper floor. Both men looked upwards.

"A cat? A settling floorboard?" suggested Pyke.

"Remember the door chain, Jem, there is someone in here. Door chains do not lock themselves. Someone is upstairs." Another creak, this time louder and directly overhead. Wiggins imagined that he saw the ceiling bulge slightly. Another creak, then another followed. "Definitely someone up there," declared Pyke glancing again at the photograph of the three children. "I'll wager it ain't no raven-haired beauty neither."

Both men unholstered their pistols and with Wiggins leading and holding the lamp aloft, they slowly and carefully made their way up the bare wooden stairs. Wiggins noted as they climbed that the bannister was thick with accumulated dust as if unused. The creaking continued, now picking an unmistakable rhythm, getting progressively louder as they reached a small landing at the top of the stairs. The landing was dimly lit and boasted two doors, both leading to bedrooms. One was completely closed whilst the other, from which the rhythmic creaking was emanating was slightly ajar, with a hint of dim light suggesting itself from within. The skin on the back of both men's forearms began to pimple and crawl and the hair on the backs of their necks seemed to stand to attention as they each heard the soft singing of an unmistakably young female voice, coming from the other side of the door. Wiggins placed his fingers on the door edge and gently pushed it open. In the centre of the room, rocking backwards and forwards in a wooden rocking chair sat a young lady. She looked painfully frail, like a small white bird, her translucent skin was as thin as tissue paper and a wild shock of pure white hair reached nearly to the floor. In her arms, she cradled a child's doll. The girl seemed not to notice the two policemen as they stepped gingerly into the room, the floorboards creaking under the weight of their feet as they progressed towards her. Oblivious, she continued to sing her haunting lullaby, rocking back and forth whilst staring lovingly at the doll cradled in her arms.

"Jem," whispered Wiggins from behind his hand. "Do you detect what I do?"

"If it's 'cause the dolly ain't no bleedin' dolly, then yes," came Pyke's hushed reply.

What had initially looked like a child's doll was, in fact, a baby of no more than several weeks old. Its eyes were closed, and it was still and silent, its skin a ghostly pale blue pallor was cracked like alabaster. Wiggins coughed. "Miss Cripes I presume?"

"Is that you Nathaniel?" asked the spectral looking girl as she lifted her sightless pink eyes towards the direction of the policeman's voice. "Our baby will not awaken, my darling, I fear she slumbers like the others." She recommenced her singing whilst gently rocking her baby. Pyke shuddered and turned his gaze away, his mind already building a picture of the wretched goings-on that had occurred within this ghost house. "I'm going to look in the other room, Guv."

Wiggins nodded and with a parting glance at the wretched apparition before him, he followed Pyke across and into the second room. After all, what could be more chilling than the cameo they had both just witnessed.

The room was fetid, the air stagnant and pungent, a smell reminiscent of rotting fruit and flowers. There was one large brass bed in the centre of the room, upon which lay three corpses. Wiggins instantly recognised that one had been dead for much longer than the other two, the remains being nothing more than skeletal. The other two seemed more recent but were still decomposed beyond recognition, what little flesh was left on them appeared brittle and hard as if dried out. At the foot of the bed sat a large crib in which the men could see what looked like the remains of two or possibly three infants, each swaddled in rough hessian blankets. Pyke turned convulsively away, staunching the limbic reaction to wretch.

Wiggins recalled the photograph downstairs. "His mother, and two sisters, I would presume. Cripes' own Holy Trinity."

"And the girl? questioned Pyke. "Don't tell me what I'm thinking Bert, it's just too gruesome to comprehend."

"I fear your conjecture already matches mine, Jem. I think we will find that the unfortunate creature next door is Nathaniel Cripes' inbred daughter, no doubt born of one of his late sisters, and the babe in her arms could be referred to as either his granddaughter or his daughter. I am sure both would be correct."

"He is a Beast all right," snarled Pyke." I feel sick to the pit of me stomach."

"We must get this young woman to a hospital for the appropriate care and document what has gone on here, no matter how unsavoury or unpleasant. Detach yourself from it emotionally and record only the data. I will contact the coroner and photographers as soon as we return to the Yard. Do you know of anyone who can come and sit with her until we can arrange transport to the hospital? A local lady whose discretion may be trusted perhaps?" enquired Wiggins.

"Not many of those around 'ere to be sure. I'll wait with her until the bus arrives. You go and take care of the coroner and send a couple of uniforms around to relieve me. After that it's straight to the Grapes for me, I need a bit of Mary's hospitality and refreshment after this evening. You still going to join me as originally planned?" Wiggins nodded and tipped his hat towards the stalwart Pyke. "Let's go uptown Jem. My treat."

As he gently closed the fractured front door as best he could, Wiggins could still hear the faint whisper of the girl's ghostly lullaby accompanied by the low creaking of Jem Pyke's heavy footsteps as he slowly laboured up the wooden staircase.

Nathaniel Cripes remained sedentary with his feet planted squarely, heels together and his hands placed symmetrically upon his knees. He was motionless and silent in the damp cold cell, a solitary flickering lightbulb spasmodically illuminating the gloom of the cell as though some tormented firefly. The only sound, the buzzing of the bulb, was rudely interrupted by the commotion to Cripes' left as Constable Bunce threw another occupant into the cell. Cripes persisted in his statuesque demeanour and remained stationary. A vision suddenly appeared directly in front of Cripes' face.

"Oh dahling, you do have the cutest little pink eyes," examined a lipstick-smeared Syphilis Phyllis in his gruff Cockney accent. "Like a cute lil' white bunny wabbit. They matches my petticoats divinely don't you agree," asked the he-she hitching up his skirts provocatively, hairs springing through the underlying red stockings.

It was as though Nathaniel Cripes had not even noticed the appearance of the apparition now before him as he continued to stare unblinkingly ahead paying no attention to his new lodger. Six-foot-tall in his stocking soles and twenty stones of sexually receptive Nancy had been bundled unceremoniously into holding cell G. The strains of "I ain't daaan naaaafink," had wrung through the corridors of Paddington police station to the obvious amusement of the attending officers, some of whom lampooned the overblown theatrics of Phyllis.

"Fancy the two of us being thrown together on this chilly evening, and only one bed as well," pointed out Phyllis flashing his heavily laden eyelashes lasciviously at Cripes. Black streaks stained their way down his grotesquely rouge-tinted cheeks, where crocodile tears had traced their way during his arrest only moments before.

"You're a quiet one," proffered Phyllis taking a few steps back. "I do like the strong silent types, especially the ones who pretend not to be interested. They're the ones who really want it most I can assure you," he pouted salaciously at Cripes who sat unflinching, silent and emotionless. Phyllis looked furtively around the holding cells. "Look! All the other rooms are empty. Tis Kismet dahling!" uttered Phyllis clapping dramatically before bursting into song.

Let me call you sweetheart, I'm in love with you … let me hear you whisper that you love me too … la, da, da, di, di, da … oh, I forget the rest but it could be our song for this evening dahling. It is my absolute favourite."

"Shut your filthy hole!" spat Cripes abruptly, emphasising each syllable, spittle shooting forth from his mouth. "You are a repugnant atrocity of nature and an obscenity to the Lord you unholy sodomite! If a man lies with man as with a woman, both have committed an abomination; they shall surely be put to death; their blood is upon them. Leviticus twenty, thirteen."

"Oh, hark at you, Holy Joe!" mocked Phyllis, his mascaraed lashes widening in shocked parody. "I could just sit on you and have my wicked way in any fashion I so choose you know. Shall I do that little boy? Shall I let you know who mama is?" Cripes rose from his seated position slowly and mechanically from the knees until the two men were nose to nose.

"Do you know who I am … whore?" whispered Cripes. Phyllis looked him up and down rather haughtily. "Some little plaything DI Wiggins has offered up to me I do believe. Someone to keep old Phyllis warm and lubricated this evening. Isn't he kind and thoughtful?" Neither man backed down from the face-off but only one was blinking.

"I am the Beast they all seek, and I do believe DI Wiggins has offered me one final sacrifice before I stand in judgement with the Lord. Are you ready?"

Nosher Ash carefully scraped the dottle out of his bulldog pipe making sure that every last remnant of his previous smoke was gone, and his bowl was as clear as it could be. He always took a great degree of satisfaction in the ritual of lighting up a new pipe. The scraping, the filling, the tamping, the lighting. All individually pleasant activities which resulted in the final gratification of smoking the fragrant tobacco. Nosher was thumbing some Cavendish rough shag from his tobacco pouch when he heard the first scream.

"Get me out of 'ere now!" came the screech from the holding cells. Nosher snorted a little as he laughed, an involuntary habit which continued to annoy his wife, even after eighteen years of marriage. *'That'll teach the pink-eyed deviant,'* he thought, satisfied that Big Phyllis would be putting the fear of God, and possibly something even more unwelcome, into the petrified Cripes. He tamped the tobacco down into the bowl of his pipe with his thumb and proceeded to light it, each puff reddening the embers and producing a satisfying sizzle and a plume of sweet-smelling purple grey smoke.

"For God's sake someone 'elp me! Get this monster away from me!" The screams were getting louder and more frantic. "Noooooooooo! Heaven help me! Let me out!"

Nosher laid down his pipe, careful not to upset its contents. *'That did not sound right,'* he thought, now a little worried. He turned to the two constables who were laughing at the tea station and signalled them to be quiet. "Hush lads, let me listen." Nosher pulled his thick mop of hair away from his ear and listened intently. All he could detect under the monotonous ticking of the station wall mounted clock was a long, low wailing noise. The wailing was piteous, almost animalistic rather than human, like the mewling of a puppy in need of milk.

Nosher grabbed one of the young constables by the elbow. "You come with me, Jacks." Nosher unlocked the steel gate to the cell corridor and the two men trotted down the corridor to the furthermost cell. Holding cell G. Nosher shouted "Stand back from the door, lads," as his key tumbled the lock and he heaved open the steel door.

Nathaniel Cripes sat on the solitary chair bolted to the floor in the centre of the room, his rat pink eyes staring straight ahead, unblinking, and seemingly focused on nothing at all. His milk-white hands, their pale blue venous tributaries pulsing beneath his translucent skin, rested upon his knees. His feet were still planted firmly on the cold concrete floor, ankles seemingly grafted together. A tremor of a smile ran across his insipid lips as the two police officers barged through the cell door.

Nosher crossed himself, "Holy mother of god." Syphilis Phyllis sat on his haunches in the furthermost corner of the room as if trying to squeeze himself into the very walls themselves. He rocked back and forth, his massive bulk, quivering like jelly, his hands lifted to his face covering his features. Blood dripped from between his fingers as if he were squeezing a particularly juicy orange and fell into a small pond of fresh urine on the floor beneath him. "He made me take me eyes, Nosh! Me own eyes for Gawd's sake! He made me take me eyes out!" he moaned. Nosher looked aghast at Cripes, then back to the weeping mass in the corner. Cripes' tongue ran briefly across his lips. "And the Lord said, if thine eye offend thee, pluck it out, cast it from thee. Matthew eighteen, nine." Constable Jacks, ran from the room, thinking of his mother and wishing he had taken her advice and joined the Post Office Service.

"Cripes is a deviant monster to be sure. His daughter and no doubt his late sister, would, I am sure, testify to that. But what unearthly power enabled him to make a twenty stone 'man' of the world pluck his own eyes out in a locked police cell?" questioned Wiggins. Pyke lifted the rim of his derby to scratch his head. "I don't know but it ain't natural, gives me the Portland Bills just thinking of it. Phyllis was a Nancy through and through, but he was a big old lump of a bloke. I'm only too glad that the little pervert is safely locked away in Saint Luke's. Anyway, wouldn't our Beast not delight in removing Phyllis' eyes personally?"

"You are most probably right Jem, but we still cannot rule Cripes out yet. He is a plausible suspect. His deviant behaviour, his past involvement in butchery, the psychosexual personality all point towards our killer. At least we have him under secure observation pending the outcome of our investigations," responded Wiggins.

The two men each nursed a pint of porter in the secluded snug nook in the Ship and Shovell in Craven Passage behind Blackfriars Station. Wiggins took a long slake of his drink and leaned back in his chair. He looked around, the tiny pub was full of patrons as always, its small booths resounded with chatter and laughter.

"Time for another, Guv?" asked Pyke hopefully, his thirst stimulated by the first refreshing pint. Wiggins nodded and slid his empty glass across the table towards his Sergeant. He watched Pyke chatting to the barmaid as she drew another two foaming pints from behind what he mused must be one of the very smallest bars in London. His attention was drawn to a company of four people who were departing one of the booths to his left. He absentmindedly noticed how the leather upholstery of the bench retained the impression of its previous occupant, soon to be covered by the rear end of its next customer.

Pyke finished his chat with the barmaid and eased his way back into the snug with a pint in each hand and a smile beaming from his face. "That's me sorted for tonight," a wink accompanying his grin. Wiggins lifted the glass to his lips and gulped. "Radasiliev, Jem. I would wager that Cripes was infected and controlled by Radasiliev. Recall how the Russian somehow, and rather too easily, brought out the worst in us, our weaknesses, fears, and aggression. Imagine what he could do with an individual such as Cripes. Already a deviant of the highest degree. If he can influence the likes of us, I fear the control he could muster over the feeble minded, criminally insane and depraved masses of our City Jem. Given time and careful selection Radasiliev could potentially turn London into a writhing mass of insane mayhem."

Chapter 12 - The Organist

R ose Harsent faithfully completed her familiar routine. She settled herself squarely on the organ bench in the Church of Saint John of Jerusalem, in South Hackney, positioning her feet upon the organ pedalboard and made herself comfortable. Rose always took her seat with a profound sense of pride and fulfilment. It was sixty-five years since the Church's expansion, a project planned and executed mainly to accommodate the rebuilding of the Church's famous pipe organ. Since the exalted Henry Bonavia Hunt had become choirmaster, some forty years previously, only the country's leading organists had been appointed to the privileged position at Saint John's.

Rose had always regarded herself as a talented musician but had never expected to be so well respected and recognised by her peers within the world of religious music. Music, after all, was Rose's overriding passion in life. Reading and interpreting the music and giving recitals had seemed to come naturally to Rose from an early age. She was devoted to the church and lived the solitary, contented life of a middle-aged spinster with her two cats, Leo and Banjo, in the nearby small terraced house she had inherited from her late mother. Her father had died of consumption when she was a young girl and it was at that point that her mother had become completely absorbed into the welcoming arms of the Church. Mathilda Harsent had found solace and strength in her rekindled faith, and in the faith of those around her, so much so that young Rose would be taken to mass each day after finishing school. Soon she had come to love the sense of familiar comfort provided by the ceremony and rituals of the Church, with evening Eucharist being her particular favourite. The sights, the smells, the peaceful atmosphere, but most of all she delighted in the gloriously uplifting music. Rose had swiftly risen from playing the piano for the children to sing along to at Sunday School to the position of lead organist. She would imagine the music as a living entity of which she was an integral element, filling the huge stillness of the organ pipes as lungs inhale and exhale air, literally breathing life into the instrument, the building and the massed congregation.

Rose was an uncomplicated person who treasured the solitude of her evening rehearsals, particularly on chilly evenings such as this night. Rector Batty could always be found bumbling around somewhere within the building or perhaps in the adjoining Rectory, but otherwise, she was quite alone, just as she preferred. She began her now-familiar ritual of removing her spectacles and placing them on the bench to her left. She wiggled her fingers for several moments until they were warmed and primed for the performance ahead, then she sang a few scales in her mezzo-soprano range, accompanying each across the keys. She liked to refer to this as 'flexing her musicality.' She proceeded to place her right foot upon the balanced swell pedal and with her left foot free to pump the expression pedals she launched into a rendition of 'Oh Night Divine,' a particular favourite since childhood.

Rector Batty sat at his desk struggling with what would be tomorrow's sermon. He was a tubby little fellow who looked dry, as if his skin was dusted with talcum powder. He took a small sip of the sherry that always accompanied his writing and contemplated the underlying theme of his forthcoming homily. *'Perhaps the emerging importance of women within the establishment of the Parish,'* he wondered. Gone were the days where women were seen only as being capable of arranging flowers and driving cake sales. Now women such as Rose Harsent were taking more active roles within the Church and society as a whole. Batty considered using Rose's musical virtuosity as an allegory to illustrate the diverse talents of these emergent, empowered women. Batty sat back, satisfied with himself at devising such a clever little twist for his sermon and treated himself to another tiny sip of sherry. As he did so he could hear the organ music rise from the chapel. *'Rose is starting her evening rehearsal,'* he thought happily, *'a most welcome accompaniment to my little jottings.'*

Absorbed as she always was in this peerless hymn, she failed to notice the dark shadow shifting and darting amongst the pews and cloisters behind her, its elongated form flitted from wall to column whilst stretching its slender angularity across the tessellated tiled floor. Rose's voice sang out the chorus, revelling in the solitude her isolation afforded. Her voice was sweet but none the less powerful for such a small woman.

"Fall on your knees! O hear the angel voices!"
You will only hear the Devil voices!
"O night divine, the night when Christ was born."
I hunger, I thirst! Flesh, I need flesh. Blood, I crave blood!
"O night…"
They call me the Beast, but I am more than that.
"O holy night…"
I am the life taker. I am the life-giver.
"O night divine."
They will all recoil at my rage. YOU will repent!

Rose was lost in the reverie of the music, her eyes squeezed tightly shut, all her senses detached from her surroundings and focused purely on the hymn she joyfully played. Only the music existed in that instant.

The shadow slowly rose behind her, taking nightmarish shape, engulfing this earnestly religious woman, her fragile frame lost within its indelible darkness. Rose shrieked in absolute terror as the clammy skeletal fingers of the shadow grasped each of her shoulders and moved with incredible speed towards her neck. The organ fell silent.

The Rector awoke abruptly, his head nodding to attention the way ones does when slipping into a deep sleep only momentarily. He presumed however that he must have nodded off at some point soon after Rose had started her practice. This was not an uncommon occurrence these days, particularly where a drop or two of sherry was involved. He could hear only silence now. He must have slept longer than he had thought. He reasoned that Rose must have finished and left for home. Batty creaked his ageing body aloft from his mahogany swivel desk chair, pushed the sherry glass aside, stretched out a yawn and straightened his cassock. '*Better go and check that Rose has snuffed out the candles and locked up behind her*,' he thought. The obsessive in Batty ensured that, even though in all the years that Rose had been carrying out her nightly rehearsals she had never once failed to lock the main doors of the church on her departure, he must always carry out this unnecessary check.

Suddenly he stopped in his tracks. The music had unexpectedly resumed, but this time the notes made no sense whatsoever, an incoherent tumult as if played by an overexcited child. '*There is something awfully wrong here*,' thought Batty striding towards the main enclave of the church where candles were still obviously lit, casting shadows along his route. '*She must be ill. That cannot be Rose.*' The musical cacophony increased in volume, its deconstructed notes bawling out a harshly disjointed crescendo of ear-splitting clamour. The Rector hurried from the Manse across the short gravel path and into the side door of the main church. He ran in short little hops as best he could. The disjointed music grew louder and louder as he entered the church, reaching an intense climax as Batty shuffled as quickly as he could into the transept.

What he saw took his breath away. What appeared to Batty to be an enormous black crow was hunched over the organ, cackling and screaming whilst it thumped the extended fingers of its hands randomly against the keys of the organ, all the time pulling wildly at the organ stops. The onslaught of sound stopped abruptly, and the crow turned what seemed to be its enormous head, topped with a crest of flying greying hair towards the now shocked rigid pastor. The creature's inky black eyes turned upon the Rector and the vilest of blood-drenched smiles spread across what

Batty reasoned was the face of the Devil himself. The rector fell to his knees grasping his rosary to his chest in silent prayer before passing out into blessed unconsciousness.

"It ain't him, Guv. It ain't Cripes. Can't be!" shouted Pyke excitedly as he flung open the door to Wiggins' office. "Apologies for not knocking Sir but there's been another slaying, same modus operandi."

"And not unsurprisingly our friend Cripes is safely incarcerated in the security of Saint Luke's, wasting our valuable time, energy and resources. Damn him! That vile man has cost another life, let him rot in Bedlam," raged Wiggins rising from his chair and grabbing his jacket. "To where do we head, Jem?"

"Saint John's Church in Hackney, Guv. It's the lady organist. A Rector Batty just rang. He was in a frightful state having discovered the body. Almost incoherent he was. Also says he saw the very Devil himself playing the organ, of all things," continued Pyke. "I've sent some uniforms down to secure the scene and ordered them not to touch anything until we get there."

"Photographer?"

"On his way."

"Best get your hat, Jem."

The two policemen made their way up Lauriston Road and parked on the gravel driveway outside Saint John's, its copper-clad spire reaching for the clouds of the moonlit sky. Pyke scraped his boots on the cast iron scraper at the front door as he followed Wiggins into the nave of the Church. As they walked up the aisle Pyke experienced the customary unfamiliarity he felt when he entered a place of worship. He always felt uncomfortable at exactly what to do and when to do it in a Church. He also knew that Wiggins and his wife attended regularly but Pyke's experiences of Church going were mainly restricted to attending the funerals of friends and colleagues.

Rector Batty sat in the front pew before the chancel where he was being comforted by Constable Murray. Wiggins was not surprised at this. He had often considered Murray a natural carer and protector, a kind yet fearless man. "It was the Devil Lucifer himself. The wings of a black angel of death. Played an unholy lament on our organ," spluttered Batty as he turned to Wiggins. "The very Devil himself I tell you, Inspector. Lord save us."

Pyke tapped Wiggins on the shoulder and nodded that he should look in the direction of the side transept. On the side wall hung a large crucifix, perhaps eight feet in height, on which a plasterwork statue of the crucified Christ was nailed. Hanging from Christ's neck was what remained of the ravaged body of Rose Harsent, her ankles tied securely around the icon's neck so as her head and arms dangled downwards reaching towards the feet of the Lord. Her neck and torso had been ripped apart and blood had spilt into a pool at the foot of the crucifix. A vile soup of Rose Harsent's heart, liver, her lungs and kidneys, all ripped asunder from her body, lay upon the floor just inches from her terrified, still open eyes.

Wiggins blew out his cheeks. "Only our Beast would be sick and vile enough to remove an Organist's major organs. This was planned, the victim was carefully chosen, Pyke." The Detective Inspector crossed himself. "Take those photographs as quickly as you can Constable and get that poor woman down from there this instant."

"We must end this, Guv. This cannot go on," demanded Pyke, shaking his head.

After staring at, and processing the grizzly scene before him, Wiggins turned to Pyke. "This begs the question, why did our Demon spare the man of God Pyke? Batty quite clearly stated that the Beast saw him. Would his sacrifice at the altar not be the ultimate atrocity?" questioned Wiggins. "There will be no killing in the House of our Lord!" shouted Wiggins as he turned and headed towards the door. His face bore an intense look of anger that Pyke had never before encountered.

Chapter 13 - The Study

His ashtray was full of cigarette stubs, the fire had long since guttered out and his coffee pot was empty. It was three twenty-two in the morning and Albert Wiggins sat huddled over the roll-top bureau in his top floor attic study. This secluded enclave was where he did his greatest thinking, free from the perpetual activity and buzz of the hive of Scotland Yard. He was inwardly astounded at how little sleep his body required when he was immersed in such a case. '*What was he thinking? There had never been such a case!*' He seemed to thrive on the sustenance of intrigue and mystery, reason and thought. He had investigated hundreds of crimes during his service, but nothing could ever come close to replicating the atrocity of the current situation. His profession was to serve and protect the denizens of the great city. That was what he had sworn to do all those years ago as a raw recruit. That had always been his underlying mantra. He had never in his career felt such a sense of acute failure and inadequacy. He had to push on through what he regarded in his darker moments as the hopelessness of it all, the answer was there, somewhere. He knew it.

The last four hours had been spent poring over previously solved and unsolved murder cases and meticulously researching and approaching the current one from divergent angles. He was acutely aware that it would be a mistake to twist facts to suit theories. Each evening over the past few weeks had mostly followed the same vein, intently studying the data, reinterpreting it, and analysing every element of the current case in his customary fastidious manner.

There was nothing in his study that was not required to be there. No frippery, no decoration, no unnecessary adornment. Only the tools of his profession. The room seemed smaller and more cramped than it was on account of the floor to ceiling bookcases that aligned three of the four walls. Two of the bookcases contained a library of criminal themed texts and general reference books, each shelf indexed by subject and each book alphabetised by author surname. The remaining bookcases contained his library of case notes and reference files. These files contained newspaper clippings, photographs and reports from around the country. Three neatly stacked piles of recently acquired books lay on the floor, awaiting cataloguing.

The one free wall housed a large school blackboard that Wiggins had acquired and on which he scribbled ideas, drawings, pathways, lists, keywords and such. Differently coloured chalks were used for specific subjects; red for facts and truths, blue for ideas and notions, green for names and objects, and white for any miscellaneous jottings. The list of all possible culprits, written in blue chalk, numbered nine. Some names were crossed out and some underlined or punctuated with question marks. Three neatly arranged stacks of paperwork adorned the bureau. A copy of National Geographic lay open at a treatise on the cannibalistic Korowai tribe of south-eastern Papua New Guinea. A small pad of handwritten notes lay beside the publication. Wiggins habitually wrote using only capital letters. "Less ambiguity equals less uncertainty, Pyke," he had always expounded.

Detective Inspector Albert Wiggins had made it his mission to understand exactly what it was that drove murderers to kill, the compulsion to commit their heinous acts. His conclusions thus far were many-fold and complicated. Almost all murders were perpetrated by men. Multiple killers were often abused emotionally, physically or sexually, by a family member or someone they knew. Impulsive killers were generally less intelligent than murderers who had plotted their crimes. Killers who had committed crimes of passion and who had murdered out of rage bore different neuropsychological and intellectual mindsets to those that meticulously and strategically planned their crimes. Existing data at his disposal highlighted that premeditated murderers were almost exclusively more predisposed to depression, mental issues and mood disorders than those individuals who killed on impulse. Spontaneous murderers were also more likely to have intellectual and cognitive impairments than cold and calculating killers. Alcohol or drug use was almost always a factor for impulsive murders who were more likely to be mentally impaired and less intelligent to some degree, whereas predatory and planned murderers displayed more evidence of psychotic disorders.

Wiggins threw down his pencil and stood up and stretched his spine back into normal alignment. He lit a cigarette and moved to the window. He parted the curtains and raised the sash by its brass finger lifts, breathing in the cool night air. It was a clear, moonlit night and from the vantage point of the fourth floor of his Marylebone home on Park Crescent, he looked eastwards across the rooftops towards Limehouse and Whitechapel. *'Where is the demon tonight? he wondered. What is he thinking? What is he scheming? What is his next infernal move?'* His gaze fixed upon an indiscriminate point in the distant panorama, never wavering, as he recalled the horrors that had already transpired, and which would have made the Almighty turn on his heels and run. He gritted his teeth. "I will catch you!" he whispered.

Chapter 14 - The Samaritan

The City had reluctantly awakened and was now approaching full throttle as Wiggins made his way along Northumberland Avenue towards Victoria Embankment. It was an unusually late start for him but given that he had worked on the case until the early hours of the morning, he felt justified in leisurely taking his time. He invariably walked to work each day feeling that it afforded him some personal thinking time during which he could review his current cases without any intrusive influences.

His morning stroll also allowed him the opportunity to observe his fellow Londoners. The Avenue was busier than it normally was during his morning constitutional which afforded him plenty of scope to indulge in his favourite mental pastime. He would pick out random pedestrians and endeavour, through observation and deduction, to ascertain their occupations and habits, and in some cases even their names. There an ex-cavalryman, here a housemaid, yonder a carpenter who habitually played billiards. Each was identified by the cut of their clothing, the bearing of their walk, the condition of their hands or the tone or staining of their skin.

Motorised carriages vied with those of the horse-drawn variety, creating a clamour and underlying background noise which Wiggins reasoned would only intensify over time due to Mr Ford's petrol-driven machines inevitably winning favour over their equine rivals.

The morning was frosty but relatively clear of fog and Wiggins could feel that the sun would soon burn through the blanket of cloud. The pavements were busy with the flow of human traffic which coursed through the veins of the great metropolis, giving life and purpose to the City. This constant surge of humanity created the trade and vitality which fed the greatest commercial hub on the planet. Millions of worker ants constantly feeding an insatiable Queen at the centre of a vast nest, mused Wiggins.

He was looking forward to a productive day when he unexpectedly felt the gentle but forceful grasp of a hand at his right coat sleeve. "Remain calm and continue walking but turn apace, Detective Inspector Wiggins. Trust that I am a friend. We are in mortal danger," came a low controlled voice. The hand guided him forward, forcing him to quicken his pace. Wiggins left hand immediately went to his shoulder holster. "No need for that yet. Trust me. Just stay stride for stride with me," came the authoritative voice. Wiggins glanced to his right in an attempt to see who his self-appointed guide may be, but the man was at least five inches shorter than Wiggins and wore a large felt fedora which fully masked his features from the detective. A faint hint of Blenheim eau de Cologne stimulated a distant memory. He could sense that his new companion was an older gentleman. His voice and bearing attested to this.

"There are two Burmese dacoits following us, approximately thirty yards behind and to the right at seventeen hundred hours. A further is shadowing us in the horse-drawn Hansom which imminently approaches," the stranger informed Wiggins. The Detective Inspector noted that his self-appointed guardian had positioned himself nearest the roadside, acting as a human shield between Wiggins and any potential attack that may be forthcoming from the approaching cab. Wiggins could hear the clatter of hooves of the Hansom's horses on the cobbles, getting louder and more thunderous as they approached.

"When I say 'now' immediately crouch down on your knees and lower your head as if in prayer," instructed the voice. Wiggins felt a strange allegiance with, and confidence in his apparent protector and accepted his bizarre instructions almost without question. He knew instinctively that this man could be trusted. The Hansom's approach grew closer and closer. He could almost feel the hot breath snorting from the fast-approaching horses when his companion whispered in his ear, "Now!"

Wiggins crouched as swiftly as he could, lowering his head to stare at the pavement. A blast of air passed over his head as a crossbow bolt all but pierced his hat and embedded itself with a reverberating thud in the splintering timber of an adjacent door. Just as the word, *now*, left his lips, his companion instantly drew his pistol and simultaneously spun one hundred and eighty degrees and, using the taller man's crouched back as a steadying armrest, fired off two shots at the now fleeing cab. The bullets ripped through the side of the cab as it hurtled towards the Embankment.

Although slightly deafened by the ringing in his ears, Wiggins was conscious of hearing the muffled shouts and screams of confused people all around them. Both men now stood upright and turned towards the two other dacoits. "Clear the Cobbles!" shouted Wiggins, firing his pistol at a vertical trajectory into the air. People turned and scattered into the nearest shop, café or any other doorway or alleyway that afforded protection. Others fell to the ground and clung to the pavement as if to the edge of a cliff. The two Burmese, realising that they were now hopelessly exposed, turned tail and began to frantically flee southwards towards the river. The man in the fedora raised his pistol for a second time. Two shots rang out. Instantly, deep red holes appeared at the base of the neck of each of the fleeing Burmese and their throats exploded, their arms flailing involuntarily as if they were about to attempt flight. Their faces bit the paving stones and their bodies flipped unnaturally.

"I wager a fiver I got the blighter in the cab as well," asserted the good Samaritan. "Fancy a morning coffee in the Northumberland Arms? I am familiar with the landlord and I am positive we can persuade him to open slightly earlier than his normal hours of custom. The establishment has a telephone so you can call the Yard and inform the necessary authority of what has just transpired."

Wiggins stood open-mouthed in astonishment. Not only at the acute accuracy of his companion's shooting and the efficiency and speed of his actions, but also at the calmness exuded by the elderly gentleman who stood before him. His initial instinct had been correct. His rescuer was an older man. Older by almost an entire generation.

Two constables were already on the scene ushering the public to safety and securing the area. Wiggins walked towards them and related his version of what had occurred, cleaning up any loose ends or concerns the constables may have had. Not only were his ears still ringing but his head was still reeling from what he had just witnessed. He turned to see the marksman rapping on the door of the Northumberland Arms with the silver hound's head of his walking cane. "Open up Jenkins. Surely you couldn't have slept through that infernal racket, you Dullard!" After a few moments, the lock clicked open and a young girl opened the door. "Ah! Edith, how delightful to see you again. May we trouble you for two cups of your finest coffee my dear?" intoned Wiggin's companion almost apologetically.

"Why of course Doctor Watson, please do come in. I'm afraid father is shakin' off a rather heavy one, so you'll have to make do with me," smiled Edith.

'*Of course, Doctor Watson!*' thought Wiggins, mentally kicking himself.

"A pleasure Edith. Wiggins, won't you join me? Some Colombian refreshment to start your morning shift should do you the world of good." Wiggins followed Watson into the bar, still somewhat bamboozled at what had just transpired. Edith re-bolted the door behind them and drifted behind the bar, throwing the elder gentleman a smile as she did so. Both men settled into opposite sides of a four-man booth and placed their hats on the table. Wiggins was still flabbergasted. The Great Detective had formed him, his way of thinking and reasoning. Tutored him in the science of deduction and reasoning but sitting before him was his hero. The man who had mentored him through his childhood. A man whose bravery, sense of justice and loyalty knew no bounds. A man who had selflessly and without a second thought to his own safety, risked his life countless times for his colleagues, his fellow man, his monarch and his country. Here sat the awe-inspiring Doctor John Hamish Watson.

THE REIGN OF THE BEAST: A DI WIGGINS ADVENTURE

"Ah, coffee," enthused Watson as Edith set the cups and saucers before them. "I am afraid I have become as addicted to its simulative charms as our mutual friend once was to an altogether more hazardous substance," admitted Watson.

"I'll just bring you sugar and milk gentlemen. You can have the cream off the top Doctor Watson," said Edith again smiling brightly at the Doctor. Watson winked and Edith giggled. *'He is actually charming her, and she's young enough to be his granddaughter,'* thought Wiggins, smiling to himself. *'His charisma is such that she barely notices any age difference nor indeed my presence.'*

After a few sips of the strong, piping hot coffee Watson broke the silence. "My dear Wiggins, or should that be Digger? I am sorry about that infernal mess outside, but I just happened to be taking the morning air when I noticed both you and your imminent predicament. Being an old soldier and all that you know…"

"Fully armed my good Doctor, on a Monday morning stroll. I somehow think not," interrupted an admonishing Wiggins regaining some of his customary composure. "Much as I appreciate you saving my life, for what is, I might add, definitely not for the first time, I doubt very much that your presence here this very morning is entirely serendipitous."

"Such a long word, Wiggins, you certainly have come a long way!" chuckled Watson signalling the eagerly attendant Edith for a refill. "Why, you have me bang to rights, as they say. I had hoped that my retirement in beautiful Perthshire would have been more permanent or at least longer-lasting, but it seems that the salmon and grouse of the land of my fathers will be breathing a sigh of relief for a little while longer".

"Surely salmon would not breathe?" puzzled Wiggins.

"A logical and literal mind to be sure. I wonder where you inherited that from?" Watson hunched forward. His hair was greyer and slightly sparser than Wiggins' last remembered, but the square jaw and honest open countenance remained unchallenged by the effects of the passing years. His eyes still twinkled with a wicked enthusiasm for the chase. "Before it slips my mind, how fares Constable Murray?"

"You know of Murray? I am surprised," responded Wiggins absent-mindedly stirring his coffee. "He is an exemplary constable and will soon, no doubt be an equally exemplary officer. He is due for promotion later this month. A dedicated and resourceful, not to mention brave and caring individual. You know of him how?"

"I know not him, but I knew his father, without whom I would not be sitting here with you this morning. Thirty-three years ago, during the Afghan War, Murray's father was my orderly and single-handedly rescued me from the battlefield of Maiwand after I had carelessly taken a Jezail bullet in the shoulder. I am glad to hear that the apple has fallen close to the tree. When young Murray was in search of a position, I called in a favour from Inspector Lestrade, who kindly took him into the constabulary," reminisced Watson. "But I digress from the subject at hand. I have been asked to help, my dear boy. To keep an eye, report back, that sort of thing. He is most anxious that no harm comes to you or yours."

"You mean Mary? Surely she is in no danger?" stuttered a suddenly worried Wiggins. The idea that his wife may be at risk had never entered his mind until now. "Just a precaution, old fellow. You know how He thinks of every eventuality," reassured Watson. "Of course," said Wiggins, although not entirely placated.

"These are indeed dark times and He finds himself unfortunately otherwise detained on the Continent. Hamstrung though He is by various forces of evil, he has managed somehow to get a message through to me and has asked that I pass on some words of advice. Trust in Van Hoon. As you know, and despite what the general public was told, he was instrumental in assisting us in apprehending the Ripper twenty-five years ago. He is a valuable ally. The greatest threats are these Oriental Devils. Whatever the Chiswick Papers are they must be protected and must not fall into their hands or the consequences could be monumental. He seems to think that your superior, Chief Superintendent MacDonald, knows more regarding these matters of State than he may currently be acknowledging. Whatever occurs I am to be at your service."

Wiggins was at once proud that this man still cared enough for him and his wife to jeopardise his own safety, but also felt vaguely slighted at the presumption that he needed protection. His mind however then quickly returned to the fact that no more than twenty minutes before this man had saved his life and had demonstrated his readiness to take a crossbow bolt in his lieu.

Watson smiled once more as he drained his coffee and placed his hat atop his head. He rose to take his leave and smiled a parting farewell to Edith. "I am staying just across the road in the Northumberland. Professor Sigmund Freud is also staying there currently, and I am delighted to say he does make for a most entertaining and stimulating supper fellow! You can contact me there as you require. Room number sixty. Make no mistake young Wiggins, the game is most definitely afoot."

Chapter 15 - The Actor

"The King was in his Counting House, counting out his money." The four little girls sang as they skipped after each other merrily, ropes in hand on the slippery cobbled Soho lane. The morning was all but gone and the sun was struggling to penetrate a chill hazy sky. Less than a few hundred yards away in the basement of a Gerrard Street restaurant, Mr King sat on his ornately carved cherry wood throne, his verdant eyes concentrating intently on the intricate work he was conducting.

"The Queen was in the parlour eating bread and honey." Rosie was farthest ahead in the girls skipping race, pleased as Punch with the new rope her Daddy had given her for her birthday the day before. She was convinced that the rope was a magic rope which made her skip faster than all the other girls.

Jabez Rubenstein winced as he witnessed King's scalpel carefully carve away another diamond-shaped piece of skin from the cheek of the comatose man's face.

"The maid was in the garden hanging out the clothes." Rosie looked anxiously over her shoulder. Jeanie Taylor was gaining on her. '*Running instead of skipping,*' thought Rosie chewing on her cheek, '*that's cheating!*'

"Down came a blackbird and pecked off her nose." Rosie halted suddenly almost falling over her magic rope. Her abrupt scream brought her little friends running to her side. Jeanie Taylor ran into the back of her almost causing Rosie to stumble forward onto the body of the man lying face down on the cobbles. He was lifeless and twisted. Broken like Rosie's old dolly, Mrs McHuggles.

Each afternoon between matinee and evening performance, Sheridan Sweet held court in the old Lyceum Public House on the Strand. Habitually frequented by theatre land's actors, stagehands and writers, the old pub also drew crowds of both early evening and after-show theatre goers. As such it was an ideal haunt for 'Sweet Sherry' as he was known to everyone but the bill writers and his long-suffering bank manager. Sweet was a chronic alcoholic, his once distinguished handsome face now swollen and threaded with tell-tale red veins. He suffered dreadful psoriasis caused by his alcohol consumption and his shoulders were permanently covered in the dry flaking skin his scratchings had caused. His now palsied hand had once shaken the hands of Sarah Bernhardt, Henry Irving and Ellen Terry. Sweet was now almost entirely unemployable due to his heavy drinking, his inability to remember lines and his unhealthy interest in rough trade. His aristocratic bearing brought him the occasional small part in minor plays, normally cast as a noble grandee of little import and even less dialogue.

That evening Sweet was at his favourite table in his favourite pub, projecting forth in his most melodramatic tones, his sweeping gestures and booming voice reverberating around the crowded bar. "And of course, Irving's Hamlet was untouchable, superior even to his Macbeth in my opinion. I told him so darlings, I sat in this very chair whilst the adorable, sainted Ellen sat next to him exactly where you are my dears." The young impressionable actors that had gathered around Sweet hung on his every word, fascinated by stories of his glory days, and enjoying oiling the bottomless source of anecdotes with repeated glasses of Gin and Dubonnet for the old soak. "Of course, his Shylock was his grandest masterpiece," flourished the ageing thespian with his one good hand as he accepted another glass from an unknown benefactor. "My reviews as Launcelot Gobbo were utterly flattering of course, my most memorable performance at the Lyceum."

So long as he had an audience the anecdotes could continue all night. The beautiful boys, the ghastly directors, the tumultuous applause, the encores, the beastly actresses who saw him as a rival. All the stories he had told the previous night and would retell the next and the next. Gradually the acolytes drifted away leaving Sweet, as always, on his own staring at a table so encumbered by empty glasses that he struggled to find a space to place his gin.

"Certainly, my conscience will serve me to run from this Jew, my master. The fiend is at my elbow…" mumbled Sweet struggling to pronounce each word, belching into his nearly empty glass, quoting Gobbo's opening line. No matter how inebriated Sheridan Sweet became he was always able to recall the words of his lines from the Merchant of Venice. He had, after all, performed it triumphantly on hundreds of occasions. Sweet hiccupped and drained his glass, the gin now tasteless on top of its many predecessors. "… Not a poor boy, sir but the rich Jew's man; that would sir that my father shall specify."

"Time gentlemen, please. Down it or lose it!" boomed Harry the landlord, a robust, balding but moustachioed barrel of a man as he swept around the pub clearing glasses and sweeping up stragglers. "That means you too Sweets old luvvie," said Harry placing a kindly hand on the old inebriate's bony shoulder.

"Of course, my Liege," pronounced Sheridan Sweet rising unsteadily to his feet. "Tell him there is a post come from my master, with his horn full of good news!"

declared Sweet repeating his character's final line from his favourite play. "I bid you good night and Adieu!" Sweet bowed with a flourish and toppled headlong onto the floor. Harry looked skyward and lifted the snoring thespian to his feet. "Wake up Sweets. You ain't sleeping here, old boy."

The thespian nodded and puffed out his cheeks stifling a wretch then weaved a meandering route out of the pub and into the ice-cold air of the London night. Sweet lived in humble lodgings above a music publisher in Denmark Street. "Only temporary of course, darling," as he would always emphasise. Sweet turned right as he exited the Lyceum and headed down the Strand, concentrating on keeping one foot in front of the other, mostly successfully. So far so good. The fresher air seemed to be having the desired effect, giving him a second wind. A right turn into Charing Cross Road saw him proceed towards Soho in search of some late-night lubrication in one of its many unregulated underground drinking dens. The Cocktail Club perhaps, or Black Angus's Rendezvous Club. Either would be accommodating for Sweet. As he weaved his way, hiccupping along the streets of London's theatreland, his alcoholic haze kept him blissfully unaware of not only the two stealthy shapes that trailed him but also of the large black sedan that slowly shadowed closely behind.

Sweet stopped, fumbled in his coat pocket, and extracted an old tin cigarette case, along with half the lining of his pocket. After further fumbling with his working hand he produced a Pall Mall from the tin and tried unsuccessfully to strike a match in the belligerent breeze that whipped at his coattails. "Blow, winds, and crack your cheeks! Rage! Blow! … Bloody wind," he mumbled and stepped into a convenient side lane in the hope that it may offer some shelter. After much concentration and exaggerated coordination, the old drunk finally managed to light his cigarette. He raised his head in triumph. Blowing some upwards into the sky from his first inhalation. It was at that point that he was blinded by a set of large headlights shining directly into his eyes.

The large sedan blocked the entrance to the narrow lane. The driver sat as still and silent as the engine. Inside the car sat Hercules Chin and a small lizard-like oriental chauffeur. Chin felt uncomfortable, squeezed into a relatively small car that felt less to him like a vehicle and more like an overcoat. His back was hunched over and his knees raised almost to his eye level.

"This is the one Father King wants, Big Boy. You are to bring him back to the master. He has a part to play. You know what to do," instructed the driver. Sheridan Sweet stood in front of the car holding his good arm up to shield his eyes from the glare of the Sedan's headlights.

"What is the meaning of this outrage?" blustered the old thespian in his most stentorian of tones. "I am a man of the stage. Pray allow me to pass." Hercules Chin grunted his acknowledgement of the situation and slowly extricated himself awkwardly from the car. The alley was so narrow that the door of the car struck the brickwork of the alley wall. The driver stared at Chin in admonishment. Chin shrugged his enormous shoulders and continued to ease his way out. As he did so the springs on the car's suspension groaned an appreciative sigh and the chassis rose several inches, such was its relief at the exit of the giant.

"Who goes there? Let me pass," bellowed the now frightened Sweet. He was about to say more when he saw the colossal form of Chin lumber towards him. Backlit as he was by the beams from the car headlights, the giant Chinaman presented a monstrous silhouette. Sheridan Sweet shrieked a high-pitched shriek. "Holy mother of God preserve us." He turned to run but seemed struck immobile by fear, his eyes transfixed by the figure looming menacingly towards him. "It is a monster!" he trembled. "Some enormous monster!"

A giant hand, bigger than Sheridan Sweet's head, grabbed him by the collar and lifted him aloft, three feet into the air. The face that met his was monstrous indeed, the sallow complexion, the dull drugged eyes under a Cro-Magnon brow. Chin smiled and a deep rumble of satisfaction echoed from his throat. Sweet felt sure that he would faint but somehow his fear translated itself into aggression. He went into a frenzy, kicking and clawing at the giant Chinaman, even trying to bite the enormous hand that grasped him. Chin groaned once more and shook the actor like a rag doll to stop the resistance. Stop it he did. Chin heard a sudden, sickening snap and Sheridan Sweet's, pompadoured head flopped forward onto his chest. His frail neck was shattered. Chin moaned at the realisation that he had broken this man that Father King wanted.

Chin looked down, still holding the body of Sweet Sherry aloft. The two Shang Twins and the driver stood beside him looking up, all three shook their heads. "What you done, Big Boy? You killed the man the Master wants! Numbskull!" The Shang brothers sniggered as one, while Chin groaned. "What we do now?" demanded the driver. Chin shrugged his huge shoulders resigned to the fact that King would not be best pleased.

The driver turned out to be a more resourceful fellow than even he had expected. "Throw him down on the ground as hard as you can. Police will think he jumped or fell from window," explained the chauffeur pointing upwards towards the side of the building. "No one here going to say anything." Chin nodded and grabbed Sweet by the neck with one hand and the back of his coat by the other and hurled him face downwards with as much force as his giant muscles could muster. The chauffeur winced at the snapping crackle of Sheridan Sweet's shattering vertebrae and rib cage.

Mr King's scalpel sliced cleanly down the length of the man's nose, loosening a flap of skin which he delicately folded back with the tip of the blade. The man's eyes stared wide with terror, traumatised by the agony he was experiencing, but unable to move due to the heavy dose of opiates he had been administered and the tight leather straps securing him to the low table that separated King from the Jewish crime lord. "Death by a thousand cuts, Ruben," explained King unnecessarily. "No doubt you have heard of our unique form of retribution, but so few have been privileged enough to witness it in the flesh, as it were," chuckled King excitedly.

"And what has this poor unfortunate done to deserve such an end, my friend?" enquired Rubenstein, trying vainly to avert his eyes from the grisly scene being played out before him.

"He failed me, my dear Rubenstein," replied the Chinaman enigmatically, flaying the slice of skin from the length of the man's nose. "I do not tolerate failure. It is not a habit I wish to encourage amongst my employees." The man strained against his bonds, his body convulsing with pain as he bit into the leather gag that somewhat ingeniously tightened with each movement he made. "The last man who suffered such a punishment was a scout for the Giorgiano family. He was returned to his paymasters in Chicago in a box, every piece of skin flayed from his body save the patch on his right forearm which featured the Family's signatory tattoo of a red circle. We have heard little from the Giorgianos since."

Rubenstein diverted his gaze from the pleading eyes of the flayed man towards the tall fig tree standing in a large willow patterned ceramic pot to the right of King. Rubenstein recoiled suddenly as the fig tree seemed to twitch and come to life. An albino granite Burmese python thicker than a man's arm began to uncoil itself slowly from amongst the branches of the tree, its pale forked tongue flickering from its mouth tasting the air for a scent of fear.

King peeled another segment of skin from the doomed man's forehead and casually dangled it between his thumb and forefinger, offering it to the great white serpent as it slithered towards its master.

"Feed, Apep, feed. A little morsel for your supper my dearest," oozed King, stroking the serpent's head as its tongue feathered the tissue before grabbing and swallowing it. King laughed the gleeful laugh of a lunatic.

The Jew was a man who had spent his life inflicting intimidation and fear upon others. A life of many experiences. A life of violence. He exploited the weak and murdered his rivals, but sitting here in front of this satanic Chinaman, Rubenstein knew that he was out of his depth. A lifelong criminal, he felt intimidated, inferior, and genuinely afraid of King. The devil before him flaying the skin from a dying man and feeding it to an enormous snake chilled the very blood in his veins.

King sensed the Jew's fear. He could smell it almost as well as his ghost snake Apep could. Comfortable that he now had the old head of London's Undzer Shtik exactly where he wanted him, King decided to proceed with his proposal. "Jabez, my friend. I need you to do me a service."

As if on cue the Shang twins appeared from behind a crimson dragon emblazoned wall drape and sidled their way towards their master's side. The twins emanated menace, moving almost as one being, each appearing as the other's evil shadow. Rubenstein swallowed hard. The combination of the twins, the flayed man, the ghost constrictor and the satanic figure of King all merged into such a nightmarish scene that Rubenstein knew that he would acquiesce to anything to escape from the Chinaman's sanctum.

"I believe you have a nephew who is an employee of the Home Office, Jabez," enquired King, the words seeping from his mouth in a serpentine hiss as the phantom snake unwound its body from the fig tree and began to coil around the back of the Chinaman's chair.

"Young Arnold, yes, he is a junior clerk within a minor department, nothing more," stuttered Rubenstein nervously.

The snake coiled silently around King's shoulders. The Chinaman seemed not to notice and if he did it was as natural to him as a child hugging a mother. "A minor department, no doubt, but one I know in which his position would give him access to certain plans."

"Plans?" questioned Rubenstein. "What plans, may I ask?"

"You may indeed enquire," smiled King. The snake's head, which was the size of a grown man's fist, stretched out from the Chinaman's shoulders towards the Jew's face, its tongue flickering continuously, tasting the atmosphere for a hint of fear, searching for another piece of flesh now that its hunger had been awakened. "I require your nephew to acquire the plans of the Cruciform building in Euston and then pass them to you. You are then to safely store them in one of your most admirable pawnbroking establishments, from where I shall arrange for them to be stolen." Rubenstein nodded, somewhat relieved at what appeared to be a relatively simple task. "Why not allow me to simply bring you the plans?" he questioned.

King stroked the head of Apep, the serpent coiling back toward its master. "The police are always alert my dear Rubenstein. The more steps on the ladder, the more likely a rung will snap," he hissed enigmatically.

Jabez Rubenstein had never been more relieved to leave someone's presence as he stepped out into the busy throng of people flowing up and down Gerrard Street. He steadied himself against the wall of a shopfront and caught his breath for a second or two. He realised he was trembling, adrenalin coursing through his body. He was nauseous. He inhaled deeply, steadied himself and hailed a cab.

Wiggins and Pyke approached the cobbled Soho Lane. Constable Potts greeted them. "Body is that of a gentleman in his sixties I would think, Sir. Looks as though he's jumped or fallen from the roof four stories above."

"Has the body been moved or interfered with in any way, Constable?" enquired Wiggins surveying the scene. A small throng of people loitered around the periphery of the secure ring set up by the uniforms. "It is as it was when we arrived Sir," answered Potts.

"No guarantee that the old boy's pockets weren't rifled before you got here though," observed Pyke casting a knowing eye amongst the crowd. "Who discovered the body, Pottsie?"

"A seven-year-old girl called Rosie and some of her friends. They were playing in the lane. They are with their families now, but I have their names and addresses," stated Potts looking at the body. Pyke grimaced. "Ain't no type of sight for a little lass to see."

Wiggins nodded and crouched at the side of the prone figure. "It certainly looks as if he has hit the cobbles with a destructive amount of force. His back and neck appear broken. Hullo!" he exclaimed, "There is an injury to the back of his neck. A large swelling and contusion that looks inconsistent with a fall to the road from the building."

"Perhaps he hit his head on the way down?" suggested Potts. Wiggins scanned the facade of the building. "No obtrusions other than windowsills. It is possible, I suppose, that he may have collided with one, but unlikely I would wager."

"What's that ruffing and tear on the back of his jacket, Guv?" Pyke pointed to an area of the corpse's clothing that seemed to be raised and gathered as if it had been suspended from a hook or had caught on something during the apparent fall. Wiggins had already noted the strange anomaly and was closely examining the ground around the body.

"Nothing here. Help me turn over the body Pyke. Let us have a look at our poor unfortunate," asked Wiggins. The two men stooped and turned over the body. As they did so Wiggins let out an almost imperceptible gasp. "Why this man has an extraordinary resemblance to Lord Grey don't you think Pyke?"

"He certainly does Guv but it ain't Lord Grey. This is, or rather was Sheridan Sweet, or Sweet Sherry as 'es known around Soho and the West End," confirmed Pyke. "He does have more than a passing resemblance to his Lordship, now that you mention it. Sherry was an actor. Quite high profile at one time but now not so much. He had a big drink problem and an even bigger boy problem if you know what I mean," Pyke stood and scanned the crowd. On the periphery he spied the shadowy figure of a slim young lad leaning against the alley wall, cigarette in mouth and cap lowered to shield his face. "Pottsie, go and pick up that bobtail over there will you. Knowing Sherry's proclivities, he may just know something about this." Potts hurried off to apprehend the youth. Pyke turned to find Wiggins examining the brick walls at the alley entrance with his ever-present magnifying glass. "What you got, Guv?" asked Pyke.

"Paint transfer, Jem. Black paint. Could be new. Looks fresh. Looks like it is at the correct height for a car door perhaps," said Wiggins miming opening a car door.

"Are you thinking someone's opened a car door and hit it against the wall?"

"That's what it looks like," Wiggins had moved from the wall and was now walking towards the end of the lane, carefully examining the ground. "Hullo! What have we here? Quick Jem look at this." Wiggins pointed to an area of the street where the cobbles had dropped. The resulting depression had filled with moss and mud.

"Sweet Baby Jesus," groaned Pyke. "It can't be human. That's the biggest damn footprint I have ever seen."

Wiggins winced. "The Chinese Giant, Jem. Hercules Chin. No other man on Earth could make a footprint of such dimensions. This was no suicide, Jem. This was murder. But why murder an old has-been actor who had no money?" Pyke raised the front of his derby. "We're going to need a lot of plaster of Paris to take a cast of that big boy."

Chapter 16 - The Entertainer

The Top Hat Club, Soho, four-thirty in the afternoon. Mary Munday twirled her decorative parasol as she coquettishly glanced over her shoulder, winking cheekily at the eager crowd of London's theatrical underworld as she launched into a rather risqué version of "My Grandfather's Clock." Accompanied by Franklin 'Fingers' Butterworth on the upright piano, Mary's little spot on the Top Hat's variety matinee show was going down a storm as usual. Glasses and hats were raised and backs and thighs were slapped, laughter and applause rising at every decidedly unsubtle innuendo.

Doctor Watson and a rather awkward looking, off duty, constable Murray took their chairs at one of the rustic tables situated closest to the stage. Tables where it was impossible to hide from the intrusive interaction of the acts a mere few feet away. Murray loosened his collar and looked around anxiously at the cavernous cellar club, awash as it was with noise and infectious raucous laughter. The enormous basement venue was completely without windows and as such the atmosphere was heavy with lung choking smoke and the heady alcohol-laden air seemed intoxicating enough to Murray to impose a potential hangover without ever having the need of actually having imbibed.

Watson straightened his neck, smiled his most engaging smile, and held his hand aloft signalling for service. Two young waitresses battled somewhat comically with each other to reach the Doctor's table first. "Ah, Jeanie. Good afternoon, you look as stunning as ever my dear. How is your mother, fit and well I hope?" enquired Watson with the brightest of twinkles in his eye.

Jeanie giggled. "Mother is fine Doctor, thanks to your good self. She ain't never hacked another cough since you gave her that tincture, Sir. What can I get you, gentlemen?" Watson interjected before Murray had the opportunity to open his mouth. "Two glasses of Young's Best and two London Gin chasers, please my dear. The driest you have." Watson removed his hat, brushed it with his sleeve and offered Murray a cigar, which was refused politely.

"Thank you, Sir, but I don't partake," replied Murray. "I likes the smell and all, but I just can't get a taste for it. It's like coffee Sir, smells wonderful but tastes the opposite of its aroma. Bitter even with sugars added."

"A clean-living constable. Very good. Clean living stimulates clarity of thought which fosters accurate decision making," beamed Watson, snipping the end from a cigar. "Your father of course was exactly the same. Cut from the same cloth you might say. An admirable man."

Murray smiled and nodded appreciatively as he began to look around him with a greater amount of attention. The club was brimming with patrons, even at this hour. Reduced prices until the evening performance never ceased to enliven and engorge the establishment. There were three stepped stages. The main, highest one, upon which Mary Munday was currently rolling out the old music hall standards illuminated with every double entendre known to man, as well as two others, both slightly lower, each set up with instruments and instrument stands, presumably ready for forthcoming performances. The centre of the vast underground hall was dominated by a massive barrel-shaped wood-burning boiler, its chimney disappearing off somewhere beyond the multi-vaulted brick ceiling that topped the vast cellar venue. The boiler was stacked full of crackling logs and the open cast iron hatch spat flames as the body of the boiler pumped out the heat required to keep the chill out of the cavernous space.

"What is this place Doctor, and why have you brought me here?" questioned a slightly nervous but inquisitive Murray just as Jeanie arrived, half walking, half dancing, holding a laden tray displaying their four drinks. "Here you go, Doctor Watson, Sir. I broughts you some crackers 'n all. Soak up the ale like."

"Why thank you kindly Jeanie, you are so very thoughtful. I presume they are heavily salted to instil further thirst," grinned Watson knowingly. "Perhaps the same again in thirty minutes if you would be so kind?" smiled Watson handing her what a surprised Murray was convinced was a silver threepence.

"Of course, Sir. Half an hour Sir," gasped Jeanie skipping off happier than ever that she had won the race over the other waitress. Watson settled back, and puffed upon his cigar eagerly, the smoke exiting from his nostrils, before taking a thirst-quenching draw upon his beer glass. He wiped the residual froth from his moustache with a scarlet handkerchief, placing it in his outside top pocket and turned to Murray. "I brought you here to get to know you better, Murray. I thought perhaps a little late afternoon entertainment along with some liquid refreshment might be in order." Watson indicated towards the stage on which Miss Munday was performing as he raised his gin glass. "She really is quite good. She could even make the Palladium one day if she censored some of the saucier interludes."

"Yes, she is," agreed Murray, wincing at the first sip of gin as it assaulted his taste buds. The room continued to resound with uproarious laughter and unbridled applause as Mary finished off her rendition of 'My Grandfathers Clock' and launched unbridled into 'Maybe it's because I'm a Londoner.'

"Ha! Very good," ejaculated Watson. "What is this place you asked me a few moments ago? Well, this is a club frequented by London's theatrical oddities. You see before you performers on their way down and hopefuls on their way up. Buskers and theatrical agents, broken clowns and alcoholic ventriloquists, singers, dancers and prestidigitators, all desperate to impress, and all in search of the next booking. All in search of fame and riches. He and I would come here frequently when pursuing a case. He believed that the theatrical underworld of London was as rife with information as its criminal counterpart, and almost certainly more willing to part with it. You see, young Murray, virtually every one of the denizens of this establishment is a performer of some description, a show-off, and many of them have supplemental careers on the darker side of the divide. See there, the skinny fellow with the long nose sitting with the enormous lady wearing the yellow frock?"

"I do indeed," acknowledged Murray, gradually getting accustomed to the sharp tang of the gin.

"His name is Parker. A virtuoso on the Jewish Harp, but also on occasion, a masterful garrotter of some considerable repute." Murray's eyes squinted as he swallowed hard. "A rather unfortunate surname for one endowed with such a magnificent proboscis," added Watson with a chuckle.

"The large coloured fellow sitting next to the Great Dane dog is Demerara Smith, a Jamaican rum runner-cum-master percussionist who also does an extremely fine line in broken bones upon request. He once, it is rumoured, murdered a rival smuggler with nothing more than a drumstick. An altogether unsavoury chap, I can tell you." Murray's mouth was agape at what he was hearing.

As Watson regaled his younger companion with lurid tales of the characters he could identify within the surrounding hoard, Mary Munday finished off her matinee spot for the early evening. The crowd whistled and roared, some stood and clapped and as Mary took her final bowing curtsey, the stage trap door directly beneath her feet flung open and she plummeted like a stone, screaming into the bowels of the undercroft below her. The crowd erupted, their roars and cheers getting louder and louder, at this unexpected and surprisingly entertaining finale.

Watson's brows furrowed. He rose slowly pushing his chair rearward with the backs of his thighs. '*This does not feel right he thought. This is not part of her act!*' His senses alert to danger amongst the uproar around him, he looked at Murray who was laughing along with everyone else. The cheering echoing around the room was so loud that Watson, close as he was to the stage, could not quite hear the muffled screaming that came from beneath the boards. It was only as he began to take a few tentative steps towards the stage that he saw the first spurt of crimson spring from the gaping dark hole in the stage. He immediately vaulted over the prompter's box and onto the stage, leaping down through the trap door. He landed in the gloom of the theatre's underbelly, instinctively aware that something was dreadfully wrong. Before his eyes could adjust to the darkness a flash of razor-sharp blades slashed towards his face. He jerked his head back just in time to avoid being sliced open although the blades managed to rip through his cheek superficially. He fell backwards and as he did, he pulled his pistol out of his waistband and fired from his hip in the direction of a moving black mass that shifted in front of him. The large crow-like shadow seemed unaffected by the shot but began to recede into the blackness of the stage void. He could hear maniacal cackling as the phantom disappeared. He turned his attention to the prone form of Mary Munday that lay prostate next to him, blood pulsing from an open throat wound that Watson immediately knew was a death knell. In an attempt to staunch the flow, he clasped his hand to the wound, closing it as best he could, hot, sticky blood trickling through the gaps between his fingers.

Mary tried to speak but a frothy gurgle of crimson spilled from her mouth. "Quiet, my dear, be quiet," Watson pleaded. "Help will be here soon." He heard Murray's boots hit the dusty floor next to him. "The Beast, lad, it was the Beast," exclaimed Watson. He threw his pistol towards Murray. "Go after him, Murray, that direction," he barked pointing in the direction the shadow had vanished. Murray fumbled and dropped the gun. "For Christ's sake man, get after him. I will tend to this good lady. Aim for his heart or his head, but just get him."

Murray could hear the screeching laughter of the escaping Beast as it crawled on all fours like a giant black cockroach through the guy ropes, supports and cogs of the machinery hidden in the sub-void of the stage. Murray pointed the gun and fired. The bullet hit a large steel stanchion, the light from the resultant spark illuminating the crouched shape of the back and shoulders of the Beast as it began to clamber up the rear backstage staircase. Murray's heart was pounding like a jackhammer. The realisation struck that he, and he alone was pursuing the dreaded Beast. He felt exposed and frightened as well as strangely invigorated at the prospect. He reached the bottom of the wooden staircase and looked upwards. Five storeys met his gaze.

He began climbing, legs pumping, thighs screaming, lungs gasping for air. A door crashed open one flight above and he launched himself up the final few stairs. He reached the open door. "Police!" he shouted. "I am armed and will shoot to kill. Put down your weapons and surrender yourself this instant!" His order was met with a devilish screech of insane guttural laughter. Murray fired twice through the open door and dived onto the flat roof rolling for cover behind a nearby chimney. He could see the ghoulish figure of the Beast appear before him. An image manufactured in

Hell if ever there was one. It smiled grotesquely at Murray, blood drooling from its gaping maw, then whirled on its heels and ran full pelt towards the edge of the roof. The cloaked figure took a prodigiously powerful leap, spring-boarding from the parapet coping stones and sailing into the murky air, as if for all the world, like a monstrous vampire bat. Its black cloak whipped through the evening sky like the sail of an airborne plague ship. The Beast landed with a bone splintering thud on the asphalt of the adjacent building more than fifteen feet away.

Murray levelled the pistol and fired three more times in quick succession, each bullet narrowly missing its target. He cursed, quickly considered his options, and whipped off his jacket. He steadied himself and inhaled deeply then took half a dozen steps backwards before launching himself at the parapet. Ten or more strides and he would be ready to leap with all his might, but he had misjudged his stride slightly. As realisation struck him, he tried to pull up but his forward momentum was too great. His heels slipped on the parapet and he began to desperately swing his arms backwards in a circular motion in a final effort to counterbalance and stop himself tumbling over the edge. He could hear the laughter of the Beast ringing mockingly in his ears. His heart leapt from his chest as he realised that he was going to fall off the building. He closed his eyes tightly and clutched frantically at thin air.

Watson's right hand snapped out and found Murray's collar just as he pitched over the edge. His left hand grasped at one of Murray's flailing wrists, clenching it as tightly as he could muster and tensed every muscle in his sixty-year-old body in preparation for the wrenching that he knew must come. Watson braced himself as he took the weight of the falling constable. An intense bolt of pain shot from his left shoulder and racked through his entire body. The agony was virtually unbearable, a searing neural pain that burned through every muscle fibre. He could not let go despite the severe acute pain he was experiencing. He pulled with all his might, his left arm now feeling as if it no longer sat within its socket or even belonged to him. The toes of Murray's shoes scraped frantically at the brickwork as though he were riding an invisible bicycle. He gained the slightest of purchase in some loose pointing and this, combined with a Herculean effort by Watson, saw him rise just enough to grasp the parapet copings. Watson gave one final tug, almost retching with the agony it produced and Murray heaved his elbows, a leg, and finally his entire body back onto the blessed safety of the roof. Both men lay entangled on the roof, each gasping for air at their combined exertions. Watson's shoulder was afire with pain from the rotator cuff tear he had incurred pulling Murray to safety.

"Good Lord, Doctor," panted Murray, his heart pounding like a Coldstream snare. "You saved my life. If not for you I would have been lying dead on them cobbles sixty feet below us."

Gasping wildly, the older man smiled at the younger. "A debt suitably repaid son," he grimaced. "If not for the bravery and selfless actions of your father on the battlefield thirty-three years ago, I would not have been alive and here today to save you. Give thanks to your blessed father, not to me."

Murray lay back, his head resting on the asphalt roof, clinging to its stability and safety as if clinging to life itself. Gulping in the evening air he dedicated a silent prayer to the memory of his father. "And the lady songstress, Doctor? Did she....?" Murray's question trailed off. Watson turned his head away. "She did not survive the attack, I am sorry to say."

'*Forty years ago, I may have made it,*' thought Watson, ruefully thinking of the leap. He stood and straightened in stiff instalments before brushing himself off. Looking across the fifteen-foot-wide chasm that divided the two buildings. He was astonished to see the devilish figure of the Beast staring back at him whilst sitting atop the coping stones of the neighbouring roof, his long arachnid legs dangling over its edge. The two locked eyes. The thin line of the Beast's mouth broke into a blood-chilling smile. The smile of a devil incarnate. Smudges of dried blood smeared the Beast's chin. Watson maintained the stare, as rigid as London Bridge, boring his hatred into the brain of the Beast. The Beast returned Watson's steadfast stare, its ink-black eyes as unblinking as those of the veteran adventurer.

"Where is my pistol?" Watson whispered from the side of his mouth to the prone Murray, never once taking his eyes from those of the Beast. "Sixty feet below on the cobbles beneath, I fear Doctor. It went over the edge with me," admitted Murray. "It would have been no use, Sir as I emptied every chamber." Watson grunted his acknowledgement, his useless left arm hanging limply and redundant by his side. The Beast rose, almost seeming to grow out of the roof like some satanic black corpse flower. The two pairs of eyes locked together as if by an invisible chain, neither wavering, neither blinking. The Beast's smile broadened and its lips curled back to reveal razor-sharp teeth. Watson, without breaking their stare, raised his right arm and pointed his index finger, gun-like and mimed firing a shot. "Bang!" he whispered. The Beast spat and gave a parting guttural snarl, then whirled away in a sweep of black cloak, disappearing across the rooftops of London's late afternoon.

The Top Hat Club nestled, unseen by the vast majority of the London populace that streamed by its door. It stood in the centre of the capital's theatrical heart of Soho, somewhere between Greek Street and Wardour Street. A small, simple, dirt worn brass plaque bearing the engraved outline of a top hat, and a large knuckled, round-bellied doorman were the only visible signs of its existence.

"Evening Smiffy," nodded Pyke towards the barrel bodied concierge as he descended the stone steps towards the basement club. "How's Mrs Smiffy and all the little Smiffettes?"

"Thriving Mr Pyke, thriving, thanks. Another one on the way," the doorman shrugged a knowing smile.

"You want to keep that cigar in its case every once in a while, mate," laughed Pyke. He had long since lost count of the number of children the long-suffering Mrs Smythe had been forced to unleash upon the world. The trailing Wiggins looked skyward. Once inside the club, the men were greeted by a shapely hat check girl sporting a garish deep vermillion silk top hat. "Can I take your hat Jem?"

"No chance Lois. You should know by now where I go, me hat goes," specified Pyke. He flipped a coin towards the smiling Lois who caught it adeptly and plunged it immediately into the depths of her décolletage.

"Is there a doorman or hat check girl in London that you do not know Sergeant Pyke?" enquired Wiggins.

"If there is Guv, they ain't worth knowing," came Pyke's enigmatic reply.

The two policemen descended into the huge cellar bar. The attending constables had ensured that no one had left the club, so the area remained a swirling mass of the theatrical dregs of the London underworld. Constable Potts led the newly arrived officers into a rear office. "We're taking statements from everyone in the place who can remember seeing or hearing anything," informed Potts.

"A list of names would be most welcome, Constable," added Wiggins scanning the room.

"You'll be lucky to get any genuine names. I reckon there's a few John Smiths and Henry Irvings in tonight Guv," sniffed Pyke.

The office they entered carried the name 'Garrison Ketch - Proprietor' carefully written in mock gold paint on the glazed panel of its door. The room was small and cluttered, its walls lined with theatrical bills and posters from a bygone age that spoke of former prosperity. At one time Garrison Ketch had owned a pantheon of theatres across the country. From London to Blackpool, Glasgow to Portsmouth. He rivalled Karno and aspired to Meyerfield, but Garrison Ketch was more impresario than businessman, and now he found himself resigned to running a club for London's theatrical hopefuls and its dismal failures. Bitter and broken, Ketch looked upon Karno's extravagant white elephant, the Karsino on the Thames' Taggs Island, with envy and jealousy, hoping beyond hope that this new perilous venture would be doomed to failure. The man himself sat behind his desk, his body aquiver, nervously rolling a cigar between thumb and forefinger of a puffy, knuckle-less hand. Ketch was a corpulent man with a permanently sad face framed by the most outrageous whiskers Wiggins thought he had ever seen. Seated opposite this human walrus were

Constable Murray, white as a ghost and sipping from a glass of brandy whilst wrapped in a blanket. Jeanie the waitress was finishing off pinning a makeshift sling around Watson's left arm.

"Thank you, my dear," said the Doctor. "I can see you missed your true calling." The waitress smiled as she departed "I'll leave you gentlemen to it." Wiggins took the one remaining chair whilst Pyke slouched against the door frame, the unlit stump of a cheroot gripped between his teeth and a thumb in each waistcoat pocket. "What can you tell us Doctor?" enquired Wiggins making himself as comfortable as he could. "It was your Beast, young Wiggins. No doubt about that," declared Watson emphatically.

"It were 'orrible, Sir. A devil I tell you. Claws like a lion, teeth like a wolf. An animal sir, a bloody animal," added Murray still quivering with shock. Wiggins noted the scarring on Watson's cheek. "From him Doctor?" Watson nodded. "A weapon of some design, I'd wager. I only just managed to avoid it. Another inch and it would have sliced my throat clean out."

"And our victim?" enquired Wiggins turning his attention towards Ketch.

"Mary Munday," replied the walrus. "She was one of the best things about this place, detective. Always popular. She knew how to manage a crowd did our Mary." Wiggins looked at Watson.

"Gone. Alas, I could not save her. There was nothing to be done. Her injuries were too severe, far too traumatic. Poor woman. She tried to speak at the end, but her throat had been all but removed by the Beast," elucidated the Doctor, struggling to mask his emotions. He could see Wiggins raise a questioning eyebrow. "We gave chase to the roof, but it leapt the gulf between this building and the next." This time it was Pyke's turn to raise an eyebrow at the thought of such a leap. Watson continued, "It is a Beast, gentlemen. A scion of Hell itself. The Ripper was a depraved butcher, a maniac, but we all know he was a man. This is worse. This is some type of animal, an unholy unearthly demon. I locked eyes with it for fully three minutes and I tell you Sirs, those three minutes may well have been spent staring into the eyes of Satan himself."

Chapter 17 - The Letter

"A letter for you dear," announced Mary lightly stroking her husband's well-kempt hair. Wiggins sat in the parlour of their terraced house, shirt sleeves rolled up, vigorously polishing his work boots in front of the fireplace. The flickering flames of the fire reflectively danced on the highly burnished leather. He looked up at his wife and smiled a gentle reassuring smile. *'How lucky he was to have found and kept such a devoted and loving wife,'* he reflected happily.

"Thank you, dear." Wiggins took the letter from Mary and placed it on the table at his side. He placed one completed polished boot upon yesterday's newspaper laid out on the floor in front of the stone hearth and picked up the second, inserting his hand into it acting as a makeshift last. He dipped the tip of the shoe brush into the inky paste of the polish tin and began to enthusiastically rub the boot in a clockwise circular pattern as was his daily habit. The evocative odour of the boot polish took him back to the long distant past when he would regularly carry out this task for Him and the Doctor, usually whilst sitting on the rear doorstep of the townhouse in Baker Street. He sniggered inwardly as he recalled Mrs Hudson, Mary's grandmother, warning him not to get that 'infernal' black polish on her pristine, newly scrubbed step.

"Are you listening to me, Albert?" For a split second, he thought it was Mrs Hudson speaking to him and half expected to feel the sharp nudge of a broom handle from the formidable Scottish landlady. "Albert!" It was Mary rousing him from his vivid daydream. Wiggins made a mental note of the remarkable power a scent had in evoking long-forgotten memories. "You haven't been listening to a word I've been saying have you Mr High and Mighty Detective Inspector?" questioned Mary mockingly. He could see that she was slightly irritated but was trying to sheathe her annoyance in a light-hearted way. "Sorry, Dear. I was just ruminating on the case. What was it you said?" He stopped polishing his boot and turned his full attention to his wife.

"The theatre Albert. Tonight? James and Lilly asked us last week if we would accompany them to Daly's tonight, don't you remember? They have a spare pair of tickets for The Marriage Market. It has received sparkling reviews. Gertie Millar's performance is rumoured to be worth the price of the ticket alone. Please tell me you haven't forgotten, Dear, I have been so looking forward to it."

"Of course, I've remembered Darling, I shall be home in plenty of time, make no mistake." '*Give me an evening chasing ghouls any day of the week*' he thought smiling affectionately at his wife. Mary stroked his hair again, softly kissed the top of his head and retreated into the kitchen to make their customary morning pot of tea. Wiggins finished applying polish to his second boot and reached into his shoe-shining box for the polishing rag to give each boot an energetic final buffing. He admired the final result but recoiled somewhat at the shine that revealed his tired looking reflection. This case was taking its toll on him, both physically and mentally.

He laced on his left boot, always the left one first, double looped. He placed his other foot in the right boot and stooped to lace it up then suddenly remembered the letter Mary had passed him a few moments before. He leant back and retrieved the envelope from the parlour table. '*Always examine the envelope first Wiggins. It can often tell much more than the text of its contents.*'

A high-quality bonded envelope. No sender's address, but post-marked from Geneva two weeks past. '*Unusual,*' thought Wiggins as he eagerly tore open the envelope with a rasp of his thumb. He raised the marbled parchment paper to his nose and gently sniffed. The letter had a faint whiff of tobacco. He rubbed the paper between thumb and forefinger gauging the quality and thickness. Satisfied that the paper was of an expensive grade he proceeded to examine and analyse the graphology. The writing bore a steady neat hand to the lettering with a slightly italicised slanting to the left. The hand was that of a man. A flowing, immaculate calligraphic style hinted at a confident and highly ordered intellect. Wiggins read.

Dear Inspector Wiggins,

Hoping this missive finds you in good health and that you do not find it to be too much of an intrusion. I merely intend to offer some insight and perhaps clarity on the myriad challenges and obstacles that you and your colleagues face at this time of worrying continental unrest.

Our City currently plays unwanted host simultaneously to three of the most dangerous men in the world. I will endeavour to assist from afar with what little I can do to inform your actions.

Let us firstly concentrate on the individual labelled by the National Press as the Beast of London. Seek out the admirable Professor Freud. He is, I believe, currently in London. Take heed of his methods and conclusions, he has my absolute confidence in matters of human nature. You are, as you are well aware, dealing with a misogynistic psychopath with cannibalistic tendencies. He will be a man of medicine, most likely a surgeon. He is preeminent in his particular speciality and glories in being the centre of attention. He no doubt also suffers from schizophrenia or multiple personality syndrome. There will be a methodology to the crimes. Concentrate almost entirely on the victims. That is where the answer lies. One advantage you hold over this killer is that no matter how devious he appears, his greatest weaknesses are his ego and his desire to be caught and perhaps immortalised.

May we now turn our attention to a greater long-term threat, namely that of the Chinaman, Mr King. Make no mistake, this man could well be the biggest danger to the stability of our nation and indeed our continent at this present time of conflict and unrest. Unfortunately, my current location is known to him and due to this, I find myself rather hamstrung in terms of freedom of movement and indeed communication. If this letter finds you at all, my network of aides will have accomplished a minor miracle. King is a Mandarin of the loftiest pinnacle within the Orient. A man of immense power and resource and completely and utterly ruthless and devoid of compassion. His ultimate aim is to destabilise not only London but our entire government and Commonwealth with a view to the Orient spreading its influence across Europe.

Eventually, we come to Radasiliev. I hear outlandish claims regarding this Russian, if indeed he is Russian. A conjurer of demons, a sacrificer of innocents, and a practitioner of the dark arts. This and much worse it is rumoured, but I would resist forming definitive conclusions or indeed theories without the advantage of further data. Some say there is a paranormal element to this character but let us just state however that he is a dangerous individual and should be monitored extremely closely.

So lastly onto the enigmatic Dutchman. Take heed of Dante Van Hoon, he is an asset and ally, though of somewhat dubious motives. He can open doors that no police force possibly can. His record of accomplishment shows remarkable results, though they come at a high price, physically, ethically and financially.

Above all stay safe.
Your Friend,

William Escott, Esq.

Wiggins read over the letter twice more. It did not in truth tell him much that he did not already know or had surmised, other than the revelations about King's possible wider motives and the hinted references to Radasiliev's satanic proclivities. Once again, he intently scrutinised the signature at the foot of the page. William Escott, Esq. The name was not one that he was immediately familiar with, but it did ring a vague and very distant bell. He had seen the name somewhere else before and could vaguely visualise it on a faded yellowing document of some description. The image floated in and out of his mind but he could not focus clearly on just where nor when he had seen it. He sniffed the letter once more in the hope that the faint scent of tobacco may awaken a hidden memory just as the smell of the boot polish had taken his thoughts back thirty years. He eventually set aside the letter, deciding that the subconscious cortex of his brain would eventually awaken the memory at a later time. He laced his gleaming boots and headed for the station.

Albert and Mary had arranged to meet James and Lilly in a small café in Leicester Square just outside Daly's theatre prior to the evening performance. The couples greeted each other warmly, each of the ladies admiring the other's outfit, with the men feeling awkward in unfamiliar evening suits. Half an hour of small talk over coffee and cake saw them making their way to the corner of Cranbourn Street and the portico entrance of the grand and elaborately decorated neo-classical facade of the theatre. As the two couples approached the entrance door, they passed a small shoeshine stand, its patron touting hopefully for business amongst the milling throngs of theatreland.

"Tuppence for a shine, Sir," offered the young trader as Wiggins approached. Wiggins declined politely, whilst at the same time palming the young lad two pennies as he passed, smiling at the irony of the situation given the time and effort he had expended that morning in polishing his own work boots. The Shine tipped his cap at Wiggins, "Thanking ye kindly, Sir, you're a true gent you are." As Wiggins nodded his acknowledgement his nostrils caught the unmistakable turpentine aroma of boot polish. As the scent penetrated his nasal canal, Wiggins' gaze settled upon a Theatre bill encased in a glass-fronted cabinet on the wall at the building's entrance. That was it! The switch clicked inside his head completing the circuit and the combination of scent and the billboard transported him back to an image of an old tobacco-stained theatre bill haphazardly pinned to a plaster wall. One of the names of the actors on the bill was William Escott. Instantly Wiggins knew the identity of his secretive correspondent.

Chapter 18 - The Ball

Wiggins and Pyke were in deep discussion regarding the merits of the mysterious Luca Radasiliev as a potential prime suspect for the slayings. The two colleagues were revisiting the case file on the Russian who had still not resurfaced in London since the bizarre incidents at the Russian Embassy.

"The timelines definitely fit Sir, and he is certainly responsible for several sexual assaults on women in the same area," reiterated Pyke as he flicked his ash rather haphazardly into the cut-glass ashtray on Wiggins' desk. "The murders also commenced shortly after this Russian fellow arrived in London. We know he checked into the Saint Pancras Midland Grand Hotel on the third of January this year, before quickly moving into his official quarters in Highgate less than a week later. The first murder occurred only nine days after his arrival. As we have seen, he has an alibi for the night of each of the killings, but my nose tells me that these are spurious. Anyway, guv I simply do not like the bugger. Not one little bit. We have seen what he is capable of. I only wish we had some lead on where he has disappeared to."

"Not only seen, Sergeant but also felt it. Experienced it ourselves. Besides, your steadfast dislike of all things Russian should not qualify as a case for the prosecution," smiled Wiggins glancing at the sickle-shaped scar on his redoubtable colleague's left forearm. He leant back in his chair, both hands clasped behind his head. "Although I do concede to there being a tenuous yet pointed connection between him and at least two of the deceased," conceded Wiggins. "… and, whisper it gently Pyke, but I too share your dislike of the man. There is something of the night about him. What we experienced in that interview room was certainly not natural. My experience, and more importantly my instincts, tell me there is surely a darkness there that stems from somewhere deeper than our eyes can see," added Wiggins, blowing Pyke's misplaced ash from his desk. "I am convinced that he was responsible for the lunacy we found at the Embassy the other day. I am also leaning towards your theory that he is implicated somehow in the Cripes affair. If only we could establish a connection. We must use every method at our disposal to locate him. Oh, and by the way, can you be more assured of aim with your cigarette ash Pyke?"

"Sorry boss," apologised Pyke, scratching behind his ear. "He could very well be overseas by now." Wiggins stood from behind his desk and strolled to the window. "We have been monitoring passenger lists on all legitimate liners leaving the major ports. No sign of him. He could easily, however, have travelled under an assumed name or indeed sailed on an unchartered vessel." Pyke nodded his agreement.

"Yet I feel that he is still in London. I sense his presence. I see his influence across a myriad of obscure and baffling incidents," added Wiggins, his hands clasped behind his head.

"Excuse me Sir, a gentleman to see you," coughed Potts quizzically as he slipped his head around the door frame of Wiggins' office. "At least I think he's a gentleman. Are the public permitted to bring dogs into the station house, Sir?"

"On occasion yes Potts," answered Wiggins. "Who is it?" his interest piqued. Potts glanced at the bronze foil-stamped calling card he held in his hand. "A Mister Dante Van Hoon, Sir. His card doesn't state a profession, merely his name, Sir. If dogs is allowed, how about wolves?" Potts looked sideways like a quizzical puppy, uneasy with the outlandish nature of his question.

"Wolves, Potts? Don't be so ridiculous, lad," snorted Pyke. At that moment Van Hoon strode self-importantly into the office as if he had owned it for a hundred years, his cobalt blue silk top hat cradled in the crook of his left arm whilst in his right fist he clenched one end of a taught black leather leash studded with crimson crystals. On the other end of the leash calmly padded in what looked to the two police officers, for all the world like a wild grey wolf, its piercing parti-coloured eyes locked upon the two detectives. Pyke and Wiggins both stood, coiled, in anticipation of trouble, their fight or flight instinct coursing adrenalin around their veins at the sight of such a primordial predator in such everyday surroundings.

"Sit, Mayerhofer," commanded Van Hoon patting the enormous head of the seemingly docile carnivore. "I can assure you, gentlemen, he is quite harmless, when in my command. A Siberian wolf husky, named after a particularly skilled prestidigitator I once happened upon in Vienna," extolled the Leper as he sat down with an extravagant flourish. "I once witnessed him sawing a woman in half like no other. He split her down the middle lengthways and not across the belly as other magicians. Quite a spectacle and not a single drop of blood. An absolute wonder. It may well just be smoke and mirrors, but he was far superior to that Jewish circus performer over the pond. All he does is escape from mailbags and milk churns … preposterous! Don't you agree gentlemen?" he remarked.

"Tea, Potts!" demanded Van Hoon with a chuckle, inwardly much more amused with his little witticism than he cared to display. "Turkish if you have it. If not, Tunisian will do. As strong as it comes and then stronger still my good fellow." Van Hoon waved the back of his fractally scarred left hand at the constable who retreated out the door shrugging his puzzlement to his senior officers with open hands. Mayerhofer lay down at his master's signal and rested his head upon one of Pyke's shoes.

'*I ain't moving that foot 'til the hound itself decides to leave,*' thought Pyke. '*Even if he drools on me brogues.*'

"To business then gentlemen," announced Van Hoon. "You called for me did you not?"

"We made no such request Mr Van Hoon," replied Wiggins raising an eyebrow and glancing at Pyke.

"Not to my knowledge, Sir" confirmed Pyke.

"Never mind. Perhaps I imagined it, just let us say that you did, or that you were about to. What matters may I assist you with?" continued Van Hoon fastidiously removing his white kid-skin gloves one finger at a time. He placed the gloves neatly, one atop the other, on his lap. "I do hope the search for the Beast is progressing apace."

Pyke looked at his commanding officer with widening eyes shaking his head in disbelief. "We … we were just discussing the possible merits, or otherwise, of this fellow Luca Radasiliev being our accursed Beast."

"I am loathe to admit it but the name and the individual are currently unknown to me," puzzled Van Hoon resting both hands on the serpent topped head of his engraved bocote wood cane. "Whence came he to your fair city?"

"Roughly about the same time as the killings began," snorted Pyke, joyous in the knowledge that they seemed one step ahead of the '*man who knows ever bloody one and every ruddy thing!*'

"He is, we gather, a Russian dignitary of some description. An envoy or ambassadorial representative. He appears to be cloaked in the protection of his nation's Embassy and to be brutally honest, he seems a thoroughly dislikeable sort to say the least," detailed Wiggins to the Dutchman. "We have already interviewed him, and he offers an alibi for the evenings of the murders and has, on existing evidence, a tenuous connection to at least two of the murder victims. His apparent diplomatic immunity is presenting us with a very tangible obstacle in our pursuit of the individual. He displays a remarkable talent for influencing people." Wiggins proceeded to describe the interview he and Pyke had held with the Russian as well as the chaotic unfathomable scenes they had witnessed at the Russian Embassy.

"Intriguing I must say. Could it possibly be…?" mused Van Hoon stroking the leprous scarring on his cheek. He seemed to be deep in thought, oblivious to the presence of the two policemen. "I should have been, how should I say, made aware of this gentleman before now. Luca Radasiliev, you say. The name now strikes a vaguely familiar note with me, but I cannot quite place from where or when. He is obviously extremely well protected by some means or another, be it earthly as you say, or otherwise."

"That being the case, it may be beneficial for us if you were to make his acquaintance?" suggested Wiggins. "Your vaguely familiar note may well turn into a symphony if you were to meet him in person."

"I was thinking likewise Chief Inspector. I will throw a Grand Ball, two days from now gentlemen. The attendance of the great and good, not to mention the bad and the worse shall be requested," winked the Leper devilishly. "Lords and Counts, Ladies and Countesses, anybody who is anyone and others who think they are someone. It will be irresistible to our Mr Radasiliev. We shall see the cut of this fellow's jib. I will smell any evil scent, sense any of his guilt. I have a gift for such things. Polish your dancing shoes gentlemen, and please both dress smarter than you are currently attired!" Pyke snorted as Mayerhofer continued to snore and drool over his best brogues.

Van Hoon's country estate lay to the west of Windsor near the banks of the Thames. Wiggins and Pyke arrived in an unmarked police car with their dancing shoes indeed polished. The driveway and grounds reminded Pyke of Richmond Great Park.

"I thought the Belgravia house was impressive, but this seems more resplendent still," murmured Wiggins from behind the back of his hand towards Pyke's cauliflower ear. Pyke's right ear cavity looked as though it had been filled with putty such had been the damage inflicted upon it over years of brawls. Behind them sat Superintendent Magnus MacDonald and his guest Doctor Joseph Bleak, his fellow Demosthenes Club member, and sometime police advisor on matters medical.

"What are ye twa conspiring aboot?" snapped MacDonald, uncomfortably rubbing his finger around what felt like his stiffest collar. He was irritated at missing his habitual Wednesday night debate at the Demosthenes Club. '*At least Joseph is here with me,*' MacDonald thought. '*Several free whiskies for me and we can have a one-on-one debate.*'

"Just remarking on the length of the drive, Sir," coughed Pyke. "We seem to have been driving along it these last ten minutes."

The drive was indeed a lengthy thoroughfare, with impressive poplar trees planted at regular intervals lining each side and dark, unseen, yet Wiggins guessed, well-kempt grounds beyond. Eventually, they reached the culmination of the drive which was a sweeping arc of gravel chippings surrounding an elaborate Florentine style fountain which was lit from below creating a mesmeric dancing effect. The quartet disembarked the car and stood in front of a dwelling that was more castle than stately home. The huge stone edifice which greeted them was a masterpiece of medieval architecture encompassing flying buttresses, towers and crenulations. Loopholes sat alongside gothic arched stone mullioned windows. To the West of the castle sat what appeared to be a separate chapel which was lit from within illuminating the blazing colours of the exquisite stained glass of its gigantic windows. To the East lay what looked like an extensive set of stables, garages and outhouses.

"Well I'll be a Dutchman," whistled Pyke scratching his head under the uncomfortable top hat which, for this one evening only, he had reluctantly agreed to wear in place of his ever-present Derby. A plethora of coaches and automobiles were parked around the sweep of the drive in a vehicular display of wealth, opulence and vulgarity. Chauffeurs leant against their neatly parked vehicles smoking solitarily or gathered in small groups, chatting conspiratorially. The four companions trotted up the right-hand flight of a curved double-sided stone entrance staircase towards the awaiting servant at the door.

'*No crooked, pestilent servants here,*' noted Wiggins as he took in the finest livery of the straight-backed female valet standing before them. "Your invitations please gentlemen," she enquired, extending a white-gloved hand. The strains of a demi-orchestra drifted out to them as they offered their hats, gloves and scarves to the awaiting cloakroom attendant who promptly vanished as soundlessly as she had arrived. The hall in which they found themselves was awe-inspiring. Fully thirty feet high it featured a domed stone ceiling interspersed with plaster frescos painted in the Renaissance style depicting cherubs and angels, devils and demons. Grotesque gargoyles crawled around the cornice leering down upon them. The room was dominated by a huge double spiralled stone staircase, the two branches of which met on an intermediate marble landing dominated by a stuffed Polar Bear standing fully twelve feet high. The staircase then proceeded to branch once again to either side of the landing, winding its separate ways towards the upper galleried floor. The gallery was surrounded by an elaborate stone balustrade topped with a highly polished marble handrail containing the ancient imprints of thousands of tiny fossilised shells and sea life. An enormous ornate cast ormolu girandole hung from the ceiling, its thousands of blown glass amber prisms casting a faintly orange glow upon the festivities below.

Chamber music drew them into a huge ballroom to their left. The room was a whirl of activity. Wiggins could just see the flickering image of the musicians through the dancing figures on the ballroom floor as if viewed through a magic lantern. A waitress approached and smilingly offered them each a crystal flute of champagne from a silver tray, bowing as each man took the proffered glass. MacDonald quickly swigged back the champagne whilst picking up a replacement and dragging Doctor Bleak by the arm. "Youz twa go and do your thing with the master of this house of madness. Joseph and I will circulate our way to the bar and find some proper drink. Brandy for me and some tonic, no doubt for yourself Joseph." Bleak nodded and smiled to the two detectives "You must excuse me, gentlemen, it seems Magnus has a thirst for something other than champagne." The two older men were swallowed up by the whirling crush of revellers around them. MacDonald's diminutiveness made him vanish from view whilst Bleak's head and shoulders were all that could be seen atop the mass of dancing.

Wiggins and Pyke nodded, and half raised their flutes to each other. "Thank the Lord for that," mumbled Pyke. "Old Mac could turn a wedding into a wake and no doubt about it." Wiggins could not help but smile. "Let us find Van Hoon and try and get this evening's business behind us. I am intrigued to see if our rat has been tempted by the trap."

Even in the crowded cacophony of over three hundred uproarious guests, it was the simplest of tasks to locate the Lord of the Manor. His was the most uproarious laugh, the loudest roar, the most extravagant tumult. He was the epicentre of the cyclone, surrounded as he was by fawning acolytes prostrating themselves at his every outrageous tale. Van Hoon arose from his crowded table and greeted the two approaching policemen with a salutation and a raised glass. "Gentlemen, you are most welcome to my house."

"I thought I had seen your house already," joked Pyke. "How many of these places have you got for heaven's sake?"

"More than you might ever imagine Mr Pyke. Owning property and filling them with beautiful things is another of my passions. In fact, it is my only vice. Next time you are in the high loch lands of Scotland, the grandeur of Lake Como or Florence, Vienna, Cairo or New York, you must look me up," giggled Van Hoon. "Let us retreat to the balcony, I crave some night air and a cigar." The three men stepped behind a luxurious red velvet drape that touched the marble floor and stood on the stone balcony. They looked out into the clarity of the starlit night and lit the cigars offered by Van Hoon. Pyke smiled as he lit the largest Havana he had ever seen. *'Looks as though I should flush it rather than set it alight!'* mused Pyke with a grin, *'this thing will last me a week.'*

"He is here gentlemen," stated Van Hoon anticipating the policemen's question and blowing smoke towards the moon. "Our Beast is presently amongst us. There is a darkness here, darker than that of the night that currently surrounds us."

"How do you know this Van Hoon?" enquired Wiggins.

"You might say I can hear him. Sense him. Feel his presence. I can see from inside his head. I have a gift for remote viewing, of seeing what others see. Believe me, gentlemen, whoever bestowed the moniker of Beast upon this man was exactly right for a Beast is indeed what we have on our hands."

I hunger. I thirst.

"He is near, trust me."

Flesh. I need flesh, Blood I crave blood.

"He is beyond evil, foulest of the foul."

They call me Beast, but I am more than that.

"He comes nearer."

I am the life-giver. I am the life taker.

"I sense that he is close at hand."

They will all recoil at my rage. They will all repent.

"He is here gentlemen. Be prepared."

The drapes were swept back, and a tall austere figure strolled out onto the balcony. "Do you mind if I join you, gentlemen. I noticed you escaping to the freshness of the night. The night air is so conducive to ones' health don't you think?" bowed the figure now standing before them. "Mr Wiggins and Mr Pyke, I already of course know. Luca Radasiliev at your service, Mr Van Hoon," nodded the diplomat. "So good to see the two of you again gentlemen. You have a beautiful castle, Mr Van Hoon. It reminds me so much of my own home."

Wiggins could just see MacDonald and Bleak through the open drapes over Radasiliev's shoulder. MacDonald chatting, no doubt boastfully to a pair of attractive young ladies whilst Bleak looked on, an awkward but willing witness to the conversation, rather than an active participant.

Van Hoon looked into the intelligent grey eyes of Radasiliev and shuddered ever so slightly. "You are more than welcome Mr Radasiliev. Surely we have met before my good sir." It was more a statement than a question.

"Perhaps. It is more than likely. I would imagine we have moved in similar circles during similar points in time," smiled the Russian revealing a set of perfect white teeth.

"I cannot, however, recall where or when, nor indeed can I recall inviting you to this evening's entertainment," responded Van Hoon regaining his customary composure.

"Well, someone must have invited me," grinned Radasiliev "Or I would not be here, standing before you as I am."

"Ah! of course," smiled Van Hoon raising his glass in acknowledgement, a glimmer of understanding flashed within his emerald eye.

During the exchange of pleasantries between Van Hoon and Radasiliev, Wiggins had been observing the Russian closely. The man was impeccably groomed and dressed. His high forehead spoke of a sharp intellect and his handsome chiselled features and strong chin indicated a strength of inner character. He noted again that the hair was jet black to the point of being blue and greyed at the temples creating a distinguished aura. His bearing and manner exuded self-assurance, and, Wiggins suspected, engendered confidence and loyalty, perhaps even devotion in others. His striking dark grey eyes were focused intently on Van Hoon, although Wiggins was sure that he was observing intensely all that was going on around him.

"I am aware from our initial interview, Sir, that you are a representative of Czar Nicholas' government," interjected Wiggins. The dark eyes turned to the Detective and bore into him. "That, as you very well know, is correct Inspector," nodded Radasiliev.

"Although I see you are a medical man," observed Wiggins with a smile.

"How so?" enquired the Russian, his attention and curiosity now utterly focused upon Wiggins.

"The thumb and index finger of your left hand are faintly stained with bromine. Evidence I surmise of you having recently poured some from a bottle," highlighted Wiggins. Pyke stifled a chuckle with an ill-disguised cough. "Is that not so?" Wiggins began to experience the same feeling of unease he had experienced when first interviewing the Russian.

"An impressive deduction, Inspector. You are indeed correct," bristled Radasiliev. "My background is indeed in medicine but I no longer practice actively. The evidence you so perceptively point out is due to a recent experiment conducted in pursuit of some private research I am currently involved with," defended the Russian regaining his previous composure. Wiggins nodded as if satisfied and a brief silence lay awkwardly between the two men. The feeling of unease was rapidly escalating to one of inexplicable anxiety. Wiggins glanced at Pyke hoping that his outward behaviour did not betray his inner feelings. He could see Pyke's eyes boring into Radasiliev, the vein on the side of his forehead throbbed like a surfacing earthworm. Wiggins recognised that intense anger was rising within Jem Pyke which was never a good thing. "I would like to ask you some further questions regarding some rather bizarre circumstances we happened upon across at the Russian Embassy following our previous interview," enquired Wiggins.

The Russian bowed slightly. "But of course, Detective Inspector. I am always only too happy to assist the Metropolitan Police in their enquiries. I feel it to be my duty as a Russian citizen." Radasiliev produced a card from his inside pocket. "You may send for me at this address or alternatively call around. The property is old but very, how do you say … cosy."

A palpable sense of tension was rising amongst the quartet. Pyke's distaste for the Russian was becoming ever more apparent and Van Hoon could taste a foulness in the atmosphere. Van Hoon clapped his hands together, instinctively breaking the spell. Wiggins could see Pyke's temper recede and felt his own anxiety shrink. "I hope you enjoy the festivities, my friends. There is food and drink aplenty in the banqueting hall." Van Hoon indicated the general direction with what Wiggins detected was the slightest of trembles in his hand and a very definite note of irony in his voice.

"My thanks. Please excuse me, gentlemen, I indeed feel it is now time for me to dine," grinned the Russian, bowing in turn to each of the three men before departing through the draped curtain with a smile and a flourish.

"He is our man for sure!" gushed Pyke, his anger now replaced by enthusiasm as soon as Radasiliev had departed. "See how you called him out Van Hoon. Let us take him now and end this charade of manners. We can have the creature behind bars before the hour is out."

Van Hoon raised his hand. "He is a Beast indeed Sergeant, but I fear a Beast of perhaps even greater evil and consequence than the one we currently seek. Our quarry, however, the one you call the Beast, is without doubt, here but alas it is not, I feel, Radasiliev. Evil certainly abounds in my house this night gentlemen."

Wiggins examined the calling card in his hand. As he began to read the address each exquisitely printed letter disappeared before his very eyes leaving the card completely blank.

Chapter 19 - The Opera

Van Hoon padded barefoot amongst the tropical foliage which crowded the enormous Sunroom attached to the south-facing wall of his Belgravia home. His naked figure seemed as though painted in the dancing shadows created by the myriad of plants that surrounded him. An inquisitive hummingbird in search of nectar vibrated close to his ear, feathering his lobe, no doubt confused by the sparkling diamond earring which hung there. Multi-coloured butterflies frittered their way around the room, darting from bloom to bloom as if blown on some invisible breeze. One particularly bold, iridescent violet and blue-hued butterfly landed on his shoulder and seemed content to cling there a while, imperceptibly tickling the scarring that tattooed the Leper's skin. Van Hoon remembered reading a long time before that seeing a purple butterfly is supposed to indicate that an important person may soon make an appearance in your life. He smiled a knowing smile at what lay ahead this day. Sweat dripped over his hairless chest and trickled down his lithely muscular torso to the predominant scar which ran across his taut stomach, giving the wound the appearance of a long, thin-lipped mouth, clenched shut. He held a pair of razor-sharp secateurs in one hand and a glass of Swiss absinthe aloft in the other. The strains of Beethoven's ninth symphony filled the space, echoing and reverberating around the glass cathedral. Van Hoon traced the notes of the pastoral in the air with his glass whilst, in time to the music, carefully snipping and slicing at succulent leaves and fronds with the blades in his other. His revelry and sense of unbounded bliss were cut short by a sharp ringing in his right ear. His hand came up to his ear and a finger gently pressed the device hidden ingeniously within his aural tract.

"Van Hoon, here," he said aloud, apparently to no one in particular.

"Ah, Mr Van Hoon. I am glad I have caught you. This is DI Wiggins here. I wanted to follow up with you after the Ball the other night. Most specifically with regards to this Russian fellow, Mr Radasiliev." The words came faintly and with a slight rasping tremulous overtone to the receiver inventively concealed in Van Hoon's earpiece.

"Inspector! I am delighted that you have called. How do you find my voice? Can you hear me clearly enough? Does it sound like me?" enquired Van Hoon enthusiastically.

"The line is quite faint Sir, but I can hear you adequately well," answered Wiggins.

"Excellent! Simply excellent!" rejoiced the Dutchman. "A little experiment of mine in the field of, what you may call telecommunications. I shall henceforth regard this as a resounding success, if you will excuse the painful pun." Van Hoon took a celebratory slug of absinthe. "Radasiliev you say? I must admit to being most impressed with the individual the other evening. How may I be of assistance?"

"As you know, our initial interview with the gentleman proved far from successful and our encounter with him the other evening left me, and I might wager, your good self, with more than an underlying doubt regarding the man and his intentions," explained Wiggins.

"That would be to put it mildly, Inspector. Radasiliev is no doubt a fount of evil, ready to spill forth his abhorrent, bilious influence on our society. Have you ever propagated a sedum praealtum, Inspector? Most satisfying and almost always successful. One merely cuts a leaf from the succulent, trim it to a straight edge and insert it in well-drained soil. Isn't it wonderful how life comes so easily to some species, yet to others, it appears an almost impossible ordeal?"

Wiggins stuttered, taken aback by Van Hoon's sudden apparent diversification of subject matter. "I can't say as I have Mr Van Hoon. My botanical experience is not a strong point although I know some basics. To the matter in hand, namely Luca Radasiliev. I have a request."

"Request away, good Sir. You find me in the most amenable of tempers this morning," the strains of Beethoven's greatest masterpiece underscoring his mood.
"I would like, if you agree, for you to endeavour to get closer to this man. Try to establish his motives, monitor his movements and such. You mentioned at the Ball that he represents potentially an even greater threat to our City than the Beast that we presently pursue. I find this rather fanciful and difficult to comprehend at this juncture, but I am prepared to keep an open mind regarding the matter. My resources are, as you know, limited at this time, whist yours seem to be, how can I put it, unfathomably unlimited."

"You flatter me, Mr Wiggins. Yet, I have already made it my Business to know his Business. In my World, Detective Inspector, animals such as Radasiliev come along every so often and every so often they must be removed from the arena of play. He is indeed dangerous. More dangerous than you can ever imagine. Only twice before can I recall such an underlying sense of dread and unease as this man evinced from within my soul."

"Then you will do it? You will keep a watch on him in my absence?" ejaculated Wiggins eagerly.

"I can do better than that, my dear chap. The process has already begun. My Pestilent have been as an unseen shadow to him these past few days. His every move is their every concern. Tonight, he attends the Opera at Covent Garden. I had hoped to spend the evening in the quiet solitude of bacchanalia. As you know, it is my only vice. Although I suppose a visit to the Opera will help to refuel my much-neglected cultural engines."

The opening strains of Orpheus in the Underworld resounded around the grandeur of the Royal Opera House. Luca Radasiliev locked the door of the private box gifted by the Opera House to the Russian Embassy, removed his top hat, hung up his cloak and sat back in his seat. He made himself comfortable, clasped his mother of pearl opera glasses loosely in his milk pallid hands, closed his eyes and settled back into velour cushioned comfort to absorb the performance. No more than a few minutes into the uplifting opening overture he had gradually become aware of a presence having silently appeared within the otherwise inaccessible box. He suddenly opened his eyes and turned his head to what should have been the one vacant seat to his left.

There sat Dante Van Hoon, a smile playing mischievously upon his face, intently gazing at the splendour of the Opera unfolding before him. "Orpheus," he beamed whilst conducting with an imaginary baton. "Obviously, it would just have to be Orpheus. Rather too satirical and comic an operetta for me. My own tastes lean more towards Madame Butterfly I must admit, but I can understand why you would feel that Orpheus would be the Opera for you. I suspect unfortunately however that in a thousand years from now the name of Puccini will still be revered, whilst Offenbach will be lost in the midst of time. A tragedy really. One is only truly dead when nobody remembers you any longer. I expect therefore that we will both live for an exceptionally long time don't you feel Mr Radasiliev?" Van Hoon questioned whilst remaining focussed upon events unfolding on stage.

"Mr Van Hoon, what an unexpected pleasure," spluttered a rather awestruck Radasiliev." I have heard several rumours regarding your talents, but I cannot say that I expected transmaterialisation to be amongst them. How may I ask did you manage to gain entrance into this box? I alone hold the key." The Russian shifted uneasily in his chair, momentarily taken aback at the sudden and unexpected appearance of his uninvited visitor. As he did so he reached furtively into the inner right breast pocket of his jacket. Upon him doing so, a slender but powerful leprous hand rested gently on each of his shoulders strongly suggesting that he desist the manoeuvre. A quarter turn of Radasiliev's immaculately coiffured head was enough to show him the tall shrouded presence of one of Van Hoon's Pestilent looming menacingly directly behind him.

Van Hoon continued to stare directly ahead, apparently soaking in the music and libretto. "A client of mine, you might say, is rather uniquely placed within the hierarchy of the Opera House. My friend, Erik, was pre-eminent for many years in the Wiener Staatsoper, before having a rather notorious and unfortunate period during his tenure in the Opéra de Paris. His current position behind the scenes here in London permits me free reign of the Opera House from time to time." Radasiliev slowly removed his hand from his pocket, producing a slim-line gold cigarette case which he proffered towards Van Hoon. "Turkish, extra strong, from the coast of the Black Sea."

The leprous arms retracted noiselessly into the dark shroud that retreated into the shadows of the drapery suspended behind the Russian. "No thank you," replied Van Hoon, turning his remarkable eyes for the first time towards his somewhat unsettled companion. "I prefer Moroccan. It is my only vice you understand."

"Offenbach had such a vivid imagination don't you agree Mr Van Hoon?" enquired Radasiliev, lighting his cigarette with a gold plated lighter and inhaling deeply. He stretched his neck backwards and exhaled a plume of smoke up towards the ornate ceiling of the box. A slight cough emanated from within the drapery behind him. Radasiliev smiled a smile of satisfaction. "Travelling to the Underworld in the hope of resurrecting a lost love. Absurd do you not think," said Radasiliev glancing at Van Hoon's cane.

"I think we both know that it is less an absurdity and more a romantic notion. Where would the Arts be without poetic license? Who knows what the future, or indeed the past may bring? Why you, I am sure have more than a passing association with the underworld of Hades. I do after all detect the slightest whiff of a brimstone undertone to that cologne you are wearing," parried Van Hoon. Radasiliev again turned his head towards Van Hoon who was now actively whistling annoyingly and mischievously along to the underlying refrain whilst tapping his fingers on the head of his cane. "Surely, the same could be said of yourself, Sir. Dante Van Hoon indeed? The name itself has such obvious connotations with the home of demons." Van Hoon laughed heartily. "And of course, I am sure Luca Radasiliev is your birth name?!"

The two men turned to look directly at each other. Van Hoon noted small red spots spiralling around the deep grey pools of Radasiliev's kaleidoscopic eyes. The spots spiralled more rapidly in time to the music until they resembled small whirlpools. *Drums thundered and woodwind trumpeted around the room.* Van Hoon could feel that the Russian's stare was endeavouring to penetrate his mind. *Cymbals crashed and the crescendo increased.* He began to find himself drifting, losing his mental focus, so fixated was he on the Russian's mesmeric eyes. *A whirlwind of flashing violins*, the music now heterophonic in nature. Van Hoon felt himself being pulled into a whirlwind of abstract thought, senseless images and ideas like a fantasia of music. He shook his head and with extreme mental effort broke the hypnotic gaze of the Russian just as there was a musical lull on stage. His laugh broke the silence as he again shook his head more in amazement than in distress. "I see so clearly now the foundation of your power. If you are searching for a soul Mr Radasiliev, I fear you will be bitterly disappointed."

"But surely you must have a weakness, an anxiety, an anger, a fear?" enquired Radasiliev with the raise of one quizzical eyebrow and an inspection of the leper's attire. "Vanity perhaps?"

"I am afraid, my dear Sir, that you will find that my only weakness is the enormity of my over-exercised ego and that even a man of your evident powers could not attempt to make it any larger than the passing years have already inflated it."

On stage, as Hades and Persephone began to grant Eurydice her operatic exit from the Pit, Radasiliev, in turn, stood to also take his leave. He rose and straightened the seams of his opera coat. "I feel my appetite for the remainder of this spectacle to be somewhat diluted and must beg your indulgence, Sir. I bid you good night and look forward to our next encounter wherever and whenever it may occur." He placed his top hat upon his head and bowed slightly, clicking his heels together in the Eastern European fashion. As he turned to make his exit past the shrouded figure lurking behind the drapes, Van Hoon leant back in his chair. "Bezopasnoye puteshestviye. You never know what demons and beasts haunt the London night, or perhaps you do. Do have a safe journey and be sure to get home before sunrise, Luca."

Chapter 20 - The Club

The Demosthenes Club, like its neighbours in exclusivity, The Reform Club and the Athenaeum, was located in Pall Mall, a mere stone's throw from those other doyens of the gentleman's elite; Boodles and Whites in Saint James Street. Unlike its sister club the Diogenes, famous for its patronage of Mycroft Holmes and its vow of galba adactae, the Demosthenes, as one would expect by its name, actively encouraged open debate and fostered oration amongst its members.

Several patrons sat in various areas of the large oval-shaped smoking room. Some were reading newspapers and books whilst one aged, bald grandee sat asleep with mouth agape, volunteering the occasional grunt. All possessed drinks of some description and were tended by two immaculately attired waiters whose darting eyes constantly scanned the establishment for any requesting raised hands. Heavy midnight-blue brocade drapes were closed at every window whilst two fires burned invitingly at opposite ends of the room. The air was laden with pipe and cigar smoke mirroring the fog shrouding the streets outside. A mixture of smoke, whisky, coffee and cologne blended to perfume the room.

Chief Inspector Magnus MacDonald sat in a green, wing-backed leather chesterfield chair in the intimate reading room of the Demosthenes. He sipped his Hennessey cognac then swirled the remainder of it around his balloon glass contemplating the patterns its substantial legs produced. The shades of the open fire twinkled and reflected through the sharp amber liquid as he contemplated events.

"Mind if I join you Magnus?" the softly voiced enquiry suddenly jolted MacDonald from his considerations. "Oh! Not at all Joseph. Always a pleasure, never a chore," returned McDonald rising slightly from his seat and offering its opposing neighbour to the towering figure of Doctor Bleak. "The fire is most comforting the night," observed the Chief Inspector in his Scottish brogue, "…and the cognac is going doon a real treat."

Bleak placed his copy of the Lancet on an occasional table and settled into the crumpling cracked comfort of the armchair, whilst signalling a passing attendant. "I do not partake I have to admit. I drank alcohol on only one occasion, many years ago, and it did not agree with me or those around me. A glass of iced milk please, Jephson. A vicious night out there Magnus is it not?"

"I find that most o' them are these days Joseph if truth be told. It's a blessing to leave the carnality of the East End for the warm comforting embrace of the Demosthenes. I cannot tell you how much I look forward to our wee weekly debates sitting at the round table. Takes my mind, however fleetingly, from stressful matters and traumatic times."

"Indeed," nodded Bleak, gratefully accepting his milk from the silver tray offered by Jephson who had quietly appeared at the Doctor's side. Bleak signed his receipt with an exaggerated flourish and thanked the steward with a kindly smile.

"How did you find the Ball at the Dutchman's castle the other night, Joseph?" enquired MacDonald looking distractedly into the fire.

"Not entirely to my liking, to be frank, Magnus. A little ostentatious for my tastes. I find the preening of feathers unwarranted and rather obscene. I much prefer the homely relaxation of the Demosthenes," admitted Doctor Bleak, almost sheepishly.

"I agree, of course, Joseph. Such ostentation, as you say, sits uncomfortably with a dour old Episcopalian such as myself," chuckled MacDonald.

"How goes the world of criminal investigation? Is Commissioner Gregson still of hale countenance?" enquired Bleak, anxious to move the conversation away from religious persuasions. "I have not had the pleasure of his habitual visit to my practice for some time now. I do hope he remains in good health."

"Aye, he's on guid form and continues to belie his years, keeping us all on our toes. Particularly at this especially demanding time," added the Scot. "This blasted Beast wreaks havoc in our East End and the pressure from above is very much to staunch the flow and curtail another panic like that triggered by auld Jack's atrocities."

"Of course. Indeed, these must be especially trying times for all involved. You have your best men on the case no doubt?" enquired Bleak sipping his chilled milk.

"Aye, the absolute best Sir. Make no mistake there is no better detective on the Force than DI Wiggins and no harder a loyal workhorse than Sergeant Pyke. We are indeed in safe hands and the full strength of the Force is squarely behind them. If truth be told we are awfully close to cracking the identity of this monster," announced McDonald proudly, though somewhat unjustifiably.

"Really? That is indeed most encouraging," responded Bleak. "And your erstwhile colleague, Chief Inspector Lestrade. How does retirement suit him?"

"Ach! We never hear from the man. And quite right. Living a life of peaceful retirement doon in Kent no doubt," complained McDonald secretly wishing the tables were turned and it were he living the sedentary life. "I see the Suffrage movement has garnered abundant impetus over the last few months."

"Indeed. A most noble cause, yet one that one might feel to be ultimately of little worth," observed Bleak.

"I disagree Joseph. I think the movement is now unstoppable and a good thing too." Bleak shrugged and changed the subject. "Pray what is the topic of our debate this evening then Magnus?"

"One that will suit you doon to the ground Joseph. The terminations rife among the unfortunate young women in our lower classes. No doubt you hae strong views on the subject, Sir," primped McDonald.

"Indeed, I do, although some that may surprise you, Magnus." A gong rang three times. The signal for all participants in that evening's debate to decant into the debating chamber and take their seats at the round table. "Ah, there we are. The gong. Shall we proceed Joseph?"

"Of course, Magnus."

"After you old chap. Age before intellect."

<hr>

Chief Superintendent Magnus MacDonald and Doctor Joseph Bleak were helped into their overcoats in the grand foyer of the Demosthenes Club by the cloakroom attendant. "Another fine debate this evening Joseph," smiled MacDonald who was always enthused and invigorated after an evening of measured opinions and exchanged views accompanied by multiple tumblers of cognac. "As always we seem to sit on opposite sides of the house, as it were, when it comes to the significant matters of the day."

"That's as it should be Magnus. It would be dreadfully tiresome if we all held the same opinions and had the same agendas don't you think?" replied Bleak. The two men placed their hats atop their heads and were handed their canes as they descended the polished marble steps of the great gentleman's institution. MacDonald breathed in the night air somewhat melodramatically. His chest secretly puffed with pride each time he entered and exited the Demosthenes. His massaged ego continued to be surprised that a small rapscallion from the South Side of Glasgow had risen to such lofty heights, not only within the London Metropolitan Police but also within this great City's society. Lofty enough even to have been granted membership to the Demosthenes after only three years of trying.

"Can I offer ye a lift Joseph? I see my car just arriving up ahead," enquired the Scot, inwardly eager to show the good doctor his new staff issue Bentley. The large black tourer glided to a halt at the kerb in front of them.

"No, Magnus, thank-you for the kind offer but I reside but a mere stone's throw from where we stand and to be honest, I relish the walk on such foggy nights as this. There is something about the anonymity the cloak of mist provides that appeals to me," replied Bleak with a smile and the slightest of bows.

"As you wish," nodded MacDonald, masking his inner disappointment at the lost opportunity to impress. "I will see ye next Wednesday, no doubt. Be watchful on the way home, you know that damned Beast is still at large and could attack at any moment," cautioned the Chief Superintendent, laughing nervously.

"You will be the first to know if I run into him Magnus," smiled Bleak as he touched the brim of his top hat, turned, and disappeared into the foggy night.

Chapter 21 - The Kidnap

Hercules Chin had awoken early in the morning as always, the incessant squawking of the seagulls acted as would a crowing cockerel, rousing him from the bunk he occupied on the small boat moored to the pier by Pakapuh in Shadwell Basin. The bed had been constructed out of salvaged lengths of timber and it filled the full length of the cabin of the small fishing boat. Chin liked to sleep in the boat, the gentle rocking caused by the tides of the Thames helped the giant Chinaman fall asleep. He dressed in his habitual rough serge suit, cut in the Chinese style, and made his lumbering way from the pier into the back room of Pakapuh. Chin nodded to Wang, the spherical master of the opium den as he ducked his huge frame through the doorway, his giant hand gripping the top of the door as a normal person would grab a garden gate. He squeezed through the doorway and lumbered past the many bunks, each containing a comatose occupant. Each heavy footfall created a small cloud of dust motes. Chin sat down at his usual table in the corner next to Wang as the rotund opiate dispenser handed Chin his first pipe of the day. Chin took the pipe with a nod and a grunt of gratitude and inhaled deeply.

"You at big meeting tonight, Chin?" enquired Wang, busily heating a spoonful of opium over a candle flame. Chin nodded. He watched the opium bubble turn a treacle brown colour. He gazed into the flame flicking around the spoon, mesmerised by its pyrotechnic dance. He had no concept of time other than night and day, but he did know that he had to guard Father King when all the others came today. He expected that one of the twins would let him know when his services were required. The smiling wizened old cook came shuffling happily into the back room from the kitchen carrying a massive bowl of noodles, chicken and eggs, in both hands. "Big boy's breakfast!" she laughed, placing the meal in front of Chin, her aching wrists happy that they no longer had to carry the weight of the enormous portion of food. Chin nodded towards the smiling little woman and grunted his thanks before shovelling the food into his mouth between drawing on his carved bone pipe. Once he had consumed the food, Wang handed Chin his second pipe of the morning and the giant lay back and let the pleasant feeling of numbness engulf him.

At this time of the morning coughing and snoring were the only noises discernible in the gloomy smoke-veiled darkness of the warren of rooms. Three compartments rested one atop the other to maximise customer use, roughly curtained to hide their lodgers from the gazes of others. Patrons did not want to be recognised in this wretched den of iniquity and self-loathing so there was no conversation. Oil lamps intermittently illuminated small pockets of activity where inhabitants began the ritual of forgetting memories and sins or in the hope of relieving pain and loneliness. Most reclined on makeshift mattresses in order to hold the long opium pipes over the oil lamps, which warmed the drug causing it to evaporate, allowing the smoker to inhale the vapours. Chasing the Dragon.

The disused granary warehouse in Wapping offered the ideal meeting place for the cartel of crime headed by the nefarious Mr King. The main area of the warehouse offered a huge open plan space of concrete floor, brick walls and close boarded suspended timber ceiling with steel trusses and purlins. Nowhere, on the face of it at least, to conceal anyone. In the middle of the huge open space sat the Council of Crime, Mr King's cartel of evil. Under King's masterful direction, the Cartel's raison d'être was to wreak havoc and inflict chaos throughout the order of civilisation. King's ultimate target was to dominate society through fear on an unprecedented scale. His tools where the acolytes whom he dominated, his means, assassination, extortion, opiates, torture, protection, prostitution and cruelty. There was no act too evil, no deed too devilish to which King would not stoop to achieve his dream of total subjugation through fear and intimidation. To this end, King had assembled a network of the most ruthless criminals and cutthroats in London.

King entered through the side door of the vast chamber, shadowed by the enormous, ominous figure of Hercules Chin, and flanked by the lethal assassin twins, the Shang brothers. King took his seat at the head of the table, all eight feet of Hercules Chin looming directly behind him like a behemothic headstone. The Twins lurked in the background like two inquisitive rats. King looked around him, his serpentine green eyes, beneath his shining bald head, bore into each face gathered around him. These people were hardened criminals themselves, heads of their own crime syndicates, but each of them felt uncomfortable under the sinister gaze of the fiendish Chinese crime lord.

King's two chief lieutenants sat either side of him. The Poisoner, the lizard-like chief amongst King's Burmese Dacoit and Thuggee assassins and Madame Huai, the ruthless head of King's prostitution business. The Jewish underworld boss Jabez Rubenstein sat alongside the Grice Brothers, dual heads of the East End's hardest, most villainous mob. Also in attendance were the Italian, Don Anastasi and the Irish hoodlum known as the Horse.

"Tonight, gentlemen we will move another step closer to destabilising the powers of justice," gloated the demonic Chinaman, his reptilian eyes glinting with pleasure.

MacDonald's car drew to a halt outside his substantial Marylebone home. The house was a grand four-storey stucco-covered Victorian townhouse built on a typical sweeping West London crescent. MacDonald extricated himself unsteadily from the car, a little lightheaded from the more than generous measures of cognac served up in the Demosthenes. "Thank you, James. Collect me at seven sharp the morn's mornin' if ye'd be so kind." James saluted and drove off. '*The morn's mornin' indeed,*' impersonated the driver to himself. '*Bleedin' Scotch.*'

As MacDonald made his way up the portico steps to his front door, he was saluted by Constable Chivers who stood in attendance outside the Superintendent's house that night. "Evening, Sir." MacDonald's position within the Met warranted a constant security presence at his place of residence. MacDonald returned the young policeman's acknowledgement. "Cauld night the night laddie. I'll be sure to ask my Housemaid, Millicent, to bring ye some hot tea and a lump o' Dundee cake."

"Thank you, Sir. Most kind," returned the pleasantly surprised Chivers. This was an altogether different Chief Super to the one he was used to down at the Yard every day. '*Seems almost normal,*' Chivers thought to himself.

Once inside the hallway MacDonald placed his cane in the stick rack and removed his hat and overcoat, finding a place for each of them on the nearby hat stand. He shuddered as he shook the fog from his bones and headed towards the stairs.

"Would you be wanting a nightcap, Sir?" asked the diligent Millicent, her head appearing from the kitchen. Millicent's rather too pointed nose sniffed the air. Much to her disapproval, she detected a slight whiff of strong spirits. "Some hot milk or a malty drink, perhaps Mr MacDonald?" she enquired, sardonically.

"No thank ye, Millicent. I have an early start tomorrow. I think I will just head up to bed. You might brew up some strong tea for young Chivers out there though, heat his bones a bit. Oh! And I am sure a generous slab of your wonderful Dundee cake wouldn't go amiss," remembered MacDonald as he strode upstairs. "As you wish, Sir," replied Millicent, relieved at the prospect of a relatively early night.

Chivers was blowing into his cupped hands, somewhat pointlessly he realised, given that he was wearing leather gloves, as Millicent opened the door and passed him a cup of steaming tea. He was just about to thank her and ask about the promised slab of cake when an ear-splitting scream reached them from the secluded communal garden square in front of the Crescent. Chivers hesitated "Did you hear that? It sounded like the cries of a woman!" he asked Millicent, peering into the gloom in the direction from which the scream had emanated.

"Course I did. Ain't you gonna investigate it like?" admonished Millicent withdrawing the tea. "I'll go and get 'is Nibbs." Chivers nodded and reluctantly passed his much-anticipated cup of tea back to Millicent. *'So much for the Dundee cake,'* he lamented. He ran towards the garden blasting on his whistle, whilst Millicent hurried upstairs to alert MacDonald, leaving the front door wide open. Chivers pulled at the wrought iron gate of the private garden square and saw that it was padlocked. Only the residents of the Crescent owned entrance keys. Cursing, he scaled the gate, all the time thinking in the back of his mind that he should not be doing this alone, he should have stayed at his post and waited for reinforcements. *'What if it's the Beast?'* he worried. As his feet hit the crumpling gravel on the other side of the railings Chivers heard some muffled cries and scuffling coming from the direction of a large Oak Tree that dominated the centre of the garden. "Help me!" he heard a woman's cry, just as it was cut short. Chivers ran towards the sound and was greeted by the sight of two oriental men grappling with a woman who looked as if she also hailed from the Far East. Chivers blasted on his whistle again as he approached the scene. "Hey, you two, Police! Leave that woman go!"

The two men did indeed let the woman go. To Robert Chivers' surprise, all three of the protagonists turned and smiled at him. He thought it odd that the two men looked identical. He then looked down at his chest to see, much to his disbelief and shock, that the still reverberating hilt of a dagger was sticking out his upper rib cage where it had landed home less than a second before. As he fell to his knees, the last thing Chivers saw was the shadow of an unfeasibly huge, nightmarish monster lumbering past him.

MacDonald came rushing frantically down the stairs in response to Millicent's cries. His first thought was to get to his pistol which was in the drawer of his desk in his study to the left. "What's going on Millie? Where is Constable Chivers?" demanded MacDonald, gasping and struggling for breath as he reached his housemaid who stood at the foot of the stairs, teacup and saucer rattling in her trembling hand. "He ran to the gardens Sir to answer the lady's screams." As Millicent spoke, MacDonald saw that she was now looking over his shoulder towards the door, her mouth fell open, the cup and saucer smashed to the floor and splashed their contents over MacDonald's night slippers. "Mary mother of God have mercy!" croaked Millicent, frozen in wide-eyed terror. MacDonald wheeled on his heels just in time to see a stooping monster squeezing itself through the aperture of his front door and turning its gigantic, grinning head towards him.

"Lord preserve us," groaned MacDonald. "Get out Millie, the back door quick, lass! I'll do what I can." Millicent turned and fled screaming "A Monster, it's a Monster!"

MacDonald ducked into the thankfully unlocked study and dived towards the bureau housing his gun. Hercules Chin followed behind, squeezing his enormous bulk through the study doorway, seemingly filling the room as he did so. MacDonald saw plumes of dust puff from the shoulders of Chin's serge jacket as they were dragged against and through the door frame. As MacDonald placed his hand on the drawer containing the precious pistol, the entire desk was whipped violently backwards across the floor by one giant hand and crashed into the wall, scattering books from shelves.

MacDonald found himself isolated and unarmed in front of some monster from a childhood nightmare. He turned instinctively to the fireplace and reached for the poker, tugging it from the companion set on the tiled hearth. He swung the poker towards the giant with as much strength as he could muster. Chin easily caught the poker in the palm of his massive hand and snatched it away from MacDonald's grip, dislocating two of MacDonald's fingers in the process. The Scot yelped in pain and then stood frozen, mouth wide open as the enormous Chinaman took the ends of the poker in each hand and bent it double before casting it aimlessly aside. The diminutive Scot swallowed hard, braced himself, and raised his fists, southpaw fashion, the blood of his battling highland ancestors coursing through his veins "Come on ahead then ye big galoot, or get oot o' ma damn hoose!"

'This is the one Father King wants alive,' thought Chin as he approached MacDonald. The policeman swung punches right and left as the Chinaman's huge body engulfed him. The punches had no effect upon his assailant. One giant hand covered MacDonald's head and the other grabbed both of his ankles, lifting him upwards like a human plank and battered his head twice against the ceiling, knocking the consciousness out of his now limp body, and dislodging shards of lath and plaster that fell upon the Giant's head dusting his eyes. Chin shifted the motionless MacDonald under his left arm and squeezed himself and his abductee out of the house, turning as he did so to carefully close the door behind him.

"It's the Super's housemaid Millicent on the phone, guvnor. She's goin' bananas screeching about Mr MacDonald being carried off by some giant Chinese monster! Can only be one man of that description!" announced Pyke as he crashed into Wiggins' office.

"What? Where on earth is Chivers? Was he not on guard duty at MacDonald's this evening? Send some uniforms around there straight away and contact Marylebone Station immediately. Get on to Nosher at Paddington and get reinforcements," demanded Wiggins, raising an eyebrow. "What do we know about the whereabouts of that devil, King at the moment?"

"Down Shadwell way somewhere. We lost track of him when old Beastie Boy started up. I can find out exactly where he is right now if you give me an hour," responded Pyke urgently grabbing his Derby and turning for the door.

"Make it as quick as you can Pyke. I'll go to MacDonald's residence while you seek out where King is. I suspect that if we find him, I fear we will also find the Superintendent. We will meet back here in one hour and formulate our plans. In the meantime, I will inform Commissioner Gregson," detailed Wiggins gathering his authority and composure and beginning to feel more comfortable now that he had a plan of action.

Pyke had already called into the Seven Dials, The Grapes, The Boars Head and The Crooked Man before trying the Red Pig. Pyke approached the barman "Any sign of Harry Filch tonight, Sandy?" enquired Pyke, refusing the whisky that the bulky barman had placed upon the bar in front of him. "Not tonight mate, I'm on the clock," added Pyke looking longingly at the glass.

"Nobody's seen 'Arry for a few days, Jem. Disappeared off the face, probably that god-forsaken cough of his. You looking for information?" enquired Sandy, lowering his voice as he moved his head closer to Pyke's. Pyke nodded, deciding to take the whisky anyway, swigging it down in one adventurous gulp. "Yes, information that I'd normally get from Filchie."

"Little Crumb is in the back room if he's of any use," whispered Sandy, rubbing his bristled chin, and indicating the door behind him with a raised thumb and a backward glance. Pyke thanked Sandy with a grip of the shoulder and walked into the private room behind the bar of the Pig. The room was small and smoke filled and was served by a tiny private bar, no more than a hatch extending through from the main pub. Two or three high-backed small booths made up the seating in this private room. "Everyone out!" announced Pyke flashing his badge. "Get home to your wives, children or dogs, whatever you have." The small group of hardened drinkers began to moan disapprovingly and shuffle out from their booths staring at Pyke with obvious disdain. One large Irish ragger who obviously did not appreciate being told to vacate his nook began to bristle, sniff and roll his shoulders intimidatingly. "Don't even think about it Don, I ain't got time to smack some sense into you tonight. Some other time I'll happily oblige you, now sling yer hook," growled the Detective Sergeant,

"So, you are aware of the document then?" sneered King. "Believe me it would be in your best interests to tell me what I need to know. You have already been injected with a truth serum. An anaesthetic drug called scopolamine, against which you will have no defence."

"I am a police officer, not a government official. I have no access to such high-level information," specified MacDonald.

"But Superintendent, I know exactly what you are and so do you. Magnus Andrew MacDonald, you are very much more than a mere police officer, hence your appearance here upon this table," replied King with a knowing smile. "This can be either slow and painful or quick and painful, it all depends upon you. Otherwise, you can tell me what I need to know, and I can return you to your lovely housekeeper, Millicent."

"You better not have harmed that wumin' you heathen devil. Go to hell where you belong! It doesn't matter what I say, you will kill me either way," spat MacDonald straining furiously against his bonds.

"Your powers of deduction are indeed accurate," King laughed clapping his hands rapidly together like a child on Christmas morning. The applause stopped abruptly as he reached up and turned on a tap above the copper pipe just enough to allow a drop of water to fall impacting on MacDonald's immobile forehead. "Given enough time the water will eventually bore a hole into your forehead, drip, drip, drip, but rest assured Mr MacDonald, you will have lost all your sanity before it reaches that point. I will now pass you over to the capable hands of Hercules Chin, whom no doubt you remember from your initial meeting at your house earlier this evening."

MacDonald shuddered at the arrival of the giant shadow looming to one side of him, straining his eyes sideways to try and glimpse the monster which he could not quite believe had entered his house and carried him off. He felt the touch of a giant hand rest on his stomach, covering the whole of his abdomen. MacDonald flinched at the contact. He could feel his shirt being pulled up to his chest and something being strapped to his stomach.

"A most ingenious device Magnus. You don't mind if I call you Magnus, do you Magnus?" mocked King. "A small raffia basket strapped across your stomach. Bottomless, of course, and just large enough for a starved rat to be squeezed into. Once the basket is strapped shut there is nowhere to go for our hungry little friend other than to eat his way through your abdomen. He gets fed and escapes, it's a win-win situation for the rat. Believe me, I have seen this many times before and the pain appears to be excruciating. Which will it be Magnus? Death by water, death by rat, or tell me what I need to know and Hercules here will make your demise swift and relatively free from pain."

"Damn you to hell you yellow filth," cursed MacDonald spitting in King's direction. "I will not betray my King and I will not betray my men. I would'nae gie ye the steam aff mah first shite you evil Chinese bastard!"

The last thing Magnus MacDonald heard before passing out was the gleeful laughter and child-like hand clapping of King as Chin raised a large brown rat by the tail and dropped it into the open basket before securing the door.

Wiggins, Pyke and a dozen armed police officers had surrounded the disused granary warehouse. Four of the division's trained marksmen were positioned on the roof of the building, one at each skylight. The lead marksman raised his left fist and waved it downwards signalling to Wiggins that the main chamber of the warehouse was empty. "Damn!" cursed Wiggins shooting a glance in Pyke's direction. "Looks like Crumb gave us false information." Pyke shrugged and bit his lip. "Let's get in there anyway Guvnor, there may be some other rooms. I cannot believe that little weasel lied to me. He knows what will happen to him if he has."

Wiggins nodded and gave the signal to advance. He had never known Pyke's intimidation tactics to fail on an informant yet. Even one as loathsome as Little Crumb. Very few men would risk unleashing the wrath of an angry Jem Pyke. The unit scampered from their places of concealment, weapons cocked and ready, led by Pyke who jemmied open the main door of the warehouse with a crowbar and leapt in, pistol aloft shouting, "Police! Lay down your arms and you may live."

A resounding silence greeted his order with only his own voice echoing around the large empty space. Wiggins quickly assessed the situation. "They are here somewhere," announced Wiggins his keen eyes had instantly spotted several betraying signs of occupation. The faintest sound of a dripping tap, multiple fresh footprints in the husky dust strewn floor, a set of oily handprints on a rear door, the contracting rattle of a recently used radiator, and the faint smell of oriental spiced oils. "Take care lads, be on your guard." Each policeman now felt very exposed in the large open space. Wiggins surveyed the scene around him. *'What was the fiend's plan? If he was here surely, he would not leave this place unprotected.'*

Wiggins wheeled as he heard the cry of the first officer as he hit the floor, a massive tiger fork spear pinioned in his back. Then a second, then a third fell. "Hit the decks lads!" ordered Pyke, his soldier's instinct realising that a prone man offered less of a target to a knife thrower. Several of the police officers now opened fire randomly around the room causing bullets to ricochet haphazardly around them. Panic had set in. Being in such an isolated position was not a scenario they had been trained for. Wiggins continued to look around him and spotted several open doors leading off the main granary chamber. Immediately he remembered the sound of the dripping tap and indicated to Pyke the door from which it had emanated. "They are in that one, Jem," pointed Wiggins, whispering from behind his open hand.

"Follow me lads," ordered Pyke indicating the door in question. The company began to follow Pyke who was already headed for the door. It was then that it hit Wiggins. Perhaps it was a noise, maybe some form of intuition, but he suddenly knew what was going to happen. He looked upwards at the giant steel hoppers fixed to the steelwork of the ceiling overhead. "Take cover!" he shouted, pointing upwards. "The hoppers!"

The chutes of the giant silos were released in unison by Dacoits previously concealed within the labyrinth of roof trusses and purlins. Hundreds of tons of grain plummeted from each of the six overhead hoppers engulfing most of the policemen in a mountain of suffocating grain.

"Jesus Christ!" cursed Pyke turning back towards the unfolding scene behind him, his mouth agape as he heard the final muffled screams of his drowning colleagues. "They knew we were coming … Crumb!" rumbled Pyke, "I'll kill that bastard baby!" Wiggins turned his gaze away from the granary burial mound.

Constable Potts came running towards them from out of the dust cloud accompanied by another four coughing uniforms, their faces ashen white and covered in grain dust. "Where to Sir?" asked Potts gamely. Wiggins swallowed hard, gathered his strength, and indicated the door ahead, resigned to the fact that the rest of his colleagues had met a grisly end. "Through there."

Pyke was already halfway through the door as Wiggins gave the command. Once they had all entered, they were met with an incredible tableau. Superintendent MacDonald lay strapped to a table with what seemed to be blood oozing from a basket placed on his stomach. An eight-foot-tall nightmarish monster stood at his side and the devilish looking Chinaman sat behind the table. Several dacoit thugs were also dotted around the room each carrying weapons. As soon as the policemen entered the room, the chair on which King sat rapidly shot backwards and disappeared into a concealed alcove in the wall behind him. King had made his escape.

The constables opened fire on the onrushing dacoits, who dropped as one, their shambolic attack, no match for the firearms of the police. Pyke leapt at the retreating figure of the giant who whirled and swatted the detective sideways crashing him sickeningly into the wall. Chin kicked at the door through which King had made his escape and somehow squeezed his way through it. Wiggins levelled his pistol and fired and was convinced that he had made a direct hit to the Giant's shoulder as it disappeared through the hole.

Wiggins and Pyke raced after Chin through the hidden door and found themselves on a pier extending out onto the River. Wiggins noted a motorised skip making its way back upriver carrying the fleeing Mr King to safety. '*For now,*' thought Wiggins inwardly. Pyke and Wiggins were joined by their surviving colleagues on the pier, all of them faced by the looming gigantic figure of Hercules Chin who seemed to be trying to hail the now distant boat pitifully with outstretched arms and wiggling fingers. Chin slowly turned back towards the officers and started to lumber towards them, his enormous arms outstretched. His giant body lurched backwards as the impact of a volley of bullets found their target and the enormous frame fell backwards and plummeted into the inky blackness of the River Thames.

Sergeant Pyke strode into the Station the next morning dragging the diminutive figure of Little Crumb kicking behind him like a spoilt child. The two crashed through the swing doors and Pyke threw the midget unceremoniously skidding across the floor towards the Desk Sergeant. The pocket-sized Crumb tumbled comically head over arse repeatedly until he hit the front desk and lay in a crumpled heap. "Stick him inside, Sid," announced Pyke. "Don't bother attending to his bloodied nose. He tripped!"

"What's the charge Sarge?" asked the Desk Sergeant.

"Conspiracy to murder seven police officers," snarled Pyke, hefting a boot at the man child's ribs.

"What! That's for the noose!" boomed the baritone imp. "What about me thirty quid?"

A smiling Jem Pyke removed one of Crumb's cigars out of the midget's breast pocket and gleefully lit it up. "You won't be needing that where you're going you little piece of shit. There's a whole lotta room in Hell for a little poisoned dwarf like you."

Chapter 22 - The Operation

Less than five hours previously, Doctor Joseph Bleak had been sharing a pleasant evening's discourse at the Demosthenes Club with the man who now lay prone and motionless before him on the operating table. As on-call emergency surgeon, Bleak had been summoned to the London Hospital as soon as it was apparent that Superintendent Magnus MacDonald was clinging to the last fragile remnants of life following his torturous ordeal at the hands of the fiendish Mr King.

Sergeant Pyke had picked up his senior officer's apparently lifeless body and ran with it towards one of the paddy wagons waiting outside Stephenson's Granary. "Get that engine started ladies! Move your arses!" Pyke's running gait was irregular but rapid, straight-backed, slightly bow-legged, his cheeks puffing at the effort of carrying the dead weight, battering his way past his astonished colleagues. Pyke bundled MacDonald into the back of the wagon and jumped in after him. He placed his hand on MacDonald's neck and was convinced he could feel a faint pulse. "The London Hospital, quick as you can," he screamed to the driver, banging a fist repeatedly on the side of the vehicle. The wagon lurched forward as the driver's eagerness caused him to stall the engine. "Jesus Christ, get your act together you foozler and drive like a blasted demon. Don't spare the horses. The guvnor's almost gone!" shouted Pyke.

He fumbled in his inside jacket pocket, searching for a small hip flask that he habitually kept there for 'medicinal' purposes on cold winter nights on duty. He frantically unscrewed the pewter top which slipped through his trembling fingers and dropped to the floor clattering and rebounding around like a ball in a bagatelle. He tentatively tried to pour some of the brandy into MacDonald's mouth but the bone-shaking motion of the police wagon careering over the cobbles made it almost impossible for Pyke to be accurate of aim. Most, but not all the brandy missed its mark, spilling down McDonald's chin, tracing rivulets on the topography of his bare chest and into the ghastly open wound on his stomach. As soon as the brandy hit the back of his throat MacDonald's gag reflex spluttered into gear, jerking his head upwards and forwards. Blood sprayed forth from his mouth covering Pyke's hand and sleeve. "Faster!" yelled Pyke, again punching the wagon's carapace. Pyke partially wiped the blood spatter from his face with the back of his hand. He had seen wounds like this on the battlefield. He had even tried to staunch a few himself; Johnny Jessop, Spud Watson, Jocky Donaldson and Fred Onions. None of them had survived more than a few hours. Pyke could see inside the abdominal cavity and what he saw did not look good. He removed his jacket, waistcoat and shirt before wrapping the shirt as tightly as he could around MacDonald's stomach, trying as best he could to bandage the gaping wound and tourniquet the blood flow. '*How in God's name do you tourniquet an entire body?*' he wondered at the enormity of the task. He stuffed the waistcoat into the cavity and pressed in an attempt to staunch the wound "Come on you stubborn Scots bastard, keep breathing for me," he spat through gritted teeth.

As Pyke was hurtling down the Mile End Road towards the hospital, Doctor Joseph Bleak was being transported in an equally ferociously driven cab towards the same destination. Wiggins had somehow managed to get a call through to Bleak's house to raise the alert. Bleak opened the window of the car and gripped the edge of the door to steady himself, his bony knuckles straining white at the effort. From what Wiggins had told him the injury to his friend was most severe, and Bleak realised that to save MacDonald would be a feat of miraculous proportions. He began to calmly rehearse the operation over in his head, visualising the wound and extensive damage to the soft tissues and surrounding organs. Anticipating the procedure he would have to perform, he pictured the instruments he would need. Retractors, artery forceps, tenaculum, sutures, packing materials, transfusion equipment, ice and possibly a trocar for blood withdrawal from the wound site. He realised he would have to distance himself from his good friend and use science and surgery instead of emotions and hopes. Even if MacDonald managed to survive his injuries and the operation, there was an extremely high chance of fatal infection, given the presumption that a rat had gnawed into and perhaps out of his abdominal cavity. Joseph Bleak involuntarily shivered while staring at his patent leather shoes.

The cab swung violently through the hospital gates, almost overturning as it did so. It came to a sudden, jerking halt. Bleak lurched forward and steadied himself with both outstretched hands. Time seemed to have stood still for the Doctor, it seemed only a matter of minutes since he had left his Whitehall home, but he realised that the journey must have realistically taken a full fifteen minutes. He thanked the driver with a thump of the roof and dashed up the main entrance steps three at a time before bursting through the pallidly painted front doors.

"Professor Godlee is in the process of scrubbing up Sir," announced the nurse who had been awaiting his arrival and was to assist during the operation. "He arrived nary five minutes before you," she said in a composed and confident voice.

"Thank you, Nurse Dowds," smiled Bleak as he raced down the corridor to the preparation room while the nurse struggled vainly to keep apace behind him. '*So, Sir*

Rickman Godlee was also to be in attendance. CID has gone straight to the top,' thought Bleak. Godlee was the current president of the Royal College of Surgeons, Surgeon to his Majesty, and the preeminent medical man of his day. The first man in history to ever have removed a brain tumour and greatly respected the world over. *'The authorities are obviously desperate to save MacDonald,'* ruminated Bleak. Perhaps, the persistent rumours and the Scotsman's subtle boastings were in fact true. There was a prevailing school of thought, not actively discouraged by MacDonald, that the office he held as Superintendent was a cursory one and that he was actually involved in something of much higher import. Secret government work or some such. The presence of Sir Rickman Godlee would certainly reinforce this premise.

"Friend of yours I believe," stated Godlee nodding a welcome to Bleak on his entering the preparation room. Bleak noted pointedly that this was a statement rather than a question. "Yes, we are friends and fellow members of the Demosthenes Club in Pall Mall."

"I know of it. Too much chitter-chatter for my liking. I am an Athenaeum man myself. I listen to and give talks and lectures every single day and I so relish the silence my club offers. Time to actually think! Let me know if you want in old boy, I could arrange it. A step up from the Demosthenes," grinned Godlee. Bleak politely declined as the two surgeons, having completed their ablutions, entered the operating theatre simultaneously.

"I will lead on this one Doctor Bleak. I was instructed by the highest authority in the land to attend to Mr MacDonald's injuries. I can only imagine that your Demosthenes friend is of extreme importance to the Realm itself. Your assistance and expertise will, of course, be most valuable. By the look of the task in front of us, an extra pair of experienced hands will most certainly be required."

Bleak noted that the anaesthetist in attendance was Doctor Atkins, again, a man at the very top of his professional tree. Atkins bowed the slightest nod of recognition to the two surgeons. Nurse Dowds stood to the rear of the operating theatre ready for any requests. The atmosphere in the theatre was heavy and tense, the situation before them, grave.

"Then let us begin gentlemen," announced Godlee with a flourish of his gloved hand. The chest wall was all but obliterated and it was obvious that there was major trauma to MacDonald's right lung. "It is most fortunate that the vermin took the shortest route of escape as this has left the major organs almost entirely intact," proclaimed Godlee. "The resultant pneumothorax caused by the trauma requires one lung to be sacrificed but we can deal with that secondarily. The most vital thing at hand is to halt the bleeding. The huge loss of blood and the pressure this misplaced blood is having upon his vital organs is a major concern for failure occurring. If we can quickly staunch the bleeding and patch up this infernal mess, I believe he may still have some remote chance of survival. We must use phenol extensively as an antiseptic agent to counteract any bacteria present but even then, there is the very real chance of haemorrhage, sepsis or systemic infection still occurring. The Reaper's scythe is raised but not yet swiped," extolled Godlee in his rather melodramatic manner.

"Doctor Bleak, can you please extract the pooled blood so we can properly ascertain our priorities more clearly," instructed Godlee. The trochar remained stationary on the instrument table. Bleak stood motionless as if spell-bound, his lower left eyelid twitching almost imperceptibly. "Bleak!" roared Godlee. "Snap out of whatever entrances you man. This patient, your friend for Heaven's sake, desperately requires our intervention. Now!" Bleak suddenly snapped from his fugue state and swiftly administered gauze sheets to soak up the copious amounts of blood collecting within the wound cavity.

Wiggins sat sombrely at his boss' bedside. A bedside that contained an experimental new contraption, that of an iron lung. It was constructed out of a set of huge bellows and a sealed iron cage which enveloped MacDonald's chest, allowing him to breathe more easily after his pneumonectomy. Sir Rickman Godlee and his South African collaborator, Dr William Stueart, had been developing the instrument over the previous seven years in conjunction with Oxford University. Their latest working prototype was requested by the government specifically for MacDonald's treatment. Wiggins rotated his hat by the brim repeatedly, keeping in time with the exhalations of the bellows. He had been sitting there thinking for several hours, ever since Doctor Bleak had informed him that, despite several worrying and alarming moments, the near fourteen hours of surgery had gone as well as they could have ever expected. Antibacterial therapy was now being administered by a team of nurses every four hours. '*Time was now the healer*,' thought Wiggins. '*Only time and the Chief's will to survive can save him now.*'

The shrouded figure glided silently down the corridor, its rheumy eyes searching for the room. The Master had said that the police guard would not be here at this time. Feather did not question how the Master would know this, he simply accepted that it would be the case. The master was never wrong. He located the room and reached out a heavily scarred hand to noiselessly turn the doorknob. Feather was, as his name implied, ideally suited to this type of work. He was blessed with a lightness of touch that enabled him to almost float unseen and unheard in places where others could not. Once inside the room, he closed the door and drifted towards the bedside of Chief Superintendent MacDonald like a wraith. MacDonald was unconscious, the iron lung's gentle metronomic wheezing filling the room. Feather gently undid the iron lung's clasts and lifted the hinged middle portion of the machine, before withdrawing a parchment envelope from beneath his robes. From this, he removed a fine translucent webbing, unfolded it and applied it gently to the wound across MacDonald's abdomen. The light from the lamp suspended above the prone police officer caught the Leper's outstretched arm and highlighted the faint silver feather tattoo lightly inked into his forearm.

Once the webbing was in place Feather produced a hypodermic syringe. Carefully, as the Master had shown him, he found a prominent vein in the back of MacDonald's hand and depressed the plunger until all the liquid within had found its home. Satisfied that his task was complete, he gently stroked MacDonald's brow, lowered his pock-ridden face, and whispered in the Detective's ear. "Sleep well, my Prince." Feather disappeared phantom-like back to the leper house within the grounds of the hospital.

Nurse Dowds knocked fervently on the office door of Professor Godlee. "Enter!" came the stern reply. She entered and stood before Sir Rickman whose eyes were fixed firmly on some research manuscript he was critiquing. "Yes, Nurse. How can I help you?" he enquired slowly lifting his head, his spectacles resting precariously on the very tip of his nose.

"It's the patient in room twenty-two, Sir. Something strange with his vital signs, Sir."

"What do you mean exactly by, something strange?" questioned Godlee, somewhat intrigued.

"Best you see for yourself Sir," responded a hesitant Nurse Dowds, turning for the corridor.

The two medics soon stood at MacDonald's bedside. "You see his pulse has slowed to an almost comatose rate Sir. His blood pressure is impossibly low at sixty over forty. Notice if you will the bruising that has emerged on the back of the patient's hand, as if he has been injected with a hypodermic needle," detailed Nurse Dowds. Puzzled, Godlee unsecured and opened the outer casing of the iron lung which now did MacDonald's breathing for him. "What is this covering the wound? Some sort of webbed dressing," exclaimed the Professor. "What on earth is going on here?"

Both Nurse Dowds and the Professor turned their attention from the prone form in front of them to the owner of the voice who stood nonchalantly leaning against the door frame of the side room. The striking figure tipped his hat at the nurse and smiled. "Spider silk. From the Darwin bark spider to be precise. It is constructed from protein fibres and is five times stronger than tensile steel of the same diameter and thirty times finer than your traditional sutures. The cells in human skin absolutely adore its adhesive bonding properties. I am not entirely sure why yet but mark my word, I will find out. It has proved an extremely efficient accelerant to the human healing process on many an occasion. I can personally testify to its efficacy." He smiled once more at Nurse Dowds who seemed fascinated by the exotic stranger's miscoloured eyes and facial scarring.

"Who the devil are you and what are you doing in my hospital?" roared Sir Rickman. He looked to MacDonald and then back to the interloper. "More to the point what have you done to my patient! How dare you! This man's life is in severe jeopardy."

"It was but is now less so. Let me introduce myself, I am Van Hoon," bowed the Leper, resplendent in his usual finery, his head almost reaching the hem of his three-quarter length turquoise frock coat. "I am an ally and a friend, and as you may have already guessed a dabbler, you may say, in the natural and organic sciences."

"I don't care who you are, I want you out of my hospital immediately," shouted an irate Sir Rickman, approaching Van Hoon threateningly, his already florid face turning a deep shade of puce. "This is a hospital, not some medical sideshow for charlatans and purveyors of snake oil." Van Hoon laughed as he unsheathed his sword cane and waved it nonchalantly in the Professor's general direction, peacefully thwarting the surgeon's approach. "I would halt where you stand Sir. There is nothing that would appeal to the aesthete in me more than to slice off those ghastly mutton chops you sport. Just because they are fashionable it does not mean they are correct. Besides, I sense that your increased heart and pulse rate serves your blood pressure no good whatsoever."

Nurse Dowds suppressed a giggle behind her hand. Whilst Sir Rickman raged inwardly. The observant nurse glanced once more at MacDonald's hand. "What have you injected him with? It seems that whatever it was has slowed down his metabolic rate so as all bodily animation has been suspended."

"Suspended animation! Inspired!" returned Van Hoon gleefully. "How accurately descriptive a turn of phrase my dear. I shall refer to it as such henceforth." Van Hoon could see that Sir Rickman had slumped, bewildered on to a bedside chair. "The parasitic wasp of the South Americas, Sir. Its sting injects a venom into its prey which, whilst keeping the victim perfectly alive, immobilises it by slowing down its metabolism to the point of near death. This allows the Senorita wasp to lay its eggs inside the sleeping prey and eventually, once hatched, use the unfortunate victim as their first food source. Nature can be so unnecessarily cruel at times don't you think nurse?" asked Van Hoon. Nurse Dowds nodded hesitantly in response. "The solution that we have administered to Superintendent MacDonald has already lapsed him into a coma which will shut down all but the most vital functions of his metabolism, allowing his body to pinpoint the area most in need and recuperate and heal more quickly. The serum accelerates internal organic healing whilst the webbing accelerates the external epidermis to recover more rapidly and effectively. You could classify it as a win-win situation."

Sir Rickman stared at Van Hoon shaking his head slowly in disbelief. "I have never read of such matters in any journal. You must publish your research findings. Why, this could be a revolutionary leap forward in post-surgical healing, man!" he exclaimed rubbing the nape of his neck.

"You may call it revolutionary, Professor, Mother Nature calls it evolutionary," smiled Van Hoon. "Your expert surgical skills have given Mr MacDonald an excellent chance of recovery. All I have done is hastened his healing process." His enigmatic gaze turned to Nurse Dowds. "Now my dear, I hear that there is a most agreeable teahouse no more than a brief stroll from here. Would you care to join me?" The nurse threw a questioning glance back towards the bewildered surgeon as Van Hoon gently guided her by the elbow.

Wiggins had been summoned to the bedside of MacDonald later that week. He arrived at the hospital to be greeted by an uncharacteristically animated Nurse Dowds, her normal professional composure seeming to have been temporarily replaced by an excitement that Wiggins found surprising and uplifting.

"Mr MacDonald has regained consciousness much earlier than anyone would have expected Sir," she enthused as both she and Wiggins marched purposefully along a freshly painted corridor. Wiggins was always slightly suspicious of the smell of fresh paint. He had always prompted his young protégé that it may in some cases indicate a desire to cover up or obliterate some sort of evidence. "His healing has been greatly accelerated under the most remarkable of circumstances."

"How so, nurse?" enquired a relieved yet curious Wiggins. "A gentleman of a most striking nature assisted us with some rather unconventional treatments, all of which have produced rather miraculous results." Realisation dawned within Wiggins. "Would this most striking gentleman go by the name of Van Hoon perchance?"

"Why, yes Inspector. Do you know him?"

"We are most definitely acquainted, although I believe no man on earth can say they *know* Dante Van Hoon. Though I must say with some caution that his motives and methods are questionable, to say the least."

"Well his methods have certainly helped save your colleague's life and I can only imagine that he did so for the correct motives," countered a rather prickly Nurse Dowds. "Besides, I found him to be most charming." Wiggins frowned. "I am obliged to warn you of any sort of dalliance with Mr Van Hoon, no matter how casual. He is, without doubt, one of the most dangerous men in the world and to say he moves in circles that are perilous is an understatement."

They walked together stride by stride turning into the short corridor that served the private ward where MacDonald was being treated. Wiggins could sense a slight tension emanating from his companion. As they approached the door to MacDonald's side room, Wiggins halted. "What is the Superintendent's medical status nurse?"

"Normally what he has gone through would have resulted in almost certain death. However, Professor Godlee's surgical skills along with Mr Van Hoon's radical new treatments have certainly given him an increased chance of survival. The very real threat of infection from the rat bites is enormous, but for the time being, he is stable although he remains in a critical condition. When he regained consciousness earlier today, he immediately asked for you to attend his bedside." Wiggins nodded thoughtfully.

They entered the room quietly. Wiggins was taken aback at how small and frail MacDonald looked, lying as he was in the hospital bed. The previously vibrant and energetic Scottish warrior now appeared shrunken and diminished. As MacDonald's eyes focused on Wiggins, he began to attempt to raise himself up. Nurse Dowds attended him, helping to prop him up with pillows. MacDonald beckoned eagerly to Wiggins in a weak voice, "Come here laddie, I need to talk with ye urgently." Wiggins sat down on the edge of the bed beside his superior officer as Nurse Dowds began to ready her thermometer.

"Away with ye lassie stop fussing. I'm the same temperature I wiz ten minutes ago," protested MacDonald in what Wiggins noted was a mere whisper in comparison to MacDonald's normal bark. "I think it may be prudent if you were to give us some time alone, Nurse," reassured Wiggins. Nurse Dowds nodded and made to make her departure. "No more than ten minutes now," she instructed. Wiggins turned to MacDonald who was now clutching weakly at the younger officer's wrist. "How do you feel, Sir? It seems somewhat of a miracle that you are still with us after that dreadful ordeal. Nurse Dowds tells me that Van Hoon has played quite a part in your recovery."

"Never mind any of that laddie. I'm afraid I might have told them," writhed the Superintendent.

"Told them what, Sir? What did they want from you?" questioned Wiggins pre-empting and preparing for a shock.

"I couldna' help it, you understand. The pain was unbearable, and they had injected me with some sort of narcotic to make me blabber the truth to them. The rat was merely a twisted evil maniac's way of serving me a slow and painful death," MacDonald shuddered at the recollection. Wiggins could see that the older man was close to shedding tears of shame. He took MacDonald's hand in his. "There is no shame here, Sir. You fought as bravely as any man could. What is it they want? What do you suspect you told them?"

"The plague, Son. It's the plague they want," moaned MacDonald his chin lowering to his chest.

Wiggins was astounded. "But London has been free from the plague for generations, Sir. It was eradicated." MacDonald lifted his weary eyes back towards Wiggins. "It is here, laddie. It has always been here."

"But where, Sir. Where?" pleaded an oddly confounded Wiggins.

"The virus exists here in London. It is kept under high security within the laboratories of the Cruciform Building in Euston. They want it to control absolute power with the threat of mass death and, knowing the evil ways they work, there is the very real fear of them causing a cataclysmic event. Get it, laddie. Get to it before those yellow fiends or London will be engulfed once more by the walking death of the black plague."

Chapter 23 - The Clerk

'*I'm only an office clerk! I've only been here six months for Heaven's sake.*' Harold Rubenstein had only just turned sixteen years of age, but he had been feeling sick to the pit of his stomach for over a week now. That hollow empty feeling of nervousness and apprehension at the prospect of what he had been ordered to do and at what he was now on the verge of doing. '*HaShem, why am I doing this? Why am I even attempting this? I'll lose my job.*'

He had been secretly holed up in a ladies' water closet on the ground floor of the Home Office building in Whitehall, hiding there for over an hour waiting on the vast majority of staff to leave for home for the day. He had decided that the ladies' WC would present a safer squirrel hole than the Gents. He knew of only two women that were employed in the building, one of them being a cook with a squint eye and an unpleasant penchant for teenage boys, and the other a cleaner who ambled around, despite the apparent affectation of rickets, aimlessly mopping floors that she had mopped but hours before. '*Could even end up in Pentonville and for what? All for the sake of Uncle Jabez wanting some wretched architectural plans.*' Young Harold knew that Uncle Jabez was not a man to be trifled with. He was a ruthless man of great power, and would not countenance failure, even on the part of his youngest nephew.

Harold had discovered a new hobby and had been practising it for the past sixty minutes. He was seeing how far he could spit a fingernail. The ends of his fingers were now almost bereft of alpha keratin as his nervousness and excitement had necessitated him eschewing his grandmother's grave warnings of biting his fingernails. "Oy vey, oy vey, you chew enough of your nails, a horn will grow out your back sonny!" she had decreed sternly one day. He did not know how much actual truth that bizarre sentence contained, probably absolutely zero, but a warning from Grandma Mandelbaum was a warning to be heeded.

Thwupt! Another sliver of protein disappeared over the cubicle door. He had discovered that distance was controllable, but direction was an entirely uncontrollable arbitrary affair. With no more fingernails remaining he looked at his watch. Seven-twenty it read. It was time to make Uncle Jabez an immensely proud man, either that or he would end up in the Tower for treason or worse still, beheaded at the King's royal request. Young Harold Rubenstein removed his shoes, tied their laces together, looped them over his neck, took a deep breath and composed himself for his mission.

Two security guards operated during the back shift as it was termed. Harold knew that one stayed firmly rooted at the front door reception desk for his entire shift due to a mixture of lethargy and apathy. The other, he understood, wandered the corridors in a rather random fashion, which made his ascent and access to the third-floor office to which he needed to gain entry, a rather risky endeavour.

The secret to him successfully completing his mission, he had decided, was to remain as silent as possible during the whole undertaking. The darkness of the building at night was a kindly and welcome accomplice but any sudden or unexpected sounds could bring a crashing halt to the assignment with which he had been charged. He slowly opened the door to reveal an empty corridor down which he proceeded to walk on the tips of his stocking soled feet. This simple passage seemed to take an age to traverse but he was as silent as a church mouse and as stealthy as the cat hunting it. Having successfully made his way to stairwell number two, he stopped and peered up through the two further levels. He could see nobody, and his ears were met with reassuring silence. Harold's heart thumped within his chest like a piston in a well-greased engine, and he made a concerted effort not to succumb to his rising adrenalin levels. He nimbly negotiated the two flights of stairs, albeit slowly, adhering to his predetermined method of progress. After all, he had all night to make good his task. There should be no rush. He pictured an Arthur Rackham illustration in a book of Aesop's Tales he had read the previous year in which a smiling tortoise triumphs over a hare in a race.

Up ahead stood the frosted glass-fronted door to the room that he knew contained Uncle Jabez's particular golden fleece. A brass door sign read 'Architects Drawing Studio'. Harold rather oddly and inopportunely found himself questioning the validity of the sign's punctuation. *'Should the word architects be punctuated with an apostrophe or not?'* he puzzled. He knew that Security locked all office doors at six-thirty, but nevertheless, he tried the door handle, more in hope rather than expectation. It was, as he expected, locked. He pulled, from his waistcoat, a small device given to him by his Uncle Jabez specifically for gaining entry to a locked room. His Uncle Jabez had been given this special lock-picking tool by a man called Alfred C. Hobbs thirty years before during a meeting with the renowned American locksmith. It consisted of a small set of several long, pointed iron picks of various shapes and peculiar angles and profiles. Harold turned his attention to the door lock barring his entry. His furrowed forehead knitted in concentration, whilst his hands flitted about the lock with faint metallic scratching sounds. Perspiration stung his eyes making it difficult to angle the appropriate lock pick. It was, however, a relatively simple lock design and within ten minutes, and having used three different picks, it opened with a sharp click. Harold held his breath. There came only silence.

On entering the room Harold immediately recognised the long-drawered blueprint cabinets used for storing architectural plans. His heart sank as there seemed to be hundreds of these drawers but on closer inspection, he found that fortunately, each was alphabetised. He pulled out the first drawer labelled 'C' as deliberately and as quietly as he possibly could. To his horror, the drawer squeaked like a dying mouse. Harold's face wore a fixed grimace until the drawer had been fully extended. Leafing through the plans, as one would fan or pan a deck of cards, he noted that the contents of each drawer were also internally alphabetised. Cruciform, he thought to himself and proceeded to slide open the second from last drawer labelled 'C'. A most definite lucky strike! Fortunately, it did not take long for Harold to locate the set of plans for the Cruciform building on Gower Street and he set about rolling them into a tube and securing them with a length of twine. He then returned the drawer and headed for the door.

Harold peered out into the corridor before beginning his return journey to the ladies' water closet where he planned to wait until morning to make good his escape. He glanced at his watch. It was now almost ten o'clock. It had taken him over two hours to make the painstakingly slow journey and he suspected it may yet take another hour of stealth to complete the return trip. As he was nearing the same staircase he had ascended, he heard the unmistakable sound of footsteps followed by the light beam of a hand-held petrol lamp leave a room at the farthest end of the corridor. Harold stopped in his tracks and gently leant against the wall hoping the darkness would not betray his whereabouts. He was immobile with fear and did not notice that he was involuntarily holding his breath. The guard locked the door he had just exited and proceeded to start down the stairs of stairwell one at that end of the hallway. An idea instantly came to Harold. As the light dimmed and the guard began descending the stairs opposite, he swiftly leapt from his stationary position onto the bannister and glided silently down and around the stairs reaching the bottom before the guard had even reached the first-floor landing. He then slid like an ice skater along the polished floor tiles and silently returned to the Ladies' whereupon he sat in a toilet cubicle awaiting morning when he would make his leave and deliver the plans to his Uncle Jabez.

Chapter 24 - The Speech

The town hall in Bethnal Green was standing room only. 'Votes for Women' was emblazoned across a printed banner that hung high above the stage. A stage where the striking figure of Miss Agatha Harkness, the daughter of Viscount Lord Harkness, now stood. She was to close the rally with a few words, and she had intentionally dressed down for this evening's talk. She had deliberately not worn any jewellery or applied any makeup before attending. After all, she was speaking to, and trying to impress and recruit, ordinary working-class women to the cause. The last impression she wanted to give was one of privilege and wealth, ostentatious or otherwise. As she saw it, the only difference between her and the audience gathered before her was genetics. The packed hall was comprised, almost exclusively, of women of varying ages who clapped politely at her arrival, eagerly anticipating what she had to say. Oblivious to the hullabaloo, a pretty little girl sat on her mother's lap playing contentedly with a homemade clothes-peg doll. "Be still Pamela," her mother whispered in her ear.

"Friends and fellow citizens, I stand before you this evening as a member of the Women's' Social and Political Union. A union founded by my close friend Emmeline Pankhurst. Since 1903 our campaign to gain the right for women to vote has slowly been building credence and gaining momentum and indeed favour amongst differing levels of society. As I look out, I can see some familiar faces. Faces that stood alongside myself, Emmeline and Christabel during the Mud March. That was six whole years ago now and I find myself asking what has changed?" She paused. "Nothing has changed. Why, only yesterday, the Speaker banished our hopes of an amendment to include women in the Reform Bill. I am sick to death of all these reform bills, even the name Bill is male!" several chuckles emanated from the crowd.

"This vile beast that runs amok slaying innocent women in our city … do you think for one moment that this is the work of a woman? Why only a man can behave in such a perverse and evil manner."

"So, we must continue to fight, to protest, to educate. Of course, there are difficulties and yes, of course there are dangers, but we need actions, not mere words, to make a proper fist of this. A fist strong enough to finally punch the democratic process of our great country smack in its chops and bring it headlong into this still virginal century." The audience again laughed, and Miss Harkness smiled in return. She let a few seconds pass, lowered her tone, before becoming more serious.

"Yes, we must be rebellious. Yes, we must be brilliant as well as militant. So long as we as women allow us to be unfairly governed, we will be. As Emmeline stated, I would rather be a rebel than a slave. Any means of success is validated. We can chain ourselves, we can fire raise, and we can starve ourselves. Yes, we have been abused, and yes there have been deaths, but we must continue to fight, to protest. To win! We can all be heroes but together we can be heroic. Together we can unite and transform this land. So, come forth and join us in the fight. A fight that is just. A fight that is true. A fight that is long overdue. A fight that will conclude with half the population of this country having been given a voice. Deeds, not words, ladies!"

Pamela's doll fell to the floor as her mother stood with the enthusiastically applauding audience. DCI Wiggins, one of only three gentlemen in attendance, stood silently at the rear of the Hall, mesmerized.

The large Irish Ragger sidled awkwardly up to Pyke. "Moind if I join you Sergeant Pyke?" asked the heavily tattooed big man, dragging a stool across the flagstone floor to sit his six-foot-two-inch frame next to Jem Pyke. Pyke hunched over a whisky, both elbows resting on the ring stained hardwood bar, nodded his head "Free country ain't it Don. Help yourself." Pyke continued to use his penknife to trace over the groove of some long before scratched autograph on the mahogany bar top. The first two letters were S and E.

Once he had ensured that Little Crumb was safely incarcerated at Scotland Yard, Pyke had decided to come straight to The Grapes that afternoon. His excuse of following up possible leads with some of his informants had not entirely fooled Wiggins. However, the detective inspector knew his Sergeant well enough to realise that he would be of more use out on the cobbles mixing with the underworld with which he had so many connections than waiting helplessly at the hospital bedside of Superintendent MacDonald. Pyke's penknife dug away at the remaining letters etched into the bar top, V, E, R, I and N, unclogging years of greasy dirt from their grooves. *'Who was Severin?'* he wondered.

The stool let out a painful creak as the Irishman lowered his powerful frame upon it. He waved a hand to Hungry Mary. "I prefers me whisky spelt with an 'e' so two drops of the proper Oirish Mary. I've been paid today so none of that rotgut you usually serve up," he joked with a mischievous twinkle in his eye. Pyke turned towards the Irishman. "You now have my undivided attention, Don. What's on your mind? Not another brawl?"

"Sorry for the other night, Jem, you caught me right in the middle of what you might call a transaction."

"No harm done, well not to me anyways," sniffed Pyke swallowing back the whisky in front of him. He shot Mary a friendly smile as she placed the two freshly poured glasses of Jameson's on the bar.

"You do know they're double the price of the normal stuff Donnecha?" explained Mary so as there would be no possible confusion about payment.

"Paying double for the privilege of drinking something that is distilled instead of something that is distasteful is worth every penny, Mary me gal. And anyways, I got well paid today. Bit of a result." There was a brief silence between the two men as their glasses clinked together.

"Sláinte."

"Cheers to your health as well, Donnecha Savage."

Both men swallowed and slammed the empty glasses upon the bar. The Irishman nodded to Mary who topped them both up. "Fancy a beer with that Don?" asked Pyke wiping the back of his hand across his mouth. "Why not Mr Pyke. Might as well be hung for a sheep as a lamb."

"So, to what do I owe this display of unexpected camaraderie then Donnecha?" asked Pyke accepting a glass of frothing ale from his favourite barmaid. The Irishman coughed. "I heard about your pals, the coppers who were killed. Mostly young uns I heard. An awful thing. That bastard Little Crumb deserves to take the long walk for that, else put him in a room with the bereaved relatives," snarled the Irishman swilling back the whiskey with relish. He wiped the back of his hand across his bushy black beard and slammed the empty glass down onto the bar. "Two more, Mary, Luv."

"What can I do for you Savage?" asked Pyke turning to the ragger. Donnecha Savage drew a deep breath and leaned closer to the policeman. "Well, Jem, me and some of the lads around here just wanted you to understand that we'd like to help in any way we can. There are some terrible people in these parts and some of them do terrible things from time to time, but we all have wives. For Christ's sake Jem I have two daughters. It could be any of them next time that Beast of yours pounces. Can't bear to think of it. We may be a disparate mob of characters, but despairing times need desperate measures. We all want this monster off the cobbles and thrown away to rot. Even better, we want the scum dead, and there's plenty around here, meself included, who would be more than willing to do it, and at no cost neither." Pyke looked at the shaven-headed Irishman and nodded knowingly in agreement.

"You're an old soldier Jem," continued Savage, "... and you now have at your disposal a ready-made army willing to stand beside you, right here in Limehouse. Some say you to be the toughest man in all of London, and if so, I'd wager there ain't too many between you and me, so why not have me and the lads at your side and see this nightmare end. Now."

Pyke slugged down the remainder of his Jameson's. "This is definitely a superior drop this Irish. Potent with an honest kick to it. Could describe yourself, Don, to be honest. I appreciate your offer and I will, how do they say? Take it under serious consideration." The big Irish rogue smiled, rolled his enormous shoulders and slapped Pyke on the back. "That's settled then, Sergeant Pyke. That's for another day, however, so ready yourself for a sore head the morn, boy, some incoming Irish. Mary! How much for the remains of that there bottle?"

Chapter 25 - The Bad Seed

Shifty Simpson cursed as he jemmied open the ground floor rear door of the pawnbrokers in Fishbone Alley. '*Toots!*' Shifty cursed inwardly. '*Blasted Hymies always have the best locks,*' he thought admiringly. He had always marvelled at how much better Jewish businessmen protected their property in comparison to their gentile brethren. Shifty realised that he should have known better by now than to break into one of Rubenstein's places, but an order from King was an order from King after all. No one, but no one crossed the Chinaman, not even the Italians or those lunatics the Grice Brothers, and Shifty should know. He worked for all of them. He did not discriminate where money was concerned. He could spend a Shekel just as easily as a Yuan. If there was one dock rat in the Thames Basin that you went to if you wanted someone's something to become your something, it was Shifty Simpson. And now that Harry Filch seemed to have vanished from the cobbles altogether, Shifty's unique talents were in even greater demand than ever.

The previous night Shifty had watched the premises for comings and goings, surveyed it one might say. The derelict tenement building next door had been simple enough to enter. Although derelict and decrepit, it was not empty, occupied as it was by numerous down at heel families, each risking life and limb residing in what was essentially a death trap. He had walked gingerly up the unstable staircase, holding a grubby handkerchief over his mouth and nose in a vain attempt at masking the stench of human depravity and ordure. He stepped around a small forlorn looking girl of no more than five years old. She sat on the second floor flight, clutching a rat nibbled stuffed toy to her grubby cheek. Her eyes showed little if any emotion as Shifty made his stealthy way past her, flashing her what he regarded as a friendly smile whilst putting his index finger to his closed lips in an effort to keep her quiet. He clambered expertly up through the ceiling hatch and out onto the 'London' roof. He skilfully scampered up the Welsh slates of the abandoned building, up over the roof ridge and slid cautiously down the opposite slope into the lead-lined valley of the pawnbroker building. '*Damn! No skylight.*' Shifty Simpson cursed his customary curse. '*Toots!*'

Shifty grinned as his crowbar splintered the door frame. '*Nearly there.*' One more yank and he would be inside. Shifty was very thin, a real Will 'o the Wisp some said, which was especially convenient for his clandestine labours. His distinct lack of girth was especially helpful for slipping in and out of barely cracked open doors. He was once known as the Whippet. That was a long time ago now. In his younger days when he had been the fastest of the Great Detective's Irregulars, and as such, the one most often rewarded with the magical guinea piece. Wiggins was the cleverest, but Shifty had been the one they invariably turned to when they needed something whipped. Something swiped. He was the one who could shift quicker than any of the others. Fleet of foot and fast of thought. In and out like a ferret down a hole or a rat up a drainpipe.

Shifty made his way down to the ground floor jewellers. The room at the back of the shop was empty, silent save for the detached sound of an occasional cab bustling by outside. Dust particles danced in the thin beam of moonlight that shone in through the partly opened door. Shifty carefully and expertly closed it behind him and stood completely still for a few moments, allowing his eyes to adjust to the dimness of the interior. Twenty years of burglary had, he liked to think, trained his eyesight to operate more effectively in gloom and darkness than the average honest man. Satisfied that there was no sign of movement, no creaking of floorboards, he withdrew from his overcoat a state-of-the-art battery-operated hand torch. This little beauty had been an immediate boon to Shifty ever since he had convinced Christopher Grice to provide him with one on a job a year or so previously. He shone its faint beam down towards the floor, careful not to raise it above knee height for fear that it may reflect out of one of the windows and catch the attention of a passing Bobby. "Toots!" cursed Shifty as he stepped on a loose floorboard that seemed to rasp out a creak that even deaf old Mutt Lonnergan would find difficult not to hear.

King had said that the plans would most likely be locked in a safe. All Shifty had been told was that they were valuable and that they had been pawned by a disgruntled employee in order to raise some cash and stick it to his ex-employers. All he had to do now was find the safe, crack it, finger the plans, and get them to King for the biggest payday of his life. Simple!

Shifty scanned the room with his beady eyes. It made sense that the safe would be back of house rather than out front. Piles of what Shifty regarded as junk and rubbish, mixed with more valuable looking items filled the room. Shifty decided that since he was already here, helping himself to a few choice items from the front shop would be the order of the day. He tried the connecting door and smiled, he was in luck, the doorknob turned silently in his scrawny hand and the door eased open. Shifty's smile broadened and his eyes widened as he entered. He was surrounded by locked display cabinets of more valuable merchandise. China, watches, jewellery and plate. He decided that his multi-pocketed coat could amply accommodate a few prize watches, rings, necklaces and brooches. He produced a kerchief sized felt pad from the recesses of his coat, laid it on the cabinet glass and pressed down swiftly and forcibly upon it with his elbow. The glass shattered with very little noise and Shifty helped himself to as much as he could stuff in his coat of many pockets. His own private haul satisfied, he returned to the back room in search of the safe. There was no freestanding safe in evidence, so he looked behind bookcases and paintings. There was nothing concealed within the walls.

He lifted his cap and scratched his all but bald pate. '*Unlikely that it would be upstairs; too heavy,*' he surmised. Then he remembered the creaky floorboard he had just trod on. He stamped gently around to try and relocate its whereabouts. Once he had found it, he put the torch between his stumpy yellow teeth and bent down to prise up the board. Dust puffed from the floor as he removed it to reveal a glimpse of metal beneath. '*Found you, you little beauty,*' he rejoiced. Ripping up the adjacent few boards, his joy turned to ecstasy as he realised that what he was looking at was a metal box rather than a safe. '*Jews,*' he smiled, '*too tight to even buy a safe.*'

Rather than waste time trying to unlock the box where he was, he decided that the best policy was to take the box itself. He replaced it with a small jade dragon that King had given him for this express purpose. This was King's calling card and would act as a warning to the Pawnbroker that informing the police would bring nothing but further and greater misfortune in the future. Shifty carefully replaced the floorboards, escaped the way he had entered and disappeared whistling into the fog-bound night.

King pored eagerly over the plans of the Cruciform Building, greedily devouring each tiny detail. He sniggered and clapped his hands with glee, his serpentine green eyes glimmering in the candlelight. He turned to the Poisoner who was standing to his immediate left. "Get the Shangs and a few others together. Tonight, we hunt the most valuable prize in all of London."

Shifty Simpson strained his neck upwards as far as his muscles and vertebral ligaments would allow. The manacles that secured him to the chains attached to the underside of the pier cut deeply into the flesh around his wrists and ankles. He wrenched and struggled as much as he could, the freezing temperature of the rising waters of the Thames made him almost impervious to the pain the manacles were inflicting. He was panic-stricken, encompassed by utter fear. He knew he had to make his whereabouts known but it was impossible for him to shout or scream. He tried desperately to spit the balled cloth from his mouth, but it was so tightly fastened in place with two lengths of rope that it made him gag constantly. The realisation that nobody was coming to his aid struck him like a train. The river lapped at his chin now, splashes of the polluted water finding their way through the cloth and into his mouth and up his nose. He stretched his face upwards and hyperextended his neck at an almost unmanageable angle, all the while drawing in great gulps of air through his nose, but he knew it was over. He had served his purpose. King never left any loose ends. '*Toots!*' He should have known this payday would never have been realised. He was a dead man walking the moment he had handed over those plans and now he was as good as dead. As the dirt ridden waters rose above his upper lip, he remembered his childhood, scampering through the docks on an errand for the Great Detective, fishing in the mud of the Thames with Bert Wiggins for belt buckles and dead men's boots. Now those boots would be his. He gulped down his final breath of air as the murk engulfed his nose and lapped over his eyes.

Chapter 26 - The Virus

"Cheese an' boiled ham again, I'll wager," muttered Charlie Schoon as he unwrapped the greaseproof paper that his wife Mildred had so neatly and lovingly wrapped around his lunchtime sandwiches earlier that morning. "Maybes a bit of best brisket or even some corned beef with a touch of piccalilli," he mumbled optimistically as the paper rustled open under his eager fingers. Charlie had noticed that he was talking to himself more and more lately. *'No harm in it,'* he thought. *'It's just the loneliness of the job. Long hours seeing nobody so no one to 'ear me anyways.'* Charlie had been night watchman or 'Head of security' as he liked to boast, at the mysterious gothic pile that was the Cruciform Building in Euston. The building was huge and complex. So huge in fact that most people walking down Gower Street, Grafton Way or Huntley Street were oblivious to its colossal looming presence standing over each thoroughfare. Almost invisible so total was its dominance. A similar anomaly as not seeing the wood from the trees. From the outside, it resembled an endless gothic church combined symbiotically with an ancient fortress. Its name came from the cruciform shape of its x-shaped footprint but its stunning architecture cloaked a rather more secretive purpose than its clerical appearance would indicate. Internally the building was a literal maze of baffling levels and corridors, a deliberately confusing rabbit warren of laboratories, lecture halls, study rooms, libraries and storage areas. On first appearance, it was more like a cubistic optical illusion rather than gothic revival architecture.

Charlie Schoon did the grave night shift, his job, to man the front desk in the medieval stylised front foyer of the building, guarding the mosaic floored entrance like a modern-day Heimdal. Of course, there were other security guards in a building of this size and complexity, each with their own duties and areas of patrol but Charlie was especially proud that he had been given charge of this small body of men. Forced into early retirement from the Force, due to injury sustained in the line of duty, he had never envisaged that he would take up another position of trust like this.

"Cheese an' ham, right enough," said Charlie with a resigned shrug of his coat-hanger shoulders, as he took his first and indeed his last bite of Mildred's sandwich. "Always cheese an' bleedin' ham," he sniggered. He chewed and thought of some nice cold brisket, little veins of tasty fat marbling its edges. As he lifted his supper towards his mouth for a second bite, he heard a sharp rap upon the main door. Charlie looked at the sandwich in his hand, then at the door and then again at the sandwich. "Bugger!" he cursed as he returned the sandwich neatly in its wrapper. "I'll just have to finish you off later. With a nice cup o' char with George in the basement labs."

That knock again, this time a fraction louder and a little bit more earnest. "Hold yer 'orses. I'm coming," shouted Charlie as he heaved himself up from his chair. The chair let out a creaking wooden sigh of relief at some brief respite from Charlie's bulk. His injury and enforced leave from the Force had taken its toll on his health due to lack of exercise and motivation causing him to *'put on a little bit of timber,'* as he jokingly referred to it. Charlie unsnapped the stud on the leather flap of his baton holster as he shuffled awkwardly towards the large double front doors of the building. He lamented the fact that these days it took him three or four stammering steps before his back fully straightened. *'Like the Ascent of Man,'* that high educated daughter of his would say. Charlie had never fully understood Darwin's theories. *'How can we be descended from monkeys, when there is still monkeys swinging around today?'* Charlie unbolted and opened the door to see a rather diminutive oriental gentleman standing before him, his collar pulled up high around his neck. "Yes? How can I 'elp you, Sir? You do realise that this is a restricted building ... and it is closed."

"A thousand apologies, my friend," replied the Oriental in somewhat broken English. "I am lost and look for the Station of Euston Square please?" He bowed and looked up towards Charlie expectantly. Charlie smiled, at once relieved at the sight of this harmless looking little man standing submissively in front of him. "Why you're almost there, little fella," replied Charlie enthusiastically. "Straight up this road and first street to your right," instructed Charlie pointing northwards up a relatively empty Gower Street. "You've missed the last train though matey," chortled Charlie.

"A million thank yous," bowed the Chinaman, seemingly oblivious to the fact that the Station was already closed. "How you do in England?" smiled the little man offering a gloved hand for Charlie to shake. Charlie took the proffered hand and shook it with a nod of his head and a smile. "No problem, matey, have a good night." As he turned to close the door the little Chinaman remained standing at the threshold, unmoving, a huge grin fixed upon his face. Charlie staggered several steps backwards and started to gasp, his breathing was laboured, his windpipe restricted somehow. He turned his right hand upwards only to see severe blistering bubbling up on his skin, increasing in intensity as he stared at his angry inflamed palm. By now the little Chinaman had stepped over the threshold and approached Charlie, smiling all the while. Charlie crumpled to his knees, now unable to breathe, his eyes almost popping out of his head in sheer panic. As his head hit the tessellated tiled floor, he thought of Mildred his wife, his well-educated daughter and a nice piece of finely marbled brisket.

The Poisoner closed the door behind him and stepped over Charlie's convulsing body. "A million and one thank yous," he grinned. He unhitched the copious bunch of keys from Charlie's belt, gleefully jangled them in front of Charlie's now purple bloated face and proceeded to head down the marble steps to the lower level and towards the rear exits of the building.

The Shang twins stood shoulder to shoulder as always in a tiny alley off Grafton Way to the rear of the Cruciform. Behind them was parked one of Mr King's deliberately anonymous motor cars. The driver sat as still and silent as the engine. All eyes were focused upon the rear door of the building through which they fully expected to see the Poisoner emerge at any moment. Inside sat Madame Huai and Mr King himself, patiently waiting, his hands clasped tightly together. A pencil line of light suddenly appeared as the rear basement door opened ever so slightly. Both Shang twins raised their hands to signal to the car's occupant that access had been gained. King smiled the evilest vilest of smiles.

"At last! Soon I will have in my hands the power to rule the whole of London, and as we know Huai, whoever holds London holds the World." King clapped his hands repeatedly together like a delighted, demented child as he spoke. Madame Huai did not clap. At that time of night, Grafton Way was all but deserted as the two occupants left the vehicle. Only the muted sound of distant coaches and cars trundling along Euston Road mixed with the general background hum of London at night could be heard. The Shang brothers ran across the street like conjoined twins and disappeared into the light of the partially open doorway. Both King and Huai, along with several dacoit cutthroats, followed and began crossing the street. The dacoits looked carefully from side to side to ensure their way was clear of any witnesses. King refused to be distracted by such trivialities and strode purposefully towards the door.

King knew from the plans secured for him by Shifty Simpson that the object of his late-night venture more likely than not lay in the secure vault in the deepest reaches of the sub-basement of the building. He strode confidently into the Cruciform flanked on each side by a Shang twin with the phalanx of murderous dacoits in tow. The Poisoner greeted him at the door with a staccato bow. "I shall not shake your hand," acknowledged King walking past him as he and his company of killers made their seemingly unconcerned way down the rear staircase into the secretive bowels of the building.

"Where's old Charlie got to anyhow?" enquired Mickey Milligan consulting his grandfather's hunter timepiece. It was five past twelve and Charlie was never late for their midnight communal cup of tea. "Regular as me morning dump is our Charlie," he mused, snapping shut the lid of the old brass watch and replacing it in his waistcoat pocket.

"I dunno," responded Mickey's fellow night watchman, Archie Moore. "Should be 'ere by now. He's never late for his Rosy Lee." Archie scratched his head which rather comically resembled the back of a hedgehog. The two men stood either side of the double-locked steel doors directly behind them. "He ain't never missed a midnight brew these last six years." Both sets of eyes were fixed firmly on the double doors at the end of the corridor in front of them. Each man expectant that any second Charlie Schoon would turn his key in the lock and join them for their habitual midnight refreshment.

"He'll be 'ere any minute," reassured Mickey, but Archie felt a gradual feeling of unease creeping over him. He also sensed that Mickey too was slightly uneasy at Charlie's absence.

"Here he is. Must have been in the loo," smiled Mickey sighing in relief. The key turned in the lock and the double doors flew open. What befell their combined gaze was as far away from old Charlie Schoon as either man could have ever imagined. A slightly built, bald-headed oriental man strode confidently into the corridor. Archie recoiled at the evil that emanated from his face and the reptilian eyes drilling into his skull.

"Oi, you! You can't be in 'ere. Who are you?" Mickey Milligan barely got the words out of his mouth when they were replaced by a quivering dagger courtesy of one of the Shang twins. The blade sheared his mouth open vertically and struck the back of his throat. By the time Mickey had fallen to his knees, blood oozing from his throat, a dusk coloured dacoit was behind him slicing the remaining life out of him with a piano wire garrotte.

"Sweet Mary and Joseph!" implored Archie frantically. "Don't kill me! Please don't kill me. I've kids. Here take the keys, take the keys. I ain't seen nothin' please." He extended a helplessly trembling hand clutching and fumbling at a ring of brass keys. King nodded almost imperceptibly signalling one of the twins to snatch the hoop of keys so forcibly from Archie that he heard the strange click of his own fingers dislocating. So petrified was Archie that he felt not a thing as his fingers now lay at oblique angles. A dacoit placed a hand upon Archie's shoulder and pushed him trembling to his knees. Archie looked at the floor and sputtered out a quick prayer, his eyes clamped tightly shut, fully expectant of a bullet to the head or a knife to the throat. '*Some security guard I turned out to be,*' he thought to himself ruefully.

He heard the key turning in the lock. Archie recognised the tumblers roll as the vault door was opened. He could hear the familiar creak of the hinges. He sneaked a quick look at poor Mickey, blood pooling from his head onto the cold tiled floor. Archie started to sob uncontrollably, snot dribbling from his nose and tears from his eyes. He was kicked violently to the floor and lay on his side looking distraughtly into the dead eyes of his best friend who lay only inches away.

King stepped over Mickey's prone form and entered the secure underground vault of the Cruciform Building, confident in the knowledge that within lay a vial containing the pestilent virus with which he could wipe out half the population of London and have the other half do anything he so desired.

"Get rid of this one," he announced to no one in particular whilst waving in the general direction of the unfortunate Archie, "… and bring in the cleaners."

An oversized nondescript black van drew up to up to the kerbside outside the rear door of the Cruciform Building. So dense was the fog that a pedestrian standing on the opposite footpath would have been unable to discern anything but the vague outline of an indistinct shape. They would certainly have been completely incapable of reading the light grey lettering that adorned the side of the vehicle identifying its owner's occupation simply as 'Removals and Storage.'

"After you, Mr Critch," espoused a nasally feminine voice.

"Not at all, my dear. After you, Mrs Critch," responded an equally nasally male voice.

It has been speculated that pet owners subconsciously select pets that resemble themselves. In the case of the Critches, a casual observer could not but notice that, on occasion, the same could be said for one's selection of spouse. Mr and Mrs Critch descended from their van simultaneously, he straightening his high neck collar, she straightening her skirts. Both were dressed entirely in black and resembled nothing more than a pair of undertakers about to embark upon their duties. This assumption, had it been made, would have been remarkably close to the truth. Both were thin, wiry individuals with long angular features. Each had a nose so upturned that it may have proven a disadvantage in a heavy rainstorm. Neither wore a hat, a fact which exhibited one of the couple's few discernible physical differences. He was completely bald and utterly clean shaven. She sported jet black, dry and brittle hair which was pulled back into the severest of buns.

"Deathly night, Mrs Critch," observed Mr Critch in his thick Welsh accent.

"A right thick London Particular and no mistake, Mr Critch," responded Mrs Critch in her equally heavy Celtic brogue.

"All the better for the work ahead of us," smiled Mr Critch.

"Is it all right to come out now?" rumbled a low resonant voice from within the carriage of the van.

"Yes, come down Leonard, make a shift on son. Mr King has important work for us this night and time is a wasting," instructed Mr Critch.

The figure that lurched awkwardly from the cabin was that of a large, heavyset lad, sloping of shoulder and brow. It seemed impossible that this hulking lummox could possibly have been produced by the genes of two such slight individuals as Mr and Mrs Critch. Leonard opened the back doors of the van and lowered a ramp with a metallic clatter.

"Quiet boy!" hissed Mrs Critch "How many times have I told you, lad? You must make no noise." Mr Critch looked at his long, pointed shoes and shook his head.

"Sorry, mummy," bleated Leonard. "I won't makes no more sounds, I promise."

Mr Critch looked to the heavens. Leonard shuffled up the ramp and, as silently as he could, and soon re-emerged pulling a large tarpaulin covered cart, complete with vulcanised rubber tyres. The trio entered the building and was greeted by The Poisoner who escorted them to the scene of their upcoming activities.

"You have exactly twenty minutes to cleanse the area and remove all evidence of us having been here," ordered King as he strode directly past the Critch family. "The usual remuneration will await you in the usual place upon completion." As King departed, he held a cube-shaped leather case in which was secured a stoppered vial that contained approximately half of the viscous, deep yellowish ochre-coloured fluid that had previously been held within the strong room of the Cruciform. The other half, King had left in place, having gleefully topped it up with a pre-filled test tube of his own urine. "The fools will never notice that we have taken the deadliest form of virus known to man." He threw back his head and cackled with laughter.

The Critches stood aside and nodded as King and his entourage passed and proceeded to their grisly work of bleach and mop. The removal of the bodies would be swift and complete. The Critches always saw to that.

"It is probably nothing, officers, but I thought it prudent to advise you of the disappearances, given the secure nature of the Building and its contents." Professor Ericson Abel was a tall lithe man in his fifties who sported a trim goatee beard and a slim waxed moustache, curled at each end in the fashion off a Persian slipper.

Although his beard was manicured to within an inch of its life, his mop of curly hair was wild and unruly.

"Nonetheless, Professor Abel, you were wise to call this to our attention," responded Pyke scribbling in his notepad. Constable Murray peered at Pyke's customarily misspelt scrawl and decided to make his own notes, anticipating that they would prove more legible once they had returned to the Yard.

"So, three security guards vanished but nothing else stolen. No cash or securities? Items of value? Confidential documents?"

"None that we can ascertain Sergeant. We have carried out a full search and can find nothing amiss," confirmed the academic.

"Only we did hear a rumour that a certain flask of, how can I say it..." Pyke glanced at Murray, "...virulent liquid may be under threat."

Ericson Abel blustered, taken aback by the surmise. "If you are referring to what I think you are referring to, Officer, I have no idea how you have knowledge of such sensitive matters, but I can assure you, hypothetically speaking, that if such a substance was within our guardianship, it would have been the first item to which we would have looked. Putatively, nothing is missing."

"Quite so," added Pyke, one knowing eyebrow raised. "Look, Professor, there are no signs of forced entry and no indications of foul play. Is it possible that these three men simply decided to call it a day and walked out on their posts?"

"I could not possibly comment, Sergeant," answered an increasingly tetchy Professor. "All were of long-standing employ and of upstanding character. I find the whole affair quite baffling."

"Baffling indeed. Sir. We will contact the gentlemen's families and pursue our investigation down that route. Thank you for your time and for bringing this little mystery to our attention." Pyke shook the Professor's hand and strode for the door, closely followed by Constable Murray. As he marched over the stone threshold, he noted a slight scuff mark as if left by a bicycle tyre. He stopped, considered it for a few seconds, shrugged his shoulders and headed for Gower Street. "Fancy a swift pint Murray? The Euston Flyer is just around the corner, lad."

Chapter 27 - The Rebirth

Day was breaking and the sun had begun to rise through the early dawn mist revealing London's ghostly silhouette. The water appeared inviting and silvery from the sun's reflected glows but in truth the waters of the Thames estuary around the Isle of Sheppey still carried some of the City's filth, although a great deal of the detritus had been filtered and diluted by the time it had reached the Kent and Essex coasts. A small group of people, each carrying a sharp knife and with large wicker baskets slung over their shoulders, slowly waded out through the water in rows of seven, creating a strange, slowly advancing wave of threshing humanity. The group that laboured in the reed beds each day searching and slashing were mainly Bangladeshi immigrants. Once harvested and dried, the Bangladeshis would skilfully use the reeds to weave baskets and mats that they sold at markets. Their work was hard and laborious but was the only way available for them to make enough money to survive and support their extensive families.

The reed croppers spent every daylight hour harvesting their raw material, wading out until the water reached their chests and then wading back until the water barely covered their ankles. Again, and again, hour after hour. Their movements dislodged anything underfoot, creating silt which leeched between their toes and clung unremittingly to what little clothes they wore during their work. At this time of the year, it was bitterly cold, so they took it in turns to wade into the Thames. The hours of darkness would see the women drying the reeds over fires and weaving the grass into functional, intricate baskets of all shapes and dimensions.

The small band of croppers routinely dredged many strange items of debris from the murky waters. Most proved to be worthless, but now and again, small treasures such as silver buckles, coins, padlocks, and brooches found their way out of the mud. Boots, shoes and bottles were regular finds. Almost every week an animal carcass of some description would drift its way down river from the Meat Houses of the East End and find itself tangled in the reeds. On this morning, however, the river was about to regurgitate what was to be its strangest, most extraordinary and unexpected offering.

The group were about to finish their shift for the day and the light was fading fast. Their bodies were beginning to weary and shiver in the chill of evening. A roaring fire and the spicy mutton broth that always awaited them promised an inviting reward for their hard day's labours. It had been a respectable day's gathering with many full baskets of valuable reeds now ready for the drying out process. As they swept as one towards the shore for one final effort it was Faysal who initially tripped over something hard, hurting his foot. It startled the young man so greatly that the dao he was clutching dropped from his grasp and spilt into the water. Instinctively he reached down into the reeds where his knife had splashed. He rummaged around in the muddied water. He first dislodged a hand, a goliath sized hand, then, bubbling up through the watery reeds, a gargantuan monolith of an arm followed.

In utter shock, Faysel screeched out a high-pitched scream and ran, his knees pumping high out the water in fear of the apparition he had just disturbed. "Mr̥ta! Mr̥ta!" he shrieked. The turbulence he had created in his escape allowed the remainder of the mammoth hulking body to bob to the surface. Only a face resembling a huge Chinese mask was discernible at first, the rest of the body being half submerged in the water and reeds. The skin was icy blue and the lips had a dark purple hue. Faysel and his companions slowly approached the body. Suddenly and shockingly both eyes abruptly opened wide whilst the cavernous mouth gasped and spluttered frantically for life-giving air.

Old Father Thames had just given rebirth to Hercules Chin, delivering London's most feared henchman back into the world of the living.

Chin lay motionless on the bed with his eyes closed. The bed was far too small for him and his legs dangled at the knees where it ended. His throat was burning with a ferocity which frightened and confused him. Each breath wheezed out of his chest, his lungs seemingly reluctant to expand and contract. What had happened? Where was he? He was not entirely sure he even knew who he was. His head was full of fuzzy, half-remembered images. He recalled the frightening pain of the bullet impacting his shoulder. He recalled the feeling of the piercing icy water against his skin and that he had had no strength to escape its frozen embrace. Every muscle had been frozen rigid. He remembered the darkness closing in from all sides, engulfing him like a deathly shroud. The darkness was of a deep dark purple. Panic and fear had taken grip of his very being. He had never felt so helpless. His lungs were aching, his chest was fit to burst but he could not let go of this breath. This was the only air he had left! Semi-conscious with his brain and senses exhausted by oxygen depletion, he could only peer at the under-surface of the murky water. He then felt serenely peaceful as he floated downwards. Down. He saw his mother, then he saw Jao, the only two people that mattered to him. Then his thoughts ceased, his mind went blank and all was black.

It had taken enormous effort and a great length of time for the Bangladeshi basket weavers to transport the unconscious Chinaman to the place they now called home. It was Faysel who had pumped on the Chinaman's huge chest until he spewed out several mouthfuls of water. As soon as Chin had gasped for breath Sadik had recognised instantly that their discovery could be a huge asset to their work. Surely this amazing specimen of humanity could do the work of two if not four men!

Chin opened his eyes to the sight of an elderly dark-skinned woman offering up a bowl of steaming broth to his severely swollen lips. His entire body felt so distended and bloated that he found it difficult to move. He thought that the woman had nice kindly eyes. She smiled at him, offering up the hot spicy soup which he gladly accepted. The soup stung his throat ferociously causing him to gasp and cough. The room, he could see, was small and dimly lit by a single candle which gave off an aroma of cinnamon and tamarind. The giant Chinaman realised that he had been rescued from Death's clutches by a group of strangers. This thought made Chin feel good, wanted, loved.

Chin's recuperation at the hands of the Bangladeshi family took nearly three long weeks. The gunshot wound was cleansed and dressed daily using the soothing and healing properties of the bladderwrack seaweed found on the shoreline. His strength was gradually rebuilt on soups and spicy stews which, he eventually began to enjoy, the more his throat recovered. The air was fresher this far away from the City and it helped hasten the repair to his damaged throat and lungs so he could again talk if he so wished. Ojana was amazed at how copiously the Chinaman ate. She now had to radically increase the amount of food she prepared for the family meal, but she did not mind as she had grown to like her patient, so much so that she began to treat him just as she would any of her five sons. Ojana could speak no English and Chin could speak no Bengali but together they managed to converse through mime and facial expressions; mainly by pointing and gesturing but mostly by smiling at each other.

After several days of convalescence, Chin felt physically strong again. Although he felt replenished and healed, he now sensed something was missing from before. He could not determine exactly what or who was missing, just that something was absent. Something he longed for and needed but could not remember. How could he not remember, he thought? There were no memories of who he was, where he had come from or what had befallen him. He was just grateful to the family that had fished him from the water. A family Chin now found himself being a part of.

He liked the simple work of collecting reeds from the river all day, even on cold rainy days it was nice being outside instead of being confined inside the shack for days on end during his recovery. However, he disliked the wind, whipping up spray and hindering harvesting, but when the sun did shine Chin could daydream and make up stories in his head allowing the hours to pass by easily and swiftly. He would gaze at the gulls and imagine himself soaring through the fluffy clouds or picture himself on board a cargo ship happily bound for some faraway destination. Chin was also happy that he consistently produced the fullest baskets at the day's conclusion and felt proud that he could carry six at the one time. Most of the others could only struggle to carry two at best.

Evenings were spent with the men and children playing noisy games of Pitto while the women dried out the reeds ready for their weaving the following morning. His existence was one of simple contentment in the moment. His amnesia offered no past to dwell on and no future to concern him. He felt wanted and cared for.

Each evening before retiring, the eldest man in the family, Vidhu, would endeavour to teach Chin to read rudimentary English using any old scraps of newspaper he had found on their walk back home from work. Although Chin could speak rudimentary words and phrases, he had never had the opportunity, nor the inclination to learn to read. To begin with, Vidhu would pronounce each letter deliberately and phonetically and get the Chinaman to repeat it back several times. Then the elder would use several words containing that letter. Chin was a quick learner and he enjoyed the task being asked of him and besides, there was very little to do once the children were fast asleep? He began putting together the letters to pronounce the unfamiliar words he saw until he could read entire sentences from newspapers, hoardings, signs and street names.

The weeks passed, each day not dissimilar to the previous. Most days followed the same pattern with the harvesters rising at first light, and while they dressed, Ojana prepared each of them a bowl of oats mixed with rice and a little hot water. A finely diced apple would be sprinkled on top as a special treat on occasions such as birthdays or days when they had managed to sell a respectable number of baskets. If there was any spare time during the day Chin liked nothing more than to play with the children. All the youngsters adored him and were comfortable around the gentle genial giant. Chin liked to annoy the small ones by pretending to unscrew the tops of their heads with his massive hands and he would let the little ones win at Lukochuri by intentionally showing his huge feet or big behind sticking out from his hiding place. The 'seeker' would squeal with delight at finding the Chinaman then they would all collapse together in a heap of laughter.

One evening after feasting on dahl and flatbreads, Swapnil, the youngest of the five brothers, attempted to explain to Chin the circumstances surrounding his discovery in the reed beds. Chin watched intently and shook his massive head in disbelief as Swapnil traced waves in the dirt before holding his breath until he turned ruddy-faced, eventually capitulating and gasping for air. *'How could this be?'* thought the giant Chinaman, staring at the depiction of water drawn on the ground. This made no sense to him. Even he knew that if you swallowed and breathed in water you would drown and die. *'Why am I not dead,'* he wondered whilst loudly cracking his knuckles.

Each night Chin would gently lay his head on a jute pillow and close his eyes on another day. He would lie on his back in the darkness hoping there were would be no nightmares that night. He did not like his frightening dreams. Strange, vivid flashbacks began to regularly interrupt his sleep. A huge angry elephant, its huge foot poised to stamp down upon his face. A wolf with bright red eyes and large pointed fangs snarling at him within the darkness. A man with the head of a serpent. A windmill made of knives going round and round and the ever-present dark hole which terrorised his tormented dreams. The ominous pitch-black hole was a recurring theme, awakening him from his sleep on many occasions. He also experienced a heart-stopping, indescribable recurring dream of being both inconceivably large whilst simultaneously being microscopically small. Little did the giant Chinaman realise that he was, in fact, suffering from opium withdrawal and once awake he found it almost impossible to return to sleep. These episodic night terrors forced him to lay until dawn on perspiration drenched linen, his terrified eyes locked wide open. At times, he had even resorted to drinking Sadik's Bangla, a fermented rice juice, in an effort to sleep but he did not much care for its bitter taste and the way it burned his chest when he swallowed. *'How could Sadik and Swapnil drink this brew every single night,'* he puzzled.

'This would be a good exercise,' Vidhu thought to himself as he handed Chin the scrap of newspaper he had found earlier in the day. An almost complete front page of the Daily Mail with a big, bold headline. A nice little test for his pupil, he thought offering today's lesson to Chin.

KING VISITS HOSPITAL - CROWDS ECSTATIC

Chin excitedly took the piece of crumpled and torn paper and hesitantly read each letter firstly in his head then forming the words before speaking. "tee, hitch, eh … THE … dee, ah, eye, el, why … DAILY … em, ah, eye el … MAIL. The daily mail," uttered Chin looking up for Vidhu's validation. "Good, well done," replied Vidhu enthusiastically. "Now what does the rest say?" Chin returned his attention to the paper, "ki, eye, en, gee,… king …" he stammered. He paused to comprehend what he had just said.

"KING!"

Suddenly a torrent of bitter memories came crackling back into his brain like forks of lightning. An overwhelming tsunami of imagery and feelings flooded his consciousness with such ferocity that it almost knocked him to his bended knee. His synapses flashed and fired opening a floodgate of emotions and hidden recollections, each one hitting Chin like Indra's very own thunderbolts. Pain, brutality, death, Jao, humiliation, being attacked, fear, death, hatred, Pakapuh, and Him! King himself! His serpentine eyes boring into Chin's very core. Hercules Chin looked at the sheet of newsprint repeatedly, shaking his head more violently with each look. He could feel an uncontrollable rage rising deep from his gut to his gullet. Tears blinded his eyes as he began to remember the killings, so many killings and at his hand. Countless killings. The throats he had crushed, the spines he had snapped, the skulls he had smashed. All with these giant hands of his. He now realised who he was and what he was destined to forever be. He sat staring at the palms of his hands held upwards towards him on his lap. Hands reaching out pleading for a forgiveness that he now knew would never be granted. He glanced towards the distant smokestacks of London and slowly rose to his full height and having looked around him, he slowly started to walk away from the new home he had grown to love. He did not want any of the children he loved to see his departure.

He could see Whitechapel Road. He was there. He was back amidst Victorian London, albeit the depravity of its downtrodden East End. He could smell it. He could taste and hear it but could not touch it for some reason.

He walked along the cobbled street peering up its myriad of dingy slum alleys. The Rookeries they called them. Alleyways that respectable inhabitants avoided as if they were still plague-ridden. He noted very few gas lamps working in Dorset Street which was particularly terra incognita for the gentry. Small cramped tenement buildings with grimy windows selling everything from sweetmeats to books, from eels to abortions, from women to boys and anything in between. He was a lad again. A mudlark. A rapscallion. He was an Irregular.

He could smell the frightful aroma of the sewage ridden Thames. It mixed with the smell of rotting horse dung, soot, and smoke intermingling with London's great unwashed. A dreadful, nauseating stench you had to acclimatise to unless you could afford the luxury of a Vinaigrette.

He could once again hear the noise of horse's hooves on cobbled streets, the iron-clad wheels of barrows trundling through teeming thoroughfares full of all kinds of strange characters. Costermongers hollering, beggars hunched against walls, the cries of street sellers and newspaper vendors, prostitutes and pimps, all going about their daily routines. He heard the ever-present melodious sounds from grinders turning their barrel organs near and far. Too many tunes to actually pick out a tune.

He could hear it all again. Smell it all again. Taste the London acridity in the back of his throat again. He saw the occasional crossing sweeper earning a penny for brushing aside the horse muck to create pathways that respectable folks could follow. He saw the blind beggar, Willie, and the legless whistler with no name. There were queues of raggedy destitute folks standing in line for some broth and bread at the Salvation House; all with dirty hands and most with dirty thoughts. Thoughts they could camouflage by uttering a prayer in order to get a full belly for a few hours or a night's sleep slumped over the ha'penny rope. He spied barefoot children no older than babes scampering hopefully around the street vendors for scraps.

He sees the fog rolling in to briefly cloak London's ugliness. How can this be the richest city in the world? Why is there no colour? Do we not dream in colour? Everything seems so grey … so dreadfully …

"Albert. Albert!"

"Wake up Luv, can't be wasting a beautiful Spring morning like this," trilled Glenys the Nurse with her customary smile. "Cuppa with milk and two sugars as usual and here's your porridge as requested ma' Lud."

Albert stares blankly, first at Glenys then at his breakfast tray and back to her cheery ruddy face once more. Every mealtime is a surprise for Albert Wiggins these days. He can never remember what box he had ticked on the menu card the previous day.

Chapter 28 - The Sewers

Wiggins peered intensely at the London City ordnance map weighed down by paperweights on his desk. This was not the first time he had examined every minute detail of the map. Alongside the document sat the various paraphernalia one would expect to see on an office desk, albeit all positioned in their own very particular place. A single glance around the office would have immediately informed the casual observer that this was an ordered and fastidious, albeit humble workplace, qualities that accurately reflected its occupant. Pencils, inkwell, blotter and rule all sat right angles to each other. Or should that be 'correct' angles? Albert Wiggins was, after all, a particularly correct individual. A cut-glass ashtray containing several smoked Woodbines sat beside a silver vesta case with a blank cartouche. The vesta had been positioned centrally so as each of its corners were equidistant from those of the larger matching cigarette case underneath. Reams of paper sat in wooden trays positioned at each corner of the desk. Several newspapers were bundled neatly. Topping the pile was The Illustrated London News with its headline proclaiming, "Beast strikes again!"

Wiggins sat back in his chair and stroked his neat, closely manicured beard and glanced towards the single framed photograph which sat on his desk, slightly to his right. He looked at the picture contained within. A pleasantly attractive young woman beaming joyously out of the photograph whilst holding her infant son. His son. Their son. A boy taken cruelly from them far too early by the Grace of God and the cruel hand of pneumonia. His son, John Hamish, named after the bravest man with whom Wiggins ever had association, a doctor who had shown him the importance that character and honesty play in the making of a man. The man he so wished his son had been granted the opportunity to grow to resemble. Wiggins had great faith, despite the evil and degradation he witnessed around him each day, and his belief in an afterlife was unshakeable. It had to be. How often he had imagined watching his Son grow into a man. Every day he missed the child and the man that John would have become. He envisaged each day, a future whereby he played with his grandchildren in some sun-soaked village garden, a lifetime away from the grime and debauchery of London. He wondered if John was with his own unborn children, somewhere in God's holy kingdom, embracing them in love, awaiting the father he never really knew.

Wiggins swallowed back the lump blocking his throat, wiped the corner of one eye, blew his nose on a fine cotton handkerchief, and puffed out his cheeks. He stood up, pulled on his overcoat, thrust his hands into his pockets, and turned his attention to the larger scale map of central London tacked to one wall of his office.

The location of each crime scene was indicated on the map along with accompanying photographs of the appropriate victim. The map was defaced with colour coded pencil lines, scribblings and arrows and stars mapping out routes, ideas and possibilities. On his desk, lay a file for each incident containing all the forensic details, photographs and evidence garnered to date, along with biographies of each victim. No matter how many times he analysed all the data he possessed he was unable to identify any steadfast connection between the murdered women. No fingerprints, no remnants of clothing, no discarded weapons at the scene and no witnesses forthcoming. The only single connection being that they all lived and died at the hands of the same unholy Beast. Unlike the Ripper case, only one of the victims to date had been a prostitute. All were of different ages and differing appearance and varied occupations. None of the women were raped, which, to Wiggins' mind, ruled out a sexually motivated individual. Some had children and some did not. Some had siblings and some did not. None of their pasts seemed in any way intertwined and as far as he had identified none knew of the other. The most remarkable thing about these women, thought Wiggins, was that nothing at all seemed to link them in any perceivable way. Why were they singled out? Were they in fact singled out at all or were they totally randomised, in the wrong place at the right time for the Beast? He remembered the letter advising him that the answer lay with the victims. '*Damnation! There must be some connection!*' demanded Wiggins of himself.

'*Maybe Van Hoon will come up trumps with a lead that traditional police work has so far been unable to achieve,*' he mused, hopefully. '*The Leper's record of accomplishment with this type of case had in the past been remarkably productive after all.*'

Wiggins returned to his desk once more to re-examine the street map, his glittering eyes devouring every last detail. Each of the crime scenes, London Path off Narrow Street, Butcher Road, Lauriston Road, Greek Street, Spert Street, were all within a few miles of each other. His instinct was telling him that the answer lay directly in front of him somewhere, someplace, somehow.

Sergeant Pyke sat leaning back in his chair, his outstretched legs crossed at the ankles, reading the latest speculation regarding the Beast in the previous day's edition of the London Evening News. "Says here that we are chasing the Son of the Ripper, Sir."

"I would ask that you desist from the scandal sheets and instead turn your attention to the matter in hand Pyke, namely the recent murder of four innocent women, seemingly unconnected by anything other than the locale and the nature of their gruesome demise. How fare we with new information?"

"Nothing, Sir. I can't track down Harry Filch. Nobody can. The Heap reckons it was a werewolf to blame and the rest of our informants are silent on the subject," admitted Pyke, suitably chastened. "The crime boys have gone over every inch of the latest scene. Not a sausage. Radasiliev is in the wind and we have no further suspects. It is as if he were a phantom, sir."

"I think you will find that the definition of a phantom means one with no substance, as in a dream Pyke," retorted Wiggins. "This beast is definitely of substance and is, in fact, the thing of nightmares!" Wiggins sat back in his chair ruminating, his hands clasped over his stomach, whilst looking at the ceiling rose above him. "Don't they say, Pyke that a perpetrator's downfall is returning to the scene of his crime? Let us pay a visit back to Narrow Street and see if we can cast any new light upon the darkness that surrounds us."

"I'll get me hat Guv."

Less than thirty minutes later both men stood on Narrow Street facing the junction of Thames Path which was still sealed off using timber picket fence panels. One uniformed constable stood in attendance. The street was abnormally quiet for the time of day. Ordinarily, it would be bursting with all manner of activities and individuals going about their daily business but the presence of the constabulary and the horrific crime was still raw with the local residents and most people still chose to remain at a distance in fear of being cursed or tainted.

"Afternoon Murray," acknowledged Wiggins, throwing a friendly nod to the constable on guard duty whilst pulling back a fence panel and entering the alley. The two officers stood and looked around them taking in the high-sided flanks of Sun Wharf and the brick houses that stood as gatekeepers to the narrow thoroughfare which led directly to a drop off into the Thames. Both men stood surveying the precise spot where Mary Harrison had lain drowning in her own blood.

"Where in damnation did he go, Pyke? He crouched right at this very spot did he not, then was gone in an instant. Within our grasps, one second, vanished the very next."

"Nowhere to escape up there, Sir," nodded Pyke indicating the insurmountable edifices of the gables on either side. "And he certainly didn't run into the Thames, nor did he barge his way to our direction."

"Perhaps not Pyke," mused Wiggins as he lit a cigarette and threw the spent vesta to the cobbled ground at his feet. Glancing at the landing place of the discarded match, Wiggins crouched down as if to retrieve it. "You are correct in your summation Sergeant. Indeed, I wager it is not upwards to which we should be focusing our attention, but downwards. Looking, rather aptly, not upward to Heaven but downward to Hell. Note the double manhole cover here, just underneath this lamp standard. Right here where the victim lay Pyke! I suspect our rat fled to join his brethren in the sewer beneath our very feet."

Pyke could hold his breath no longer. "It stinks to high heaven down here he spluttered, trying his best to suppress the retch in his throat. "How on earth can you work down here?"

Jasper Babbitch of the London Municipal Water Management Company chuckled, his rosy cheeks shining like polished apples in the gloom. "Here, tie this around your mouth and nose, Sir." Babbitch offered each of them a neckerchief soaked in some fragrant smelling oils. "It acts as a kind of nosegay, peppermint and almond oil and such. Helps to mask the dreadful odours," giggled Babbitch, pinching his nose and throwing the policemen a wink. Pyke grasped the neckerchief eagerly as if it was his salvation. He knotted it around the back of his neck and breathed in deeply. "That's better. You not using one?" he asked of Babbitch. The permanently jolly Babbitch chuckled again, his chins wobbling. "When you been working down these sewers as long as I have you find yourself getting used to the stench. You become immune and your nose redundant."

"Olfactory fatigue," interjected Wiggins. "Also more commonly known as nose blindness, Pyke. It is that temporary inability to smell a particular odour after being exposed to it for a time," explained Wiggins. "As when you first enter a restaurant. Initially, the smell of food is obvious but by the time you've sat at the table and ordered your meal, that same smell fades dramatically or may not seem present at all."

"Very interesting, Sir. I have no doubt Mrs Babbitch looks forward with rare anticipation to your return home of an evening," joked Pyke, wiping at his now watering eyes. Babbitch smiled but chose not to respond to the remark. "The miracle of the modern age these tunnels are, gentlemen," elucidated Babbitch like a proud father as he swept his arms around showing off the spoilt grandeur of their surroundings. "All this great architecture and no bugger sees it. Saved millions of lives this did. Joseph Bazalgette was an absolute genius in my book gentleman. He cured London of its miasmic filth. No more great stinks for us, no more slops in the street, nor poison in the conduits."

"We have studied their layouts on the City ordnance plans, Mr Babbitch," espoused Wiggins interrupting Babbitch's homily of the London sewage network, but I must admit nothing would have prepared me for the grandeur of Mr Bazalgette's phenomenal feat of engineering. It is hugely impressive, more impressive perhaps even than his bridges that span the Thames. This main branch runs to the sewage treatment works at Beckton via the pumping station at Abbey Mills, does it not?"

"Indeed, it does Sir. The pumping station at Abbey Mills is a particularly striking example of Victorian architecture. I would be more than happy to arrange a future visit if you gentlemen so desired," replied Babbitch, impressed and pleased at this detective's knowledge. There was nothing Jasper Babbitch enjoyed more than talking about his beloved sewers, that is, apart from working in them or indeed showing them off. "Three hundred and forty million bricks, gentlemen, just think of it, three hundred and forty million, all laid by hand. Half a million tons of concrete n'all! Over a hundred miles of tunnels," Babbitch paused for effect to let the policemen absorb the enormity of the numbers involved. "This is the northern outfall sewer. To be honest, we ain't been down this stretch for several months due to some major upgrade works on the Southern branch going into Crossness which has kept us more than busy. What is it you expect to find down here, apart from rats, shit and grease banks as big a man?"

"Grease banks?" enquired Wiggins with a raised eyebrow, expertly avoiding the jovial maintenance man's question. "You know, big lumps of grease, Sir. From restaurants and the like. We had a clog, as we calls them, a few months back under Gerrard Street that were bigger than me, Topper an' Bert here put together, and Bert likes his food nearly as much as I do! Don't you Bert?" roared Babbitch convulsing hilariously and nodding to the larger of his two colleagues. Bert looked sheepish, not making eye contact. "That Chinese food sir. Must be full of fat judging by what they wash down the drains," shrugged Babbitch.

Wiggins took a map from his pocket, unfolded it and smoothed it as best he could against the permanently damp brick walls of the sewer. "No need for that sir, you just tell me where you want to go," offered Babbitch puffing out his chest proudly. "I know these tunnels likes the back of me hand I do and no mistake."

"Very well," smiled Wiggins who was growing to like the amiable, sewer loving Babbitch. "We want to proceed West from this point," detailed Wiggins pointing to Narrow Street, under which they currently stood. Wiggins' hypothesis being that the perpetrator would live or work in a better class of neighbourhood towards the West of the City rather than amid his range of operation. He hoped that they would find some sign, some piece of evidence that pointed to their theory that the Beast was indeed using London's network of sewage tunnels as his means of traversing the City unseen.

"We are particularly interested in any areas of the system that widen out, Mr Babbitch. Anywhere that would allow a base from whence someone may operate in this maze of tunnels. The plans indicate that there may be several such secluded areas?"

"Indeed, there are Inspector. There are several along this stretch leading off the Northern outlet sewer all the ways back to Paddington," acknowledged Babbitch. "Working Stations, we calls them. Gives the lads somewhere less cramped to do little jobs, repair their tools, have their tea and boiled eggs and such like Sir."

"Can we hurry this along Guv? I'm beginning to feel rather queasy, especially at the thought of eating in this stench hole," beseeched Pyke covering his mouth. Constable Potts threw a sideways glance at his Detective Inspector and grinned. "You'll be laughing the other side of your face son if you don't quit," threatened Pyke in jest. "I ain't never going to get this stench out of me hat." Pyke was the only one of the company who had directly refused to wear a lighted helmet, foregoing safety in favour of his beloved ever-present Derby.

The troop of six men proceeded to wade through the foul discharge of the great City. Wiggins had the feeling they were encased in the bilge of a giant ship, ploughing through the oceans, disgorging its waste as it went. Now and then an inlet pipe spewed forth its flushed effluent, sloughing liquid and solids into the main flow. '*This is truly disgusting,*' thought Pyke. '*Even if I was some deranged lunatic I wouldn't run around down here.*' He was beginning to doubt the validity of their theory.

The walls were covered in a perpetual slime which dripped echoingly around the labyrinth of redbrick tunnels. Rats scurried along the narrow kerb ways and disappeared up the inlet pipes and into holes and crevices. Pyke shuddered. He had no liking for Ratus Ratus. After approximately twenty minutes of wading, they came to the end of the branch tunnel and hit the main Northern Outlet. Here the tunnel was wider with narrow dedicated concrete walkways on either side of the sewage stream, just wide enough for the group to gain access to a drier walkway and to progress in single file. The temperature was high at this depth underground and the intrepid little troop were beginning to sweat heavily under their protective boiler suits. The beams from their helmet-mounted Davy lamps bounced and danced around the walls and arched soffit of the sparsely lit tunnel creating an eerie, ghostly effect.

"We will be coming to a workstation on our right within a couple of hundred yards," announced Babbitch who continued to lead the group. As they neared the recessed section Babbitch slipped on something underfoot. "What the Dickens?" exclaimed Babbitch almost falling on his back as the heel of his rubber wading boot skidded on the offending article. '*Probably a chunk of working man's morning best,*' chuckled Pyke inwardly.

Babbitch regained his self-assurance and stooped to pick up what looked like some liver coloured seaweed. "Offal of some sort I'd wager. These oriental chaps don't half eat some appalling stuff," pronounced the shiny-cheeked maintenance supervisor holding his discovery aloft between the finger and thumb of his gloved hand.

"If you would kindly pass your find to Constable Potts, he will put it in an evidence bag," ordered Wiggins, his, and the mood of his companions had taken a decided downward turn. There was an air of dread in the atmosphere, each man becoming gradually aware of what it was that Babbitch had just literally stumbled across.

"Is it human?" squeaked Babbitch, his nose raised in disgust, as he dropped the section of intestine into the bag offered by Constable Potts.

"I fear that may well be the case," nodded Wiggins. "Let us proceed to this workstation you talk of." As they turned the corner into the recessed concrete platform the smell became instantly something even more fetid than the sewer. The six men struggled to take in the sight that met their disbelieving eyes. The platform was roughly twelve feet by six feet and offered a workspace for the maintenance crews. In the middle of the space was a makeshift trestle table on which lay various parts of human anatomy. Wiggins could identify organs, muscle, bone, and even a set of false teeth. Sheets of what appeared to be skin hung from meat hooks suspended from the ceiling. Most grisly of all a china plate, a blood-stained pewter tankard and various carving knives and cutlery lay abandoned randomly on the table. Babbitch, the man who lived and breathed the sewers, bent double and threw up. Constable Potts followed suit almost immediately.

"Look at the Walls Pyke," whispered Wiggins nodding towards a series of erratic scratchings, the words scrawled repeatedly into the brickwork. Some characters were huge, others minuscule. Some written backwards and some upside down.

I hunger. I thirst. Flesh, give me flesh. Blood, I crave blood. They call me the Beast. But I am more than that. I am the life taker. I am the life-giver. They will all recoil at my rage. They will all repent.

Interspersed between the repetitive mantra Wiggins could see the names *Peter, John, James, Bartholomew, Judas, Andrew, John, Philip, Thomas, Matthew, Matthias* and *Thaddeus* scrawled randomly, as well as the word *Apostles*, again some of the script in huge letters and some so small as to be almost illegible.

"I want a photographer down here straight away. I think there may have been more victims than we were previously aware of," uttered Wiggins trying to take in the horror of the scene.

Chapter 29 - The Suffragette

Miss Agatha Harkness had just left the Passmore Edwards District Public Library, where she had attended a meeting with Christabel Pankhurst and a delegation of the Equal Rights for Women League to discuss a forthcoming suffrage campaign in Manchester. The hope was to disrupt a Liberal political meeting in a few short weeks. Happy with the way the meeting had progressed, Miss Harkness turned a sharp right upon leaving the building and walked briskly towards the Hyde Park end of Curzon Street where her chauffeured Royal Humberette automobile awaited her. She was in high spirits, buoyed by the success of the meeting and feeling energised at the momentum the movement was gaining nationally. Agatha had decided that she would walk through Hyde Park after the meeting and had asked her chauffeur to collect her at Cumberland Gate fifteen minutes after the meeting concluded. She would never appear at the gate.

She strolled into the Park and started walking northward enjoying the quiet solitude of the West London night. The trees reinvigorated the smoggy air making it sweeter and more breathable. She could see crows roosting in the branches of the trees, settled for the night, shrouded against the forthcoming frost. Her breath spread before her as she strode along the path, admiring the first, explorative efforts of emergent snowdrops and daffodils.

A dark, steel taloned claw flayed the white peeling bark off a nearby silver birch tree as it grasped its trunk.

After five minutes brisk walking she could just make out the hazy luminance from the Humberette's cycle-car lamps piercing the fog up ahead, two dim amber eyes behind the gauze of the London fog. She was blissfully unaware of the atrocity about to befall her and oblivious to the fact that she now only had only a few precious minutes to live.

It had stalked her mercilessly. It observed her every movement through bloodshot eyes as it silently shadowed her through the fog-bound night. It could smell her underlying scent of primaeval uncertainty. A hunter carnivore pursuing its prey. As the spectre inched ever closer, the fear and flight instinct began to grow within Agatha. It relished her fear and lusted after the sustenance it would provide. It had followed her to the Library and patiently waited, and waited, cloaked within the dark shadows and swirling fog, swallowed by the night, anticipating the optimum instant to strike.

To kill once more will be glorious.

The urge to quench its thirst for blood was consuming its every fibre. Its murderous, pitiless fury was about to be unleashed upon another oblivious victim. The anticipation of another barbaric attack excited the Beast to a point of inner frenzy. The shrieking voices increased inside its tormented skull.

I am the life saver. I am the life taker.

All the while It hunted her as would a wolf, stealthily, ravenously, following her path in a silent lust of anticipation. Miss Harkness began to sense that she was being stalked. She looked behind her, first over one shoulder, then the other, convinced that she was being followed. Her skin crept at the thought of unseen eyes following her. She shivered involuntarily and could feel goosebumps pimple her flesh. She repeatedly looked anxiously over her shoulder and began to grow more frantic with every quickening step. She was beginning to regret her decision to take an isolated route through the now seemingly endless park. Was that a shadow she glimpsed behind her, a slight movement of a bush, the indistinct sound of snapping twigs and foliage crunching underfoot? Had she heard a laugh?

'Pull yourself together Aggie. You are not in the East End now. You are far from Limehouse. There is no danger here.'

Suddenly a murder of crows fled from their lodgings as with an intense burst of energy the Beast launched its savage attack, springing out of the misty fog like a savage uncaged animal. The self-manufactured leather glove consisting of four integral scalpel blades slashed down her back like the talons of some mighty raptor, effortlessly ripping through her overcoat and bodice and shredding the skin, muscle and ligaments beneath. Blood sprayed forth gushing through yellowish adipose tissue discolouring the scene in a deep sticky scarlet. As she collapsed forwards on all fours the Beast seized her by the hair and turned her head to face his.

This is the last thing you will ever see!

She tried to crawl away, the great black Beast straddling her back. Her screams were silent, her vocal cords were no longer where they should have been and her throat had been obliterated, torn asunder by threshing blades and canines. Her fear was all-encompassing, and the Beast was feeding upon it, feeding on her. The blades easily sliced off an ear before the monster's teeth ripped at her nose like a rabid dog firstly shredding it from her face and then spitting it directly back at her. Mercifully, by this point, Agatha Harkness had already breathed her last.

The Beast picked up the prone form of what had once been the energetic campaigner, Miss Agatha Harkness, and with all its strength lifted her body above its head and forcefully dropped her, impaling her onto the park railings.

The carnage was over in a matter of seconds. The Beast threw back its head, stretched its neck and screeched at the fog-bound moon. It looked upon its carnage, then turned and fled the sickening scene, drifting back into the darkness as quickly as it had appeared. A 'Votes for Women' pin-badge lay a few feet from Miss Agatha Harkness' lifeless body, a small island of hope in a sea of hot blood.

My thirst is sated. My hunger fed. For now.

Albert Wiggins was still in his office signing off some paperwork and contemplating calling it a night. He could hear a rising commotion coming from outside his office. His desk telephone rang simultaneously with Pyke bursting through his door. Pyke looked visibly shaken. "There's been another one, Sir. Out West this time and you ain't gonna like it. You ain't gonna like it one little bit."

Wiggins held up his hand as if to silence Pyke and picked up the telephone. His face paled and his stomach lurched as the news was communicated to him. "Of course, Commissioner Gregson, Sir. We will attend at once. Yes, Sir, the lady was known to me. I understand. Yes. Yes. She will have our highest priority and uppermost respect."

Wiggins slowly replaced the receiver into its housing, his mind lost in confused thoughts of disbelief and horror. "We must hasten to Hyde Park Pyke. Commissioner's orders. I fear the victim is Miss Agatha Harkness." He shook his head, leaning back in his chair pulling his hands through his hair.

"The car is ready sir," returned Pyke nodding his head door wards.

The two companions stood in front of the railings trying to absorb the ghastly cameo which lay before them. What remained of the Viscount's daughter hung impaled on the ornate cast iron finials of the Hyde Park railings, the tips of which extruded from her sternum, left buttock and left thigh. Her body hung at obtusely abnormal angles making it difficult to comprehend it as a human form. Several constables busied themselves around the grisly scene securing the area and searching the surrounding grounds whilst a Coroner's assistant attended to the body. A police photographer was already on the scene recording the gruesome scene for posterity.

Wiggins lowered his eyes to the ground. "In the name of Jesus what manner of Beast are we dealing with here Pyke? This innocent, vibrant woman has been ripped to pieces, utterly dehumanised as if displayed in some butcher's window."

"One who hates women and is completely off his rocker. Should be locked up in Bethel if you ask me Sir," observed Pyke lighting a cigarette and offering it to Wiggins who accepted his smoke with a blank expression. "Thank you. This is unquestionably the same perpetrator, no doubt about it but why here? Why has the beast strayed from its typical hunting ground? This escalation is of the most alarming degree Pyke. Obviously, he can no longer control his urges and cravings. He no longer cares who or indeed where he kills. We cannot merely patrol Limehouse and its surrounding areas any longer. His area of operation has now migrated farther afield. Whatever slight fear of capture he may have once had, now seems totally absent. He could have chosen no higher profile a place in London if he had slaughtered the poor woman in Piccadilly Circus and pinned her on Eros' arrow."

"Do you think he knew her Sir? What I mean is did he know she was a leading Suffragette?" ruminated Pyke as he shielded his vesta from the slight breeze and lit a cigarette for himself.

"How so, Jem?"

"The railings, Sir," answered Pyke killing the flame of the match head between two spit covered fingertips. "They chain themselves to railings in protest for their cause, do they not? If he hates women so, will he not also hate their campaign for equality," suggested Pyke taking a long drag upon his cigarette.

"Of course, Pyke, I like your train of thought, excellent detective work. The brute has symbolically tethered her to the railings as she herself would desire. Desire? Perhaps he is impotent? Perhaps he is the one that is chained … chained by a lack of masculinity or virility. This would explain his having not sexually assaulted any of the victims do you not think?" Weeks and weeks of thoughts and postulations were now flowing from Wiggins' mind. "A maniac who has a homicidal fear and loathing of all women, no matter what age or standing. Where could such a monster spring from? From what background would such a bestial hatred ferment, brew, and indeed grow? One dominated by a mother or one where he has been abandoned or abused by a strong female matriarch? An orphan perhaps? Has he previously been an abused victim of punishment and chastisement? Learned behaviour? What would such a boy grow into Pyke? How does he earn his living? Where does he operate from? DAMN him!" Wiggins' mind was racing with differing trains of thought. "So many questions remain unanswered. Where is Van Hoon in all of this? What does he do to aid us?" spat out Wiggins. "Where are our informants Pyke? Where is Harry Filch, where is Jim the Lock, the Heap and the rest of them?" exclaimed Wiggins rather too loudly. The attendant constables turned their heads at this uncharacteristic outburst. He felt

Pyke place a strong hand on his shoulder. "This is not their battle Sir. Not their duty. It rests with us," specified Pyke in his colleague's ear.

"Of course, Jem, of course. You are right. It is down to us to apprehend this maniac. We must reinforce our efforts and evolve our thinking," nodded Wiggins. '*Where would he be without the strength and clear thinking of this stoutest of Yeomen?*' The constables returned their attention to their tasks. "Anyways, Harry Filch has vanished off the face of the cobbles, Sir. No one has seen hide nor hair of him for weeks now."

'*Harry Filch,*' thought Wiggins, his mind wandering back to a time when he and Harry and been part of the same gang of Irregulars, the street urchin arm of Scotland Yard as the Great Detective had called them. He and Harry had trod different paths since then, each on opposing sides of the law to the other, but still, their lives had intertwined professionally. And what of the others. Inky John, killed by a horse in The Strand when he was no older than fourteen years of age. Small Paul, now a respectable although alcoholic bookkeeper in the Home Office. Little Tommy Hagan, now tall as a reed and a successful and prosperous builder making a fortune from redeveloping the sprawling City. Whippet Simpson, these days a jobbing thief. Others whose names he now struggled to remember accurately. Strange that he reminisced nostalgically for a time when he had less than he had ever had. He realised it was not the time he missed but the companionship of friends, brothers in arms of a sort.

Pyke interrupted his meanderings. "We need some answers to your questions sir, perhaps a course of action would be to ask one of those psycho quacks I've been hearing more and more about. Seemingly they can get into the heads of such men," shrugged Pyke drawing the last of the nicotine from his cigarette and flicking the butt spiralling into a nearby sewer inlet. He smiled as he heard it fizzling out.

"You're full of clever ideas tonight Jem. You are not the first to have suggested this course of enquiry, although I must admit up until now, I had resisted the temptation to call upon such unorthodox resource," acknowledged Wiggins. "Let us seek out the most prominent of such men in London at the moment." Wiggins took a final look at the once striking woman who now hung in front of him suspended like a disjointed marionette from the cast iron grandeur encircling London's most prominent Park. The most grotesque of bunting.

Wiggins had lost patience with the activity and fussing that was surrounding the victim's body. "In God's name would someone get her down from there and cover her up," he roared. "Or I will do so myself." The two men turned and walked solemnly back towards their motor car.

Professor Sigmund Freud was only too happy to help the London Metropolitan Police with their highest-profile case since that of the Ripper murders. His itinerary was relatively free for the evening, ensconced as he was amidst the luxury of the Northumberland Hotel in Northumberland Avenue just south of Trafalgar Square. Freud was currently the toast of London's scientific and literary society, feted by the Capital's greatest scholars and medical aristocracy. The Austrian neurologist was at the height of his influence, touring Europe espousing his new and controversial theories regarding the treatment of psychopathology through the application of psychoanalysis, an innovative form of treatment which involved deconstructed dialogue between psychologist and patient. Only the previous evening Freud had met with his great friend Carl Jung to discuss the possibility of a forthcoming collaborative tour of Europe's capital cities and universities.

Wiggins and Pyke sat in the anteroom of the suite where the renowned Professor temporarily stayed. Pyke was wondering how much a hotel like this charged for a night's rest whilst Wiggins was wondering who was paying for it. The door to the anteroom opened and a short, slightly built, bearded man, whom Wiggins judged to be in his mid-fifties, entered and invited them into a sitting room that was thick with cigarette smoke. "Please do come in gentlemen," indicated Freud, his accent still heavily Germanic, although his spoken English was impeccable.

Freud indicated that they all sat and lit himself a cigarette. "I am anxious to help you in whatever way I can gentlemen. I understand from Commissioner Gregson that you have some questions that I may be able to assist with." The Professor lent forward and poured them each a small cup of strong black coffee from a silver Cafetière.

"We do indeed Professor. You no doubt are aware of our ongoing pursuit of a Beast that preys upon the women of our great City," explained Wiggins foregoing any preamble and getting directly to the matter in hand. "Well, we are attempting to build a profile of the man we are dealing with."

"I see," said the Psychoanalyst. "A most progressive and modernistic approach to police investigation, may I say. One that I highly commend."

Wiggins could see that he had snared the Austrians attention and so proceeded to describe each murder in as much detail as he felt appropriate given Freud's unofficial standing in the investigation. The three men were only halfway through their second cup of coffee and Wiggins had noticed that Freud had smoked half a dozen cigarettes by the time he had completed his review of the case.

"After what you tell me, and having familiarised myself with the newspaper articles, there is no question in my mind that you are dealing with a homicidal psychopath with overriding deep-held misogyny. That is, an individual with a personality disorder that manifests itself, in this case, in murderous behaviour and who is completely amoral and without regret or conscience for his actions or how they impact upon and affect others. He has no empathy with humankind. His hatred of women will no doubt stem back to a broken or failed or fractured relationship with a woman of major consequence in his life, probably a lover, possibly his mother or even a sibling. He obviously cannot function in this state daily and must exist outside of his psychosis in the normal world, presenting an ordinary face to his colleagues and family. I do not say 'friends' as I suspect he does not make acquaintance and foster friendships very readily. Hence, I would postulate and expect that he also suffers from dissociative identity disorder or is the occupier of multiple personalities. He will swing between two or possibly more of these personalities at any given time and he will most likely hear inner voices that torment him and determine the direction of his behaviour. It may be what you call the evil part of his soul expressing itself over the good side of his soul. It may also be that such extreme psychosis may bring on physical changes, may heighten his senses and physical prowess. I feel his latest atrocity shows a marked increase in his psychomania, as he is being more daring and is losing what little control he previously held I feel," discoursed the Austrian, all the time flicking his cigarette into an overflowing tray by his side. He stubbed out the latest in a long line of cigarettes, his fingertips disappearing below a small Vesuvian shaped mountain of ash.

"And what makes him switch from what to all perceptions would be a normal man to being a cannibalistic murderous Beast?" enquired Wiggins stroking his beard.

"There will be a trigger. An event, a noise, perhaps even a word or a smell that will inspire the change from Man to Beast," confirmed Freud. "Mankind has continually struggled when left to one's own singular devices. We are after all pack animals and when this pack hierarchy does not exist the opportunity to be the only alpha male is overriding."

"So, it could be anything then?" tutted Pyke placing his now empty cup a little too forcibly on the table.

"I understand your frustration Sergeant but given the information you have made available to me, I would hazard a guess, gentlemen, that the trigger will be either of a sexual or religious nature, perhaps even something connected with the act of consummation or the act of birth itself. I would surmise that the man himself may be impotent and therefore frustrated and sexually repressed. The act of eating human flesh can be argued as a substitute for the sexual act," informed the Professor. "Cannibals also hold the belief that consuming the flesh of another endows the cannibal with some of the characteristics and power of the deceased." Wiggins and Pyke exchanged glances of surprise with eyebrows raised. "And what of the man's profession? Can you point us in any direction?"

The Professor sat back, fingertips together, his left hand grasping his long white beard. "He must be in a position of authority or power, possibly respect, to be able to gain access to the resources he needs to maintain his double life. Perchance a member of the upper gentry, aristocracy or of the superior professions. An educator, a legal counsel, a man of Science. Most likely though, given the circumstances you describe, and the wounds you have defined, I would state that you are looking for a man of medicine," concluded the great Austrian.

"A Doctor," nodded Wiggins. "A Doctor, of course, it could be a Doctor."

Chapter 30 - The Return

He identified that he had originally come from up the great river so that was the direction he followed. He stuck as much as he could to the riverbank, trying to keep it within sight wherever possible. He knew that if he walked against the flow of the current, he would eventually reach the large City. It had been almost two days since Hercules Chin had commenced his journey to return to Pakapuh. He had no real understanding of the location or where he was in relation to it, but he had followed the course of the Thames and fortunately, the weather had been obediently kind and had remained mostly calm. He knew only that the opium den was on the north bank of the long river somewhere.

Of all the weather conditions he encountered on his journey, Chin detested the wind most of all. He found the wind whipped up by the river, was, on occasion, just as powerful as he was, and at times it took his breath away. He would walk against the wind, head down, watching his feet take step after exhausting step. Occasionally, when there was no obvious pathway he would be forced to walk on the riverbank, the mudflats and small pebbled beaches, making progress underfoot even more difficult and time consuming. The ungainly and awkward way of walking sapped his energy. At first, his progress was ponderous and frustratingly slow as he always travelled at night, in the hope that the cloak of darkness combined with the seemingly ever-present fog would help to veil his hulking shape and keep him safe from ridicule and judging eyes. He felt oddly soiled and ashamed hiding in the shadows. *'Only bad people hid away from others like this.'* His long trawl gave him time to think. Sometimes he wondered if he was a bad person. After all, hadn't he killed many men for Father King? So many men. Were the people he had killed the bad ones as Father King had told him or had he lied? The questions confused Chin and hurt his head so much that he would often walk for hours on end thinking of nothing at all, his head blissfully empty of any feelings of guilt or remorse.

Other times he would think too much. He remembered being happy with his childhood friends in his village, how he had been vilified, ridiculed and punished in the well, and how he had been lauded and adored when he was the star attraction in the circus. All these memories made him weep but, he realised for different reasons.

But still, he had never wanted to frighten people. He had never desired that. He realised that he was different from all the other people he had ever encountered, and he was also beginning to understand that many of the people he had trusted had used the fact that he was different for their own gain. As he reminisced on his life since the circus, he began to formulate an understanding that he may indeed be a bad man. He thought of Father King and how he had made him do terrible things. This made him feel wretched. He also thought of how King had fled and abandoned him to the mercy of the police, saving himself whilst leaving Chin to die. This made him feel sad, then angry, then confused.

His overriding thought now was to seek out King and ask him why he had abandoned him as he had. He yearned to fill in the gaps his memory had intentionally failed to recall. His reasoning and thoughts were now clearer and keener than they had been for many years owing to the lack of opiate surging through his system. Clearer thinking however brought its accompanying tortures. The realisation that his village had renounced him all those years ago tormented his thoughts. The confusion and disgrace he felt at knowing that his own father had not only disowned him but effectively sold him festered queasily in the pit of his empty stomach causing it to leap and lurch. '*What had he done to all these people to warrant such treatment?*' he silently pondered as he trudged upriver. All he had ever tried to do was to help them as best he could, and they had rewarded him with rejection and pain.

Eventually, the estuary wetlands began to give way to the furthermost tendrils of the sprawling metropolis. He could make out the rising, indigo grey silhouettes of the distant City buildings. The taste of the air became different, heavier and more soot laden, London's industrial acrid breath began to reach his nostrils. As he trudged ever forward the fog began to wrap him in its bronchial blanket. The oast houses of Kent had long since given way to the dock buildings of Dartford and Woolwich, the fresh Kentish air with the polluted exhalation of Gotham.

He proceeded through the night from doorway to alleyway, from boathouse to storage shed, brickworks to salvage yard, all the while struggling to hide from the gazes of the worthies and nocturnal misfits of the London night.

Chin's dream of his mother comforting and singing to him was brought to an abrupt halt. "Whotcha there, big fella!" exclaimed the gravelly voice within the darkness of the railway arch. Chin opened his sleepy eyes and stared inquisitively at the raggedy little man with the yellowing skin who was cuddling at his side for warmth. "Ya wanna lubricate your tonsils with a little tiddly wink?" Chin stared like a confused puppy at this strange little man and of his even stranger tongue. "There's ain't much left to be fair mate, but we can shares what little there is. Heat those big old bones of yours," he giggled a coarse chuckle whilst offering up a brown paper bag with the neck of a bottle peeping out from the opening. "I thinks I may 'ave a little cheroot someplace as well if you'd rather?" he said checking drunkenly through the pockets of his filthy clothes. "Where the chuffin' hell is it now? There's a good couple of drags left in the thing." Chin sat in silence trying to fathom out what language the odd swaying little fellow was slurring. "Ya daan't speak much do ya me oriental mucker. Can ya not speak? Is that it? No bother Skip, I can't read but I'm a bit of a chatterbox make no mistake. I can rabbit on for hours I can," he smiled a lopsided grin before seemingly falling asleep with his head now resting on Chin's shoulder. Hercules Chin waited several moments until his inebriated companion was lightly snoring. He gently rose to his knees, smiled, and carefully shook the drunk's hand in both of his. He settled the bottle so that it would not topple. Rising delicately and gingerly he then backed away before finally turning to leave. "I'll maybe's see you around again my large friend. May Gawd go with you … and if he doesn't, just have another snifter until he changes 'is mind," waved the inebriated little fellow, his darkly circled eyes remaining closed all the while.

It was early morning as Chin left the relative safety and seclusion of the archway. He was no longer concerned if it was daylight. He made his way from Woolwich towards Greenwich, tending to stick wherever he could to the side streets, common ground and parks. As he turned a corner leading into a park, he could hear a dog barking followed quickly by raised voices. A terrier rushed towards him and stopped short of his bootlaces, baring its teeth and snarling, whilst hopping around, its ears pinned back in a signal of aggression. The first stone hit Chin on the back. "Monster! It's a Monster!" cried the first man. Children screamed and ran to their mothers. The second stone hit him on the shoulder, more painfully than the first given that it hit his scapula with force. Chin whirled and snarled at the thrower who backed off warily. "It's the Beast!" came the second cry. Women began to clutch their children and scamper from the scene. The tiny terrier worried at the cuff of the giant's trouser leg. Chin looked down at it and roared a gargantuan primordial roar. The little dog whimpered and took to its heels as fast as its short legs could muster. By now a hard-core group of men were approaching wielding walking sticks and makeshift whips pulled from the nearby shrubbery. Chin shielded his face and head as more stones came hurtling his way.

"It's a Monster, I tell ya. A bloomin' real-life Monster!" bawled the ringleader of the group. "Let's get 'im troops," came the cry. Chin stood confused, desperately trying to dodge the incoming rocks and stones. The mob seemed to grow with each passing second. Chin realised there was no way he could outrun all of the people. '*I will just have to kill them all*,' he thought with a resigned sadness.

Suddenly a large, black, four-horse carriage drew up behind Chin. The four black stallions reared rising as one, their hooves pawing the air, their frozen breath snorting from their flaring nostrils into the frost hardened morning air. A large powerful, yet deathly pale hand, beckoned from within the carriage, summoning Chin to enter.

Chin turned to face the onrushing mob. He bared his teeth and snarled, flung his head back and roared once more. The mob hesitated, unsure of itself in the face of such unbridled ferocity. Chin roared once more and advanced a single pace throwing up his arms aggressively. A few of the more hesitant members of the multitude decided that a brief period of guilt over their lack of bravery was perhaps the order of the day, rather than run the unpalatable risk of becoming embroiled with the roaring giant in front of them, and beat themselves a hasty retreat.

"Come to me," came the firm stentorian voice from within the carriage. The mighty hand once again beckoned. "I can give you blessed shelter." Hooves rattled the cobbled street, the coachman struggling to control the worried horses.

Chin turned towards the carriage and grunted. '*Shelter,*' he thought. '*This is what Father King had promised him.*' He whirled and snarled once more at the approaching mob which recoiled as one. Chin decided that shelter was indeed preferable to the effort of killing these stupid bothersome people and strode towards the carriage. As he did so a large stone was thrown with an accompanying "Monster! Clear off, we don't want no more monsters 'round 'ere!" The stone hit Chin on the back square between his shoulder blades, but the giant seemed not to notice. He merely grunted. He was transfixed by the corpse white hand that was now opening the door of the carriage from within, inviting him to enter.

The carriage lurched as it took the enormous weight of the giant. Chin had difficulty squeezing his prodigious frame into the carriage, his mysterious saviour aiding him with a strength that surprised even Chin. The large shadowy figure was dressed in the highest of finery, a silk top hat with a grosgrain ribbon crowning the oversized misshapen head. The face of Chin's benefactor was shadowed from sight by the high upturned collar of his coat. The stranger rapped the roof of the carriage with a silver-topped cane fashioned in the shape of a wolf's head and the carriage pitched forward. A few errant projectiles bounced off the outside of the vehicle but soon the four powerful black stallions were making good speed and distance.

"I shall take you to My Father's House," rumbled the deep voice of Chin's saviour. "There I can offer you sanctuary. You will be safe there, some rest and sustenance."

Chin picked up on the stranger's words. My Father's House. Chin smiled "My Father's House, yes. That is where I want to go," he stammered in his broken English.

Chin thought for a moment. "They called me... *monster*," he questioned, rolling his shoulders to try and erase the pain that the last brick had caused. "What is a monster?"

The stranger's head nodded. "I too have been called Monster. A monster is something that ignorant people do not yet understand. An age ago they called me Wretch. They treated me as they now treat you. Men are weak, my friend, in body and in mind. They fear what they do not understand and try to destroy what they fear."

The two sat in silence for what to Chin seemed like an age. He wanted to speak to this stranger but struggled to form the right words in his head. As he peered out the carriage window, he could see that they were now crossing the Bridge of Towers to the other bank of the big brown river. "My father's house, this side," he smiled, nodding his head, and clutching eagerly at the sleeve of his companion. Chin's excitement grew as he saw that the coachman had veered the foursome to the right in order to turn eastwards. He knew from the flow of the river that this was the correct direction in which to travel to reach Shadwell Basin. Chin pointed one enormous arm, "My father's house."

The stranger's hand rested reassuringly on Chin's forearm, "First, you must rest and dine, my comrade. We shall stop at my sanctum before seeking out your father's house on the morrow." Another forceful double tap on the roof of the carriage from the stranger's cane signalled an acceleration in the speed of the ebony foursome. Chin understood and relented, and sitting back on the cracked Brunswick green leather, he succumbed to his exhaustion and closed his eyes.

Chin awoke as the carriage came to a lurching halt. It rose dramatically as both occupants alighted into an evening thick with the London Particular. They had travelled far and the last of the sun now beamed valiantly through the fog and illuminated the gothic church up to which they had drawn. "My father's House, as I refer to it," indicated the stranger with a sweeping arc of his powerful arm. Chin looked around in all directions. A graveyard surrounded the church on all sides, visibly ancient lichen festooned tombstones littered the grounds, protruding from the overgrown grass at various obtuse angles. Stone crosses, some adorned with skulls and crossed bones, stood beside ornately carved angels guarding the mausoleums that peppered the grounds between the graves. The mist crept like a snake through the deathly monuments, caressing each one as a lover sensually caresses a loved one. The church itself appeared equally ancient, partly derelict, and clearly no longer used as a house of worship.

The stranger saw that Chin looked uneasily from one gravestone to the other. "Other than Bartram, my coachman, these are my only other companions now. The phantoms and lost souls of the long departed are preferable companions to me than the company of the living. They make no demands and offer no questions."

The stranger strode towards the darkly stained, studded double entrance doors and producing an oversized key from his innermost pocket, proceeded to unlock the door. "Welcome to my home, my friend," rumbled the Stranger. Chin looked at his host and could see that he was not as other men. He was tall, probably the tallest man Chin had encountered aside from himself, but still, the Chinaman judged, a good half a yard shorter than he.

"My name is Friedrich," explained his host with a slight bow as he guided Chin inside. As he removed his hat and overcoat, Chin could see that the man was of powerful build and that he moved rather awkwardly, in a somewhat ungainly fashion, not unlike Chin himself. He could also see the reason why his saviour had referred to himself as Monster. His facial skin was of a translucent yellowish pallor and interwoven by severe scarring that spoke of some horrendous past accident. His eyes were a pale, deathly grey, seemingly lifeless orbs in red-rimmed sockets. "I see even you, whom they call Monster, recoil to some degree at my features my friend," muttered Friedrich in a somewhat disappointed drawl. "Let us sit. You must be hungry?" he questioned. Chin nodded in agreement as Friedrich showed him into one of the many rooms into which the disused church had been divided. Chin observed that for once he had no need of ducking or squeezing himself through the doorways, such was the grand scale on which the Church had been converted. Everything around him was outsized sufficiently as if it were a bespoke suit of clothes tailored specifically for its mysterious occupant. Even the chair in which his host indicated he should sit was large enough to comfortably accommodate his proportions. Chin felt reassured and comfortable in such surroundings.

"Chin," offered the giant Chinaman, as Friedrich placed some bread, cheese and a large shank of cold mutton in front of him. "My name, Chin," he said as he began to tear ravenously at the leg of mutton.

"My friend, Chin. Eat, please eat as much as you desire. Eat until you can eat no further." A glass of port was poured and handed to Chin. He accepted this with a smile and swigged it back with relish. Chin coughed slightly at the unfamiliar taste of the alcohol. Friedrich smiled. "You find the vintage to be a good one, friend Chin?" enquired Friedrich with a smile of his almost non-existent lips.

"Good," laughed Chin nodding his head and offering forth his glass for replenishment. As Chin feasted to his satisfaction, Friedrich began to light a fire within a huge inglenook fireplace that was strangely devoid of any soot staining. "You must be cold my friend. I myself do not feel the cold. I grew accustomed to low temperatures many years ago in a land extremely far from here." He threw several large logs into the grate. The splintered ends of the logs looked as if they had been ripped to size as if by some gigantic titan rather than hewn by a timber saw.

The unlikely companions settled by the fire, both engrossed in the flickering flames licking at the hearth made of colossal lumps of stone. "You seek your father, friend Chin?" enquired Friedrich leaning forward to address the Chinaman.

Chin thought. He knew that King was not his birth father, but understood that he was, in a way, his adopted father. He was unable to translate this into the appropriate words so settled for merely nodding his head. Chin related as best he could his story. From his village to the well, from the Circus to King. His instinct led him not to mention the dozens of men that he had killed on the bequest of King.

After learning of Chin's background, Friedrich gave a short synopsis of his life thus far. "My father was Swiss," continued Friedrich with a note of regret in the depths of his rolling voice. "I am afraid that he abandoned me at a very early age, cast me out to wander the world in a torment of rage and sadness without my mate. My mother…" hesitated Friedrich, "…my mother, regretfully I never knew. I was born in Germany, in a small town called Ingolstadt." He glanced across at his visitor and observed that he had been talking to an unreceptive sleeping giant. Friedrich smiled and arose from his chair and placed a blanket over the slumbering Chinaman. He then stoked the fire with what appeared to be a ludicrously small poker and threw it another ripped log. He settled back into the chair opposite Chin. "Sleep well, my friend. Tomorrow we seek out your Father. I hope by all that is holy that he has not abandoned you as mine did unto me."

Chin awoke early the next morning to the chill of the vast vaulted room in which he had slept. The fire had died and only a few remaining embers winked a fading light towards him. Chin rose and stretched, his full height such that his outstretched hands almost touched the high ceiling of the room. His was a mission, he decided. A quest, that he knew would culminate today. He had now all but forgotten the reed croppers who had rescued him from the icy waters and the desire to confront King was now the overwhelming emotive driving force rising in his heart. The pointing, baying mob of the other day, the abusive shouts, the rocks and stones, the terrified crying children were no longer a relevance.

Friedrich fed him a vast bowl of porridge and some fruit to break his fast and soon they were hurtling their way back towards London under the guidance of Bartram and the power of his four magnificent steeds. The morning was clear, and Chin felt uplifted by the freshness of the air and at the unfamiliar sight of the hedgerows of the countryside that raced past the carriage in a blur of green flashes. Earlier Chin had described to Bartram, as best he could, the general area where Pakapuh was situated. He relayed its location in context with the river, the docks and the Bridge of Towers. "Sounds like you was somewhere down Shadwell or Limehouse way," offered Bartram, the worldly coachman seemingly unfazed by the size and appearance of the Chinaman. "As you is an oriental type gentleman, I thinks we should be heading towards the wharves and docks down Shadwell. I've 'eard that's where the dens of your fellow countrymen are."

Chin had nodded eagerly at the mention of the word Shadwell, which he somehow remembered from the long-forgotten conversations of others. And so, they headed, the giant and the stranger, fatefully or otherwise, towards Chin's destiny.

The carriage jostled its way through the bustling early morning thoroughfares. Upriver, always heading westwards. The huge Chinaman had not previously recognised any landmarks or faces on his way up and around the Limehouse Reach where the river now glided smoothly but he suddenly knew exactly where he was. He had spied it approximately half a mile directly ahead. The familiarity of the buildings told him that they were at Pelican Wharf and that behind the large warehouse sat the pier at Pakapuh.

All 350 pounds of this solid mass of humanity was now blinkered as he leapt from the carriage and surged towards his intended target. Anger rose within him, engulfing his being like the pressure build-up of some emotional valve. At this time in the morning, the Wharf was thriving with traders and seaman. People fled in panic from his thunderous approach, parting to avoid the oncoming Behemoth. Friedrich also leapt from the carriage and followed the Chinaman at what appeared to be a superhuman speed. The two men dwarfed everybody. A deep resonant thundering sound emanated from the ground as Chin's massive legs tore up the distance between him and Pakapuh. Unawares, he trod upon a mangy dog that got in his way, crushing it beneath the huge weight of his gait. A horse temporarily blocking the sight of the pier was shoved effortlessly aside without Chin even realising.

"K I N G!" he bellowed as he advanced upon the rickety looking doorway guarding his recent past. Without missing a stride, he crashed headlong through the doorway causing an explosion of splintered wood and dust to implode inwards. He was braced and ready, fully anticipating King's armed henchmen to be on the other side but he was met with complete silence. He scanned around in all directions. Nothing. Nobody. All was calm. The front of house part of the establishment was empty, devoid, as far as he could see of any occupancy. It was as if nothing had ever been there at all. No tables or chairs in the eating house. He was confused. He felt the strong hand of Friedrich upon his shoulder. "Be calm, my friend. Your father's house seems as empty as a lost soul."

Chin turned to snarl at his companion. He shrugged off Friedrich's restraint and the German freely let him go, concluding that it would be prudent to leave Chin to continue what he imagined would ultimately be a futile search.

Chin crashed his way through the rear connecting door and into the kitchen. "King!" he again roared. The kitchen seemed as devoid of life as the front room, the stove unattended, pots and pans stacked unused. The absence of any smell other than a mildewed dampness indicated that it had been some time since it had last been occupied. Chin now barged through into the opium rooms which were also eerily empty. Only the slightest trace of the sickening floral odour remained as a testament to their former use. Chin violently pulled back the curtains of each opium booth halting only momentarily on discovering the emaciated body of an abandoned patron recumbent within. With one swift kick, he smashed the rear entrance door clean from its hinges and stood peering at the empty pier. *'What now?'* Chin thought to himself. *'How could he possibly find his tormentor in this huge city that spread out in all directions?'* He squatted down on his haunches, crossing his arms and resting them upon his knees. The pier bell clanged as Hercules Chin stared solemnly out into the distance, the sordid glory of the city spread out before him in all directions as far as he could see.

Friedrich slumped his considerable mass down onto the straining boards of the pier next to Chin and followed his companion's gaze, absorbing the endless metropolitan vista, imagining the thoughts that were currently bombarding Chin's naïve child-like mind. "We will find him, you and I. Together we will find your father," he consoled his newfound friend.

Chapter 31 - The Teacher

I t was eight-thirty in the morning. Eleven men were dotted around the incident room. Some sat, heads bowed as if in prayer or deep contemplation. Several constables stood smoking cigarettes, or rather holding cigarettes, as they were too emotionally drained to even drag upon them. Nosher Ash rested his bulk on a radiator chewing thoughtfully on the stem of his unlit pipe. He looked at each of the younger constables like a caring father watching over his distressed children. Pyke stood arms outstretched, his palms placed on a wall as if trying to push it down or perhaps hold it up. A newly lit cigar was grasped a little too firmly in his teeth. Wiggins stood looking out the window with his hands clasped behind his back. All the men were silent. All the men were contemplating and processing the information Wiggins and Pyke had just relayed to them.

The two detectives had returned earlier from Oak Lodge School for Deaf Girls on Nightingale Lane in Balham from where the Headmistress had called for urgent assistance. The school had been opened only eight years earlier as a boarding school for deaf girls between the ages of eleven and sixteen.

Wiggins could not dislodge the image of Sarah Devitt's severed head. It was an image he would never be allowed to forget. Once seen, it was etched into his very being. The young teacher's head had been placed atop her desk facing out into the empty classroom. Her shocked eyes were still wide open. It had taken Wiggins a few seconds to grasp exactly what he was looking at upon entering the schoolroom. What had the traumatised children thought upon entering the room for that morning's gruesome assembly, he wondered. He recalled the chalk-scrawled words on the black slate board on the wall behind the teacher's desk.

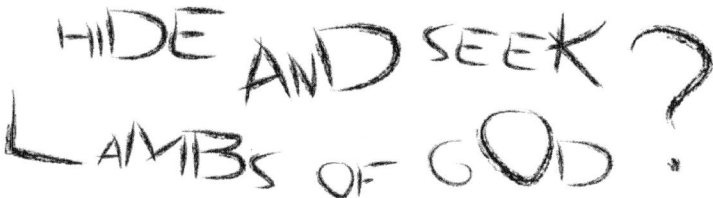

He was trying to establish if there could be any reasoning behind some of the letters being different sizes, trying to decode any cypher. Wiggins had already decided that the cryptic message was asking the schoolchildren to find Miss Devitt's body parts that, as it transpired, had been dispersed around the room. Pyke remained pressing against the wall. His eyes were closed.

The Beast had hidden behind the door, expectantly awaiting the teacher's arrival. As she entered, she had left the door wide open for the children to appear upon hearing the ringing of the school bell. The Beast had waited until his prey was approaching her desk then sprang into murderous action.

The first blow was instantly fatal and pierced her brain stem up through the back of her neck. The upwards thrust of the bladed hand had lifted Sarah off her feet, such was the ferocity of the strike. The Beast knew she was dead with that first acutely aimed blow. That was what the Beast had planned. No noise, no commotion, a quick, precise kill in a school preparing to open for the day. The body was then swiftly dissected into ten parts.

Sarah Devitt's head was severed from her shoulders and placed upon her desk. The Beast made sure that no further injuries were inflicted upon her face. Her right hand was sliced off at the wrist and concealed in the cage of the classroom's pet rat which proceeded to gnaw greedily at the fingertips. Blood had been sprayed everywhere with practically no surface or child's desk being spared the carnage of the Beast's human butchery. The teacher's left hand had been hidden in her bottom desk drawer and both feet were severed at the tops of her leather boots and placed together on the children's shoe rack by the entrance door. The macabre and sickening sight of Sarah Devitt's torso complete with dangling legs was hanging from one of the children's coat hooks resembling some horrific display in a butcher's window. Each arm was placed within the hinged lid of two randomly chosen child's desks, blood dripping through the wooden airing hole and onto the floor. Most sickening of all, Pyke had found Miss Devitt's severed nipples stuffed into the ink-well on her desk.

Every man in the room remained silent, and for the most part stationary. Wiggins shook his head and puffed out his cheeks before exhaling. He turned to face the room.

"This ends NOW!"

Chapter 32 - The Burial

The sky was darkly ominous, a leaden darkness pervaded, and the rain fell with such ferocity that Wiggins struggled to recall a more intense downpour. The total absence of any discernible breeze made the rain fall like stair rods and the noise of the drumming water upon his hat almost drowned out the eulogy being recited by the vulturine Priest. Rivulets of invigoratingly icy water traced their way aimlessly down the back of his neck and found refuge within the collar of his newly starched shirt. Although he stood towards the rear of the small throng of mourners his eye was repeatedly drawn to the lip of the graveside where a torrent of muddy rainwater disappeared over its edge in a steady stream dragging small pebbles and stones as it went. This scree pattered onto the lid of the coffin that lay within like a ticking countdown of some ghastly metronome. Every tap of every pebble seemed to pull at Wiggins' heart like the bony fingers of the Reaper plucking a resonant string on a death's harp.

'If this has such an emotional effect upon me, how must these heartbroken people feel? Her family, her friends,' thought the world-weary Detective whilst biting on his lower lip and shaking his head imperceptibly. Rainwater dripped from the tip of his nose. He always counted things at funerals. The number of people in attendance, how many trees, the number of buttons, mustachios or spectacles he could see. Counting them took his mind off the overriding sadness and insidious emotion of it all. He took the opportunity to study the Viscount, Agatha Harkness' father. He was a tall, broad-shouldered man, obviously of noble bearing. Wiggins suspected that his slightly stooped posture was a recent manifestation of the relentless grief he was suffering and that previously the man no doubt had been more commonly seen as upright and strong. His hawk-like, roman nose reminded Wiggins of paintings he had seen of the Duke of Wellington, and his sculpted chin and muscled neck spoke of a man of formidable character and physical power. The Viscount had strikingly blue eyes, almost glacial in their iciness, fringed with pale eyelashes. These haunted eyes possessed the redness and rawness that grief invariably brings from days of sorrow and tears. At that exact moment, those same troubled eyes slowly rose from the grave and settled upon those of Wiggins. The detective could feel such fire bore from

those eyes into his that he quickly dropped his gaze to regard his clasped gloved hands. Wiggins felt a mixture of guilt and shame and, inexplicably a bite of fear also, as if he was an angry parent admonishing a child. Several seconds passed before Wiggins had sufficiently regained his composure and lifted his head to return the aristocrat's piercing gaze. Much to his relief, he saw that the Viscount had taken to comforting the strikingly beautiful young lady by his side whom Wiggins assumed was Agatha Harkness' younger sister, Constance. Wiggins then saw the elderly Viscount turn on his heels and depart. Wiggins again experienced a wave of shame, this time at his feeling of relief, rebuking himself inwardly for his weakness. It had, after all, been his intention to attempt an informal interview with the Viscount immediately after the internment, but the aspect of the man had given Wiggins more than second thoughts as to the prudence of this particular course of action.

Wiggins surveyed the small neatly tended graveyard which was located next to the private chapel of the Family's Hertfordshire Estate where generations of the Harkness family had been laid to rest. He had noted that it was a mere seventy-eight strides from the chapel's door to the graveside. He was counting again. Wiggins then had an irrational vision of all those antecedents welcoming their newest and most beautiful, yet tragic member with open arms into the heart of their lifeless community, rejoicing in her presence. 'She will be looked after,' he thought again realising what a senseless waste of a remarkable life had occurred. Wreaths and sprays of beautiful flowers encompassed three sides of the grave, their colour straining to brighten the miserable scene. Wiggins could hear the distant words of the Priest dissipate to be replaced by the slough of muddy earth being shovelled onto the reluctant pine. He decided to depart silently and leave the interview for another occasion, a slightly less dreadful day. He took one final look at the grave, remembering Agatha's beautiful face and joyful, resolute attitude, he crossed himself and turned to follow the other now slowly departing mourners. At that moment he felt a gentle hand being placed upon his damp shoulder.

"A moment if you do not mind, please Inspector." The voice was melodic and youthful, almost child-like in tone. He turned to see the face of Constance Harkness smiling gently back at him as she lifted her black lace mourning veil. Wiggins removed his hat despite the rain still thundering down. "My father and I would appreciate it if you were to accompany me back to the manor house. Cook has prepared some light refreshments and I believe that father desires to talk with you," she added in a slightly conspiratorial tone. Wiggins found that she had surreptitiously linked her arm into his and was directing him towards the grand house before he had time to respond or indeed to react.

"That would be most kind ... Lady Harkness," he stumbled over the appropriate title of address making a mental note that he must consult his DeBretts on his return to the office. "How fares your mother at this dreadful time?"

"Please call me Constance, Inspector Wiggins, I have no great liking for titles or formality. I am afraid that my mother, Lady Cecilia is under sedation. This has all been too much for her constitution," she smiled what to Wiggins appeared to be a borrowed smile, her mind no doubt drifting to thoughts of her elder sister. "Did you know Agatha well or are you here in an official capacity?"

"Alas, I met Miss Harkness only once, but that was more than enough opportunity for me to recognise a woman of rare strength and character. She is a sad loss to so many. I am here to pay my respects to her and your family and had hoped that I may be able to speak briefly to your parents, and to offer my personal condolences."

"Yet you were turning to leave," stated Constance questioningly.

"I must admit, Miss Harkness that I did indeed suffer from second thoughts and felt the occasion would be better left until another time," admitted Wiggins, again with a returning pang of guilt this time accompanied by a feeling of inadequacy.

"No time like the present, as Aggie used to say," proclaimed the younger Miss Harkness who by now was almost pulling Wiggins towards the shelter of the massive colonnade that fronted the Harkness home. They walked in silence, linked together, accompanied by the constant tapping of the rain on the umbrella which Constance attempted somewhat unsuccessfully to cover them both with.

'This is another remarkable young woman,' thought Wiggins. 'Beautiful, composed and determined. She has just buried her dear sister but remains composed and erudite. Mature beyond her years and an absolute credit to her sister and her family.' Wiggins hoped that her father would be equally amenable, but very much doubted that this would be the case.

Wiggins and Miss Harkness were both divested of their outer coats by a waiting footman as they entered the hall of the great house. Wiggins' sodden top hat was also taken, no doubt to be dried and brushed ready for his departure. "This way Mr Wiggins," announced Constance striding across the marble floor, her footsteps echoing as she went. "Jeffers, can you arrange for some tea and cakes to be brought to father's study please?"

"Already there Miss Constance," said the ever-anticipatory Jeffers looking for all the world like a satisfied infantryman standing to attention.

"You are a dear, Jeffers, how would we cope without you?" called Constance with a wave of her hand and a smile as she headed across the hall. The butler's face nearly split in two with a reciprocal smile so broad that it could have illuminated a crypt, his chest swelling with pride.

'*An astonishing woman indeed,*' thought Wiggins. '*She brings sunshine where none is expected even on the darkest of days. I wonder if she at all realises how many lives she and her sister have touched.*'

Constance knocked three times in a triangular space high on the heavy oak door. "Come, Connie," answered a booming baritone from within. Wiggins noted that the Viscount had recognised his daughter's not so secret knock. The room which he and Constance entered was cloaked in oak panelling and draped on all sides by ceiling to floor shelves of bound volumes, all excepting the large triple sash window which framed the stately figure of Viscount Harkness. The aristocrat, who held a letter in his hand, rose as they entered and indicated that they both be seated. Wiggins did so whilst Constance skipped around her father's walnut desk, placed a comforting hand on his shoulder and planted a kiss on his ruddy cheek.

"What is in the letter Daddy?" she asked trying to engage her father as brightly as she could.

"It is of little import on this day, Connie. Merely a message from young Buchanan declaring that he is on his way back to London from his latest expedition and wishes to call on us once he arrives." Viscount Harkness mustered the briefest of smiles and gently squeezed his daughter's hand before he slumped down back into his chair. Wiggins could see that this great man of state, and world-renowned Egyptologist, was struggling to contain his emotions. His upbringing and position in society no doubt hindered any such outward display of anything that could be construed as weakness. Wiggins again began to feel uncomfortable. "I wish to offer my personal condolences but perhaps it is prudent that I should return another time, Sir," offered Wiggins hopefully.

The Viscount lifted his sandy crowned head and raised his glacial eyes to rest upon Wiggins. Wiggins could sense that some of the fire he had previously witnessed emanating from those reddened eyes had been extinguished. Here was a man who was barely holding himself together. "No need Inspector. What I have to say to you is brief," stated Harkness, a slight falter in his deep voice. "Put quite simply," and here the Viscount arose from his chair with a stuttering but violent surge. "Apprehend this monster!" he shouted, his thunderous voice reverberating around the house as he slammed his clenched fist down on the desk causing it to shudder. "Get this monster, kill him if needs be, or I swear by Almighty God I will have your warrant card Inspector!" He slumped back down into the chair deflated, a seemingly broken man having expended his last iota of pent up energy in his brief tirade. His chin hit his chest and his hand went to his forehead as the sobbing began to wrack convulsively through his entire body.

Constance wheeled to her father's side and cradled his heaving shoulders in an effort to console the inconsolable. "Forgive father, Mr Wiggins, his frustration and grief are incalculable. Only another grieving father could comprehend the sorrow, stress, and anger he contains within his broken heart. What he means is that our family, myself included, will do anything we conceivably can within our power and our resources to assist you in capturing this abominable fiend."

Wiggins nodded and stood to leave, finding himself utterly speechless at the outpouring of grief and rage he had witnessed, not to mention the bravery and stoicism of what he now recognised as the most impressive young lady he had ever encountered.

He thought, not for the first time that day, of John Hamish. "Sir, I promise. You have my solemn pledge that if I do not capture or indeed kill this Beast that I will be handing in my warrant card and my resignation personally," Wiggins affirmed before leaving father and daughter to console each other as best they possibly could.

Chapter 33 - The Landlady

Alf Sandalwood stood confused at the locked door. To be brutally truthful Alf Sandalwood was always in some degree of bewilderment depending upon what time of day it was. His fondness for cheap women and of even cheaper gin had caught up with him some time ago and had ravaged his body to such an extent that he was unrecognisable from the man that he had been merely a few years before. Mothers are not the only individuals to be ruined by the fermentation of juniper berries. The death of his partner and the loss of his job in Victoria Docks had been enough to destroy a week-willed individual such as Alf. He was now the humble owner of a shrunken and emaciated body, riddled with disease and the effects of his long-standing alcoholism. Jaundice and syphilis were not welcome bedfellows to Alf. His yellowish eyes blinked repeatedly, and his head thumped dreadfully from dehydration caused by the previous evening's excessive drinking. His tiny body, attired in stained and creased clothes, craved supplementary alcohol just to ease his tremors. Unfortunately for Alf, the pub was closed. 'The Grapes is never closed? Hungry Mary's is always open so long as there's money to be made and a throat to be lubricated!' he thought as he pondered as to which other drinking emporium would be open to fuel his addiction at this early hour.

"Mary. Mary!" Alf hollered as he banged on the front door and peered through the grimy nicotine-stained windows. "I needs a drink to tickle me innards Mary," he bellowed again. He craved a gin but from what he could observe the establishment was silent and empty inside. Alf retreated and craned his arthritic neck upwards to the window of the upstairs room that Mary Hallbard called home. "Mary! MAAAAARY!"

A sash window rasped open in the tenement house across the street and a threatening looking head popped out over the windowsill and bellowed at Alf. "Hoi, Mary, bloody Mary down there! Shut your cakehole or I'm gonna get more than quite contrary! Decent folks is trying to get some kip."

Alf wiped his thread-veined nose with the back of his coat sleeve, spat at the pub door then thrust his hands into his trouser pockets before shuffling off in pursuit of spiritual sustenance elsewhere.

It was two-fifteen in the morning and Mary Hallbard had just poured herself a small glass of neat gin as she prepared to lock up the downstairs pub and head to her bed to catch a few hours rest. She kept the four keys to the pub on a violet lace ribbon around her neck and close to her ample bosom. Nobody knew she wore them, and nobody would dare snatch them from her 'coker-nuts' as she referred to them. Her days were long and arduous, and she thought nothing of opening up at eight in the morning and perhaps not pouring out the last customer until four the next morning. Mary's nightly tipple was not the harsh, cheap gut rot gin she offered her patrons, but a bottle of Hayman's, secreted away solely for her much anticipated nightcap.

It had been a typical midweek evening in The Grapes with all the usual suspects carousing and, more importantly to Mary, spending what little money they possessed. Jem, her favourite Mutton Shunter, had even popped in briefly for a swift one. She had a soft spot for Jem. There was never much trouble when he was in her pub. Trouble cost money and if there was one thing Mary could not spare it was money. An ear to bend, a word of advice, these came at no cost, but in her experience, trouble meant money. She sipped at her nightly tot as she sat at the piano tinkling the yellowing ivories with one hand to the tune of 'Come into the Garden Maude.' As she played, she could not help but notice a few emergent liver spots on the back of her hand. *'Surely they weren't there last year,'* she mused. And the wrinkles, well obviously they belonged to someone else, someone much older. Sighing, she gently closed the piano lid and went to cash up before heading up to bed. An unseen shadow darted across the barroom wall. That had been the last tune that 'Hungry' Mary Hallbard would play this side of a harp.

Constable Potts looked blankly at his note pad and offered an empty open palm to Pyke. "Nothin' much to report really, Sir. Hungry Mary, ahem, Ms Hallbard, must have gone away on business or a trip of some description. Maybes a sick relative or some such? The pub was in order with no visible signs of thievery or skulduggery. Tables had been cleared and the floor seemed to have been swept. Locked up tight for the night it was. We had to force the door in fact, but we have secured it again for her return. I've left a man down there to be visible in case any scoundrel thinks of ransacking the establishment," snorted Constable Potts.

"Who did you leave there Pottsie? I hope it weren't that souse head Lewis. He will have the place drank dry before the Cock crows tomorrow."

"No, it were Bunce I left there. Lewis is off sick again Sarge."

"No doubt, Bunce is a safe pair of hands," replied Pyke, grasping his nose lightly with thumb and forefinger. "Have you ever known Mary to take time off Potts? Ever?" he asked raising his eyes questioningly towards the young constable. "No Sir, she didn't get to be known as 'Hungry' Mary for nuthin.' She opens the Grapes prompt at seven-thirty each morning as regular as me morning ablutions," quipped Potts. "Strange indeed," countered Pyke before dismissing Potts with a sideward glance of his head.

Twenty minutes later Pyke had made his presence obvious to the attending Bobby temporarily stationed outside The Grapes. "Anything to report Constable Bunce?"

"No Sir, nothing but disappointed customers and an angry delivery man. Whole crate of ale he had too," came the young policeman's instant response. Bunce was fresh to the Force, a curly-haired young man eager to make a place for himself. Bunce handed Pyke the key to the newly fitted lock which Pyke turned and entered the establishment. The smell of stale beer and even staler tobacco smoke still clung densely in the air. The silence and stillness of the pub were unsettling. It looked and felt strangely different, its use somehow redundant. The day's early sunshine penetrated the threadbare curtains casting a warm but spectral glow over the interior which seemed somewhat unnatural. Empty and hollow, not at all like the boisterous pub he was used to. However, everything did seem to be in normal order as Constable Potts had detailed earlier. Instinctively, Pyke meticulously surveyed and investigated the room rotating slowly on his axis as he did so. Taking in the scene, devouring the details.

The front door was locked. Lamps extinguished. Windows secured. Floor swept. Table leg repaired. Piano lid closed. Mousetraps set. Tables wiped. Tankards cleaned and stacked. Back door locked. Bar cleared. Cleared except for a neatly piled stack of meat pies and soft-boiled eggs placed at the farthest end. *'Why would she leave food out if she planned to be going away for a few days, especially boiled eggs,'* wondered Pyke. *'That would be a waste of money and Hungry Mary detests such waste!'* Pyke then vaulted over the bar counter to check the cash box which was secured by a heavy link chain to the wall. The box was unlocked and full of coin. He steadfastly knew from speaking with Mary about her security that the final thing she did before going to bed was cash up and lock the box, taking the night's takings upstairs to bed with her. *'Something is definitely amiss,'* he thought. He could sense it. Now he was extremely worried.

Pyke hurriedly proceeded downstairs to the cellar which was damp and dank. He manoeuvred between barrels and sporadic puddles of water diluted with spilt beer that dotted the slippery flagstone floor. Pyke's boot heel skidded momentarily on a patch of ale. He half expected to find Mary lying unconscious down there, having slipped and cracked her head on the flags. Stepping over several sandbags he noticed that the beer drop door above his head was secured with a robust hulking padlock. *'Nothing untoward down here either,'* he mused as he advanced gingerly up the rickety stairs all the while dusting cobwebs off his Derby. *'Bleedin' spiders, what's the point?'*

Pyke progressed to investigating the cramped bedroom upstairs where a solitary lamp still shone, illuminating the well-kempt but spartan surroundings before him. The walls were empty, save for a small crucifix and a cracked mirror with a crumpled paper shamrock stuffed into the corner of the frame. A floral-patterned nightdress lay neatly on the bare mattress covering the bed. There was no pillow or bolster. Looking under the bed Pyke noticed a battered old suitcase. He crouched down and pulled it out from beneath the iron bedstead. There was nothing to be found inside but a photograph of a dashing young man in uniform and a small jewellery box containing cheap trinkets, brooches and a single gold engagement ring. A handbag, complete with rouge, a tin of zinc oxide, a handkerchief and a bag of coins sat on the floor beside a timeworn pine cupboard. Pyke sat down upon the bed and picked up the engagement ring, reading the story that the room was telling him. The story of a woman that he now realised he had never really known at all. He fiddled with the ring and eventually forced it onto his little finger. *'Where is she? This is getting bizarre now,'* he thought. *'What woman leaves without her bleedin' handbag? Mary would never ever leave behind a bag of readies!'* Two dresses hung above a solitary pair of shabby shoes within the small wardrobe. No break-in. No robbery. No landlady! He pulled the ring off his finger, having to work it back and forth several times to surmount his knuckle and replaced it in the jewellery box.

Pyke returned downstairs and headed for the backdoor. He strode past the piano at which he had witnessed Mary play many times, often to quieten down rough, potentially dangerous situations. Physical violence was always a last resort with Mary but one that her formidable size and power could be administered if so required. He had forgotten to check over the Snug that lay just behind the bar. A small room longer than it was wide where customers went for a quiet drink or to conduct illicit business transactions. What next caught his eye shocked Pyke right to his very marrow. Alongside the rutted dartboard on the back wall hung a black slate scoreboard. Upon the board was chalked one solitary word written repeatedly, in tiny manic letters.

Apostles! The iciest of chills ran down Pyke's spine like a finger creating a final glissando on the keyboard. He scratched his head under his beloved Derby and sat down at the beer-stained piano. He lifted the lid and began to aimlessly peck at arbitrary keys. He had no notion at all as to how to pick out a tune but something inside him had inexplicably drawn him towards the piano stool. *'A silent piano in a room simply calls out to be played,*' he recalled someone once telling him. The ultimate soundless elephant in any room, it attracts people like a magnet, no matter what their musical ability, urging them to at least try to play. He knew middle C was the key nearest the first screw in the maker's nameplate. His grandmother had told him that nugget of data as a nipper. He hit it. No sound other than a muffled rattle. He hit it again, harder this time. Again, the muffled rattle. '*There was something dreadfully wrong here,*' concluded Pyke. He stood and lifted the hinged lid to the top of the upright. What he saw within made Jem Pyke turn away and stifle a wretch.

Mary Hallbard's corpse had been rammed so violently into the piano's innards that her entire body was sliced through by the piano wires within. It was difficult trying to distinguish an understandable human form at all due to the savagery and ferocity with which she had been stuffed inside her beloved piano. A piano now serving as some hideous coffin. Although the upright's grizzly cargo was unrecognisable, blood had pooled at the foot pedals in a very recognisable heart shape. Sergeant 'Jem' Pyke slammed down the piano lid, slowly slumped to the floor and began to silently weep.

Chapter 34 - The Contemplation

He studied the early morning mist. It took him back to the morning of the fifteenth of February, nineteen hundred, when he and his fellow cavalrymen had relieved the mining town of Kimberley from its one-hundred- and twenty-four-day siege. The mist that day, however, had been a mixture of rifle smoke and artillery shells and dust from the cavalry division's charge. He remembered leading the charge with several brave comrades, sabre grasped in hand, a rifle strapped to his back, the dry, hot wind rushing towards him, burning his gritty eyes. The trumpeting of the bugles resonated in his ears and fuelled his adrenalin. He recalled the dual surge of pride and fear that had coursed through his veins, nourishing his heart with a sustenance that gave birth to a confidence that good would triumph over evil. That same thought burned in his head about the Beast. They must triumph!

The mist today, however, clung low to the ground, hugging it, making the heath look as though it was draped in some great lake of chiffon. Birch and sycamore trees pierced the misty blanket and stretched their leafy necks curiously through the cloud as if just newly awake. The mist seemed alive and kinetic, he thought, unlike the dead and heavy fog of the city. It seemed to move and dance in time to his thoughts. A brittle frost covered everything, and his breath billowed in front of his face. The fresh, invigorating morning air purified his mind allowing for clear and concise considerations. He stretched his neck forward, revelling in the movement, encouraging the air to come to him, bathing in its iciness, eager for it to caress his battle-weary face.

When he was here, he felt unwrapped and free instead of tethered and restricted. He always sat on the same bench high up on the hill overlooking Hampstead Heath. His favourite place of solace and contemplation. Pyke knew the best way he could assist in the capturing of the Beast was to control or at least temper his anger and channel it positively into clarity of thought and precision of action. He had always struggled with impatience and rage and he greatly admired the way Wiggins appeared to remain calm and always in control of his emotions, even during chaotic and perilous days such as these. He often marvelled at how his colleague had escaped from an existence of that of a mudlark, a homeless, orphaned guttersnipe, to rise to a position of such prominence in the World's greatest police force. At least he had had his father, tough though his upbringing had been. He realised with admiration that Wiggins' resolve and determination to succeed must have been incalculable.

He flicked a barely drawn upon cigarette into the dewy grass, took a swig from his bashed hip flask and pondered further. He loved the feeling of drinking whisky on the open heath, the colder the day the better the taste.

Pyke pictured the horrific scenes that had befallen his eyes upon liberating Kimberley. Disease, decay and death were all abundant. He saw very few children and shuddered at the thought of their absence. No horses or mules were to be seen as these had become the only source of food left to the inhabitants of the gold-mining town. Unidentifiable carcasses littered the sun-baked ground, testament to just how desperate the inhabitants had become. He shook his head, determined that he would never again witness such deprivation. He threw back another mouthful of the throat warming scotch. The taste took him immediately to Mary. Beautiful, bombastic Mary. He saw the equally horrific vision of Mary's contorted body. Not the sassy and defiant person he so admired but a woman dehumanised by such savage brutality. Mercifully, he could see no face amongst the contorted torso and misshapen limbs that had intermingled with piano wire garrottes. He realised again that this monster was physically extraordinarily strong. Perhaps he should have visited the gym rather than ride out to the Heath. Build his strength for the expected physical confrontation he knew was to inevitably come. The wind flurried across his face stinging his eyes causing them to water. Or were they tears? The eyes did not blink however but remained focussed intently upon the distant horizon as the sun began to blister through the haze, illuminating the world once more. '*No matter what is going on in life, the sun always rises and darkness always comes,*' he contemplated.

The sounds of birdsong began to fill the air as the dawn arrived. The chirpings of birds always sound happy, never sad, Pyke contemplated. A lopsided smile appeared on his face. He found it peculiar that no matter how hard he strained his eyes upon the trees he could not pick out one single bird. The Beast could seemingly do the same, somehow camouflaged, moving around the streets of London as he wished. How could something so despicable and horrific be happening only miles from this tranquil haven, thought Pyke? It made no sense.

The grotesque face of the Beast flashed into his thoughts. Engulfing his memory. The vileness, the evilness, the violence of seeing its unholy countenance for the first time was forever etched into his very being. '*It was eating her heart!*' Pyke had borne witness to horrors others could only begin to imagine but he had never encountered such savagery and loathing expressed upon a face. A face so contorted with fury and bile that he had initially believed it to be some cornered, rabid animal.

The sudden sharp snorting of the horse brought an abrupt end to his contemplations. Whenever Jem Pyke needed to release his pent-up anger or cleanse his cluttered thoughts, he either visited the gym on the City Road or took his horse, Kym, for some exercise across the heath. This day he chose to ride his horse. It had been four o'clock in the morning when he had bridled Kym at the Scotland Yard stables and headed off for some solitude of thought. The majestic Grey was the envy of the Yard's mounted officers; intelligent, handsome, strong and as fast as the very wind itself. He had set his horse free this day, at first trotting their way north from the City towards the Heath, and then galloping thunderously together over the open land, his hair and her mane blowing wildly together as they charged. The exhilaration he felt always reminded him of that same feeling he had experienced leading that charge thirteen long years ago. Kym was abridged from Kimberley, named in recognition of the ten men and seventy horses that perished at the Siege of Kimberley during the Second Boer War. Cavalryman Leslie Pyke's horse, Frenchie, had perished in the successful attempt at reopening the route to the besieged and beleaguered town. He had loved that horse. He remembered the uncomprehending, petrified look in the loyal animal's eyes as he lay beside it, comforting the dying horse through its final moments. There was just no way he could bring himself to squeeze the trigger. He had witnessed enough death for one lifetime. He did not wish to see any more.

He had been taught Vedic yoga and meditation techniques by an Indian guru an exceptionally long time ago. This specific type of spiritualism was created many centuries ago by ancient yoga masters as a system of practices and movements designed to rejuvenate the body and prolong life. Van Hoon agreed with the philosophy wholeheartedly. The previous fifteen minutes had been spent stretching and posturing in his daily set routine of slow measured movements. His muscles and connective tissues were now supple, warmed and relaxed. His eyes were closed. A thin sheen of sweat glistened upon his lithely muscled torso. He sat cross-legged in a sparse chamber illuminated only by three large diameter alter candles signifying the Hindu trio of divinity. These were placed directly behind him casting his looming shadow upon the wall he faced. The small room was bathed in a vivid orange hue that softened any hard edges, adding to the serenity and tranquillity. There was no sound but his measured deliberate nasal breathing. Van Hoon had been motionless for thirty minutes and over this time he had slowed his heart rate to twenty-two beats per second. He was connecting to a parallel awareness in which his consciousness was focused within, unaware of external stimuli. His mind was clear and minutely receptive to the smallest of thoughts. Van Hoon had prepared and readied himself to visualise or remotely view, as he termed it, searching for the Beast.

The slicing sound the scissors made were relaxing and hypnotic like the sound of a distant cymbal keeping time. The transient combing and teasing of his hair only heightened the trance-like state he was currently experiencing. The scent of lavender cologne intermingled with that of menthol shaving foam amplified the calmness he enjoyed. Wiggins always found an afternoon trip to the Barbershop allowed him time to unwind and permit analyses of the data that overcrowded and burdened his already full memory. The hot towels and facial massage, the clean rasp of a precision razor. All these sensations helped him relax and focus. Was there something he had overlooked? Some minor detail, no matter how trivial, that had escaped his investigations thus far. His mind was slipping back to the grisly scene of the Agatha Harkness murder when a chirpy voice brought an abrupt end to his contemplations. "Mr Wiggins 'ere will know the answer!"

"What is that you say Johnston?" enquired Wiggins snapping out of his fugue and returning to the Barber's mirrored reflection.

"Why, me and Boniface over there were chewin' the fat the other day and wondered where the term to double-cross someone comes from," offered Johnston whilst pointing to an odd little darkly tanned fellow sitting alone at a small table playing patience. Boniface was an almost permanent fixture in Arthur Johnston's barbershop. The peculiar sight of Boniface always reminded Wiggins of the photographs he had seen of the shrunken heads of Borneo in National Geographic photographs. His oversized protruding ears were strangely positioned incredibly low on his head, and his snout-like nose enhanced the likeness. His undernourished body in the ubiquitous loose-fitting suit brought forth the image of a monkey dressed and ready for Sunday Service.

"That is a question, the answer of which my colleague Constable Pyke would be more familiar with as he is quite the pugilist," smirked Wiggins. "… but, as I understand it, in a time before the Marquis of Queensbury decided upon legislating a degree of decorum during a fistfight, there existed the term a cross-fight, or rather an ex fight. This was when one combatant had previously agreed to lose the boxing contest in preference to ending up a bloody mess, or worse. If said combatant then decided, however, not to continue with the prearranged bargain and wished to catch his opponent by surprise, then this would be termed a double-cross."

"Ha! I said so, didn't I? I knew it! I thought you'd know the answer Mr Wiggins. Hear that Brownie?" hollered the gleeful barber across the room.

"Yeah, yeah," returned Boniface with a dismissive wave of his hand and returned to his card game. A triumphant Johnston returned to trimming Wiggins' moustache and Wiggins returned to his thoughts. His eyes were closed but images rushed rapidly through his head. Slow at first then gaining momentum and getting quicker and briefer until each face remained in focus for a mere split-second. Miss Agatha Harkness, Hungry Mary Hallbard, Dante Van Hoon, Louise Smith, Constance Harkness, Phyllis, Jem, Cripes, Watson, Bleak, King, Freud. Freud! His eyes snapped open as realisation catapulted into his considerations. He distinctly recollected informing Doctor Bleak that Mary Harrison's body was found in a narrow street in the Limehouse area, but Bleak had himself stated that he suspected her head trauma was caused as a result of falling onto the flagstones that paved *Narrow* Street! There are hundreds of narrow streets in and around the Limehouse region, he thought, so why then had Bleak stated unequivocally *Narrow* Street? A Freudian slip indeed Wiggins smirked!

"Eyebrows Mr Wiggins?" enquired Johnston. "If we must," responded the detective somewhat reluctantly. His smirk had broadened to a smile.

Chapter 35 - The Housekeeper

This was her favourite part of the day. The daylight had gently faded and the evening was upon her, bringing its customary chill at this time of year. Doctor Bleak would soon be home. The mantle clock struck seven, its sonorous tones resounding from its walnut casing to fill the eerily silent house. Soon she would hear his key turn in the lock followed by his shuffle as he wiped his wet shoes on the coir entrance mat. Edith stabbed at the fire with the brass poker causing embers to jump and dance. The logs crackled and spat, and the chimney began to roar as it sucked the air upwards. Satisfied that she had stoked the blaze sufficiently she completed her fireside welcome by placing the Master's olive green Persian slippers to the side of the hearth, making sure that they were far enough away from the spitting flames to avoid accidental damage, whilst being close enough to toast invitingly. She placed his Bible on the occasional table that always sat at the side of his oxblood wing-backed Chesterfield chair, the only piece of extravagant furniture in the otherwise spartanly furnished house. Soon he would be home. She carefully folded his favourite plaid blanket and draped it over the back of the chair.

She returned to the kitchen to ensure that everything was ready for Doctor Bleak's supper. He loved his supper to be on the table as soon as he returned from an exhausting day of doing God's work by saving lives and tending to the sick and unfortunate, both of which London had in painful abundance. Only plain food, boiled rice mixed with lightly steamed winter vegetables. Bleak was not one for red meat or exotic foreign food and flavours. The antitheses of the fare they served in West End restaurants that Harley Street types frequented. Bleak had joined the Vegetarian Society many years previously and regularly visited the Concordium retreats at Alcott House in Surrey. Edith relished the strict routine they had developed in their austere household. Her strict puritan, Scottish upbringing was nourished by the environment the Bleak household afforded.

As she walked through the gloomy hallway towards the scullery, she momentarily paused at the mirror that hung from the picture rail. Doctor Bleak had hung it there himself twelve years ago. Such a talented gentleman she thought. She flicked at a stray hair that had escaped from the severe bun that scraped her brittle black hair back from her scrubbed, unadorned face. She flattened the front pleats of her ankle-length black skirt and tugged at the shoulders of her high collared blouse, straightening her back as she did so. Perfect, she decided.

She stirred the vegetables and turned the heat down to allow them a final gentle simmer before serving. He would be home any minute. She checked the rice and offered thanks that she worked for such a clean living and godly man as Doctor Bleak. Her strict upbringing had prepared her perfectly for serving such a man. She adored living in the simply furnished dark silence of the house. A house devoid of any affectation or luxury. Doctor Bleak's only treats were his books, mostly medical texts and research papers, works of religious study, and of course his beloved Bible, which, other than Edith, was his only other constant companion in the grimly sparse house.

The key scraped in the lock as the clock struck the quarter hour. She had known a few seconds before it happened that it would. *'He's home at last.'* She quickly removed the vegetables from the heat hoping fervently that they would not be overcooked and soft. "Edith I am home," came the familiar announcement in Bleak's soft but somehow resonant voice. He performed his customary shuffle on the mat as he wiped his shoes and shook his dripping umbrella before placing it into the clay spun holder by the front door. He hung his top hat, cloak and overcoat on the hat stand and unbuttoned his gloves and placed them on the simple wooden console table. He sighed, glad to be home. Another day doing God's work.

"Supper in two minutes Doctor," announced Edith as she drained the vegetables to add to the rice. She was pleased as Punch.

"I think I might take repast in the parlour on the chair this evening Edith," smiled Bleak gently. He took a quick look at himself in the mirror and ruffled his mop of now greying hair, smirking as he did so. A middle-aged man in his late forties, he stared ruefully at the dark semi-circular bags under his eyes and shrugged. *'Tempus edax rerum,'* he thought to himself. As always, the image that reflected back at him was in stark contrast to the placid looking individual he regarded himself to be. A monstrous parody of himself returned his gaze. Ink black eyes with pinpoint red pupils glared at him above a snarling mouth full of razor-sharp teeth. The lips were engorged and dripped blood copiously down his exaggeratedly pointed chin. The grimace became a silent, brain tearing scream that only Bleak could hear. He slapped at his head to make it stop and moved swiftly away from his reflection and made his way into the parlour. *'I categorically should know better by now than to offer him a glimpse of the real world,'* he admonished himself, smiling ruefully.

After Bleak had finished supper, Edith brought him a glass of hot chocolate milk and removed his plate. Bleak made himself comfortable on the chair by the hearth and picked up his Bible and laid it open upon his blanketed lap. He spent a few moments peering into the flames of the fire, watching it dance and lick around the brickwork of the fireplace surround. His eyes began to glaze and his pupils enlarged to almost fill his irises. His gaze fell back towards the book which had fallen open at the well-worn page of Deuteronomy 28:53: *You will eat the offspring of your own body, the flesh of your sons and of your daughters whom the Lord your God has given you.* Bleak's eyelids licked chameleon like over his eyes as he moistened his lips. He could taste the blood on his tongue as though it were fresh and hot. The combination of the flames, the heat and the evocative passage transported him back twenty-five years.

'*The imbecilic fools,*' thought Bleak. They had unwittingly built their new Temple on the very site of his first kill. Where better to dispose of the partial remains of his very first victim all those years ago, than in the very bowels of their own New Scotland Yard. How ironic that the Headquarters of the World's leading criminal investigation body was built upon the foundation of the most notorious unsolved murder case of its time. '*Even now that fool of a primped up Scottish Peacock, MacDonald, struts around his office in a building that he full well knows represents his beloved Metropolitan Police Force's greatest failure,*' thought Bleak. '*Good debate tonight Joseph. Lovely evening for a stroll Joseph. Look at my new car Joseph… blah, blah, blah Joseph*'." Idiot!" he spat.

The 'Thames Torso Murder' one paper had called it. Another he recalled christened it 'the Great Whitehall Mystery.' Of course, the Ripper was suspected which offered perfect cover for young Joseph Bleak's first lapse from humanity.

He was once again sat in front of a roaring fire in the Cheshire Cheese pub just off Fleet Street. The pub was a favourite haunt of the rather worldly innocent intern doctor freshly ensconced at Saint Bartholomew's Hospital and relishing the challenge of his new career. Even back then however the voice was continually ranting and raving inside his head, quoting scripture and the Epistles, screaming evil obscenities … and much worse.

The Cheese offered a secluded refuge not far from his then humble lodgings. Its low beamed ceiling and convivial medieval surroundings made him feel comfortable and safe. Although a brilliant student with a startlingly bright future ahead of him, Bleak did not relish company and actively shunned interaction with his peers. He was painfully shy and awkward in social situations and had not yet learned how to cloak his inner lack of confidence and a constant feeling of isolation. His father had been a brutal man who, after the premature passing of his beloved mother to the blight of typhoid fever, had beaten his frustration and anger out on him relentlessly.

He could not quite believe it when Maisie approached him. She with her buxom chest and swishing broche satin dress. As she blocked the fire in front of him, he could just make out her shapely thighs silhouetted sensually through her skirts. Bleak began to blush, redness searing through his cheeks. She had been from up North somewhere he seemed to recall, Leeds or perhaps Bradford. Her accent intrigued him and her sturdily built body and curves appealed to him. Although they were of an age, she seemed to Bleak to be much older, much more mature, wiser and experienced than he. Much to Joseph's surprise they both enjoyed each other's company that evening and left The Cheese having spent all his money on gin, ale and pork pies. They strolled along the embankment towards his lodgings, but, unfortunately for Maisie, they never made it beyond the construction site of the New Scotland Yard Building. A stolen kiss, a quick cuddle, a frenetic fumble. "Oh Joseph, what would your sainted mother think," she had giggled. He could still see her squirming with pleasure as she uttered those fatal words. The words were her very own death warrant.

The flames in the hearth licked and another log cracked and spat embers onto the rug at his feet. He remembers the ferrous taste of her hot blood as he bit through her jugular vein and ripped it out with a ferocity that shocked him. He remembers using a wood saw he found lying atop a pallet of bricks in the construction yard to dismember her lifeless and bloodied body. Unsurprisingly it did not take him too long to achieve. His surgical training, as the scandal sheets were later to speculate, enabled him to carry out quite a "proficiently professional job under the circumstances". The torso he wrapped in her black petticoat and deposited in a small vault in the newly constructed cellar of the building. The limbs he weighted down with bricks and tossed into the Thames. And the head, well the head still stared blankly at him each day from the shelf of one of the bookcases in his surgery office. An anatomical representation not only of the human skull but also his most prized trophy. As Edgar Alan Poe postulated, "If you want to keep something hidden, hide it in plain sight."

Bleak's chin hit his chest and his head instinctively recoiled with a sudden jerk, abruptly awakening him from his memories.

"Will there be anything else Doctor?" enquired Edith eagerly from the kitchen.

"I think not Edith," replied Bleak shaking his head from side to side in an effort to clear the demons. "You can retire early tonight. I will sit here a while and continue to decipher the meanings of the scriptures."

How would she taste?

"Are you sure, Doctor? I could warm you some more milk."

Raw, stringy flesh. Tough to chew. Stick in your teeth.

"Not at all, I will be perfectly fine, thank you."

Hot glutinous blood.

"Very well Doctor, Good night."

He could hear Edith ascending the creaking stairs, the noise of each footfall echoing through the deathly quiet of the dreary old house.

"Good night Edith. May God grant you a restful night."

As Edith climbed the stairs, she thought to herself just how lucky she was to have such a thoughtful employer. Such a considerate and godly man. Such an abstemious and pious man. She looked forward to the comfort of her bed and a good night's sleep, hoping eagerly that it would be filled with dreams of her good doctor.

Bleak spat violently into the fire. Blood sizzled as it hit the flames. Blood that came from biting upon his inner cheek. He rose from his chair and cast his bible aside as if it were no longer of any consequence to him. He raised his now entirely oily black eyes towards the ceiling and bared his teeth in a chilling maniacal smile. A high-pitched scream screeched inside his tormented brain. Saliva dripped from the upturned corners of his mouth and he felt a vague rumbling in his gut.

I hunger. I thirst. Flesh. I need flesh. Blood I crave blood. They call me the Beast, but I am so much more. I am the life taker. I am the life-giver. They will all recoil at my rage. They will all repent.

The tread of the first step of the staircase creaked as his weight pressed down upon it and he pulled himself upstairs to wish Edith one final good night.

At the same instant, less than two miles away, Dante Van Hoon sat meditating by a trickling fountain amongst the leafy serenity of his garden in Belgravia. His extraordinary eyes suddenly snapped wide open.

"Aha! I can hear you. At last, I have found you! I have you. I know who you are. How fare thee honourable Doctor Joseph Bleak, or should I call you the *Beast?*" Van Hoon's head snapped back as he roared with laughter before once again returning to his meditation, smiling contentedly to himself as he did so.

Chapter 36 - The Plan

Wiggins' office was a little less tidy than normal. He stood leaning against his desk, arms folded upon his chest, reviewing and analysing the data laid out before him. A frayed Union Flag slightly obscured the simply framed portrait of King George V which hung directly behind and above his desk. The commissioned painting may have been relatively new but the paint on the wall where it was displayed was flaking and in a somewhat distressed state. A state that DI Wiggins was himself familiar with as he surveyed the profiles of all seven murder victims. *'Would the seven deadly sins end here, or would they continue onto an eighth victim?'* he speculated inwardly.

On each of the three windowless walls of his office was pinned the body of the case. One wall was dominated by a photographic reconstruction of the scrawled writings he, Pyke and Potts had found in the hellhole within the sewers. Alongside were photographs of the body parts, the instruments, the butchery table and the other sickening pieces of associated evidence. A second wall was draped with a large-scale ordnance street map of London indicating the locations of the scenes of the crimes accompanied by forensic photographs and mini-biographies for each victim. On the third wall hung a large chalkboard full of Wiggins' observations, thoughts and theories. This blackboard was dominated by linking arrows and several underlined question marks. The word 'Apostles' was written vertically in large neat letters on the chalkboard directly in front of the table where he stood. The wall clock chimed four-fifteen in the morning and except for the Desk Sergeant, a few Constables and the Turnkey, there was little activity and very few personnel in evidence within the Yard at that hour. Pyke sat rather comfortably on a nearby tub chair, his legs outstretched, his feet propped on Wiggins' desk and his Derby covering his face, shielding his eyes from the lamp light. It was impossible to distinguish if he was sleeping or not.

"Why don't we just go round his house and arrest him, Sir?" enquired Pyke from under his hat. "Van Hoon is convinced he *heard* Bleak utter this very mantra," he pressed, waving rather aimlessly at the photograph of the graffiti-strewn sewer wall. "Not to mention the fact that old Professor Freud informed us that we were looking for a medical man. Not forgetting his narrow Street reference. It all adds up and points to Bleak. Let's just go and collar the Beast and have done with it."

Wiggins stroked his bearded chin thoughtfully. "We still have no hard evidence that Bleak is, in fact, our man. We need unquestionable proof to send him to the gallows and his subsequent onward journey to Hell. What do we really have, Jem? A leprous, master extortionist's assertion that he read the thoughts of the Beast whilst meditating in his garden? Too many glasses of absinthe perhaps? A slip of speech, one word out of place? Dubious and tenuous to say the very least and it certainly would not hold any water with a jury. Granted, Bleak does fit the profile provided by Professor Freud, and Van Hoon seems convinced, but we need solid conclusive proof."

"Get him in here and I'll knock a confession out of him within five minutes," replied Pyke cracking the knuckles of his rock-hard fists as he stood and began to prowl around the office.

A wry smile spread across Wiggins' face "I somehow doubt that strong-arm tactics will extract much from this maniac, why he would probably rather enjoy it for some masochistic reason. Besides, we must remember that Joseph Bleak is not only a member of the Royal College of Surgeons but also a fellow of the Royal Society of General Practitioners. He is an upstanding member of London Society and a friend, not only of the Metropolitan Police Force but also of Chief Superintendent MacDonald. If he is indeed our man, then we need to either gather enough solid hard evidence to ensure his conviction or we need to apprehend him red-handed, as it were." Wiggins regretted the unintentional pun as soon as it had escaped his lips.

"And how on God's green earth are we going to do that Sir!" raged Pyke, thumping the heel of his hand against the wall with frustration. "We have no idea where or when he is going to strike next. It is like the Beast himself doesn't even know! There is absolutely no pattern here other than his savagery, these mad scribblings and an all too apparent hatred of women. Do we follow his every move? Surely a man of his intelligence would soon realise he was being followed and no doubt the charge of unfounded victimisation would soon follow."

"There *must* be a motivation Pyke. Some infernal trigger to his actions. If we can find out what that is, we can lay a trap that would prove irresistible to him. The answer is here Jem, somewhere on these walls. Somewhere before our very eyes. We just have to see it and unlock it," reinforced Wiggins adjusting his reading spectacles. "Let us see. The mantra regarding hunger and thirst, flesh and blood strikes me as the ramblings of a lunatic, yet this repetition of the names of Christ's Apostles intrigues me. There is some sanity amongst this madness. Some insane purpose. I can feel it. In the name of the Apostles? For the Apostles?"

Wiggins rewrote the word 'Apostles' in capital letters across the top of the blackboard, underlining and writing the name of the twelve apostles in alphabetical order underneath it. "Why is he writing this term over and over again Jem? What is his motivation? Why does he slaughter these women?"

"Did Van Hoon not have a clock within that cavernous house of his that used the Apostles as the hours of the day? Can there possibly be a connection there? Is Van Hoon, in fact, our man? Is he leading our attention away from himself and incriminating Bleak?" mused Pyke, the notion becoming more plausible the further he contemplated it.

"It is not beyond the realms of possibility, but I suspect if Van Hoon were a killer, he would have been active for a longer time period than these recent murders. We would have had some indication long before now," highlighted Wiggins. "Let us look at our victims, there *must* be a connection … there simply MUST."

"There is Sir. They were all killed by this savage cannibal. We've been over this a hundred times before and there ain't nothing that ties these seven unfortunates together other than the horrific manner of their demise," snorted Pyke. "Some rich, some poor. Some young, some not so young. Brunettes, redheads, blondes, thin, fat, comely and plain. A teacher and a Suffragette, daughter of a Viscount. An actress and a prim church organist. A whore and a pub landlady and a sideshow entertainer. You couldn't possibly make up a more diverse group if you tried."

"And yet, they are a group. Our group. A group of individuals that we must redress and avenge," determined Wiggins, biting the stick of chalk clenched between his teeth. He began to write the names of the victims next to those of the apostles. "Perhaps there is a connection between the names of the apostles and the names of the murdered women," he offered.

"If that's the case we still have five more victims to come," offered Pyke rubbing his coarsely stubbled chin whilst shaking his head.

A knock on the door was quickly followed by Constable Pott's eager to please smile. "You might want to see this, Sir," offered Potts biting his lip and handing Pyke the early edition of the Standard. Pyke snatched it decisively from Potts' hand, "Come in lad, we need all the brain cells we can muster on this one. Balls!" exclaimed Pyke thrusting the newspaper towards Wiggins. "That sneak Babbitch has blabbed to the press. I'd wring his blubberous neck if I could get me hands around its girth."

The headline emblazoned across the front page read '*Apostle Beast's Underground Lair Uncovered*.' There followed a blow by blow account of their visit to the sewers. "Unfortunate to be sure," bemoaned Wiggins. "This could well put our man into hiding, or at the very least curtail his activities for some time, certainly in the short term. Our degree of urgency has just multiplied several-fold. We must concentrate our efforts on discovering this Beast's motivation in order to flush him out and snare him in the very act."

Wiggins was staring intently at the crime scene photographs of the second victim, thirty-four-year-old actress Mary Harrison. He rifled through the well-thumbed Manilla file scrutinising every available scrap of evidence they had collected, digging for clues they may have previously missed. Miss Harrison was an unmarried woman with no children and was found by Wiggins and Pyke, being butchered by the Beast in Narrow Street at approximately two-thirty on a foggy night. It was thought she was returning home after a performance at The Pavilion on Whitechapel Road, Mile End, where she was playing the lead in a production of The Pearl Girl. There was a newspaper cutting extolling her portrayal. 'Harrison Excels as Madame Alvarez,' critiqued the article enthusiastically. There was no evidence of sexual assault, nor robbery, only the ferocious attack that had ripped out the victim's throat. Wiggins mulled several ideas over in his head and placed her file neatly to his left whilst reaching for the case notes for the first victim, Louise Smith.

Miss Louise Smith was aged twenty-six years. '*Same modus operandi*,' thought Wiggins. "What is most perplexing about this victim Pyke is that although she was indeed working the streets as an active prostitute, again there was no apparent sexual or deviant motivation appropriated from the killer. Don't you think that as odd?" He stood quizzically staring at the blackboard, whilst gnawing on the end of the chalk before turning his attention and regained concentration upon the folder notes of the third victim.

"The first two victims were of approximate age, height and build. Correct? But this third victim, the church organist Rose Harsent, was a fifty-four-year-old portly widow." Looking towards the ceiling rose Wiggins then lit a cigarette and inhaled deeply. "The chosen victims have absolutely nothing whatsoever in common that I can decipher Pyke." Look here, the fourth victim was Lady Agatha Harkness an aristocratic Suffragette then Miss Mary Munday, an entertainer, became the sixth unfortunate."

"Couldn't be farther apart than the South Pole and Captain Scott's frozen arse," quipped Pyke from underneath his hat.

"Then there's our very own 'Hungry' Mary Hallbard the landlady at The Grapes and the subsequent slaying of Mary Devitt, the teacher."

The three men stared at the blackboard, the map, the biographies, each racking their brains and delving into their combined knowledge of the case and the individual crime scenes. Several silent minutes passed.

"J .. e .. m," intoned Wiggins slowly. "Isn't it so that all through this infuriating investigation we have supposed rather than understood that these were random opportunistic murders carried out by a monster in the heat of the moment."

"True, Sir," came Pyke's instant response. "But what if we have been misguided and wrong in that assumption these past months!" offered Wiggins. "What if these women were precisely targeted and chosen for slaughter by the Beast? Each carefully selected with a particular aim in mind, a reason for it being them." Pyke stubbed out a cigarette and looked up curiously to see Wiggins standing facing the chalkboard with his hands placed squarely upon his hips. He had neatly written several words alongside the term 'Apostles'.

A	Mary Harrison	Actress
P	Louise Smith	Prostitute
O	Rose Harsent	Organist
S	Agatha Harkness	Suffragette
T	Sarah Devitt	Teacher
L	Mary Halbard	Landlady
E	Mary Munday	Entertainer
S	???????	S ???

"We have it Pyke! Actress, Prostitute, Organist, Suffragette, Teacher, Landlady, Entertainer," proclaimed Wiggins desperately trying to retain his composure. "It is their occupations don't you see! The key is unquestionably in the letters. Although not murdered in alphabetical order, the first letter of their respective occupations, none the less spell out the word *Apostle*. We have one victim for each letter other than the final one, the 'S'. The word he scrawled repeatedly on that wall was *Apostles* so he will inevitably continue to drive his torrent of murder until he has another final trophy, the death of a woman whose description can be classified by the letter 'S'. I am sure of it." Wiggins punched one fist enthusiastically into the open palm of his other hand. "Now that we have found his rationale, we must look to capitalise upon it. We need to bait the trap. Good fortune prevails at last. I suspect we may just have discovered a device that will enable us to lure the Beast out from his lecherous lair to catch him in flagrante delicto," smiled Wiggins touching his index finger to the tip of his nose. The excitement in the room was palpable.

"I thinks you mean that *you've* discovered a way to get him and if 'flugranto dedicto' means red-handed Guv, I'll be right by your side!"

Simpsons on the Strand was one of London's oldest and most highly respected eating establishments. The restaurant situated at Savoy Court, just off the Strand was famous for the quality and enormity of its roast dinners and traditional English cuisine. It was at this venue, a particular favourite of Wiggins and his wife Mary, that the Detective Inspector had arranged to meet the bereaved younger sister of Agatha Harkness, Miss Constance.

Wiggins had been extremely impressed with the Viscount's younger daughter when he had first encountered her at her sister's funeral. Her heartfelt and determined offer of whatever assistance she could extend to the investigation came foremost to Wiggins' mind as the statuesque young lady entered the oak-panelled dining room. Wiggins stood as Miss Harkness approached the white linen clothed table which he had chosen. Constance Harkness was almost as tall as Wiggins' six feet and one inch and her beautiful, alabaster toned face with glittering agate blue eyes was framed by thick raven black hair that cascaded in waves. The whole presence of this striking young woman oozed confidence and composure. Wiggins offered Miss Harkness the chair opposite his as he resumed his seat.

"How fare thee, Miss Harkness? I regret having to ask to see you again so soon after your sister's service. I hope your family are bearing up under the enormous strain of your tragic loss. Your mother and father, how are they?" enquired a concerned Wiggins as he snapped open his white linen napkin and placed it on his lap.

The younger Harkness sister looked defiantly into the eyes of the detective. "They are stolid, high bred people Inspector, but I fear that neither of them will ever recover from the dreadful loss of their firstborn. Father now seldom leaves his study and his matters of business seem to go unattended, whilst mother is distraught and, I suspect close to complete nervous collapse. Our entire household is in the most depressed state of mourning," stated Miss Harkness trying nobly to keep her composure.

Wiggins nodded his understanding as a pristinely aproned young waiter handed them each a leather-bound menu. Wiggins could not help but notice the sideward glance the waiter threw at the striking young lady opposite him. "Can I offer you a drink, Miss Harkness? Some tea perhaps?" enquired Wiggins noting that the lady before him was struggling to keep her emotions in check.

"I think a glass of something stronger may be more appropriate considering Inspector," suggested Miss Harkness. Wiggins consulted the drinks section of the menu. "A bottle of the Chateau Laffite please," he directed to the waiter. "An excellent choice, Sir," nodded the waiter, retreating.

Once they were alone Miss Harkness enquired. "So Inspector, much as I appreciate being asked to dinner in such splendid surroundings, I cannot help but suspect that you have a motive other than to offer me some fine dining?"

"Your suspicions are, unfortunately, well-founded," admitted Wiggins, spying the imminent approach of the young waiter armed with the requested bottle of wine. Once the awkward preliminary wine tasting was completed and the subsequent ordering of their food had been dealt with, Wiggins exhaled deeply and continued. "You mentioned to me previously at your sister's funeral, quite adamantly as I recall, that you would be willing to do anything to assist in the capture of her killer. I would like to ask if that is still the case, or was the offer made in, how shall I put it, the heat of an extremely emotional occasion."

"On the contrary, Inspector, I remain more than eager than ever to do whatever I can to assist you in apprehending this Beast. He has broken the hearts of my family and I would welcome any opportunity to bring him to justice, or preferably, to hasten his demise."

Once again Wiggins marvelled at the bravery of the young lady sitting opposite. *'This is a truly remarkable young woman,'* he thought to himself, swallowing hard as he tried to imagine the grief and anger that must be pulsing through her soul.

The waiter brought their dishes, roast silverside of beef for Wiggins, and poached Salmon for Miss Harkness. After placing two silver salvers of vegetables the waiter topped up their glasses then left them to their meals. Wiggins nodded his thanks to the waiter. "I have a proposal for you Miss Harkness, one that is fraught with danger but one that could ultimately result in the capture of your sister's murderer."

"Continue Inspector, you have certainly piqued my interest," replied Constance Harkness raising one inquisitive eyebrow as she delicately forked her salmon.

"We have identified an extremely viable suspect but need to flush him out. We need someone to allow him to show his hand as it were," stuttered Wiggins, unsure as to how to put this proposal, despite having rehearsed it in his head several times over. *'How could he ask this delightful young woman to risk her own life so soon after losing her sister? Surely he could produce another plan.'* He had almost decided to withdraw the idea and change the subject when Miss Harkness boldly interrupted his ruminations. "It sounds as if you require me to be the bait in your trap, the worm on your hook, Inspector. I agree."

"But you have not heard what the proposal is, Miss Harkness. There is a definite level of personal danger involved that would be unprecedented," returned Wiggins, again impressed by the substance of this young woman. "This individual is a savage beyond compare."

"I care not, Inspector. If this scenario offers a chance at capturing or killing him, I will do it, no matter what danger it may attract," replied Miss Harkness straightening her back resolutely. "If I have any opportunity to avenge the death of our beloved Aggie, I will grasp it wholeheartedly and enthusiastically with all my heart."

Wiggins sighed, shrugged and related to her the story of Bleak, the lair in the sewer and the police's theory regarding the significance of the word *Apostles*. "So, you see, he desperately needs another 'S' to complete his insane collection."

"And I, of course, being the Sister of a previous victim, his Suffragette, offer the most appetising full stop imaginable," replied Constance, understanding at once the detective's thought process.

"Precisely," confirmed Wiggins, somewhat downcast at what had, in theory, sounded like an attractive, sensible plan but now, in the cold light of day, he was staggered that he had not fully considered the jeopardy involved.

"As I specified before Inspector, I will do it. Nothing you have told me will deter me from that resolution. There is to be but one stipulation on my part and that is under no circumstances must my parents hear of these matters. May I suggest that I visit Doctor Bleak at his practice tomorrow? I will feign some condition or other, perhaps founded in the recent passing of my beloved sister and see if he rises to the bait. I am sure I can emphasise the *Sister* aspect enough for him to do so. I will endeavour to arrange to meet him alone and inform you of whatever agreement we make."

Wiggins nodded. "Be sure, Miss Harkness, we will protect you at all times. I promise that no harm will come to you. You have my personal guarantee." Constance Harkness smiled and resumed her meal, seemingly unperturbed by their preceding conversation. "The salmon is most agreeable Mr Wiggins. How is your beef?"

"It is rather delightful, strong of taste and tender in aspect." Wiggins smiled and inwardly resolved that no matter what the future held, no harm would come to this remarkable young lady, whilst he breathed.

Chapter 37 - The Revelation

Wiggins arose from his supper table at the staccato sound of belligerent knocking upon his front door. "Who can that be Albert?" asked Mary knowing all too well that this was doubtless police business. *'This job is invading our lives too much,'* she thought wistfully.

"I can only assume that there has been a development that necessitates a visit rather than a telephone call, darling. We are awfully close to a culmination in the case," explained Wiggins reluctantly leaving his boiled ham and potatoes and making his way out of the parlour towards the hall. Mary replaced her knife and fork precisely on the table, primly dabbed at the corners of her mouth with her linen napkin, straightened her pinafore and followed her husband into the hallway. *'No doubt it would be Sergeant Pyke,'* she thought. *'It is high time that man settled down to a sober life with a good woman.'*

Wiggins unlocked and opened the front door. As the chill evening air stole into her Marylebone home it brought with it the most exotic fragrance of eau de cologne that Mary Wiggins' nostrils had ever encountered. She could not place the smell but could see that her husband was somewhat taken aback at the identity of their unexpected caller. *'Not Jem Pyke for sure,'* she realised.

"Mr Van Hoon, what an unexpected surprise!" greeted Wiggins rather hesitantly.

"And no doubt a delightful one for the household," responded the resplendent Dutchman standing on the doorstep. "I am sure your home is as warm as the welcome and as delightful as the surprise of my visitation, if only one could gain entry to view it."

"Oh, excuse me, of course. Do come in." Wiggins stood aside to allow Van Hoon entry, at which point Mary caught sight of their visitor for the first time. She was convinced she had let a small gasp of amazement escape from her open mouth.

Van Hoon strode over the threshold he removed his cobalt blue silk top hat with the widest of flourishes accompanied by the lowest of bows. "The delight continues I see. You must be Mrs Wiggins?" Van Hoon reached for Mary's trembling hand, bowed yet again, and placed the most delicate of kisses on the back of it. She could feel the warm breath escape his nostrils and caress her hand. Mary was dumbstruck. She was sure the kiss had been longer and more lingeringly intense than custom should dictate. She had been in the presence of this man only a few seconds but already she felt weak of knee and girlish. "You did not tell me that you were fortunate in having such a beautiful wife, Inspector. I am impressed. How would your sparring-partner Pyke say … you punch above your weight?" smiled Van Hoon audaciously.

"Mary, this is Dante Van Hoon. Mr Van Hoon is, how should I say, acting in an advisory capacity in connection with the case of the Beast. He is assisting us with our enquiries," explained Wiggins beginning to feel rather inadequate standing in the hallway of his own home next to the enigmatic Leper.

"How extraordinary," interjected Mary, finally finding her voice and trying to disguise her fascination at the extraordinary figure before her. "Won't you please come in, Mr Van Hoon. I am afraid you find us at supper."

Van Hoon smiled the broadest of smiles. "Capital!" he pronounced." I just adore supper! Such a quaintly English repast. Samuel Johnson, as I recall partook of it several times a day!" He flowed past Wiggins as if he instinctively knew the way, passing him his hat as he did so, and took Mary by the arm and waltzed her into the parlour.

Wiggins looked at the hat in disbelief and tossed it onto the nearby hat rack where it rocked back and forth like a sartorial pendulum. He gazed at the ceiling, listening to the light laughter that was already emanating from the parlour, composed himself and strode into the room confidently.

"Such a comfortable house, Mary. May I call you Mary? I must say you have worked wonders with it," pronounced Van Hoon flashing another charming smile at Mrs Wiggins. "You must come to visit me in Belgravia, my dear. I am sure you would love it. So full of beautiful and interesting things I am positive you would adore. But first, and foremost, I am afraid I must whisk your husband away from his evening meal forthwith."

"What is this Van Hoon? How did you know where I live?" enquired Wiggins.

Van Hoon looked startled like a little boy who has been caught lying for the first time. "But my dear Wiggins, I am … Van Hoon," he pronounced majestically. "I know everything that needs to be known." Mary tittered behind her hand. "I have had a visitation from our Beast, Inspector, and I have come to take you to him this very night."

It was Wiggins' turn to look startled. "A visitation, you say! You mean you have met with the Beast?"

"Not exactly. I will explain all to you on the way. Mary, it has indeed been an absolute joy making your acquaintance. I look forward to welcoming you to my own humble abode as soon as this ghastly Beast business is over and done with." Van Hoon bowed and turned to Wiggins. "Come, come now, Inspector. I grow eager to introduce you to our infamous Beast." Van Hoon kissed Mary's hand once again and wished her a hearty adieu. He beckoned Wiggins to follow him, retrieved his hat and ran down the porch steps towards his awaiting car. *'He moves like a ballet dancer,'* thought Mary curiously.

Wiggins looked at his wife open-handed as if pleading for assistance, and at the same time puzzled and taken aback at this tornado of charm and elegance that had invaded his home. "Go, darling. Accompany Mr Van Hoon. I am sure all will be well. I will see you when you return. Be careful," she reassured him as she kissed his cheek and handed him his hat.

"A most impressive vehicle, to be sure," remarked Wiggins trying vainly to hide his admiration at the splendour of the Rolls Royce in which they nestled. The pristine cream and silver exterior contrasted with the deep oxblood leather interior that engulfed him in luxurious comfort and an irresistible smell. He had noted the enigmatic number plate VHN 1 as they had left his house.

"I am glad you like it, Inspector. Modes of transportation are my only vice you understand. It is so rewarding to possess such wonderful objects, don't you think?" offered Van Hoon as they sat side by side in the rear of the six-cylinder, seven litre Silver Ghost. "Rather splendid vehicle is it not?" Wiggins nodded his agreement. "The Roi-de Belges tourer, a gift for services rendered, you might say, from Mr Rolls. Or was it Mr Royce? My memory very seldom fails me. Let me think a moment. Ah yes, it was Charles Rolls, the one who died only a few years ago, killed in an aeronautical accident down on the coast. The tail of his aeroplane snapped clean off. Dreadfully young, appallingly tragic. Did you know he was a balloonist of great repute? A glorious pastime, peaceful, serene and all together indulgent."

Van Hoon observed that his companion's gaze had turned towards the neck of the chauffeur in the driver's seat in front of them. Its bovine proportions were tattooed with a coil of interwoven serpents that sneaked their way through the tangled mass of shoulder hair protruding from his collar. "His name is Ilhan, Inspector. Far easier to pronounce than it is to spell. He is mute and as such he is reliable and trustworthy, and almost utterly immune to torture. He is also a Turk. As are most of his nationality, he is both prone to violence and ostentation. As such he is the ideal driver of a car such as this."

Wiggins once again shook his head in disbelief at the world in which Van Hoon existed and in which he was now inescapably entwined. "If we are to visit the Beast, should we not call on reinforcements?" he asked weighing up action and consequence as his training warranted.

"You misunderstood me, Mr Wiggins. We are merely going to call upon your Beast, not actually meet him in the flesh, if you pardon the unintentional slip of the tongue. Oops, there goes another. There will be no danger involved other than perhaps to your sanity, and I judge that your mental resources are hardy enough to withstand what I am about to show you. You are both intelligent and receptive, and therefore the ideal recipient."

"I am also perplexed, Sir," offered Wiggins, now thoroughly confused.

"Not to worry, Inspector. All will become abundantly clear. Ah! We are here," rejoiced Van Hoon with a customary flourish.

"Why we have only travelled but five minutes if that?" replied Wiggins quizzically as the car drew up to the kerbside. "We are but in the Marylebone Road."

"An indulgent extravagance, I admit, but how else was I to show you my gift from Mr Rolls?" quipped Van Hoon. "No matter, here we are. Our destination awaits. I do so hope you are looking forward to this as much as I am?" enquired the Dutchman with a lopsided grin.

Van Hoon patted Ilhan on a seemingly iron-clad shoulder and the diminutive though substantial Turk exited the car and proceeded to open the rear passenger doors, first for Van Hoon and secondly, with the slightest of bows of his chauffeur-capped head, for Wiggins. A small crowd of onlookers became fixated initially with the magnificent car and then subsequently with the remarkable figure that now stepped out of its luxurious interior to stretch himself onto the pavement. Van Hoon looked around him and raised his cane "You are free to look, by all means, ladies and gentlemen, but please, under no circumstances, touch. That is the vehicle, not the driver. I cannot account for the actions of Ilhan here if a single grubby fingerprint despoils his beautiful darling." Ilhan stood on the running board of the car, arms crossed over his unfeasibly wide chest and wore the most intimidating scowl across his burnished face. His appearance was of a man as wide as he was tall and as ready and willing to protect as he was to breathe.

Wiggins looked at the building alongside which they had parked. Madame Tussauds Wax Museum was well known to him. "Why are we *here* Van Hoon?" he enquired rather curtly as the Dutchman ushered him through the glazed oak front doors.

Once inside, the world-famous exhibition house, it became apparent to Wiggins that he and Van Hoon were the only individuals, other than those fashioned from wax, within the building. "What of the patrons and employees?" he asked, looking around him.

"I have given both them and the staff the evening off. I am sure they can find some more memorable pursuits to occupy them," announced Van Hoon speedily making his way towards the basement staircase as he beckoned Wiggins to follow him. "Come, come, Inspector, do keep up." Wiggins shook his head and marvelled once more at the influence that this enigmatic man seemingly extended across all strata of society. Van Hoon raced lithely down the stairs like a cat chasing its prey.

They stood amidst the eerie silence of the infamous Chamber of Horrors, a testament to the foulest and most noteworthy villains and murderers in history. From the historic figures of Genghis Khan and Vlad the Impaler, through to more recent defilers of humanity such as Percy Lefroy Mapleton and Israel Lipski. Wiggins felt a cold unease creep across his flesh as his skin goose-bumped, the normally busy chamber now as silent as a mausoleum. A crypt of evil. The shoes of the two men tapped on the flagstone floor as they slowly made their way around the exhibits, Wiggins' highly polished brogues followed the lilac spat covered patent leathers of Van Hoon. They passed a reconstruction of the execution of Charles Peace alongside a tableau of Doctor Crippen standing in the dock awaiting his fate.

"Fascinating, don't you find, Inspector? That the masses will pay hard-earned coin to view wax facsimiles of the most notorious killers in history. To look upon such grisly goings-on cannot be a natural desire of your average person. Then, of course, who am I to question their motives? I am hardly an average person," postulated Van Hoon as he surveyed the gruesome ugliness around him. "Ah! Here we are, Inspector."

They stood in front of an exhibit portraying the story of Jack the Ripper. The man who only a generation earlier had held London in a grip of mortal fear. The tableau was staged to show a looming black, unidentifiable shadow crouched, ready to submit another victim to a horrendous end. The victim, presumably Mary Jane Kelly given the surroundings, noted Wiggins, lay upon a bed in a small unkempt room, her face the very personification of fear. Wiggins raised a questioning eyebrow towards his companion. "What do you seek to prove by bringing me here Van Hoon? Surely you do not think the Beast we seek is the ghost of Jack, returned to wreak more carnage on our City?"

"Not at all Inspector," responded a grinning Van Hoon.

"Then if you know the identity of our Beast, why not simply tell me and dispense with this self-indulgent charade and we can proceed towards his apprehension."

"I much prefer a touch of the dramatic, my friend. I not only want you to hear who he is, but I also want you to see him." Wiggins removed his hat and shook his head in confusion. "I confess I am utterly baffled, Sir."

"You will note that of all the representations in this chamber, his is the only figure not to be a recognisable waxwork of the subject. As I recall the late Madame Anna Maria Tussaud telling me over tea at the Dorchester many years ago, it was her rigid policy that models would be made only of those whose features were known.

Jack's face, other than to a select few who cannot now tell, was never known. I must say, however, that the body shape portrayed here is remarkably close to the reality."

Wiggins could feel his gaze being inexorably drawn towards the faceless blackness of the stooping silhouette standing before him. The arm raised, the dagger poised, the positioning of the figure all highlighting the imminent, savage thrust to come. The sense of evil was so tangible that he imagined that he could smell it.

Van Hoon sensed Wiggins' engagement. "Good, Inspector. Continue to feel, continue to penetrate reality. Allow your mind to open to what you already suspect, to what you already know." Van Hoon's voice took on a melodious, hypnotic tone. "See what stands before you. Observe and comprehend. Embrace the truth, let it embrace you as would a lover."

Wiggins' peripheral vision clouded with a blurred haze, his stare concentrated fully on the faceless figure crouched before him. His eyes probed eyes that were not there, searched for a face that was not there.

"He is here. He is here now. Hear him, see him," continued the mesmeric voice of Van Hoon.

Wiggins' eyes widened and his pupils dilated. In front of him, he could see a face slowly begin to form where there had previously been but blackness. Red rimmed, onyx black eyes emerged from the face and returned his stare. A cruel, thin-lipped mouth materialised as if tearing a rent through the darkness. A long-hooked nose, flaring nostrils, a furrowed brow and a strong pointed chin, all took shape in front of his very eyes. He shuddered involuntarily, lost in the image that was gradually appearing before him. The eyes blinked, their hooded lids descending as if in slow motion. The head turned slowly towards him, the satanic eyes meeting his. The corners of the mouth upturned in a horrendous smile. Breath steamed from the nostrils.

"Bleak! It *is* Bleak," stuttered Wiggins, his mind struggling to accept what his eyes were seeing. "How….?" his question faltered.

"I have heard him, my friend. Or rather I have heard the voices that he hears. Terrible, chilling voices the like of which I have never before heard. He is as polluted a human being as I have ever encountered," stated Van Hoon placing a hand upon the shoulder of the trembling and emotionally drained policeman. "… and I have encountered many I can assure you."

"But he is here. I can see him," evinced Wiggins. "What have you done?"

"It is not what I have done, but rather what you yourself have done Inspector.

What you see is only a manifestation of what you already know, or suspect, my friend. All I have done is provide the setting, the emotion and the ambience, shall we say, enabling *you* to see *him*."

Wiggins stood in disbelief as the evil smiling face of the creature in front of him began to fade and recede into the darkness from which it had materialised. "We must set our trap and prepare our plan. The reign of the Beast shall soon be at an end."

Chapter 38 - The Entrapment

Miss Constance Harkness was ushered into Doctor Bleak's office by his dowdy receptionist. The almost overpowering smell of chlorine was immediately apparent to her as she strode towards the hunched figure at the desk. Constance had prepared and rehearsed for this moment several times since the previous day with Wiggins playing the part of her tutor.

As she moved through the doorway, Wiggins' words came back to her. "You must, above all, stay calm," he had instructed. "Remember that you are there to accomplish a task and you, and not he, is the one aware of the nature of that task. Play the part as we have rehearsed it and he will suspect nothing."

In precaution of anything untoward and unplanned occurring, she had secreted a Webley & Scott point two-two calibre pistol in her garter. Several hours of tuition from Wiggins had seen her became reasonably proficient in its use.

Her absolute hatred and loathing for the man sitting in front of her were boundless. However, she knew that she must compartmentalise her revulsion for this Beast and use it against him to enable their plan to be a success. She tiptoed into Bleak's consultancy room coquettishly, her head tilted slightly to the side in preparation of removing her black-veiled mourning bonnet. As she did so, she let her raven hair cascade onto her shoulders just as she had carefully practised.

Bleak half stood as she entered and indicated that she take the chair opposite his desk. He cleared his throat. "Good morning … erm … Miss Harkness," he invited, glancing briefly down at her notes. "I believe this is your first appointment with me. What can I do for you this good morning?"

"Well doctor, it is a somewhat embarrassing situation for a lady to be quite frank, but I fear not seeking medical advice could be a grave misjudgement on my part," Constance offered, feigning embarrassment. She sat down hitching her dress up ever so slightly to partially expose her ankles.

"Come now Miss Harkness, I am after all a man of medicine so I can assure you there is very little that I have not been witness to during twenty years in practice," replied Bleak, suppressing his desire to stare downwards at her legs. "You are very kind and reassuring my good doctor," she smiled flirtatiously. "Continue please Miss Harkness if you will," replied Bleak extending an open hand.

"Well, there seems to be a small, perplexing swelling to my left breast. It has been present for only a few weeks but to be brutally honest my family have suffered enough bereavement without having to worry about the state of my health as well."

"Does it pain you Miss Harkness?" enquired Bleak matter-of-factly.

"My sister's death? Why, of course it does, what kind of an insensitive question is that doctor?!" replied a furious Constance with a waspish tongue.

"No, no please, no you misunderstand me Miss Harkness, I was enquiring about the swelling … does it pain you?"

Bleak's mind sped, his synapses flashing quicker than he could process. '*Harkness? This cannot be mere coincidence. Bereavement? This is surely too fortuitous to be true. Sister? How glorious it will be to kill and feast upon two sisters. Pray to all that is unholy, the "S" of my Apostles has just revealed herself to me!*'

"No Sir, there is no pain to tell of, just a small hardening beside the underarm. Somewhat like a pea or the head of a vesta," replied Constance.

"Is there any bleeding or discharge to the site?" asked Bleak somewhat lasciviously.

"None whatsoever that I can tell doctor."

Bleak's thumbs began to caress each adjacent index finger in a slow circular motion as if he was rolling together bits of loose thread. "I feel I have no alternative but to examine the region you describe if I am to give an informed opinion Miss Harkness. Obviously if you consent, I will, of course, ensure a female observer is present during the examination. My receptionist, Ms Dykes, is quite accustomed to being engaged as a chaperone in delicate situations such as this."

"Oh, there will be no need to waste her valuable time Doctor Bleak," Constance instantly responded recognising that being alone with Bleak would be best suited to the prearranged plan. "You are a man of medicine and I trust you as implicitly as I would a Priest."

Bleak's heart began to pound and his hands now writhed and squirmed behind his back. His nostrils flared with lust and anticipation. '*No Priest can save you from me now you foolish bitch,*' Bleak gloried.

Constance Harkness stood behind a changing screen and removed her overcoat before unbuttoning the jacket of her tailored morning outfit. She then deliberately and nervously removed her black silk blouse before unstrapping her corseted underwear just enough to expose her left breast. She knew it was vital to hide her tangible fear and mortal embarrassment during this dreadful ordeal, so she concentrated by focussing upon the eye test chart at the far end of the room. *E, F, P, T, O* … Bleak appeared in her periphery. *Z, L, P, E, D* … her body stiffened at his touch. '*These are the very same devilish hands that took my sister from me! Stay calm Connie,*' she repeated over and over to herself.

Bleak slowly and purposely cupped her breast in one hand and proceeded to palpate the area she had previously described to him. His long slender fingers caressed and probed the pale white flesh of her bare bosom. She was longing for this agony to end, her hand poised over the secreted gun, ready to blow his vile brains out at any moment she chose. '*Why not just do it now?*' she thought. '*Surely justice would be served. But no, she must adhere to the plan. His capture or demise at the hands of the appropriate authorities was more amenable than to expose herself to prosecution.*'

Her stomach was bilious and lurched at the thought of what he had done to her beloved sister. He continued to massage and stroke for what to Constance seemed like an eternity. His grip was getting stronger with every passing second.

The poisonous desire to bite off her nipple was almost unbearable to him. '*S I S T E R S !*'

Bleak shook his head, fighting back the voices in the darkness of his twisted mind. "I am pleased to say I can find no lump whatsoever Miss Harkness and I pride myself in the sensitivity of my touch," his hands visibly shaking due to a combination of adrenalin and desire. "I suspect what you may have felt was perhaps a small air-filled cyst that has been absorbed naturally by the body. Or possibly a temporarily blocked sebaceous gland. No matter, there is no cause for concern on your part. You are young and perfectly healthy," he explained nervously smiling whilst wiping his sweated forehead with his handkerchief.

"Thank you, doctor, you have certainly put my worried mind at rest," offered Constance as she hurriedly dressed. Perspiration trickled its way down the canal of her spine. She felt soiled and nauseous at what she had experienced at the hands of this monster but the thought of his execution and everlasting suffering in Hell was motivation enough.

Whilst Miss Harkness continued to compose herself, Bleak continued, rather excitedly from the other side of the screen. "I am pleased you came to seek medical advice, Miss Harkness. I hope your mind is now settled regarding this. It is always best to be properly examined and to know exactly what you are dealing with in such situations. Better the Devil you know, as they say. I do wish more women would look after themselves as they look after their husbands. Now, is there anything else I can do for you today?"

"Well now you mention it doctor," paused Constance. "I am due to give a speech tomorrow evening at a small Suffrage meeting to some schoolgirls at Saint Olave's Grammar School and I really could make use of something to settle my nerves. My sister's death has left an emptiness within my being that I am understandably struggling to cope with. Anxiety and tension knot my stomach as though it is besieged by a plague of butterflies. It is the first time I have presented in public since my sister's funeral and I fear I may crumble in front of an audience."

"I fully understand your situation," sympathised Bleak unsympathetically. He turned to the medical cabinet behind him and fumbled in one of its drawers. Constance's gaze was drawn towards a human skull that sat on one of the cabinet shelves. It seemed to her to grin out a warning. *'Leave this place. Leave this place now. Trust me. This man is evil beyond evil.'*

Bleak produced a small brown bottle and handed it to Constance. "Laudanum pills, my dear. A modest dosage. Take one tablet before you retire this evening and another after breaking your fast tomorrow morning. This should relax you sufficiently to get through your ordeal. By the way, Miss Harkness, what time are you due to give your speech tomorrow?" asked Bleak. "I would not mind making an appearance."

"That would be delightful Doctor Bleak. I will arrive before the crowds at approximately a quarter after eight, so I do look forward to seeing you there," replied Constance as she headed towards the door.

"Kind regards Miss Harkness. I look forward to seeing you there also."

'... more than you can imagine!'

Chapter 39 - The Preparation

Dante Van Hoon stood in the centre of the second-floor room of the octagonal tower of his gothic Belgravia mansion, arms outstretched, offering his leprous valet a cruciform position on which to dress his finery for the evening's adventure. Van Hoon's body was lithe and hard, lightly muscled and sinuous. The fractal-like leprous scarring extended from his neck down the left side of his torso to his waist. A shockingly large, long-healed white scar ran from one side of his rib cage to the other, traversing his stomach like a pale thin smile.

The valet hung one of his master's preferred black silk shirts on his frame and buttoned the pearl buttons. A dark grey vest waistcoat was then added, and the silk ties tightened at the back to afford a comfortable fit. Van Hoon gave a nod of satisfaction and indicated his three-quarter length greatcoat which the hooded attendant proudly offered up, slipping one arm in and then the other, brushing off the back, satisfied and proud at the job he had done. Van Hoon regarded himself in the free-standing mirror and nodded his approval.

"Very good Jacobus. You can help prepare the car now if you will. The large Bentley Tourer is most appropriate for this evening's business I feel," instructed the sartorial masterpiece. Jacobus bowed, "Yes master," and ran off to inform Ilhan the chauffeur of the necessary arrangements.

Van Hoon turned to a ceiling height bureau in the room, pulled out one of several small drawers and carefully extracted a silver ring fashioned in the shape of an upturned cat's paw, along with a tiny screwdriver similar to those used by opticians and jewellers. He carefully placed both items on the desk section of the bureau. From within another drawer, he carefully removed a small silver vial and a pipette dropper. The vial contained the most lethal venom known to man, namely that of the Taipan serpent. Van Hoon smiled as he untightened a minuscule screw on the back of the cat's paw revealing it to have a small hollow chamber within. He then extracted some of the fatal venom using the pipette and fed it drop by careful drop into the ring. Once satisfied that the ring was replete, he returned the screw to its housing and placed the ring on the index finger of his right hand. One scratch from the claws of the tiny ring would now result in virtually instant paralysis followed closely by almost certain death. Van Hoon knew that any victim would first experience vomiting and acute headache, which would quickly lead to collapse and convulsions, followed by major organ failure then ultimately death. All within approximately forty minutes. He knew that no human could resist the bite of the Taipan and he was certain in his knowledge that this Beast they hunted tonight, monster though he was, was most definitely human.

Next, the enigmatic Lord of extortion turned to his armament strongbox. This box was constructed of solid steel and built flush into the wall of his octo-room like a wall safe, albeit, one large enough for a man to walk into. Less a strongbox, more a strong wardrobe room. Once inside Van Hoon selected a pair of ivory-handled Colt Forty-Fives which he placed in the holsters of an ornately embossed leather gun belt strung around his waist and concealed beneath his greatcoat. He subconsciously ran his tongue across his teeth as he recalled that both the pistols and the gun belt had been a gift from an infamous American dentist. He turned to a small chest holding multiple drawers of ammunition and pulled at one drawer and removed a solid silver bullet, one of many contained within the velvet-lined compartment. He first rolled it between his fingers as if judging the quality of a fine hand-rolled cigar and then weighed it in his palm, gently tossing it up and catching it.

'*Not since that night of foul savagery in Bucharest nearly fifty years ago have I had call to use such a bullet,*' he reminisced whilst subconsciously rubbing the line of scar tissue that adorned his stomach. '*Perhaps they might be called for this evening?*'

He decided to load one colt with the silver bullets, the other with standard ammunition. He then filled a leather pouch with a mixture of both and strung it over his shoulder. A miniature Derringer was then added to the leg of one boot and an Arabian Kriss dagger to the other.

He exited the strong room, locked it and secreted the key in a panel behind the wall. He then checked his fob and saw that as always, as in all his dealings, he was precisely on time for what he hoped would be a surprise rendezvous with Wiggins and Pyke. He took his favoured silk top hat from the hat stand and a silver serpent topped black ebony cane from the cane stand. As with all Van Hoon's canes, its intricate carvings displayed the nine levels of Dante's inferno descending from Pope Celestine being pursued by insects in the upper vestibule of Hell to the very depths where Judas is held in the mouth of Lucifer himself. He whistled nonchalantly as he twisted the cane, confident in the knowledge that the sword blade contained within was also tipped with the deadly venom of the Taipan serpent.

The metronomic slapping of the rope on the sprung wooden floor was the only sound that interrupted the silence of the gymnasium. At this time of the morning, Jem Pyke was a lone figure in the gym. He knew jumping rope aided his footwork speed whilst affording better coordination of his lower limbs and fostering quicker agility of foot. *'Speed will help tonight,'* he thought to himself. His black leather boxing boots were a blur as he concentrated on his rhythm. He was sweating profusely now, his hair darkened with sweat as the rope flashed, increasing in speed to the point where it became a blur then disappeared completely. He breathed only through his nose as this kept him calm and concentrated. Calmness would help tonight. The small grubby gymnasium was accommodated in a room above the Ten Bells public house on Commercial Street in Spitalfields. Not too far for Jem to drag his carcass to whenever he had the time or inclination. How ironic that in his preparations to confront the Beast that the pub he now occupied held so many memories of the Ripper.

Surrounded by medicine balls, batons and benches, he draped the rope over a set of wall bars and made his way to the heavy bag suspended from an exposed ceiling beam. He struggled on the worn brown leather gloves. Fortunately, the gloves were a snug fit as the tie-strings had long since been snapped or lost. After years of punishment, the knuckles of the gloves were cracked like petrified mud after years of hard drought. Jem rotated his shoulders several times then sent a hefty left hook followed immediately by two stinging right jabs into the bag. He weaved and bobbed in front of his imagined opponent before unleashing two right hooks to the side of the bag. All the while he envisioned that vile hate-filled face staring up at him from what remained of Mary Harrison. Bam! Bam! Hard numbing, rib-snapping punches. Bobbing and feinting, he proceeded to pummel the sand-filled bag causing it to sway alarmingly on its housing. For five three-minute periods, he continued to batter upon the bag until the lactic acid build up in his arms forced him to cease the onslaught. He was gasping for breath and his heavily muscled body was covered in a sheen of perspiration. As a final act of vengeance, he kicked the bag thunderously with the heel of his boot with all the force he could muster. "There'll be no need to abide by Queensbury tonight," he muttered under his breath as he wiped sweat from his reddened face and proceeded to unbind his fists.

She carefully slid the gun into her garter in readiness of the task ahead. Miss Constance Harkness once more recalled Wiggins' instructions on how to fire the Webley & Scott point two-two calibre pistol. They had gone over it more times than was necessary, but it was a safety measure in case the plan they had devised were to go horribly wrong. "You have to be close to the fiend for it to have any devastating effect. Damn near right in his face!" she remembered him explaining. The plan was indeed for her to be close to him. Closer than she ever wanted to be … but that was the plan. She opened the silver locket around her neck and stared thoughtfully at the photograph of her sister. "Watch over me Aggie. I *will* avenge you."

The Lyons Tea House on the corner of Piccadilly and Coventry Street offered the sort of sophisticated but affordable table service that suited the temperament of Albert Wiggins. He took his usual place at a single table positioned in the front of the café offering a clear view of the main front pontil marked paned window and door, his chair back resting against a wall.

He ordered his usual pot of strong Colombian coffee. "Thank you, Elise," he smiled at the young waitress as she placed his order on the table. He poured the coffee, neglecting to add any milk, and stirred it gently, even though he added no sugar. Six times clockwise as always followed by six times anti-clockwise. The first sip warmed his mouth and throat. Already he felt invigorated. He sat back and opened his copy of the Evening Gazette. Headlines regarding the latest atrocity of the Beast screamed out at him. Although intimately aware of the details, Wiggins read the dramatic yet ill-informed article, his temper gradually rising with each badly phrased sentence.

He took another sip of coffee and sat back, fingers positioned together as if in prayer. '*Soon this will be over. Soon he will be no more. Thanks to Van Hoon they now knew who he was. Thanks to the bravery of Constance Harkness the trap was set, and the bait would be in place, the snare a' ready,*' he thought to himself. '*Jem Pyke is champing at the bit, set on revenge, the uniforms instructed as to their roles, and Donnecha Savage's local horde drilled as to their part in blocking off any routes of escape.*'

He lifted his cup with a now slightly trembling hand. The adrenalin of anticipation coursed through his body. '*Tonight, we end the reign of the Beast.*'

Chapter 40 - The Bridge

The scalpel gloved hand slashed through the fog ripping the throat from its victim, who slumped convulsing to the ground.

It was a particularly foggy night even by London's extraordinary standards. The precise form of swirling, impenetrable fog that Wiggins had prayed would not transpire this night had revealed itself during the early evening. '*Not tonight of all nights,*' he pleaded to himself. It was now too late to change to another plan. The game was now truly and inexorably afoot!

Wiggins and Pyke sat in silent anticipation in their darkened car in an unlit corner of Lafone Street. Waiting. Each engrossed in their own private thoughts. Wiggins ran over the plan, repeatedly, exploring possible permutations that may interfere with the desired outcome, whilst Pyke decided which would be the most satisfying method of killing the scum. They sat waiting to put an end to the abhorrent nightmare they had found themselves part of for the past few months. Tensions ran high but minds were cocked and alert. Nothing had been left to chance. Constables had been strategically stationed at half-mile intervals secreted along the intended route towards Saint Olave's Grammar School in Queen Elizabeth Street. Wiggins had ordered that all manholes along the route be secured. Donnecha Savage's unofficial Limehouse battalion was stationed at strategic points blocking off streets and alleyways that may potentially offer the Beast a route of escape. Constance Harkness' safety and the capture of Bleak were paramount. Wiggins wanted the Beast alive, Pyke wanted him dead. They had talked about this eventual outcome for many long hours but, no matter what the conclusion may prove to be, they both intended to see the wretch rot and suffer in Hell for eternity and a year. Pyke's knuckles whitened as he recalled the fate of his friend Hungry Mary. The sight of her body mangled within her piano would haunt and torment his thoughts for the remainder of his life.

Miss Constance Harkness sat in the rear of her car. Constable Potts and her Chauffer sat up front, both unusually quiet. The motor vehicle cautiously navigated through the darkened streets of London along the carefully selected route that had been meticulously and methodically planned. Its front lamps struggled to illuminate the impermeable gloom and seemed only to serve to make the murkiness appear even thicker and more menacing. They were headed towards Saint Olave's where Miss Harkness was due to give her short talk to a group of its young ladies. Although her nerves were almost completely shredded at the thought that Bleak could appear at any time, she tried admirably to hold her composure. She trusted Wiggins implicitly and urgently wanted to avenge her dear sister's murder but inwardly prayed that the Beast would not make his presence felt. *'How could he attack her in a room full of people? A room full of schoolgirls, for heaven's sake.'*

The tension and silence in the car were tangible. "Isn't it a ghastly evening Constable Potts?" she offered in an attempt to break the deafening silence. There came no response which spoke volumes about the apprehension of the situation given that Potts was normally a complete chatterbox. "I said awful evening Constable Potts!" her voice rising in exclamation as she prodded his shoulder lightly. Potts' head and shoulders lurched forward alarmingly, and his limp body slumped down into the passenger chair with a low moaning groan. At that instant, Constance Harkness' mouth opened. She instinctively knew something was terribly wrong. A chill of fear sizzled down her spine and she immediately looked towards the Chauffer with a growing feeling of impending doom lurching in her stomach. As she did so a sinuous hand reached upward and slightly adjusted the rear-view mirror such that her eyes looked upon his accursed ugliness. The inky blackness of Bleak's eyes returned her now petrified stare. As he turned around to face her, he removed the Chauffer's cap from his head and wedged it on that of the lifeless Potts. The same cap he had removed from the beheaded driver only thirty minutes earlier. Bleak began to giggle, then to laugh, then to shriek with maniacal glee. Constance's hysterical screams were intermingled with his high-pitched frenzied laughing.

Bleak drove like a demon, sometimes with both hands on the steering wheel and sometimes with only one, the other slashing in a frenzy at the underpane of the car's leather roof. Rather than heading towards Queen Elizabeth Street, the vehicle veered sharply past the junction of Lafone Street towards Tooley Street, mounting the kerb and scraping painfully against a gas lantern post as it accelerated for Tower Bridge Road.

"Damnation! That's her car Pyke. Drive man. Something dreadful has happened. Something has gone wrong. Catch them … now!" Pyke instinctively plunged the accelerator to the very floor and the car shot out onto Tooley Street narrowly missing a lamp-lighter crossing the road. The police car screeched towards the other, down Boss Street before turning alarmingly onto Queen Elizabeth Street.

"Give it everything you can, Jem. We must not lose her. We simply must not." The car in front could barely be seen through the fog but it now sped furiously down Horselydown Lane with Wiggins and Pyke in close pursuit.

Constance Harkness' first instinct was to get out of the car, but the speed at which it careered along the London streets made it impossibly dangerous to do so. Buildings and people sped by in a blur. Remembering the gun, she frantically hitched up her dress and reached for the Bull Dog revolver in her garter belt. The erratic shaking of the vehicle and the sharply acute turns made her bounce around and she struggled desperately to break the pistol free from its makeshift holster. '*Careful, careful Connie,*' she thought. She pulled back the safety catch, remembering how Wiggins had shown her, took as careful aim as she could considering the bone-jarring jolting of the car's motion, closed one eye, and gently pulled on the trigger. An almighty gunshot resounded around the cabin making her dizzy and lightheaded, but she could see that she had hit her intended target. Bleak squealed in pain like a trapped animal, and as he reached to his shoulder where the bullet had penetrated, he lost control of the car crashing it into storage crates near Butler's Wharf Pier. The car was still.

Hissing steam emanated from the radiator and the ringing in Constance's ears had effectively rendered her temporarily deaf. Her head spun and she was groggy as she opened her eyes to see Bleak slumped over the steering wheel. She realised by the excruciating pain and the unnatural angle of her right arm that she must have badly fractured it during the collision. '*Where's the gun? Where is the blasted gun?*' She panicked, vainly fumbling and scrabbling around the car floor. The force of the discharge had dislodged the pistol from her grasp. Just then she saw Bleak slowly drag his cloaked body from the driving seat like some huge, hellish bat. She was frozen with fear, unable to move, unable to even scream. Bleak reached ominously over the back of the driver's seat. "SISTER!" he spat insanely at her. "I HAVE SISTERS!" He slowly and deliberately raised his scalpel glove and made a long slicing incision on his left cheek as if to reinforce their sharpness, before swinging it towards Constance's face. Just then, out of nowhere Constable Potts flung his body protectively on top of Miss Harkness and the blades sheared through his uniform and back causing blood to gush onto Bleak's shocked face.

Pyke screeched the car to a ninety-degree halt and the two policemen instantaneously bounded out of the car doors with pistols drawn. Bleak was incandescent with rage at the car's unexpected arrival. The Beast was confused and angered at the thwarting of his ultimate goal. He violently tore himself away from Potts, ripping the flesh from the brave Constable' back as he did so, and with an ear-piercing scream of unbridled rage, he bounded off into the fog. Pyke fired a single shot in the air to alert reinforcements of their approximate location before racing after Bleak.

"Get the bastard Jem!" hollered Wiggins. He flung open the rear door of the vehicle to see Potts lying prone with Constance Harkness safely underneath his lifeless form. She was sobbing uncontrollably as Wiggins gently moved the Constable's selfless body and cradled her in his arms. "Help is coming Miss Harkness," consoled Wiggins, dabbing at her tears.

"Your young officer bravely saved my life with the last ounce of his strength Inspector," implored Miss Harkness before again breaking down in fitful tears.

"Yes, I knew he would," replied Wiggins nodding his head in agreement whilst biting his bottom lip to staunch his emotions.

"I managed to shoot the monster, so he is injured but I know not where," added the sobbing woman.

"I must leave you now and apprehend the Beast Miss Harkness, you will be safe with Constable Bunce here. Thank you for everything and I am sorry we failed you."

"You will only fail me and my family if you do not capture and destroy that animal Inspector. Now go!" pleaded Constance with a clenched fist and an exhausted smile. Wiggins unclasped her hand and stormed after Pyke as furiously as his body could manage.

The two policemen raced after Bleak for several hundred yards, following his mad yelps and screams through the dense fog. Possessing pistols in the thickly misted night was virtually pointless and their torch beams only reflected and intensified their temporary blindness. Wiggins could see up ahead that Pyke was almost upon the Beast. One final surge and Pyke threw himself headlong towards the Beast's shoulders.

Bleak ferociously ripped himself free from his cloak and left Pyke clutching at thin air as he sprang from the detective's grasp and ran furiously up Tower Bridge Road in the direction of the Bridge up ahead. The moon illuminated the looming gothic towers of London's greatest river crossing as they pierced the night sky. The Beast's silhouette hurtled towards the Bridge's twin spires. Pyke hurled the expensive cloak into the Thames with undisguised disgust at what it represented. As the coat floated slowly downwards towards the inky blackness like some giant wounded bat, Wiggins glanced upriver and spied a large steamship heading towards the bridge. Instantly, an embryo of a plan formed in the Detective's keen mind.

"After him men!" shouted Wiggins unnecessarily as he could already see Pyke's coattails flapping as he sped after the fleeing Beast, his arms and legs frantically pumping like the pistons of the oncoming steamer. "Force him on to the bridge lads." Pyke raised a thumbed hand over his shoulder in a gesture of acknowledgement of the command and continued his exhausting pursuit. The three constables gave chase behind Pyke but despite being younger than their Detective Sergeant they looked as if they were running in Thames mud compared to the bullet-paced blacksmith's son. Pyke was once more rapidly gaining on the long spring-legged figure of Bleak who seemed to almost fly across the wet cobbled roads beneath him like some monstrous pond skimming beetle. Wiggins followed as fast as he could, confident in his plan, and even more so, in his redoubtable Sergeant.

Bleak ran onto the Bridge, emitting a maniacal high-pitched laugh, almost leaping with each pace. Blood spattered from his mouth as he ran, the result of him having bitten through his lips in a psychotic frenzy of euphoria at the excitement of the tumultuous chase. He too spotted the steamship approaching the Bridge and realised, even amid the turmoil of his mania, that the Bridge would commence its slow rise and that he would soon be trapped. His options were to either stop and fight his pursuers, run as fast as he could in an effort to jump the gaping chasm of the rising bridge or to vault over the blue and white iron parapet and take his chances with the currents of the ice-cold river below. He could see the vague shape of the giant Irishman, Savage, standing on the opposite side of the bridge, defiant arms crossed, at the head of a large group of men determined to block the Beast's path to the North Bank. The diminutive figure of young Billy Skew stood next to the hulking ragger.

Looking upwards, Bleak explored the notion of climbing up the steel suspension girders and fleeing at high level across the bridge walkways. The sane compartment of his brain was dismissing all these options as impractical possibilities even as he ran, laughing like a lunatic bathing in the glow of the full Hunter's moon overhead. He could hear the tacks within the hard leather soles of Pyke's shoes sparking against the cobbles, getting closer and closer with each passing second. Bleak could almost feel Pyke's hot breath on his neck, like a pair of pumping bellows. He furtively glanced over his shoulder and saw that the Policeman was once again almost upon him. He shrieked demonically with anticipation and the pleasure of what was about to unfold.

Pyke launched himself downwards at Bleak's legs, his arms outstretched in a makeshift attempt at a rugby tackle. Just at that moment, the Beast side-stepped acutely towards a doorway, and Pyke received a sharp kick to the mouth from the heel of Bleak's trailing boot as he thudded to the street, winding himself painfully.

"Hell!" cursed Pyke, wincing from the impact. "Get that bleedin' animal boys! Watch out for his hands and let us nail his worthless carcass."

Bleak pulled at the door and smiled grotesquely as it flew open before him. He plunged down a flight of concrete stairs, his strides gobbling up half a dozen at a time, his berserk psychotic laugh echoing around the stairwell as he descended.

The three pursuing constables raced past Pyke just as he sharply leapt back to his feet, cursing the fact that he had lost his beloved hat somewhere during the pursuit. He re-joined the chasing group, and all four men hurtled down the concrete staircase after the fiendish Beast following the sound of his rabid shrieking. As they gained on their quarry the Beast abruptly stopped and wheeled around, teeth shining in a wide grin of pure, unthinking evil. The Beast was now the prey! Pyke caught a flashing glint of steel as Bleak slashed out with his improvised gauntlet of scalpels, felling one of the constables by scything through his throat. Blood sprayed sideways and upwards as Constable Jenkins fell to his knees clutching the gaping wound in an attempt to stem the flow. The second constable bravely launched himself at Bleak's midriff toppling him backwards with the force. As they tumbled to the ground, the crazed Doctor stabbed the courageous Constable Perkins in the back of the neck, roaring with demonic hilarity as the blade ripped open the front of the young man's throat. The third constable hesitated just long enough for Bleak to regain his feet and whirl around to stare coldly at him.

They were now at the bottommost part of the stairwell which ended on the observation platform of the south side bascule chamber of the bridge. Bleak was at a dead-end, directly in front of him on the staircase stood the Policemen and behind and below him lay the vast chamber with no other visible exit. Bleak vaulted over the steel handrail and landed catlike on the floor of the bascule chamber. The ceiling of the chamber, a mass of steelwork, beams, cogs and stiffeners, was in actual fact the underside of the massive bascule counterweight that filled the chamber from above as the south side roadway of the Bridge raised to allow the passing of high river traffic. Bleak shrieked with hysterical prolonged laughter, his mind had now conceded any of his remaining sanity to the psychopathic insanity of his bestial alter ego. Whatever little humanity had remained within him was now entirely absent. He spat and hissed at the officers.

Wiggins joined his colleagues at the observation platform just as Pyke began to peel off his jacket. Pyke put a comforting hand on Constable Murray's slim shoulder.

"Don't worry son. Leave this animal to me," instructed Pyke as he leapt over the flimsy handrail to confront the lunatic.

"Why don't we just shoot him, Sir?" Murray pleaded as he turned towards Wiggins, his voice close to cracking.

Wiggins raised his pistol and aimed it at Bleak but was unable to get a clear shot at the target past the onrushing Pyke. "Damn it Jem, step aside. I can end this nightmare right now with a single bullet."

Pyke feigned deafness, understanding that a shot missing its intended target would ricochet randomly around the steel-clad chamber, endangering the lives of his colleagues. '*If only I could just grab and hold the monster,*' he thought, it would give his boss the greatest chance of a clear and deadly shot.

A warning claxon suddenly began to ring thunderously around them and the bulkhead lights flashed red behind their cages filling the chamber with an unnatural pulsing glow which signalled the imminent raising of the bridge and with it, the descent of the massive bascules filling the space which Bleak and Pyke occupied. The steelwork of the ceiling groaned and creaked deafeningly as it began its inexorable descent to fill the vast chamber.

Pyke launched himself like a charging bull at the wretchedly grinning monster that stood before him. The resulting impact was ferocious. Pyke firstly grabbed Bleak by his wrists, conscious of the danger presented by the razor-sharp scalpel blades and battered his scar tissue covered rock of a skull into the upper part of the nose of his dark, fetid opponent. Bleak screamed a mixture of pain and enjoyment as the bridge of his nose snapped and splintered. Pyke's vice-like grip tightened on Bleak's wrists and he head-butted the Beast repeatedly. Blood was pouring down the brows and into the eyes of each protagonist. The onslaught was incessant. Repeatedly Pyke thundered his forehead into that of the Beast. Bleak growled and snapped like an attacking dog trying to bite at the shorter man's face and throat but the ring savvy bulldog knew to keep his head moving and bobbing. This was street fighting at its most brutal, and Jem Pyke knew he could best the Beast this way. Time and time again he cracked his now ringing head against that of the killer. The punishment each man's cranium was sustaining was brutal. Finally, blood obscuring his sight, Pyke twisted the monster's wrists and pulled off the lacerating scalpel glove. The Beast stood disarmed and hissing, his long pale face curtained in red from forehead to chin, eyes swollen to slits and grinning like a blood-drenched demon.

"I'm going to beat you to death you murdering scum. You ain't up against no defenceless Suffragette now you evil bastard!" spat Pyke through clenched, blood-stained teeth as he swaggered slowly towards Bleak, cracking his knuckles. "Let me introduce myself. I am Jem Pyke and I intend to send you back to Hell from whence you came!"

Two hundred tons of wrought iron was incessantly descending less than ten feet above their heads and getting closer with each passing second. The flashing lights continued to cast their hypnotic pulsating crimson glow onto the scene, the warning claxon now one continuous thunderous drone, rising in pitch as the mass of steel machinery descended closer and closer. Wiggins' view of what happened next was obscured by the lowering section of the roof. He and Murray vaulted over the safety handrail and gained access to the same level as Pyke and Bleak.

"Leave him Jem, the animal has no means of escape, he's trapped. Either he comes to us or he'll be crushed to smithereens by that ceiling above you," shouted

Wiggins gesticulating to Pyke to join him and the young constable in the restricted safety zone of the chamber.

Pyke either could not hear the pleading of his superior above the noise of the machinery opening the bridge, or decided to ignore it, and continued his attack on the bloodied Beast. He swung a pile driver of a right cross against the temple of Bleak. "That's for Mary, you filthy bastard!" spat Pyke. Bleak crumpled to his knees all the while laughing like a hyena. Pyke threw a left uppercut that started at his knees and travelled through his shoulder to crumple Bleak's jawbone into an unrecognisable shape. Bleak fell backwards, but as Pyke moved in, he suddenly leapt up and grappled with the policeman. Bleak had the strength infused in a maniac by his madness whilst Jem had the adrenalin-induced strength of an ex-soldier. The two men rolled around together, grappling in a frenzy of blows and kicks, Pyke trying to keep the Beast's teeth from his throat. It was impossible for Wiggins to get an accurate shot.

"How very dramatic. The noble lion pitted against the unholy Beast." The unexpected gentle whisper in Wiggins' ear startled the life out of the Detective. Upon turning, he saw Van Hoon standing beside him, smiling, at his shoulder, his cane pointed towards the frenetic scene unfolding before them. "It is a rather exciting contest …" He nodded towards the descending tonnage of steelwork. "… but don't you think you should pull your boy out of there sharply Inspector? Those internal workings are getting exceedingly close. Could be exceedingly messy."

"How did you get here, Van Hoon? You're like some kind of insidious phantom," marvelled Wiggins. Van Hoon smiled, pleased with what he regarded as a compliment.

"Get out of there now Pyke! That's an order Jem!" screamed Wiggins trying to make his now hoarse voice audible against the ever-increasing pitch of the howling claxon.

Pyke could now feel the colossal presence of the bascules tickle the scalp at the top his head. '*Time to scarper Jem old boy*, he thought. '*Need to finish this off now.*' Bleak rushed towards Pyke in a final effort to rip out his opponent's throat. Pyke whirled, raised his boot to the chest of the oncoming Beast and with all his remaining strength, kicked the monster deeper into the ever-decreasing chamber. "*Go to Hell, filth!*"

The warning claxon continued to ring its deafening clamour and the red bulkhead lights flashed their unrelenting warning behind their metal cages. As Wiggins had always known they would, the massive bascule counterweights of Tower Bridge continued their slow descent filling the hollowness of the chamber to allow the raising of London's landmark river crossing. There was now less than three feet between the floor and ceiling.

Pyke's sickle-scarred forearm shot out from within the steel chasm and Wiggins grasped the proffered hand and pulled with all his might. His colleague lunged out almost free of the crushing weight when suddenly Bleak's hand grabbed Pyke's ankle and began to pull and twist his leg back into what were now the jaws of certain death.

"Pull, Digger! Pull for Christ's sake PULL!" shrieked Pyke.

Wiggins strained, beads of sweat popping out his forehead, as he attempted to rescue his colleague and friend. Pyke could feel the ominous presence of the weights descending, almost creating an enveloping vacuum of oppression around him.

Suddenly, seemingly out of nowhere, a blade swiftly flashed in front of Wiggin's eyes as Van Hoon's sword swiped like lightning slicing cleanly through Bleak's grasping wrist. The Beast's twitching hand remained clutching Pyke's ankle as the detective gratefully pulled his leg free from the machinery. Van Hoon tipped his hat at Pyke who lay gasping and bloodied at the feet of his three comrades. "That was a bit too close for comfort. Where in Heaven's name did you come from?" panted Pyke, grinning his thanks to the Leper.

Pyke's question went unanswered as Van Hoon watched Bleak's desperate attempts at clambering out of the maw of the descending bascules, his bloody stump hopelessly grappling for safety. The oily surface of the huge steel counterweights created an ever more acute and slippery slope as the ceiling of the chamber made its final approach towards its floor. Sheer panic was painted upon the face of the Beast as he realised that his only hope of escape came in the shape of the charity of his pursuers. Again, and again he frantically tried to clamber and claw his way up the ever-increasing slope only to slide back down further. He now began to scream a wordless scream, his black eyes bulging and pleading in the utter realisation of his inevitable fate. There was now only a matter of inches between his body and hundreds of tons of steelwork. Soon his feet would be crushed, followed closely by his legs, pelvis and upper torso. One final lunge saw him strain every muscle and somehow, he managed to grip the rim of the floor plate with his one remaining hand and pull himself up so as his head and shoulders were free.

"Help me, in the name of Christ Help Me!" screamed the Beast stretching his arms towards his three protagonists. Wiggins involuntarily moved towards the outstretched arms, his instinct ruling his actions. Immediately he felt a staying grip on his shoulder. Pyke looked into the eyes of his honourable colleague and gave his head the slightest of shakes. "Not tonight, guvnor. Let his Christ deal with him."

Bleak's superhuman efforts almost got him to the lip of the crushing weight but already he could feel his feet disappearing into a space where there was no space. '*Please God, make it painless!*' thought Bleak, the indelible blackness of his eyes frozen with terror.

Bleaks' arms and upper body began to writhe and shake at an inhuman speed. It was as if a high voltage electrical current were coursing through his pain-racked body. The speed of his writhing increased as the crushing weight began to slowly descend on his legs, his arms now jerking so violently it was difficult to distinguish their movement at all. The blur of motion continued even as the bascules ground to a halt stopping just short of destroying the Beast's upper body. His feet, legs, pelvis and abdomen were flattened and crushed and still the frenzied blur of movement continued. The siren eventually ceased its unheeded warning.

Van Hoon unsheathed his venom tipped sword cane from its ebony casing and calmly approached the writhing creature in front of him. Very deliberately he raised his sword and placed the tip squarely on the centre of Bleak's forehead. The Beast immediately became still as if he had been captured in some terrible cameo photograph.

As Van Hoon carefully carved the sign of a crucifix into the skin on the now motionless forehead of the Beast he pronounced, "I am the Apostle, I am the Poet, I am the Necromancer. You have heard my voice. In the name of all three and of my fallen brother the Angel Lucifer, I condemn thee to the seventh circle of his House, wherein you will dwell with Attila, and drown in hot blood for all eternity."

Van Hoon withdrew his sword and re-sheathed it, turning to the two detectives as he did so. "Our Beast is dead, gentlemen. I shall expect my usual remuneration as agreed in due course, although Heaven knows what I will be able to do with it." Van Hoon made his way up the concrete stairs twirling his cane and whistling 'The Danse Macabre' as he faded into the gloom of the chamber.

Wiggins, Pyke and Murray stood, struggling to catch their breath, in wide-mouthed amazement at what they had just witnessed. Their eyes moved to the body of what remained of Doctor Joseph Bleak who stared blankly back at them, a frozen snarl etched on its unholy countenance.

Pyke stooped, panting for breath, both bloodied and bruised hands on his knees. He mopped his sweating grossly swollen forehead as he turned to Wiggins and asked, "What the hell is a necromancer?"

Chapter 41 - The Hat

A single drop of rain tapped upon the top of the brown felt Derby. The solitary spot was joined by another, then another and another. Each spot expanded as it hit the felt of the hat, dispersing its moisture through the material, staining it from light brown to a dark ochre. More raindrops followed until the hat echoed like some watery drum, beating like a timpani as the rain now thundered off the cobbles it sat upon.

A pale slender hand reached out of the mist and picked up the hat from the puddle it now sat in. The hand raised it to a cranked nose that sniffed at the cigar smoke-infused brim. The battered and scarred hat had seen better days, but the boy knew of its value to one man. As he turned the hat over to peer inside, the light from a nearby lamppost glinted against a metallic object sewn within the hat's Brunswick green silk lining. The boy examined the metallic object closely, turning it over in his grubby fingers. It was then that he realised just why the hat was so important, why it was cherished. Why it was loved.

Professor Freud rejoiced in the comfort of the pristine white towels that enshrouded his pale undernourished body with a fluffy motherly embrace. He pulled upon a large Cabanas cigar and released the pungent smoke with a puff of gratification. Wiggins noted that this was the Professor's second such cigar of the hour. Wiggins was the only member of the company of four who was not smoking. Both Pyke and Doctor Watson each drew satisfyingly on their own robust Havanas.

"This is the life, gentlemen," declared Watson, removing the cigar from his mouth and rolling it between his fingers, inspecting it as if it were the most beautiful of women.

"These cigars are over twenty years old gentlemen," announced the famed psychiatrist. "A true Cuban Cabanas grows less potent with age but improves in both flavour and performance."

Pyke smiled. "A bit like us men, you might say, huh Prof?"

They all laughed, Watson uproariously so, taking his head out of the newspaper he had been scanning for the previous ten minutes.

"A most apt Freudian analogy," enthused the Austrian. "I may use it in my next lecture, with your kind permission, of course, Mr Pyke."

"Be my guest, Prof! After all, you provided the cigars," laughed Pyke. "And the name is Jem, by the way."

"Very good, Jem. I thank you. Jem, if I am not mistaken, comes from the Hebrew and means sent by God, which I feel can fittingly apply to you all gentlemen. Jem, you may call me Sigmund." Pyke smiled, "Right you are Prof."

The four companions had repaired to the Turkish Bath suite within the Northumberland Hotel and reposed in the leisurely atmosphere of the opulent drying room.

"My old, erstwhile colleague and I once regularly partook of these very Turkish baths on the resolution of a particularly arduous case. We always found it a most relaxing and invigorating oxymoron," recalled Watson with an air of longing nostalgia.

"Die Türkischen Bäder," added Freud. "Most luxurious and stimulating."

Wiggins glanced across to Pyke and noted that his colleague seemed to be drifting into a cloud of melancholic thought. To divert his attention, Wiggins turned to Freud. "Professor, can you explain how Bleak transformed from a highly respectable physician into a savage cannibalistic Beast?"

"I must declare, Herr Inspector, his is the most singularly remarkable case I have ever encountered. Indeed, I am convinced that he was, in fact, unique and that we will never see his like again," began Freud.

"Amen to that," puffed Watson.

"Bleak's psychosis was so deep-rooted and his ego so polluted that his condition manifested itself not only in psychotic change but also in a physical metamorphosis. Of course, there have always been stories of mythical beings that can shapeshift, werewolves and vampires and the like, but here we have irrefutable scientific proof of such a transformation occurring. You have witnessed it with your own unbelieving eyes detectives as you struggled and dealt with this monster. I can assure you, one day, in retrospect, that struggle will strike you as most beautiful. It is undeniably a case without precedent and medically inexplicable. Don't you agree, Herr Doctor?"

"I do indeed, Professor," responded Watson, somewhat honoured at being asked for his opinion. "I see here in the Standard, young Wiggins, a report regarding the mysterious disappearance of three security guards from an, as yet, unnamed secure building in central London. Is this a matter upon which you are currently acting?"

"It is, indeed, Doctor. Sergeant Pyke and Constable Murray are already looking into the matter, but at this stage, it seems to be without serious consequence, other than that of the missing individuals of course," responded Wiggins, searching out Pyke's gaze. He could see that his Sergeant remained preoccupied, his thoughts now elsewhere.

An ivory aproned attendant silently appeared at the side of Pyke as would a puff of smoke through a keyhole. So unobtrusive was his arrival that Pyke, distracted as he was, failed to notice the outstretched hand holding a silver salver until it was accompanied by a pointed cough from the turbaned courier. "A message for you, Mr Pyke, Sir," announced the attendant proffering a hand-written message from the concierge. "If you can accommodate an intrusion upon your leisure, a master William Skew requests to see you, Sir." Watson folded his paper closed in curious anticipation whilst Freud continued to puff heartily upon his cigar. Pyke glanced across to Wiggins, who nodded his approval.

"Show him in please," affirmed Pyke wondering why Billy would be calling upon him and how he could possibly have known that he would be here within the Northumberland.

Billy entered at the behest of the attendant, his eyes cast downwards staring at his threadbare shoes, his shoulders rounded, and his hands held firmly behind his back. Wiggins inwardly thought that one would not need to be a Professor of psychoanalysis to read this tableau of body language.

"Come in Billy, what brings you here, lad?" questioned Pyke cheerfully, beckoning the boy towards him. Billy shuffled forward hesitantly and the attendant, content that there was no need of his involvement in the situation, busied himself with some unwarranted towel folding.

"Begging your pardon, Sirs," stammered the lad, lifting his stare from his feet and darting a look at each of the men in front of him. He swallowed what he imagined to be a sharp object and said, "I brought somefink for you, Sir. Somefink I found in the street, you see. I recognised it as yours, smells of you it does. I thought you might want it back." Billy slowly produced the brown felt Derby from behind his back, took a sheepish step towards Pyke and held it out at arm's length towards him. "I saw what was inside it, Sergeant Pyke. I knew it must be valuable like so I thoughts I would bring it to you, you know. Seeing as how you was so kind to me the last time we met, like. Mr Jem, Sir."

Pyke stared open-mouthed at the hat, his hat. He looked to Billy and smiled whilst nodding his head, at that moment unable to reply to the boy, instead ruffling his hair with a thick calloused hand. "Thank you, Billy. This means so much more to me than you could ever realise," he finally managed to stutter. Pyke peered inside the hat at his Kimberley Star medal carefully stitched securely into the lining of the hat. His mind, as it always did when looking upon the decoration, drifted back to his lost comrades, their wasted lives, and their acts of ultimate bravery in defending the besieged town. He also thought fondly of the inhabitants of Kimberley that the Cavalry had managed to save. "Thank you very much lad, you've made an old soldier incredibly happy. How did you know I would be here?"

"I tracked you down, Sir. Made a few enquiries, you might say, Sir," admitted Billy, not sure whether he was saying the right or the wrong thing. "I called round the Yard, but you wasn't there and that big beefy Sergeant wouldn't tell me where you were. So, I asks Blind Johnny Jewlip, you knows, the beggar who sits outside Charing Cross who ain't blind a bit, if he'd seen you around. And he says you an Inspector Wiggins 'ere were headed towards the hotel, not an hour before. So, I steals around here and asks Millie the flower girl on the corner, if she's seen you go in 'an she says she as, but you ain't never come out yet. Rest was simple as shelling peas, you might say, Mr Pyke, Sir."

"Admirable detective work, young man," interjected Wiggins. "Most impressive, lad." Wiggins looked across at Pyke, urging him to compliment the young boy. Pyke nodded in agreement.

From where Watson was sitting, he could see a glimpse of the inside of the Hat and instantly recognised the situation. "Young man…" he announced, "…you demonstrate great resource and bravery in coming here, not to mention extreme honesty in returning this item to Mr Pyke. Many a lad of your age would have taken such an item straight down to Rubenstein's and traded it for as much as they would offer for such an item." The old campaigner smiled so his moustache rose in a reciprocating smile of its own. His eyes twinkled as he fumbled in his discarded jacket, and producing his billfold, extracted a crisp new pound note and passed it to an awestruck young Billy. "Here is your reward. Make sure you spend it wisely, some aniseed twists may be in order, what?"

Pyke saw the joy in the boy's eyes and immediately realised it would be short lived. The Heap could hear the rustle of a pound note at a hundred yards and would soon have it commandeered off the unfortunate Billy for his own use. He made a decision. "Billy, take a fiver out of me wallet. You'll find it in the left inside pocket of that jacket hanging behind you there."

Billy did as instructed, attempting to subdue the fever of euphoria rising within him. He now held six whole pounds in his grasp. This was more money than he had ever seen in one place at any time in his life. He looked at Pyke, mouth slightly open, wondering what to do or say next. "You know where I live Billy, don't you?" Billy nodded his head, his skewed features trying to mask his swelling excitement. "Good. Now take this money there and tell Red Noreen, who you've already met, that I told her to give you a bowl of her mutton soup and some fresh bread. After you've eaten ask her to take you and that money down the market and use it to buy you a new set of clothes and some shoes that ain't full of holes. If there's anything left over, you might ask her to find you a small Derby hat, maybes." Pyke threw young Billy a wink. "Now get out of here, lad before I change my mind. I'll see you when I get home."

"Thanks, Mr Pyke, Sir. Thanks Mr, I means Doctor Watson," enthused Billy as he ran full pelt out through the drying room door, upending a newly stacked pile of towels onto the floor as he did so. The eyes of the attendant rolled silently towards the ceiling.

The four men laughed. Watson reacquainted himself with his newspaper and Freud busied himself in selecting his next Cabanas from his carved cigar box. "That was an admirably noble thing you did there, Jem," acknowledged Wiggins.

Pyke sighed. "Least I could do really. The lad deserves an even chance, Guv, besides I've been looking to get one over the Heap for a while now. He ain't going to be best pleased, I can tell you."

Wiggins nodded sagely. He knew that below that hardest of exteriors beat the heart of a fine decent man, honourable in the extreme. "I take it there is room within that battered old hat of yours for another piece of silverware, Jem?" he queried. Pyke looked puzzled. "The King's Police medal for bravery for instance? I had wanted to inform you in a more formal setting, Sergeant, but Commissioner Gregson confirmed to me only this morning that you are to be honoured for your unparalleled bravery in single-handedly confronting the Beast."

Watson turned, lay his newspaper on his lap, and started a slow round of applause, Freud joined in, as did Wiggins. Pyke shook his head and drew upon his cigar attempting to disguise his pride and mask it with his customary indifference.

The heavy oak door cracked open with a splintering rent. The blue pink moon hid behind an enshrouding cloud as the pale but powerful hand disdainfully discarded the short crowbar to the ground. Lighting cracked overhead, illuminating one side of the cruelly handsome face. The hands gripped the door edge, pulled and the door creaked open, its arched top struggling against the overgrown ivy that gripped it to the surrounding stonework. The howling wind whistled through the yew trees and tombstones of the ancient graveyard and a distant fox screeched like a banshee. Once inside, the tall lean figure heaved the heavy door to, interrupting the invasive flow of dry leaves that were blowing their dancing way into the church entrance. Luca Radasiliev slowly and carefully looked around him, surveying the space he now occupied. A muted undertow of unease ebbed in and out of his soul. His face split into a sinister smile. '*This will do nicely*,' he thought. '*Yes, this will do very nicely indeed.*'

"Each was an inebriate beggar, a life without life, each an existence of no import. As such they will not be missed, not even by their low life contemporaries," smiled King, his oblique hooded eyes glinting with pleasure as he surveyed each of the unconscious forms laying before him. Each one was strapped to a hard timber bench from forehead to ankles. "We have given each of these unfortunates a varying diluted solution of the virus to determine the optimum potency for our purpose. Ingenious, don't you think, my dear Rubenstein?"

The old Jewish crime lord shuddered and found it impossible to hide his revulsion at the sordid scene he was being forced to witness. He took another bracing slug of his brandy, drained the glass and placed it with a trembling hand on the jade inlaid cherry wood table at his side. "So, you mean to use the virus to hold the authorities to ransom?" ventured the Jew, trying vainly to disguise the tremble in his voice. '*This man is not human*,' he thought. He felt as though he were standing before the very devil himself.

King cackled the mad laughter of the truly insane. "You underestimate me, Rubenstein. I mean to use the serum not only to extort but also to kill. I have the power within my grasp to annihilate half the population of London. Imagine it Jabez, not only the pathetic public but also government officials, the police, leaders of industry, the ruling classes, perhaps the very Royal Family themselves." Rubenstein swallowed hard, a clammy fear creeping through his soul.

"How does it taste, Jabez?" asked King, looking at the emptied glass at the old man's side. King's laughter rose to a shrieking cackle of madness.

Chapter 42 - The New Life

Wiggins puffed out his cheeks and exhaled a rapid deep breath as if he was cleansing his body for the task ahead. He and Miss Constance Harkness, her now plastered arm in a sling, swallowed hard and approached the front door of the modest terraced house in Upper Hoxton. The area was somewhat run down and neglected but Wiggins observed that the front step of the little house was scrubbed clean and the tiny front garden, as it was, was tidy and well kept. He glanced sidewards at Miss Harkness and smiled a half-smile that was intended to be reassuring as he rapped the shining brass door knocker twice, paused then rapped another three times.

Inside, Jennifer Potts was polishing the kitchen table. *'Why is William knocking?'* she thought, *'he must have forgotten his keys again.'* She hurried away the duster and tin of polish, shouting "Just a minute Billy" as she straightened her pinafore. She could see the rippling obscured shapes of two blurred heads through the frosted glass panel in her front door. That is when she instantly knew.

Wiggins was just reaching for the door knocker a second time when the door opened hesitantly. Jennifer Potts stood in the open doorway her mouth agape, her head shaking and her body trembling overwhelmingly. She reached her arms out as if in supplication. "Oh my God No! Please no … not my William, not my Billy Boy," she pleaded with tears now pouring down her flushed cheeks. She faltered and stumbled backwards as if on the verge of collapse. Wiggins stepped forward and clutched her at both elbows, steadying her from crumpling before them.

"Please Mrs Potts. May we come in?" he intoned, a feeling of complete desolation and inadequacy sweeping through him.

"Not my Billy boy. What am I to do? What are we to do?" she cried cradling her obviously swollen stomach. Wiggins looked at his feet. It was just too much to bear. Miss Harkness was immediately by the stricken woman's side, comforting her, guiding her into the pristinely clean parlour. "Come, Mrs Potts, sit down. Inspector, would you be able to muster some tea?"

"I will do it, my lady," mumbled the house-proud Mrs Potts seemingly in a trance, rising to head towards the kitchen.

"Don't be silly," insisted Miss Harkness, nodding towards Wiggins and indicating the kitchen. Mrs Potts was quite obviously in shock, tears streamed down her face and the emptiness within her body felt as if her heart had suddenly exploded. In a matter of seconds, her World had ended.

Wiggins stood immobile. The woman's grief was a palpable thing that enveloped the room, coating its contents in misery. She convulsed uncontrollably into sobs, rocking back and forth in the chair by the fire that she had lit and tended to only minutes before, awaiting the arrival home of her beloved husband.

Constance Harkness put an arm around Mrs Pott's shoulders and hugged her tightly as a mother comforts a distraught child. "How? How did it happen?" her tear-filled eyes lifted towards those of Constance. Wiggins coughed. "I am afraid your husband died in the line of duty Mrs Potts. He died a hero, sacrificing his own life that others may live. His bravery and selflessness were immeasurable and without bounds."

Mrs Potts wailed. A wail that came from the very depths of her soul. She then recoiled as if hit by a sledgehammer, doubled up in grief. "How can this be Sir? He is but a policeman, not a soldier. What good is his bravery to us now? How will I live without him? How will I raise my child without its father?"

Wiggins gritted his teeth, tears welled in his eyes. Tears of sorrow for this woman's plight and tears of pride at the bravery of his young Constable. He opened his mouth to speak but nothing emerged. He realised that nothing he could say could possibly help this now empty woman. '*Sometimes silence is more appropriate than trying to fill a silence*,' he thought. At once she had been at home awaiting her husband's return, looking forward in anticipation to a fireside supper, and now she would never see him or hear his voice again.

"Our Landlord, Mr Levinsky will soon have us out the door, Sir. And what of the funeral? What of my baby? What of our lives?" Wiggins stood in silence frustrated at his inadequacy to source any words in reply to her pleas.

Constance Harkness took Jennifer Potts by the shoulders, one hand on each. "Mrs Potts. Look at me." Jennifer's nut hazel eyes looked into the azure blue eyes of Constance. "Your husband breathed his last breath saving my life. I promise you here and now, Mrs Jennifer Potts, that you will want for nothing in this life any longer. You and your baby will come to live with us on our Hertfordshire Estate. You will be my companion, not a servant you understand, and your son or daughter will receive the best of educations and we shall endeavour to offer the love your heroic husband would have bestowed upon you both. I owe you that much at the very least. Since my sister Agatha's departure there is a void in my life that only another young woman can fill. You will be as a sister to me, and your soon to be born as my Niece or Nephew."

Mrs Potts dropped her head and gasped for air, wiping her tears. "You would do this for us? Me and the child?" she spluttered.

"I will do it for both of you and especially for your husband," nodded Constance "You have my solemn oath." Wiggins shook his head, once again amazed at the compassion and resourcefulness of this young lady, and quietly shuffled towards the kitchen in search of a teapot.

Four months later a small congregation gathered in the Harkness private chapel on their Hertfordshire Estate. Sunlight streamed through the stained-glass windows warming the chapel. The bright colours cast through the glass seemed inappropriate for the darkness of the day now upon them.

"In the name of the Father and the Son and the Holy Spirit, I hereby christen you, William Albert Potts, in the presence of our Lord God," proclaimed the Bishop making the sign of the cross on the child's forehead and gently sprinkling holy water three times on the head of the baby resting calmly in his doting mother's arms. The Godparents, Wiggins and Constance Harkness, exchanged smiling glances of knowing understanding. Viscount Harkness nodded as if satisfied and content and shook the hand of the Bishop.

Pyke winked at the babe in arms and made a funny face by crossing his eyes whilst pulling at the corners of his mouth. The baby gurgled with glee. "Here's to you Pottsie," said the hardest man in London, dabbing the corners of his eyes with a pristine white handkerchief. "May you be just half the man your father was."

Jennifer Potts looked around the scene before her and mentally pinched herself for what was the umpteenth time that day. She gave thanks to her late husband's memory once more, marvelling that in death he had managed to bestow upon them a better life than he could ever possibly have given them when he was alive. She sat in the sprawling drawing room of the Harkness family, her newly christened baby son sleeping serenely in the cot by the side of the chaise that she shared with Constance Harkness. She looked long and lovingly into her child's face, picking out likenesses between father and son. Viscount Harkness sat in a great wing-back chair, a balloon of brandy swirling in his hand, his glacial eyes staring intently into the ever-changing flames within the hearth. Albert and Mary Wiggins sat together opposite Jennifer and Constance, each engaged in conversation with the heiress to the Harkness Estate, whilst Alexander Buchanan, newly returned from Egypt looked on admiringly. Behind them, Jem Pyke and Doctor Watson were exchanging animated stories of adventures and shared acquaintances whilst Magnus MacDonald looked on and occasionally interjected from his state-of-the-art wheelchair. Lady Cecilia Harkness fussed around making sure that the staff kept every glass full.

A sudden laugh from Watson jolted Viscount Harkness from his melancholy. "And then, of course, we handcuffed the little madman and he spat at us; *I have royal blood in my veins. Have the goodness to always address me as Sir!*" roared Watson. Pyke howled with laughter and slapped the old campaigner on the shoulder. "By the Kaiser's beard, I thought I had seen it all, but your tales take some beating, Doctor."

The two old soldiers' verbal sparring was suddenly interrupted by a sharp clinking noise signalling their attention. All in the room fell silent and turned towards Viscount Harkness who stood at the fireplace hitting a fork against his crystal goblet. At a nod from his Master, the ethereal Jeffers proceeded to pass everyone a flute of Dom Pérignon. "And take one for yourself, Jeffers," nodded the Viscount. The obedient butler took a glass and held the now empty silver tray down by his side.

Wiggins noted that the Viscount cut a stately figure that no man in the Kingdom could hope to match as he raised his glass, first to the lifelike portraits of his wife and deceased daughter that hung above the mantle of the grand fireplace and then turned to salute the dozing babe in the cradle. "A toast ladies and gentlemen, to young William Potts. May he live to grow and prosper in a world free from beasts, ghouls and monsters."

The company raised their glasses and replied "Here, here," as one. Wiggins felt a strong hand grip his shoulder and recognised the force of nature that was Jem Pyke. Jem leant forward slightly and whispered in his ear "Sounds like we have our work cut out for us, Guv!"

Chapter 43 - The Fee

"Schijt!" cursed an exasperated Van Hoon under his breath. He carefully wiped the beading perspiration from his forehead with a silk Paisley handkerchief. "Lastig, very tricky indeed."

The huge arc light beamed down, illuminating the scene. He stooped industriously over his work, concentrating intensely on the complexity and sheer volume of the task he had set himself this time. It was challenging work on a scale of intricacy not previously encountered in the hundreds of specimens he had worked on over the intervening years. He had once made a rather agreeable purse out of a sow's ear but this current payment in kind presented perhaps his greatest taxidermic restoration to date. The materials he had been left to work with were not what he would have desired. The damage inflicted upon the body by the crushing weight of the steelwork within the bascule chambers had decimated practically everything below the sternum leaving almost no identifiable parts from which to recreate a semblance of the Beast. A Beast that had been snarling viciously back at him only a few weeks before.

Reconstruction was a major challenge, albeit one that Dante Van Hoon relished. He believed nothing to be unsurmountable. He had proved that many times over the decades. He was Dante Van Hoon after all. Providing that the features and visible limbs were concentrated upon accurately and precisely, clothes, detailed brushwork, wool and polyurethane could complete the illusion of what lay underneath, of what was unable to be reconstructed.

Doctor Joseph Bleak's flailed and dried skin was now draped and ready, positioned over the wire-framed mannequin Van Hoon had previously sculpted to portray a crouched and hunched form. The upper torso and face were almost complete in their entirety and intensity. "Should I maintain or camouflage the cross I carved upon his forehead?" he asked to no one in particular. *'Perhaps he should leave it,'* he thought. A unique feature and testament to a unique being, and a memory for him to savour in future years. The pelvis he had reconstructed from the bastardised pelvic girdle of a pig which offered splendid suspension points from which to hang the reformed lower limbs.

Van Hoon wore a pair of brass jeweller's loupes of his own design, the right lens of which, at the touch of a tiny lever, could be greatly magnified for minuscule, intricate work such as he was currently conducting. After accurately adjusting the intensity of the magnification to reduce the increasing strain being placed upon his weakened eye, he resumed stitching with a precision rivalled only by that of the most well-regarded surgeons in the land. He carefully began to intricately stitch and reattach the severed hand to the Beast's right forearm. This was going to take some time. He smiled.

Chapter 44 - The Visitor (1953)

He could hear the twittering of the birds accompanying the hesitant patter of a light early morning shower as it hit the windowpane. His eyelids were closed against the morning sunshine.

For the past four years, he has sat in this easy chair. The term 'easy' being a misnomer as there is nothing easy about getting in and out of it these days for him. It is one of those chairs that elderly incontinent people sit in most of their day. Waterproof, stain-resistant and fire retardant and upholstered in faux leather to make it look as though it is not at all designed for an incontinent, dementia sufferer like Albert Wiggins.

Sherrinford Care Home for the Elderly & Infirm in Hertfordshire is where he now exists. His dementia began several years ago now. Initially, he kept mislaying things. Forgetting silly little things like why he found himself standing in the garden in the rain with no shoes on. Wondering why he had found a pair of socks in the oven; stupid trivial things. Worryingly he soon found it difficult to solve problems and remember things, which was ironic as these were the two things Digger was famous for. It was his job after all. His stock and trade. Thoughts were now irregular, drifting and see-sawing from the here and now to the then and when. Clouded memories to a half-imagined past which at times seemed to belong to someone else entirely. Not his memories. Not Albert Wiggins. Not Digger. He had been orderly, meticulous. Organised and analytical to an obsessive degree.

He does remember they once called him Digger. The called him Guv. Follow one lead, lose it, and dig out another. That was how he worked; dogged, determined, like some huge hound on a scent. He was forensic in his investigations and meticulous in his work. That was back when he could remember every detail of a case. Back when the Old King was still on the throne. He met His Majesty once. A very brief encounter during the days when he helped Him out from time to time. He seems to recall someone, maybe Glenys or one of the other nurses, telling him that there was a new Queen now. A young, pretty one.

Back in the days when he was a lad, when every day was hard, mud-larking on the Thames, digging to find treasure in the stinking, black-grey, oil heavy ooze. Ooze that sucked between your toes with every laboured step and blackened your nails and dried like cement in your hair. The stench stuck with you day and night, an ever-present prurience in your nostrils. On a good day, you may have discovered a scrap of builders' debris or a piece of lead or a length of copper that could get you a few pennies from Pikey Pierce down Limeharbour Yard. On a particularly good day, you would get the word that He had a job needed doing. Something exciting and dangerous to keep your wits about you, running around the City looking here or there, for this or that, him or her.

Nobody knew London like him and his mates back then. Every alleyway and mews, every brothel and opium house, every alehouse and butcher shop. Albert and his gang knew them all. Every inch of the docks, every rope makers yard, warehouse, tobacco store and rat run. He knew shortcuts to shortcuts and secret passages that could make him seemingly vanish into thin air and outwit any pursuing ne'er-do-well. And He knew it. That is why they would get the call, a shilling a day for each of them and a sparkling, palm-heavy guinea for the lucky lad who fingered the final prize.

Albert's room is cosy and homely. A single bed, which is comfortable enough, apart from the feel of the cold metal framework against his arms as he tries to manoeuvre his position during the night. It reminds him of the hospital bed he spent almost three months lying in whilst recovering from the American's poorly aimed revolver. *'Back in '13 … or was it '14?'* Whichever year it was it is still almost forty years ago, and despite his dementia, he can still hear the blast from the Webley .38 pistol and see the white scar tissue on his chest. It still pains him when he wheezes or sneezes or coughs, which is often these days.

The room is sparsely furnished with a bedside table with nightstand, a wardrobe and chest of drawers and a small table. There are sadly very few possessions for a man of his age. A few photographs that occasionally rekindle memories of good and bad persuasion, a bashed silver vesta case, his wedding ring that is now too loose for his finger, and an emerald tiepin which appeared on his bedside table one day a few years back. Albert cannot even remember owning such a pin, but he likes the way the emerald catches the light and winks mischievously at him. Maybe Mary gave it to him.

His chair faces a window that looks out onto the well-maintained gardens. The sun streams in on bright days like this and warms his now almost permanently chilled and translucent skin. The manicured lawns and neatly tended flower beds remind him of what he called his Little Yard where he would tend out back of the house in Finchley. The home Mary and he had moved to when he was eventually persuaded to retire from the force twenty years or so ago. At first, he found it difficult adjusting to life outside of Scotland Yard. He knew nothing else. The job was a vocation where every case would be all-encompassing, becoming an obsessional crusade. Although with Mary's help and love, he eventually settled into a more sedate lifestyle. He hung up his blackjack and warrant card, and just as he had swapped digging for scraps in the Thames for digging for sinners in the foul-smelling underbelly of The Smoke, he then found himself digging for weeds in a tranquil north London suburb. Digger, right enough. Always digging.

"Can I perhaps trouble you to enquire as to how Mr Wiggins is today Nurse?" asked the tall elderly gentleman standing before Glenys. "He's in fine physical health this morning Sir but his mind is not his own I'm afraid. It wanders even worse than when you last visited."

"Would it be possible if I sat with him for a short while? My journey should best not be wasted, and I can converse well enough for the pair of us. We share many memories Nurse, although unfortunately, he cannot recollect them as he once could. One vitally important one to me especially," explained the elderly gentleman removing his cloth cap to reveal a mop of snow-white hair.

"Of course, you can, Mr Escott. Can I fetch you a pot of strong black coffee as usual Sir?" replied Glenys with an encouraging smile. "That would be most refreshing thank-you," his thickly tufted eyebrows rising above his intensely piercing, intelligent eyes in delight at the prospect.

The tall, gaunt visitor made his way along the corridor to room twenty-four. He strode purposely and moved lithely for someone of such advanced years. He was dressed in a modern tweed suit which sat oddly with the accompanying old-fashioned Ulster over-jacket. He drew up a chair and sat beside Wiggins.

Albert sees indistinct shapes move beyond his eyelids, shadows in the light. His mind sees the man with the lighting on his cheek, the tall handsome Russian. *'What were their names?'*

The smell. *'What is that smell? The smell of Brazilian burley?'* A long-lost memory. *'Where did that come from?'*

He shudders and whimpers as he sees the Beast. A horrific blood-curdling vision that makes him shake his head. He feels the gentle reassuring touch of a calming hand upon his.

'The smell of Moroccan leather. A beautiful smell but what does it remind him of?'

The shapes behind his eyelids shift. The sun's rays grow stronger. The sound of the rain becomes the drumming of horse's hooves, the whistling of the birds, the clamour of men. Shouting and selling. Spitalfields, Limehouse Docks. His memory finds his friend, his protector. Jem, he remembers his name. The bravest man he ever knew.

'Greek pitch. What is that smell?'

He sees the Chinamen, the monstrous giant and the one who was more evil than the devil himself. Once more he whimpers and shakes his head. Once more he feels the comforting hand stroking his. He begins to calm. He sees Mary. He smiles. Mary his love. His eyes well with tears. He feels the light touch of a cotton handkerchief dab at the corners of his eyes. He smiles. The heat of the sun warms him.

'*A mixture of tobacco smoke and strong coffee blended with rosin. What is that smell? Where is it coming from? It is His smell!*'

He hears His voice.

"My dear Wiggins, old chap! How does this fine day find you?" he proclaimed in a fast, high-pitched voice on entering the room. He removed a jar of homemade honey from his inside pocket and placed the gift on the nightstand next to Wiggins' bed. "Have you seen today's edition of The Times my good fellow?" he inquired excitedly. "We have conquered Mount Everest! Would you believe it? Someone has grasped the summit of the world." Albert Wiggins offered no response and displayed no emotion. It was as if his caller had not blustered into the room at all. "As you may know, I possess an inordinate dislike of mountains, but this is indeed a great accomplishment by our very own Hillary and some fellow called Tenzing. I suspect the success can chiefly be attributed to the Sherpa, a thirty-nine-year-old Nepalese mountaineer of great repute." He took a short pause for breath, staring at his languid host, before continuing at a hundred miles per hour, "Why does the editor of The Times think we are in any way interested or concerned in every individual's age? It is a most unhealthy modern habit they obviously have no desire to discontinue. No matter who the person, what the story, or how great the achievement they will insist on printing everybody's age!"

Glenys appeared in the open doorway with a tray upon which stood a pot of steaming black coffee and a bowl of sugar alongside two custard cream biscuits on a paper doily. "Here you are, Sir. I know you never eat the biscuits, but it would be amiss of me after all these years if I was not to continue our little charade," she admitted snorting back a nasal laugh.

"Very good, Nurse, you have excellent powers of deduction," replied the visitor with a lopsided grin.

"Did you see they hanged Derek Bentley, *aged 19*, for the murder of Police Constable Sidney Miles earlier in the year?" inquired the elderly visitor emphasising extra enunciation upon the young man's age. "I have been following the case closely and I fear they may find that they have rather unfortunately condemned the wrong assailant in this matter. Not like John Christie however who was most definitely another Beast." He paused momentarily as he thought he had seen a glimmer of recognition in Albert's features. The slightest of twitches. "Do you remember

Constable Miles, Digger? The jury's verdict was 'party to murder' but I find this to be a rather tenuous conviction and one that unfortunately cost him his own life."

After pouring himself a second cup of black coffee with two sugars he returned to his copy of The Times to find snippets worthy of discourse. "I know how greatly you appreciate the game of football, young Albert, so it may be of interest to you that Blackpool won the FA Cup final. You may recall that John preferred the games of Rugby and cricket, whilst my modest endeavours stretched only as far as the boxing glove and the rapier. A solitary sportsman rather than a team player, you might say. Anyway, Blackpool triumphed in a 4-3 victory over Bolton Wanderers. Stan Mortensen scored three goals by all accounts, but I suspect that this game will go down in history for the heroics of Stanley Matthews as he was instrumental in the winning of the game. It would not surprise me in the least if they awarded him a Knighthood for kicking a spherical object around a field of muddy grass! Perhaps you managed to watch the match on the new television in the communal room?"

"Oh, before I forget I must obtain a copy of 'Casino Royale' for my next visit. It is a rather splendid novel about a secret service agent that was published only a few months ago. Not a great literary effort, and I suspect it doesn't purport to be, but one that I am confident you will appreciate as a fellow sleuth. It will certainly pass a few hours for you. I sincerely hope the author, an Ian Fleming, writes a follow-up novel."

"You really must permit me to get a word in edgeways for once Wiggins, old fellow!" he jokingly added.

'The smell again. That smell once more. His smell!' Wiggins smiled. He remembered the smell. He remembered the seventeen steps on the staircase that led to His rooms. He remembered Mary's grandmother and the heroic Doctor.

Albert slowly opened his eyes to a most remarkable countenance. A sight he thought he would never again see. A vision that defied both logic and time. An astonishing, beautiful absurd sight, one which quite frankly he thought was categorically impossible.

The sight of Sherlock Holmes.

"Mr Holmes! Mr Sherlock Holmes? Please tell me my eyes do not deceive me again Sir. That I'm not once again dreaming of that time long ago? It surely must be a trick of my damaged memory. It can't be … you must be over 100 years old for Heaven's sake!"

"A mere ninety-seven," interrupted Holmes with a lopsided and barely perceptible grin.

"Good Heavens," retorted Wiggins.

"Amazing really when you consider the treacherous lifestyle I chose to pursue. Cocaine, criminals and hoodlums, tobacco, pistols, opium, devil hounds, strong coffee and poison, whilst not forgetting a certain Reichenbach Falls, are not I should think, the best prescription for longevity. Not to mention Professor Moriarty and Colonel Sebastian Moran. Excepting the minor hip pain and the arthritic fingers, I do not feel any different than I did when I was eighty-three," winked Holmes. Wiggins smiled. He felt elated and content at the same time. The sun shone on his face.

"Arthritis is rather an annoying bed-fellow. A dreadfully frustrating affliction, especially when one has a Stradivarius sitting idle at home, staring at you, pleading to be played. There can be few things worse than a musical instrument forced into silence don't you think? Sound is its sole reason for being after all. Nothing screams louder than an unplayed instrument."

"I have visited a few times over the intervening years, but you have either been asleep, at repast or ... best occupied. Very few people appreciate that I am still alive so there is no requirement for disguise these days you understand. You were asleep upon my last visitation when I placed the emerald tiepin on your dresser. A wicked little clue to prick at your memories. Wiggins glanced at the pin with a blank expression, a lone tear tickled and trickled a meandering path down his cheek. He was enraptured at the company of this inspirational man.

"Lord! Look at the time," ejaculated Holmes as he glanced at his Rotary wristwatch. "I have taken up far too much of your valuable time. It is rather a long train journey to Eastbourne, but it does pass some splendid countryside. I must earnestly get to the point of my visitation. I have watched your career from afar with immense pride and no prejudice. Observing Wiggins, the irregular street urchin turned regular solver of crime, has been a rewarding distraction for me at times. I must admit that for my analytical mind most cases have required very little intricate investigation, no great powers of deduction, but there was one case that has escaped even me. I am affronted and to some degree ashamed that I cannot resolve one final element in ... the Case of Doctor Joseph Bleak!"

"My dear Wiggins, I know why it was done, I know where it was done, and I know how it was done. These are all elementary, my dear Wiggins, I am Sherlock Holmes after all. I dread to count how many pipes I must have inhaled mulling over the data of this case. For the last forty years, I have retraced thoughts, eliminated factors, ruled out possibilities, discarded probabilities, developed new theories and discarded them also ... but for the life of me, I am at an impasse like no other I have ever encountered. A literal dead-end! For my entire life, it has been my business to know what other people do not know so please offer me up the final piece of this mysterious jigsaw puzzle. You have bested me." Holmes paused to allow the question to register in Wiggins' mind.

"My dear Digger, our time is limited, and I suspect our paths may never again cross. My great age and your diminishing memory testify to the fact. My mind was once like a racing engine, but it merely idles this past while. We both know there are certain rare crimes which the authorities cannot touch, and which consequently justify private revenge and this is one such case so I implore you, I beseech you … what did you do with the body? It was never recovered, absolutely no trace of it and it remains a complete mystery today. I beg of you Wiggins, satisfy an old man's curiosity. What did you do with Bleak's body?"

Epilogue (2013, One hundred years later)

Van Hoon winced slightly as he carefully inserted the cannula into a vein on the back of his right hand. Despite having performed this procedure countless times over the years he still found it impossible not to flinch somewhat as the needle penetrated its target. Any slight discomfort, however, was soon replaced by the relief of the icy surge of the life-prolonging solution that began to trace through his cardiovascular system delivering renewed vitality throughout his body.

The elixir was a cocktail of his invention. A blend of various enzymes and cells extracted from the immortal jellyfish, Turritopsis Dhornii, the regenerative asexual starfish, Linckia, and the cancer-resistant tiger shark, Galeocerdo Cuvier. All now combined with medicines of modern science producing a treatment that permitted the transdifferentiation process to revitalise the cells throughout his ancient, though outwardly ageless body.

Van Hoon sighed and sat back on a large carved oak chair, inlaid with an alabaster and bronze relief of Seraphim. He contentedly surveyed his Collection Room which made up the expansive basement of his Belgravia Mansion whilst sipping absinthe from a sixteenth-century Murano glass.

So many years had passed, so many loves lost, so many adventures survived, so many centuries lived, and yet still he revelled in the magnificence of the collection set out before him. All painstakingly preserved and resting in row upon row of individual taxidermy display cabinets. Brass plaques inscribed with names and details for each one in the assemblage. From under his coloured glasses, Van Hoon's eyes darted excitedly between the display cases. He never ceased to enjoy observing his exhibits.

He surveyed the name plaques. The Marquis de Sade (*French Aristocrat, 1740-1814*) and the diminutively abhorrent Louis XIV (*King of France, 1638-1715*). He gazed for several minutes upon Alphonse Gabriel Capone (*American Gangster, 1899-1947*), admiring a particularly challenging exhibit considering the mobster's syphilitic ending. A larger display cabinet containing Bonnie Elizabeth Parker and Clyde Chestnut Barrow (*American Outlaws, 1910-1934, 1909-1934, respectively*). Theirs was another problematic operation due to the number of wounds that had ravaged their bullet-ridden bodies. A true test of the master taxidermist. To the right stood Peter the Great (*Tsar of Russia, 1672-1725*) and on the left, Elvis Aron Presley (*American Entertainer, 1935-1994*).

Van Hoon wandered over to a case containing Elizabeth Báthory de Ecsed (*Hungarian Countess, 1560-1614*). He touched the palm of his left hand to the glass the way a grandfather touches the head of a grandchild. He had treated and preserved her skin almost as well as she had attempted to do during her lifetime.

Wolfgang Amadeus Mozart (*Austrian Composer, 1756-1791*). '*Tragic that those fingers would never again move or create,*' he mused when he had displayed the great composer. James Warren Jones (*American Cult Leader, 1931-1978*). '*Particularly unpleasant lips to do,*' he shuddered. Ivan IV Vasilyevich (*Grand Prince of Moscow, 1530-1584*). '*Terrible in life but majestic in death,*' he chuckled at his witty epithet. Lee Jun-fan (*Cantonese Martial Artist, 1940-1973*). '*An individual so swift rendered motionless,*' he ruminated admiringly at the way he had successfully achieved the illusion of rapid movement in the stationary man before him.

A huge smile spread across Van Hoon's face as he approached the display case of Charles Spencer Chaplin (*Comic, Actor, Filmmaker, Composer, 1889-1977*). He chuckled as he recalled how this particular remuneration was almost never concluded due to the reckless circumstances surrounding the body snatchers' attempt at blackmailing him. '*Very messy business,*' he remembered.

Van Hoon walked past Idi Amin Dada (*President of Uganda, 1925-2003*), dressed in full military uniform, looking as though he could stride out of the display case at any moment to greet visitors. He looked deeply into the eyes of the monster and imagined the carnage he had witnessed.

He had placed a smile upon the lips of Pol Pot (*Cambodian Prime Minister, 1925-1998*) betraying the fact that this little man committed the genocide of three million of his own people. '*A rather jolly looking little fellow,*' Van Hoon thought to himself.

Row upon row of historical figures perfectly preserved and painstakingly displayed. Van Hoon's collection of the dead. Despots, desperados, demigods and demons. How he loved his human Menagerie of the Departed.

The Leper observed that some of his older exhibits were displaying signs of deterioration due to the rudimentary techniques he was enforced to employ at the times when he had received the rewards. Although Van Hoon could control the ravages of time he faced personally, he found it extremely frustrating that he could not rewind the clock, thus enabling him to rework his exhibits with the more modern taxidermy techniques now within his possession.

As he scanned the room, his eyes as always, settled upon the two exhibits in the central display case. His masterpieces. Magisteriis eius. His neighbours from Hell. Doctor Joseph Bleak (*The Beast, 1866-1913*) stood alongside Jack himself (*The Ripper of Whitechapel, 1854-1891*). Today, over a century since their disappearances, the public remained completely unaware of their capture and of their preservation. Both corpses had been awarded to Van Hoon as his reward for his part in their ultimate fate. His remuneration.

Van Hoon sat back down and allowed himself a few moments of satisfaction whilst recalling the role he had played in removing both monsters from the world. His actions had made the world a better place. A safer place. How many lives had his interventions saved he wondered? Then, as the heavenly elixir began to course through his veins, he turned his attention to an onyx and marble chess set placed on a low, mother of pearl inlaid table before him. After a full minute's intense concentration, he gently moved his ebony bishop in an attack against the opposing ivory King. Slowly, without moving his head, he raised his eyes towards his opponent who sat rigid as though set in deep concentration, his aquiline chin held in his strong, long-fingered hand. Van Hoon, with the slightest of grins, whispered,

"Your move I believe, Mr Holmes."

"When a doctor goes wrong, he is the first of criminals."

Sherlock Holmes - The Adventure of the Speckled Band

Bibliography

Researching this book has been a labour of love and has greatly informed us of Edwardian London, its people and cultural events of the time. Today, as researchers, we are spoiled with a limitless amount of data, as Wiggins would say, at our fingertips. It would be impossible for us to cite every single reference point, and far easier just to state Wikipedia, but we have tried to include the most used and most accurate and effective sources.

1)   Baring-Gold, William S. *Sherlock Holmes of Baker Street: A life of the World's first consulting detective*, Wings Books, 1995.

2)   Conan Doyle, Sir Arthur. *The complete illustrated Sherlock Holmes*, Omega Books, 1986.

3)   Lewis, R.W.B. *Dante: A Life*. Pheonix, 2002.

4)   Sharma, Meher. *The development of serial killers: a grounded theory study*, Master's Thesis, University of Illinois, 2018.

5)   Shpayer-Makov, Haia. *A Work-Life History of Policemen in Victorian and Edwardian England*.
     https://www2.clarku.edu/faculty/jbrown/papers/shpayer. pdf.

6)   https://bakerstreet.fandom.com/. Online encyclopaedia of all things associated with Sherlock Holmes.

7)   https://www.culture24.org.uk/history-and-heritage/tra43336. All about the Chinese community in the Limehouse region of London at the turn of the 20th Century.

8)   https://www.geographicus.com/P/AntiqueMap/London-smith-1892/. Antique map of London.

9)   https://christianhistoryinstitute.org/magazine/article/dante-divine-comedy-recommended-resources /. Dante Alighieri and the Divine Comedy resources.

10) https://www.british-history.ac.uk/old-new-london/vol3/pp329-337/. Scotland Yard and the history of the London Police.

11) http://www.nationalarchives.gov.uk/suffrage-100/. The history of the Suffrage movement in Britain.

12) https://www.historicalemporium.com/mens-edwardian-clothing.php/. Everything you need to know about Edwardian era clothing.

13) https://londonist.com/pubs/pubs/wapping/. Public Houses in and around Wapping and Limehouse.

14) https://www.britishbattles.com/great-boer-war/siege-of-kimberley/. The siege of Kimberley during the second Boer War.

15) https://www.historic-uk.com/HistoryUK/HistoryofBritain/Opium-in-Victorian-Britain/. Opium dens in Victorian and Edwardian Britain.

16) https://theodora.com/encyclopedia/s2/slaughterhouse.html/. Background information regarding slaughterhouses and slaughtering techniques.

17) https://www.towerbridge.org.uk/about-us/how-does-tower-bridge-work/. The Home page of London's Tower Bridge.

18) http://atkinson-swords.com/collection-by-region/south-east-asia/burma-myanmar/. Burmese knives and weaponry.

19) https://www.jack-the-ripper.org/. Information on all things Jack the Ripper.

20) http://victorian-era.org/victorian-era-actors.html/. Turn of the Century stage actors.

21) http://www.edwardianpromenade.com/resources/a-glossary-of-slang/. Dictionary of slang terms used in Victorian and Edwardian eras.

22) https://www.britannica.com/topic/Orpheus-in-the-Underworld/. Information on Orpheus in the Underworld opera.

23) https://heritagecalling.com/2019/03/28/the-story-of-londons-sewer-system/. Background on the London sewer system.

24) https://www.ucl.ac.uk/wolfson-institute-biomedical-research/cruciform-building/. Information on the Cruciform Building, London.

25) https://www.nhs.uk/conditions/dementia/about/. Dementia Guide.

Coming Soon from Ian C. Grant

The Gallery of Death: A DCI Wiggins Adventure, <u>excerpt</u>.

Chapter 1 - The Caretaker

"There are always some lunatics about. It would be a dull world without them."

Sherlock Holmes - The Red-Headed League

Jonas Crake loved warming his feet by the open fire. "You'll bloody well singe those socks before the night is through and I ain't darning them again for you Jonas Crake" his wife would announce each evening. Jonas shrugged and wriggled his toes even more. *'Lovely'* he would think.

That night the rain lashed, and the wind blew. Lighting cracked overhead, rattling the toffee thin glass in the windows of the Crake cottage. The chilly air whistled through the gaps in the rotten windows of the little presbytery. "When you gonna fix 'em winders, Jonas Crake?" demanded his wife irritably.

Jonas shrugged. "No rush, Maisie. They're as good as new 'em winders" he countered, rubbing his stockinged feet together. "Last for years yet they will."

"You're a lazy hound and no mistake, Jonas Crake. My mother always said you was a no-good layabout. I should have listened to her and married your brother Arthur" admonished his wife as she went to draw the curtains for the evening. "Old Reverend Brook would be beside himself if he knew just how lazy you really is."

"I keeps the grounds spick and span, don't I? Babbling Brook never said anything abouts keeping the buildings ship-shape n'all did he now?" argued Jonas as he settled down to his evening pipe. "Besides I need to check the Church tomorrow. I ain't been up there for over a week now. Probably full of leaves, mice and damned filthy pigeons and such like."

"Here!" exclaimed Maisie as she peered out into the gloom through the unwashed grime of the little sash windows. "I thinks you'd best get up there right now. Something is going on in the old Church, I can see lights flashing around inside."

"Probably just the lightning playing tricks with your eyes" countered Jonas, determined that he would not be shifted from his cosy fireside on such a brutal night.

"I ain't goin' nowhere tonight. It's blowing up a storm out there Maisie, and anyways, me shoes are off now." He puffed on his pipe and wriggled his toes some more. '*These new wool socks are wondrous soft*' he thought contentedly.

"What if it is the lightning, Jonas? What if there's a fire brewing in the Church. The whole place is nought but kindling. Old how's yer Father will have us turfed out of here sooner than you can say, Jack Robinson. Then what would we do Jonas Crake? Then where would we be, I asks you?" enquired Maisie sternly, her hands set firmly upon her ample hips.

Jonas was resigned to the fact that the scold's tongue would eventually prise him out of his comfortable chair and away from his fireside, out into the uninviting menace of the night. He slipped on his shoes with an acquiescent look and a grunt of dissatisfaction.

The rain and wind lashed at Jonas as soon as he stepped over the threshold. The biting rain stung his face like the pricking of ice-cold needles, and he yanked up the collar of his jacket in a forlorn attempt to fend off the storm. Jonas screwed up his eyes against the rain and looked towards the distant dark shape of the church silhouetted in the moonlight. He could see a throb of light playing against the stained-glass windows as he trudged up the tree-lined lane, leaning into the wind whilst holding his flat cap atop his head. The branches of the trees whipped back and forth like numerous cat-o'-nine-tails and the wind howled to an almost deafening degree.

'*I hopes none of these trees come down,*' he thought. '*I don't care to have to chop up any of these fellows. There'll be plenty of branches to pick up tomorrow as it is without me breakin' me back.*'

As he neared the front door of the church a crack of lighting thundered overhead, hitting the spire of the Church, and illuminating the night sky for an instant. The noise was explosive, and Jonas was convinced his heart had leapt out of his mouth and just as quickly leapt right back in again through fear. A primal surge of dread coursed through his veins. "Sweet baby Jesus!" he cursed "I nearly lost me life there!" What he had lost was his cap, which went spinning off into the darkness, closely accompanied by his nerve. Jonas clutched at the cast iron ring of the door and fumbled in his pocket for his loop of keys. The rain drove into his eyes making it difficult for him to distinguish one key from the other. His fingers searched through numerous options and eventually, he identified the correct one, the largest one, more by touch than by sight. He turned the rasping key in the lock and pulled the door ajar. He could feel light and warmth ebb out towards his receptive body and, encouraged, he slipped through the narrow opening and shook the rain from his dripping head and coat. "What the Hell's going on in here?" he muttered to himself under his breath. "Probably some young rapscallions playing doctors and nurses I'll wager."

All the while he was aware, subconsciously, of a low moaning chant resounding around the fourteenth-century building, like the chanting of ghostly monks. He shook his head clear and focused his attention on the altar. What he saw there literally took his breath away and almost chased his eyes from their sockets.

A writhing mass of bodies, some partially clothed, most naked, convulsed together in what appeared to be a groaning entanglement of human carnality. Enclosing this squirming mass sat a circle of more people, cross-legged, each bedecked in a scarlet, hooded gown that concealed their features. Each of these individuals chanted a steady canticle of some ancient, long discarded language. *Moratum di Omni de fastigat Som. Moratum di Omni de fastigat Som.* The mantra was repeated steadily over and over like a low echoing drumbeat.

Above this thrashing mass of humanity, floated the seemingly unsupported figure of a man, his arms outstretched in a cruciform position, his ankles crossed as if nailed together with some invisible brad. As Jonas watched on, his mouth agape in astonishment, Luca Radasiliev levitated higher still, his head thrown back as if in the throes of orgasm.

"Rejoice, rejoice my children. Drown in the baseness of the Master's depravity. Glory in his satanic majesty. Give yourself up to the Lord of Darkness and all his unholiness" shouted Radasiliev, turning his oil black eyes towards the nest of intertwined human vipers.

Jonas Crake whimpered unknowingly. Radasiliev immediately turned those inky orbs towards the stricken caretaker. Jonas felt the Russian's stare penetrate his very soul and grip forcefully around his heart. Involuntarily hot dampness spread across his groin. He ducked as quickly as he could behind the rearmost pew of the church and crouched there panting, his heart pounding like a drum, hoping beyond hope that the terrifying floating man had not noticed his presence.

The chanting continued, growing gradually louder and faster with each repetition. Jonas Crake could feel the noise infiltrate his brain, resounding around the inside of his skull. He felt himself being irresistibly drawn to peer over the pew. He tried to resist but was unable to defy the temptation. His head slowly rose over the timber backrest of the pew. Terror surged like electricity through every fibre of his being as he found himself nose to nose with the levitating man. He could feel and smell his hot, fetid breath engulfing him. It seemed to Jonas Crake that Radasiliev's head was unfeasibly larger than his own, a black-eyed snorting bull of a head.

"BOO!"

As he fell sidewards, and just before he lapsed into unconsciousness, Jonas Crake saw that despite this face being less than an inch from his own, the black-eyed man's body remained where it had been, forty feet away, hovering over the throng of naked, squirming acolytes.

"Just some children up to mischief my dear" informed Jonas Crake to his wife as he stamped into the cottage shaking himself free of the weather. He pushed the rickety door closed behind him, shutting out the wind and the mini cyclone of leaves that had danced a reel following him across the threshold.

"I hope you ain't made a state of me hall carpet Jonas Crake" scolded Maisie from the confines of their tiny parlour, as her husband entered.

"I cannot rightly recall one way or t'other but if there is, I'll surely clean it up in the morning, Maisie" replied Jonas. "I feel a bit peculiar after being out in that storm to tell you the truth. Soaked to me very marrow and a bit light-headed and giddy. That wind would take the 'ed off Lord Nelson atop his column, make no mistake" He had made his way into the main room and sat back down in his favourite fireside chair with a triumphant grunt. "I've seen a man make do with one good eye, even manage life's struggles with a single arm, but you ain't gonna be worth tuppence with no bonce" he chuckled as he dried his hair with his handkerchief.

"You is a lazy bleeder and no mistake, Jonas Crake," stated Maisie reciting her oft-repeated mantra. Jonas seemed not to hear her. He had closed his eyes against the dwindling light of the fire and was engulfed in a torpid blackness. Shapes and shadows danced and leapt at him through the gloom like satyrs cavorting in some impenetrable forest.

Maisie sat opposite, talking incessantly about a distant neighbour whose life was the latest into which she had inserted her inquisitive nose. "Elsie Crump is having no ends of trouble with her lazy, philandering, good for nothin', lump of a husband," she preached, all the while accompanied by the incessant clicking of her bone knitting needles. "Out down the Green Dragon all hours of the day and night, spending what little money they got. Pissing it all away and running around with god only knows which piece of cheap skirt he can lay his drunken mitts on. It's disgusting I tell ya, absenlutely disgusting is what I says!" Occasionally she would lay down her knitting to look at her husband who sat immobile, chest on chin, seemingly sound asleep. "Are you listening to me Jonas Crake?" she demanded.

Crake jerked back to reality. "Of course, dear, Charlie Crump is a no-good drunken womaniser. I knew that these last twenty years woman, ain't no news to me." Inside Jonas Crake's head, an orgy of unspeakable deeds was being acted out amongst the dark theatre of his mind. The oversized head of the floating man drifted in and out of his consciousness, sometimes laughing, oftentimes urging him towards unspeakably deplorable acts.

"Don't you talks to me like that Jonas Crake. That old mucker of yours is driving poor old Elsie up the pole, I tells ya. It's absenlutely disgusting is what it is. I wouldn't stand for no behaviour like that from you Jonas Crake, and that's for sure." Clack, clack, clack went the needles as they worked ever more rapidly at the scarf Maisie was working on, the speed of her knitting increasing as her self-induced indignation continued to rumble and rise. "Don't you even begin to think abouts going on a jolly with that good-for-nothing Charlie Crump. You hear me?"

"Of course, not dear," replied Jonas, adding '*I wouldn't dare*' under his breath.

Maisie threw him a look that could have pulled a nail from a fencepost. She put aside her knitting melodramatically and strode purposely to the parlour window. She peered out into the storm. "I can still sees lights coming from the Church, Jonas, are you sure you properly chased them rascals away?"

Jonas Crake opened his eyes and shook his head causing a needle-like pain to shoot from one temple to the other. He winced and tightly closed one eye in agony.

"Don't you wince at me Jonas Crake" pounced Maisie. "I swear if you don't like the sound of what I'm saying you can fend for yourself, you lazy old goat. My mother always said I should have married your brother. He's got a proper job he does, looking after all those poor filthy people in Spitalfields for that nice Mr Grice. Makes sure they have the money to pay their rents he does. A proper job that is, not like you Jonas Crake, sweeping up some old Church that nobody ever uses as it was intended, and forgetting to repair them winders." Maisie returned to her chair and her knitting. Clack, clack, clickity-clack. "Ain't you gonna put more logs on that fire?" Clack, clack, clickity-clack.

An explosion of fury erupted inside Jonas Crake's head.

Jem Pyke strode purposely through the open door of DCI Wiggins' office scanning the piece of paper he held in his hand. "Sorry to bother you, Guv, but we've had a report of a strange one down Kent way."

Wiggins was standing at the window of his office, hands clasped tightly behind his back. He turned towards Pyke. "Strange? In what regard, Sergeant?"

"Well, you did say to keep an eye out for anything peculiar, anything that may have a whiff of that Russian Luca Radasiliev about it" responded Pyke, handing Wiggins the transcript of the telephone call received at the Yard a few minutes earlier. Wiggins turned, took the document from Pyke, and sat down at his desk. He brushed a stray trace of ash from the paper before reading. Pyke looked at the ceiling.

"Forty-year-old woman, down Kent way, name of Maisie Crake found dead in her parlour with a knitting needle rammed so deep into each ear that they almost exited the opposite sides. On first inspection, it looks as though she may also have been strangled with a scarf she had been knitting. It was found stuffed in her mouth" explained Pyke as Wiggins carefully read the report. "Been deceased for a couple of weeks they reckon, on accounts of the decomposition present."

"Husband? Any children?" enquired Wiggins in a rising tone.

"No kiddies Guv and the husband has disappeared. Scarpered. Local Bobbies reckon he's good for it. Neighbours, such as there are, reckon he was as hen-pecked as a pile of seed" responded Pyke taking the seat opposite Wiggins.

"Such as they are? What do you mean, Sergeant?"

"Well, seems they live in a presbytery cottage on the grounds of a disused church near Staplehurst. Caretakers as such. Minister's name is Reverend Abercorn Brook."

"And this has just come through?"

Pyke nodded whilst fishing in his pockets for a cigar. "Just got it from Desk Sergeant Ash."

"How is Nosher Ash coping with his new position here at the Yard, incidentally?" asked Wiggins looking up from the report.

"He finds it well, Sir. Fewer drunks to handle than he was used to at Paddington, and the desk ain't ever been run so efficiently" replied Pyke reaching for the box of vestas on Wiggins' desk, making a mental note to replace them in exactly the same position. *'Guvnor is mighty particular about that sort of thing'* he reminded himself.

Wiggins considered the report in front of him. "My initial feeling was to let the local constabulary deal with it, but you are right with your suspicions Jem, there is the distinct scent of Radasiliev about it. Why don't you and Constable Murray go and investigate first thing tomorrow?"

Pyke blew a smoke ring into the air and watched it whirl and dissipate, then blew another directly through the centre of the enlarging first. "No time like the present Guv. I'll get me hat."

About the Author

Ian C. Grant is, in fact, two people, namely brothers Grant and Ian Christie.

Grant Andrew Christie was born in Dundee and lives in London. He is married with two children. He has spent his working life as a Manager within the Building industry. He is a talented artist who has work displayed and purchased internationally. This novel stemmed from his wondering how minor fictional characters are affected by the roles they played in major events. As an ardent Sherlock Holmes reader, he turned to Wiggins, lead Baker Street Irregular, and the only one of the Irregulars to be mentioned by name.

Ian Stuart Christie was born in Dundee and is married with no children. After initially working as a greeting card artist, he has now been employed by the University of Dundee University as an Academic Skills Tutor since 1990. Ian also provides high-quality electronic illustrations for research, education and publication purposes. He designed the official Glastonbury Festival t-shirts of 2002 and 2004 and has done cover illustrations for three children's books. He recently redesigned the cover of The Foot Journal.

Printed in Great Britain
by Amazon